CONJUNCTIONS

Bi-Annual Volumes of New Writing

Edited by
Bradford Morrow

Contributing Editors
Walter Abish
Chinua Achebe
John Ashbery
Mei-mei Berssenbrugge
Guy Davenport
Elizabeth Frank
William H. Gass
John Guare
Robert Kelly
Ann Lauterbach
Norman Manea
Patrick McGrath
Mona Simpson
Nathaniel Tarn
Quincy Troupe
William Weaver
John Edgar Wideman

published by Bard College

EDITOR: Bradford Morrow
MANAGING EDITOR: Michael Bergstein
SENIOR EDITORS: Robert Antoni, Martine Bellen, Peter Constantine, Brian Evenson, Thalia Field, Pat Sims, Lee Smith
ASSOCIATE EDITOR: Elaine Equi
ART EDITORS: Anthony McCall, Norton Batkin
PUBLICITY: Mark R. Primoff
WEBMASTERS: Brian Evenson, Michael Neff
EDITORIAL ASSISTANTS: Jedediah Berry-Boolukos, Caroline Donner, Jonathan Safran Foer, Alía Habib, Jacqueline Blair Holt, Paulina Belle Nissenblatt, Andrew Small, Alan Tinkler

CONJUNCTIONS is published in the Spring and Fall of each year by Bard College, Annandale-on-Hudson, NY 12504. This issue is made possible in part with the generous funding of the Lannan Foundation, the National Endowment for the Arts, and with public funds from the New York State Council on the Arts, a State Agency. This issue also received financial support from the Foundation for the Production and Translation of Dutch Literature.

SUBSCRIPTIONS: Send subscription orders to CONJUNCTIONS, Bard College, Annandale-on-Hudson, NY 12504. Single year (two volumes): $18.00 for individuals; $25.00 for institutions and overseas. Two years (four volumes): $32.00 for individuals; $45.00 for institutions and overseas. Patron subscription (lifetime): $500.00. Overseas subscribers please make payment by International Money Order. For information about subscriptions, back issues and advertising, call Michael Bergstein at 914-758-1539 or fax 914-758-2660.

All editorial communications should be sent to Bradford Morrow, *Conjunctions*, 21 East 10th Street, New York, NY 10003. Unsolicited manuscripts cannot be returned unless accompanied by a stamped, self-addressed envelope.

Visit the *Conjunctions* web site at www.Conjunctions.com.

Copyright © 1998 CONJUNCTIONS.

Cover design by Anthony McCall Associates, New York. Cover photograph by Baron Adolphe de Meyer of Vaslav Nijinsky is from the publication *L'Apres-midi d'un Faune.* Copyright © Eakins Press Foundation, 1977, and is reproduced with permission from the publisher.

Printers: Edwards Brothers.
Typesetter: Bill White, Typeworks.
ISSN 0278-2324
ISBN 0-941964-47-7
Manufactured in the United States of America.

TABLE OF CONTENTS

RADICAL SHADOWS

Previously Untranslated and Unpublished Works
by 19th and 20th Century Masters

Edited by Bradford Morrow and Peter Constantine

INTRODUCTION

THIS PROJECT BEGAN as serendipity, then developed into an international search. Last winter, Joyce Carol Oates wrote me about an acquaintance who had completed work on some previously untranslated stories by Yasunari Kawabata—was I interested in seeing the manuscript? That same week, I happened to be speaking with Peter Constantine, himself a translator of writings from some twenty languages, who offered me a group of short stories by Anton Chekhov that had not yet seen their way into print in English. This set me and Peter, and a host of other friends, on a quest to see if we couldn't uncover works by some major literary writers from the late nineteenth century forward, that were lost, forgotten, suppressed, rare, unknown—or, at minimum, unknown in English—and commission translations or secure rights to bring them into the light.

Why *Radical Shadows?* As a title for this collection of fiction, poetry, plays and journals written by some of our great nineteenth- and twentieth-century innovative forebears—some undiminished shades of the relatively recent past—*Radical Shadows* seemed apt. But as a larger idea, one that raises some intriguing questions, *Radical Shadows* becomes more provocative than I might first have imagined. We who value literature must ask ourselves: What *else* has been left behind in the mad rush of this frenzied century? What other works remain safe but unexplored in private or institutional archives, or were published in their original languages in ephemeral reviews known only to specialists, or were until recently suppressed by governments to whom certain writers were (and are, in some cases) considered dangerous and thus have languished, out of official critical favor? How much important material has been overlooked? How many works by major writers such as Proust have been published in honorable, but very limited deluxe editions that few but book collectors will have the chance to read? What other texts have come down to us in versions expurgated or altered by members of the authors' families, such as in the cases of Vaslav Nijinsky and Antonia Pozzi? If works as interesting as Musil's play and Federigo Tozzi's stories and Dostoevsky's prison passage haven't found their way into English until now, what other remarkable literature is out there, unknown to so many readers? How was it that a magnificent poem by Djuna Barnes, once rejected by Marianne Moore when she worked at *The Dial*, until now remained unpublished along with many of Barnes's personal favorites, unknown to those among us

7

who like her Jacobean line better than Miss Moore did?

Norman Manea, the great Romanian writer who was kind enough to bring to my attention both the Cioran and delightful Ionesco works in this issue, tells me that his own manuscripts were lost when he had to flee his homeland, and that other of his papers are "locked in the censor's safebox" in Romania—unavailable not only to his readers, but to the author himself! In a perceptive introduction to a collection of political essays by Günter Grass some years ago, Salman Rushdie proposed that one of the themes central to all twentieth-century writing is that of the migrant. Rushdie writes, "The very word *metaphor*, with its roots in the Greek words for *bearing across*, describes a sort of migration, the migration of ideas into images. Migrants—borne-across humans—are metaphorical beings in their very essence; and migration, seen as a metaphor, is everywhere around us. We all cross frontiers; in that sense, we are all migrant peoples."

One need not invoke Thomas Mann, Primo Levi, Milan Kundera or anyone else (the list is long) who left home in order to survive and write, to catch the validity of Rushdie's assertion. A quick glance at the group of writers gathered here—from Seferis and Cavafy to Gippius and Nabokov—reveals how many migrated, exiled themselves or were exiled. Which again brings up the salient question about what's been lost along the way.

Radical Shadows invites, I hope, more of this sort of cultural investigative work, and an appreciation both of translators—those who "bear-across" work from one language to another—and everyone else who strives to complete the canons of our important writers.

I owe a debt of gratitude to many people who helped make *Radical Shadows* possible, above all my co-editor, Peter Constantine. Also, I would like to thank others who brought manuscripts to our attention, as well as those who helped with securing permissions, and gave us leads and suggestions: André Aciman, Beth Alvarez (University of Maryland Library, College Park), Jin Auh (Andrew Wylie Agency), Cal Barkside (Arcade), Daisy Blackwell and Georges Borchardt (Borchardt Agency), Andreas Brown, Gerald Clarke, Caroline Donner, Susan Drury (Authors League Fund), Brian Evenson, Jonathan Foer, Robert Giroux, Florence Giry (Editions Gallimard), Lynn Goldberg (Goldberg McDuffie Communications), Alía Habib, Petra Christina Hardt (Suhrkamp Verlag), Glenn Horowitz, James S. Jaffe, Robert Kelly, Chuck Kim (French Publishers'

Agency), Franz Larese (Erker Verlag), Nancy MacKechnie and Gita Nadas (Vassar College Library, Special Collections), Anna Magni, Tom McGonigle, Bruce McPherson, Alice Methfessel, George Robert Minkoff, Kenneth Northcott, Joyce Carol Oates, Barbara Page, Randy Petilos (University of Chicago Press), Alan Schwartz (Truman Capote Literary Trust), Gary Shapiro, Avi Sharon, Dan Simon (Seven Stories Press), Nikki Smith, Frederick Vanacore, Kathy Varker (Farrar, Straus & Giroux), Lawrence Venuti, Tom Whalen, John Wronowski and of course everyone at Bard College for their continued support of this project.

Postscript: Our longtime Senior Editor Pat Sims, highly respected by her colleagues at *Conjunctions* as well as the hundreds of authors she's worked with, is leaving to pursue other interests. On behalf of all of us who've worked with Pat, I wish her the best in her new career. I would also like to welcome Laura Starrett, who joins *Conjunctions* with our next issue, *Eye to Eye.*

—Bradford Morrow
October 1998
New York City

Fourteen Stories
Anton Chekhov

—Translated from Russian by Peter Constantine

> "Don't lick clean, don't polish—be awkward and bold. Brevity is the sister of talent!"
>
> *—Anton Chekhov to his older brother*
> *Alexander, February 1889*

Chekhov wrote these fourteen prose works during the early 1880s, his most productive and prolific period. He had just arrived in the big city and was energetically studying medicine, supporting his parents and siblings, and exploring the streets, taverns, markets and brothels of Moscow, absorbing the city's color and commotion and working it into quick, vivid prose. By the time he was twenty-six he had already published over four hundred short stories and vignettes in Moscow and St. Petersburg magazines.

Young Chekhov amazed his audience of the early 1880s. He was particularly interested in the absurd, and repatterned the anecdote and vignette forms of the popular press into innovative forms of writing: pieces in the guise of National Census questions, a test set by a mad mathematician, a proposal to the board of a medical school, the twisted "questions and answers" of popular women's magazines. The story in "After the Fair" is told in fragmented paragraphs—the "torn and tattered papers covered with smudged writing" that a Moscow housewife finds in her husband's pockets after the Nizhgorod fair. As she reads the bits of paper, a story unfolds. "A Lawyer's Romance, A Protocol" uses the gruff legalese of a divorce petition to tell the cynical love story of a Moscow lawyer.

Traditional storytelling with a beginning, middle and end is no longer important. Chekhov aims for effect, an uncommonly pioneering approach for the time.

Almost a century has passed since Chekhov's death, and it is surprising that these masterpieces have not been previously translated into English. Earlier generations of translators overlooked these pieces, which until recently were often considered shocking in terms of literary technique. As the Chekhov specialist Julie de Sherbinin points out in a letter to Harper's *Magazine, which had published other previously untranslated stories of Chekhov, "The gaps in English translation of his early work can be attributed to various factors: these stories were long considered products of an 'immature' writer, they are rich in colloquialisms and wordplay and thus are hard to translate, and they often depend on cultural context for their humor."*

These remarkable stories do not present the Chekhov that we know in the West. In them, one sees the exuberance, energy and craft of a young writer of genius. They are some of the pieces that made Chekhov famous in his day.

* * *

AFTER THE FAIR

A MERCHANT FROM the First Traders Guild of Moscow had just returned from the Nizhgorod Fair, and in his pockets his wife found a bunch of torn and tattered papers covered with smudged writing. She managed to make out the following:

Dear Mr. Semyon Ivanovitch:
Mr. Khryapunov, the artiste you beat up, is prepared to reach an out-of-court settlement of 100 rubles. He will not accept one kopeck less. I await your answer.
Sincerely, your lawyer, *N. Erzayev.*

To the brute who dares call himself a trader:
Having been insulted by you most grossly, I have relegated my complaint to a court of law. As you seem incapable of appreciating who I am, perhaps the justice of the peace or a public trial will teach you to respect me. Erzayev, your lawyer, said that you were not prepared to pay me a hundred rubles. This being the case, I am prepared to accept 75 rubles in compensation for your brutish behavior. It is only in lenience for your simple-mindedness and to what one could call your animalistic instincts that I am prepared to let you off so

cheaply. When an educated man insults me, I charge much more.
  Khryapunov, artiste

... concerning our demand of 539 rubles and 43 kopecks, the value of the broken mirror and the piano you demolished in the Glukharev Restaurant ...

... anoint bruises morning and evening ...

... after I manage to sell the ruined fabrics as if they were choice merchandise, I plan to get totally soused! Get yourself over to Feodosya's this evening. See to it that we get Kuzma the musician—and spread some mustard on his head—and that we have four *mademoiselles.* Get plump ones.

... concerning the I.O.U.—you can take a flying jump! I will gladly proffer a ten-kopeck piece, but concerning the fraudulent bankrupter, we'll see what we shall see.

Finding you in a state of feverish delirium due to the excessive intake of alcohol (delirium tremens), I applied cupping glasses to your body to bring you back to your senses. For these services I request a fee of three rubles.
  Egor Frykov, Medical Attendant

Dear Semyon, please don't be angry—I named you as a witness in court concerning that rampage when we were being beaten up, even though you said I shouldn't. Don't act so superior—after all, you yourself caught a couple of wallops too. And see to it that those bruises don't go away, keep them inflamed ...

⁓ BILL ⁓

1 portion of fish soup .... 1 ruble, 80 kopecks
1 bottle of Champagne .... 8 rubles
1 broken decanter .... 5 rubles
Cab for the mademoiselles .... 2 rubles
Cabbage soup for the Gypsy .... 60 kopecks
Tearing of waiter's jacket .... 10 rubles

... I kiss you countless times, and hope to see you soon at the following address: Fayansov Furnished rooms, number 18. Ask for Martha Sivyagina.

Your ever-loving *Angelica*

CONFESSION—OR OLYA, ZHENYA, ZOYA: A LETTER

Ma chère, you asked me, among other things, in your sweet letter, my dear unforgettable friend, why, although I am thirty-nine years old, I have to this day never married.

My dear friend, I hold family life in the highest possible esteem. I never married simply because goddamn Fate was not propitious. I set out to get married a good fifteen times, but did not manage to because everything in this world,—and particularly in *my* life— seems to hinge on chance. Everything depends on it! Chance, that despot! Let me cite a few incidents thanks to which I still lead a contemptibly lonely life.

First Incident

It was a delightful June morning. The sky was as clear as the clearest Prussian blue. The sun played on the waters of the river and brushed the dewy grass with its rays. The river and the meadow were strewn with rich diamonds of light. The birds were singing, as if with one voice. We walked down the path of yellowish sand, and with happy hearts drank in the sweet aromas of the June morning. The trees looked upon us so gently, and whispered all kinds of nice—I'm sure—and tender things. Olya Gruzdofska's hand (she's now married to the son of your chief of police) lay in mine, and her tiny little finger kept brushing over my thumb ... her cheeks glowed, and her eyes . . . O *ma chère,* what exquisite eyes! There was so much charm, truth, innocence, joyousness, childish naiveté, in those blue sparkling eyes of hers! I fell in love with her blond braids, and with the little footprints her tiny feet left in the sand.

"I have devoted my life, Olga Maksimovna, to science!" I whispered, terrified that her little finger would slip off my thumb. "The future will bring with it a professorial chair . . . on my conscience there are questions . . . scientific ones . . . my life is filled with hard work, troubles, lofty . . . I mean . . . well, basically, I'm going to be a professor . . . I am an honest man, Olga Maksimovna . . . I'm not rich, but . . . I need someone who with her presence . . . (Olya blushed and shyly lowered her eyes; her little finger was trembling) who with her presence . . . Olya! Look up at the sky! Look how pure it is . . . my life is just as boundlessly pure!"

My tongue didn't have time to scramble out of this quagmire of drivel: Olya suddenly lifted her head, snatched her hand away from mine and clapped her palms together. A flock of geese with little goslings was waddling towards us. Olya ran over to them and, laughing out loud, stretched her arms toward them . . . O what beauteous arms, *ma chère!*

"Squawk, squawk, squawk!" the geese called out, craning their necks, peering at Olya from the side.

"Here goosey-goose, here goosey-goose!" Olya shouted, and reached out to touch a little gosling.

The gosling was quite bright for its age. It ran from Olya's approaching fingers straight to its daddy, a very large foolish-looking gander, and seemed to complain to him. The gander spread his wings. Naughty Olya reached out to touch some other goslings. At that moment something terrible happened: the gander lowered his neck to the ground and, hissing like a snake, marched fiercely towards Olya. Olya squealed and retreated, the gander close at her heels. Olya looked back, squealed even louder and went completely white. Her pretty, girlish face was twisted with terror and despair. It was as if she were being chased by three hundred devils.

I rushed to help her, and banged the gander on the head with my walking stick. The damn gander still managed to quickly snap at the hem of her dress. With wide eyes and terror-stricken face, trembling all over, Olya fell into my arms.

"You're such a coward!" I said to her.

"Thrash that goose!" she moaned, and burst into tears.

Suddenly I no longer saw naiveté or childishness in her frightened little face—but idiocy! *Ma chère,* I cannot abide faint-heartedness! I cannot imagine being married to a faint-hearted, cowardly woman!

The gander ruined everything. After calming Olya down, I went home. I couldn't get that expression of hers—cowardly to the point of idiocy—out of my mind. In my eyes, Olya had lost all her charm. I dropped her.

Second Incident

As you know, my friend, I am a writer. The gods ignited within my breast the sacred flame, and I have seen it as my duty to take up the pen! I am a high priest of Apollo! Every beat of my heart, every breath I take, in short—I have sacrificed everything on the altar of my muse. I write and I write and I write . . . take away my pen, and I'm dead! You laugh! You do not believe me! I swear most solemnly that it is true!

But as you surely know, *ma chére,* this world of ours is a bad place for art. The world is big and bountiful, but a writer can find no place for himself in it! A writer is an eternal orphan, an exile, a scapegoat, a defenseless child! I divide mankind into two categories: writers and enviers! The former write, and the latter die of jealousy and spend all their time plotting and scheming against them. I have always fallen prey, and always will, to these plotters! They have ruined my life! They have taken over the writing business, calling themselves editors and publishers, striving with all their might to ruin us writers! Damn them!

Anyway . . . For a while I was courting Zhenya Pshikova. You must remember her, that sweet, dreamy, black-haired girl . . . she's now married to your neighbor, Karl Ivanovitch Wanze. (*À propos,* in German, Wanze means "bedbug." But please don't tell Zhenya, she'd be very upset.) Zhenya was in love with the writer within me. She believed in my calling as deeply as I did. She cherished my hopes. But she was so young! She had not yet grasped the aforementioned division of humanity into two categories! She did not believe in this division! She did not believe it, and one fine day . . . catastrophe!

I was staying at the Pshikovs' dacha. The family looked on me as the groom-to-be and Zhenya as the bride. I wrote—she read. What a critic she was, *ma chère!* She was as objective as Aristides and as stern as Cato. I dedicated my works to her. One of these pieces she really liked. She wanted to see it in print, so I sent it to one of the magazines. I sent it on the first of July and waited two weeks for the answer. The fifteenth of July came, and Zhenya and I finally received the letter we had been waiting for. We opened it; she went red, I went white. Beneath the address, the following was written: "Shlendovo village. Mr. M. B. You don't have a drop of talent in you. God knows what the hell you're writing about. Please don't waste your stamps and our time! Find yourself another occupation!"

Ridiculous . . . it was obvious that a bunch of idiots had written this.

"I see . . . ," Zhenya mumbled.

"The damn . . . swine!" I muttered. So, *ma chère* Yevgenia Markovna, are you still smiling at my division of the world into writers and enviers?

Zhenya thought for a while and then yawned.

"Well," she said, "maybe you don't have any talent after all. They surely know best. Last year Fyodor Fyodosevitch spent the whole summer fishing by the river with me. All you do is write, write, write! It's so boring!"

Well! How do you like that! After all those sleepless nights we spent together, I writing, she reading! With both of us sacrificing ourselves to my muse! Ha!

Zhenya cooled to my writing, and by extension to me. We broke up. It had to be.

THIRD INCIDENT

You know, of course, my dear unforgettable friend, that I am a fervent music lover. Music is my passion, my true element. The names Mozart, Beethoven, Chopin, Mendelssohn, Gounod are not the names of men—they are the names of giants! I love classical music. I scorn operettas, as I scorn vaudeville! I am a true habitué of the opera. Our stars Khokhlov, Kochetova, Barzal, Usatov, Korsov . . . are simply wonderful people! How I regret that I do not know any singers personally. Were I to know one, I would bare my soul in humble gratitude!

Last winter I went to the opera particularly often. I did not go alone—I went with the Pepsinov family. It is such a pity that you do not know this dear family! Each winter the Pepsinovs book a loge. They are devoted to music, heart and soul. The crown of this dear family is Colonel Pepsinov's daughter, Zoya. What a girl, my dear friend! Her pink lips alone could drive someone like me out of his mind! She is shapely, beautiful, clever. I loved her . . . I loved her madly, passionately, terribly! My blood was boiling when I sat next to her. You smile, *ma chère?* You can smile! You cannot comprehend the love a writer feels! A writer's love is—Mount Etna coupled with

Mount Vesuvius! Zoya loved me. Her eyes always rested on my eyes, which were constantly seeking out her eyes. We were happy. It was but one step to marriage.

But we foundered.

Faust was playing. *Faust*, my dear friend, was written by Gounod, and Gounod is one of the greatest musicians on earth. On the way to the theater, I decided to declare my love to Zoya during the first act. I have never understood that act—it was a mistake on the part of the great Gounod to have written that first act!

The opera began. Zoya and I slipped out to the foyer. She sat next to me and, shivering with expectation and happiness, nervously fanned herself. How beautiful she looked in the glittering lights, *ma chère*, how terribly beautiful!

"The overture," I began my declaration, "led me to some reflections, Zoya Egorovna . . . so much feeling, so much . . . you listen and you long . . . you long for, well, for that something, and you listen . . ."

I hiccupped, and continued: "You long for something . . . special! You long for something unearthly . . . Love? Passion? Yes . . . it must be . . . love [I hiccupped]. Yes, love!"

Zoya smiled in confusion, and fanned herself harder. I hiccupped. I can't stand hiccups!

"Zoya Egorovna! Tell me, I beg of you! Do you know this feeling? [I hiccupped.] Zoya Egorovna! I am trembling for your answer!"

"I . . . I . . . don't understand . . ."

"Sorry, that was just a hiccup . . . It'll pass . . . I'm talking about that all-embracing feeling that . . . damn!"

"Have some water!"

I'll make my declaration, and then I'll quickly go down to the buffet, I thought to myself, and continued: "In a nutshell, Zoya Egorovna . . . you, of course, will have noticed . . ."

I hiccupped, and then in my consternation bit my tongue.

"You will, of course, have noticed [I hiccupped] . . . you've known me almost a year now . . . well . . . I'm an honest man, Zoya Egorovna! I am a hard-working man! I am not rich, it's true, but . . ."

I hiccupped and leaped up.

"I think you should have some water!" Zoya suggested. I moved a few steps away from the sofa, tapped my finger on my throat and hiccupped again. *Ma chère*, I was in a terrible predicament! Zoya stood up, and marched off to the loge with me close on her heels. After escorting her, I hiccupped and quickly ran off to the buffet. I drank five or six glasses of water, and the hiccups seemed somehow to quiet down. I smoked a cigarette and returned to the loge. Zoya's brother got up and gave me his seat, the seat next to my darling Zoya. I sat down, and at that very moment . . . hiccupped! About five minutes passed, I hiccupped, hiccupped somehow strangely, with a wheeze. I got up and went to stand by the loge door. It is better, *ma chère*, to hiccup by a door than into the ear of the woman one loves! I hiccupped. A schoolboy from the loge next to ours looked at me and laughed out loud. The joy with which that little brute laughed! And the joy with which I would have gladly ripped the horrible little brat's ear off! He laughed as they were singing the great *Faust* aria on stage! What blasphemy! No, *ma chère!* As children we would never have comported ourselves in this manner! Cursing the impertinent schoolboy, I hiccupped again . . . laughter broke out in the neighboring loges.

"*Encore!*" the schoolboy loudly whispered.

"What the hell!" Colonel Pepsinov mumbled. "Couldn't you have hiccupped at home, sir?"

Zoya went red. I hiccupped one last time and, furiously clenching my fists, ran out of the loge. I started walking up and down the corridor. I walked and walked and walked—hiccupping constantly. I ate, I drank, I tried everything—finally at the beginning of the fourth act I gave up and went home. The moment I unlocked the door, as if to spite me, my hiccups stopped. I slapped my neck, and shouted: "Go on, hiccup! Now you can hiccup all you want, you poor, booed-off fiancé! No, you were not booed off, you were hiccupped off!"

The following day I went to visit the Pepsinovs the way I always did. Zoya didn't come down for dinner, and sent word that she couldn't see me as she wasn't feeling well, while Pepsinov spoke at length about certain young people who didn't know how to comport themselves in public. The fool! He's obviously not aware that the organs that induce hiccupping are not subject to voluntary stimuli! Stimuli, *ma chère*, means "shakers."

"Would you give your daughter—that is, if you had one—to a man who wouldn't think twice about belching in public?" Pepsinov asked me after dinner. "Ha? Well?"

"Um, yes . . . I would," I muttered.

"Quite a mistake!"

That was the end of Zoya as far as I was concerned. She could not forgive my hiccupping. For her that was the end of me.

Would you like me to describe the remaining twelve incidents?

I could, but . . . enough is enough! The veins on my temples have swollen, tears are flowing freely and my liver is churning . . . "O brother writers, our destiny doth weave fateful threads!" I wish you, *ma chère,* all the very best! I squeeze your hand tightly, and send my warmest regards to Paul. I hear that he is a good husband and father. God bless him! Pity, though, that he drinks so heavily (this, by the way, *ma chère,* is not a reproach)!

All the very best, *ma chère.* Your faithful servant.

Makar Baldastov

TWO LETTERS

I. A Serious Question

My dearest uncle Anisim Petrovitch,

Your neighbor Kurosheyev has just been to visit me and informed me, among other things, that Murdashevitch, from next door to you, returned with his family from abroad a few days ago. This bit of news shocked me all the more as it seemed that the Murdashevitches were going to stay abroad forever. My dearest uncle! If you harbor any love in your heart for your humble nephew, then I beg you, dear, dear uncle, to visit Murdashevitch and find out how his ward, Mashenka, is doing. I am laying bare to you the innermost secret of my soul. It is only you alone I trust! I love Mashenka—I love her passionately, more than my life! Six years of separation have not dampened my feelings for her one iota. Is she alive? Is she well? Please write and tell me how she is! Does she remember me? Does she love me like she used to? May I write her a letter? My dear, dear uncle! Please find out and send me all the details.

Tell her that I am no longer the poor and timid student she once knew—I am now a barrister, with a practice of my own, with money. In a word, to achieve perfect happiness in life I need only one thing—her!

I embrace you, and hope for a speedy reply.

Vladimir Gretchnev

19

Anton Chekhov

A DETAILED RESPONSE

My dearest nephew Vladimir,

I received your letter, and went over to see Murdashevitch the very next day. What a great fellow he is! He did age a bit abroad, and has gone somewhat gray, but all these years he kept me, his dear old friend, in his heart, and when I entered he embraced me, looked me in the eye for a long time and said with a timid, tender cry, "Who are you?" When I told him my family name he embraced me again, and said: "Now it's all coming back to me!" What a great fellow! As long as I was there, I had a few drinks and a snack, and then we sat down to a few friendly rounds of Preference. He explained to me all kinds of funny things about foreign countries and had me in stitches with all his droll imitations of the Germans and their funny ways. But in science, he told me, the Germans *have* gone far. He even showed me a picture he bought on his trip through Italy, of this person of the female sex in a rather strange, indecent dress. And I saw Mashenka too. She was wearing a plush pink-colored gown embellished with all kinds of costly bits and bobs. She does remember you, and her eyes even cried a tear or two when she asked about you. She wants you to write to her, and thanks you for your tender memories and feelings. You wrote that you have your own practice and money! My dear boy, do be careful with that money—be moderate and abstinent! When I was a young man I gave myself up to voluptuous excesses—but only for short periods, and with extreme caution—and yet I still repent!

My very best wishes.

Your loving uncle, Anisim Gretchnev

P.S. Your writing is garbled, but has an eloquent and tempting style. I showed your letter to all the neighbors. They thought you a great storyteller! Vladimir, Father Grigory's son, copied it out so he can send it to a newspaper. I also showed it to Mashenka and her husband, Uhrmacher, the German she married last year. He read it and was full of praise. I am going to show the letter and read it to others, too. You must write more! Murdashevitch's caviar is very tasty.

MAYONNAISE

Astronomers rejoiced when they discovered spots on the face of the sun. A case of unparalleled malice!

An official took a bribe. At the very moment of the Fall his boss entered and looked suspiciously at his clenched fist, in which the illicit bank note lay. The official was deeply embarrassed.

"Excuse me!" he called after the petitioner, holding out his palm. "You forgot something in my hand!"

When is a goat a pig?

"Somebody's goat had started coming over to our goats," a landowner told us. "We caught the goat and gave it a good lashing. But it still kept coming over. So we gave it a real thrashing and tied a stick to its tail. But that didn't help either. It still managed to get at our goats. Fine! We caught it, spread tobacco on its nose and smeared it with turpentine. After that it didn't show up for three days, but then there it was again! Now isn't that goat a pig?"

Exemplary resourcefulness:

When the St. Petersburg reporter N. Z. visited the textile exhibition last year, he noticed one pavilion in particular and began writing something down.

"I think you just dropped a twenty-five ruble note," the exhibitor in the pavilion said, handing him the note.

"I dropped two twenty-fivers!" the reporter shot back.

The exhibitor was so amazed at this resourcefulness that he gave him a second twenty-fiver.

This really happened.

Anton Chekhov

A LAWYER'S ROMANCE, A PROTOCOL

On the tenth of February, in the year eighteen seventy-seven, in the City of St. Petersburg, Moscovsky Region, District 2, in the house of Zhivotov, Second-Guild trader, located on the Ligovka, I, the undersigned, met Marya Alekseyevna Barabanova, daughter of a Titular Counselor, 18 years of age, literate and of Russian Orthodox faith. Meeting the aforementioned Barabanova, I experienced an attraction for her. Since, according to art. 994 of the crim. cdx., illegal cohabitation incurs penalties as determined in the above article, in addition to church penitence, (cf. the case of trader Solodovnikov, 1881, vol. of Court Disp., Fin. Dept.), I asked for her hand in marriage. I married her, but did not live with her for a long time. I fell out of love with her. Having assigned her complete dowry to my name, I began lounging about in drinking houses—the Livadias, the Eldorados—and did so for five years. So, according to art. 54, vol. 10 of the Civil Court Codex, a five-year absence without knowledge of an individual's whereabouts is grounds for divorce, and so, with due deference, I respectfully request that your Honor initiate proceedings for me to divorce my wife.

AFFIX
60 KOPECK
DUTY
STAMP

FOOL, OR THE RETIRED SEA CAPTAIN:
A SCENE FROM AN UNWRITTEN VAUDEVILLE PLAY

It is the marriage season. Soufov is a retired sea captain. He is sitting on an oilskin sofa, with one leg resting over the other, his arms crossed. As he speaks he rocks back and forth. Lukinishna the matchmaker is a fat, sagging old woman sitting on a stool next to him. She has a foolish but good-natured face, with an expression of horror mixed with surprise. Seen from the side, she looks like a large snail; from the front, like a black beetle. She speaks servilely, and hiccups after every word.

CAPTAIN. By the way, if you think about it, Ivan Nikolayevitch has set himself up quite nicely. He did well to get married. You can be a professor, a genius even, but if you're not married, you're not worth a brass kopeck! You've no census or public opinion worth mentioning. If you're not married, you don't carry any weight in society. Take me, for instance. I am a man from an educated background, a house owner, I have money, rank—even a medal! But what's the point? Who am I if you look at me from a point of view?—An old bachelor— a mere synonym, nothing more. (*He pauses to think.*) Everyone's married, everyone has children, except me—it's like in the song . . . (*He sings a few doleful lines in a deep baritone.*) That's how my life is—surely there must be some woman left on the shelf for me to get married to!

LUKINISHNA. On the shelf? Lordy-lord, I'm sure we can do better than that! What with your noble nature, and . . . well, all your good qualities, and everything, we'll find you a woman—even one with money!

CAPTAIN. I don't need a woman with money. I wouldn't dream of doing such a despicable thing as marrying for money! I have my own money—I don't want to be eating from her plate, I want her to eat from mine! When you marry a poor woman, she's bound to feel and understand. I'm not that much of an egoist that I want to profit . . .

LUKINISHNA. Well, yes . . . and one thing's sure—a poor bride might well be prettier than a rich one . . .

CAPTAIN. But I'm not interested in looks either! What for? You can't use a pretty face as a cup and saucer! Beauty should not be in the flesh, it should be in the soul. What *I* need is goodness, meekness, you know, innocence . . . I want a wife who'll honor me, respect me . . .

LUKINISHNA. Yes! How can she not respect you if you're her lawfully wedded husband? It's not like she'd be uneducated or something!

CAPTAIN. Don't interrupt me! And I don't need an educated wife either! Nowadays, obviously, everyone's got an education, but there are different kinds of education. It's all well and good if your wife can prattle in French and German and God knows what else—it's very charming! But what use is all that if she can't, for instance, sew a simple button onto a shirt? I come from an educated background myself. I can show my face in any circle—I can sit down and chat with Prince Kanitelin as easily as I'm chatting with you right now, but I'm a simple man, and I need a simple girl. I'm not looking for intellect. In a man, intellect is important, but a female can get by quite nicely without much intellect.

LUKINISHNA. That's so very true! Even the newspapers are now saying that clever people are worthless!

CAPTAIN. A fool will both love you and respect you, and realize what my rank in life is. She will be fearful. A clever woman will eat your bread, but not feel whose bread she's eating. I want you to find me a fool! It's as simple as that! A fool! Do you have your eye on anyone?

LUKINISHNA. Oh, quite a few! (*She thinks.*) Let me see . . . there are fools and there are fools . . . after all, even a foolish hen has her brainstorms! But you want a real idiot, right? (*She thinks.*) I know one, but I'm not sure if she's what you're looking for . . . she's from a merchant family and comes with a dowry of about five thousand . . . I wouldn't say she's downright ugly, she's, well, you know . . . neither here nor there. She's skinny, very thin . . . gentle, delicate . . . and she's kind, beyond the call of duty! She'd hand over her last piece of bread if you told her to! And she's meek—her mother could drag her through the house by the hair, and she wouldn't even squeak! And she fears her parents, she goes to church and at home she's always ready to help! But when it comes to this . . . (*She points to her forehead.*) . . . Do not judge me too harshly, sinful old woman that I am, for my plainspokenness, for the forthright truth that I speak to you with the Lord as my witness: she's not all there up here! A complete fool! You can't get a word out of her, not a word, as if she were dead as a doornail. She'll sit there tightlipped for hours, and suddenly, out of the blue—she'll jump up! As if you'd poured boiling water over her! She jumps up as if she were scalded and starts babbling . . . babbling, babbling . . . babbling endlessly . . . that her parents are fools, the food's awful, and all they do is lie, and that she has nowhere to go, that they ruined her life . . . "There's no way," the girl shouts, "that you can understand me!" The fool! A merchant called Kashalotov was wooing her—she turned him down! She laughed in his face! And he's rich, handsome, elegant, just like a young officer! And what does she do? She snatches up a stupid book, marches off to the pantry and starts reading!

CAPTAIN. No, she's not a fool of the right category . . . find me another! (*He gets up and looks at his watch.*) Well, bonjour for now. I'll be getting back to my bachelor business.

LUKINISHNA. Well, go right along! Go with God! (*She gets up.*) I'll drop by again Saturday evening with more about our bride ... (*She walks over to the door.*) And by the way, while you're getting back to your bachelor business, should I send you someone else for now?

QUESTIONS POSED BY A MAD MATHEMATICIAN

1.) I was chased by 30 dogs, 7 of which were white, 8 gray and the rest black. Which of my legs was bitten, the right or the left?

2.) Ptolemy was born in the year 223 A.D. and died after reaching the age of eighty-four. Half his life he spent traveling, and a third, having fun. What is the price of a pound of nails, and was Ptolemy married?

3.) On New Year's Eve, 200 people were thrown out of the Bolshoi Theater's costume ball for brawling. If the brawlers numbered 200, then what was the number of guests who were drunk, slightly drunk, swearing and those trying but not managing to brawl?

4.) What is the sum of the following numbers?

5.) Twenty chests of tea were purchased. Each chest contained 5 poods of tea, each pood comprising 40 pounds. Two of the horses transporting the tea collapsed on the way, one of the carters fell ill and 18 pounds of tea were spilled. One pound contains 96 zolotniks of tea. What is the difference between pickle brine and bewilderment?

6.) There are 137,856,738 words in the English language, and 0.7 more in the French language. The English and the French came together and united their two languages. What is the cost of the third parrot, and how much time was necessary to subjugate these nations?

7.) Wednesday, June 17th, 1881, a train had to leave station A. at 3 A.M. in order to reach station B. at 11 P.M.; just as the train was about to depart, however, an order came that the train had to reach station B. by 7 P.M. Who is capable of loving longer, a man or a woman?

8.) My mother-in-law is 75, and my wife 42. What time is it?

A SERIOUS STEP

Aleksei Borisitch has just arisen from a deep after-lunch slumber. He is sitting by the window with his wife, Martha Afanasevna, and is grumbling. He is not pleased that his daughter Lidochka has gone for a walk in the garden with young Fyodor Petrovitch.

"I can't stand it," the old man mutters, "when young girls get so carried away that they lose all sense of bashfulness! Loafing about in the garden like this, wandering down dark paths! Depravity and dissipation, that's what it is! You, mother, are completely blind to it all! . . . And anyway, as far as you're concerned, it's perfectly fine for the girl to act like a fool . . . as far as you're concerned, the two of them can go ahead and flirt all they want down there! Why, given half a chance you too, old as you are, would gladly throw all shame to the winds and rush off for a secret rendezvous of your own!"

"Stop bothering me!" the old woman says angrily. "Look at him, he's rambling on, and doesn't even know what he's rambling about! Bald numskull!"

"Ha! Fine! Have it your way then! Let them kiss and hug all they want! Fine! Let them! I won't be the one called to answer before the Lord Almighty once the girl's head has been turned! Go ahead, my children, kiss—court away all you want!"

"Stop gloating! Maybe nothing will come of it!"

"Let us pray that nothing will come of it!" Aleksei Borisitch sighs.

"You have always been your own daughter's worst enemy! Ill will, that's all she's ever had from you! You should pray, Aleksei, that the Lord will not punish you for your cruelty! I fear for you! And we do not have all that long to live!"

"That's all fine and good, but I still can't allow this! He's not a good enough match for her, and besides, what's the rush? With our social status and her looks, she can find herself much better fiancés. And anyway, why am I even talking to you? Ha! That's all I need now, a talk with you! We have to throw him out and lock Lidochka in her room, it's as simple as that! And that's *exactly* what I'm going to do!"

The old man yawns, and his words stretch like rubber. It is clear that he is only grumbling because he feels a weight in the pit of his stomach, and that he's wagging his tongue just to wag it. But the old woman takes each of his words to heart. She wrings her hands and snaps back at him, clucking like a hen. Tyrant, monster, Mohammedan, effigy and a string of other special curses fly from her mouth straight at Aleksei Borisitch's "ugly mug." The matter would have ended as always with a momentous spit, and tears, but suddenly their eye catches something unusual: Lidochka, their daughter, her hair disheveled, comes rushing up the garden path towards the house. At the same instant, far down in the garden where the path bends, Fyodor Petrovitch's straw hat bobs up from behind the bushes. The young man is strikingly pale. Hesitating, he takes two steps forward, waves and quickly walks off. Then they hear Lidochka running into the house, rushing through the halls and noisily locking herself in her room.

The old man and the old woman stare at each other with stunned surprise, cast down their eyes and turn slightly pale. Both remain silent, not knowing what to say. To them, the meaning behind the fray is as clear as rain. Without a word, both of them understand and feel that while they were busy hissing and growling at each other, their daughter's fate had been decided. The plainest human sensibility, not to mention a parent's heart, can comprehend what minutes of agony Lidochka, locked in her room, was living through, and what an important, fateful role the retreating straw hat played in her life.

Aleksei Borisitch gets up with a grunt and starts marching up and down the room. The old woman follows his every move, waiting with bated breath for him to say something.

"What strange weather we've been having these past few days," the old man suddenly says. "At night it's cold, then during the day the heat's unbearable."

The cook brings in the samovar. Martha Afanasevna warms the cups with hot water and then pours the tea. But no one touches it.

"We should . . . we should call her . . . Lidochka . . . so she can drink her tea . . ." Aleksei Borisitch mumbles. "Otherwise we'll have to put a fresh samovar on for her . . . I can't stand disorder!"

Martha Afanasevna wants to say something but cannot. Her lips twitch, her tongue does not obey and her eyes cloud over. A few moments pass and she bursts into tears. Aleksei Borisitch, himself teetering on the verge of tears, badly wants to pat the sobbing old woman on the back, but he is too proud. He must stand firm.

27

"This is all nice and fine," he grumbles. "It's just that he should have spoken to us first . . . yes . . . first of all he should have, properly, asked for Lidochka's hand! . . . After all, we might not want to give it to him!"

The old woman waves her hands in the air, moans loudly and rushes off to her room.

"This is a serious step . . . ," Aleksei Borisitch thinks to himself. "One can't just decide willy-nilly . . . one has to seriously . . . from all sides . . . I'll go question her . . . find out all the whys and wherefores! I'll talk to her, and then I'll decide . . . This won't do."

The old man wraps his dressing gown tightly around himself and slinks to Lidochka's door.

"Lidochka!" he calls, timidly tugging at the doorknob. "Uhm, are you . . . uhm? Are you feeling ill or something?"

No answer. Aleksei Borisitch sighs, shrugs his shoulders for some reason and walks away from the door.

"This won't do!" he thinks to himself, shuffling in his slippers through the halls. "One has to look at it . . . from all sides, to chat, discuss . . . the holy sacrament of marriage, one can't just approach it with frivolity . . . I'll go and talk to the old woman . . ."

He shuffles into his wife's room. Martha Afanasevna is standing before an open trunk, rummaging through heaps of linen with trembling hands.

"There's not a single nightshirt here . . . ," she mumbles. "Good, serious parents will even throw in some baby clothes for the dowry! And us, we're not even doing handkerchiefs and towels . . . you'd think she wasn't our flesh and blood, but some orphan . . ."

"We have to talk about serious matters and you're nattering on about bits of cloth . . . I can't even bear to look at this . . . our daughter's future is at stake, and she's standing here like some market woman, counting bits of cloth! . . . This won't do!"

"And what are we supposed to do?"

"We have to think, we have to look at it from all sides . . . have a serious talk . . ."

They hear Lidochka unlock her door, tell the maid to take a letter to Fyodor Petrovitch and then lock the door again.

"She is sending him a definite answer," Aleksei Borositch whispers. "Ha, the simpleminded fools! They don't have the wherewithal to turn to their elders for advice! So this is what the world has come to!"

"Oh! I suddenly realized, Aleksei!" the old woman gasps, wringing her hands. "We're going to have to look for a new apartment in town! If Lidochka will not be living with us, then what do we need eight rooms for?"

"This is all foolish . . . balderdash . . . what we have to do now is to seriously . . ."

Until dinnertime they scurry about the house like shadows, unable to find a place for themselves. Martha Afanasevna rummages aimlessly through the linen, whispers things to the cook and suddenly breaks into sobs, while Aleksei Borisitch grumbles, wants to discuss serious matters and talks nonsense. Lidochka appears at dinnertime. Her face is pink and her eyes slightly swollen.

"So here she is!" the old man says, without looking at her.

They sit down to eat silently for the first two courses. Their faces, their movements, the cook's walk—everything is touched by a kind of shy solemnity.

"We should, Lidochka, you know," the old man begins, "have a serious talk . . . from all sides . . . Well yes! . . . uhm, shall we have some liqueur, huh? Glafira! Bring over the liqueur! Champagne wouldn't be bad either, though, well, if we don't have any . . . well, forget it . . . well yes . . . this won't do!"

The liqueur arrives. The old man drinks one glass after another.

"Uhm, so let's discuss things . . . ," he says. "This is a serious matter . . . your future . . . This won't do!"

"It's simply awful, Daddy, how you just love to talk nonstop!" Lidochka sighs.

"Well, yes . . . ," the old man says, startled. "No, you see, I was just . . . *pour se twaddler* . . . don't be angry . . ."

After dinner, the mother has a long whispered conversation with her daughter.

"I wouldn't be surprised if they're talking pure balderdash!" the old man thinks, pacing through the house. "They don't realize, the silly things, that this is serious . . . important . . . this won't do! No!"

Night falls. Lidochka is lying on her bed awake. The old couple is not sleeping either, whispering to each other till dawn.

"Those damn flies don't let one sleep!" Aleksei Borisitch grumbles. Yet it is not the flies that keep him awake, but happiness.

Anton Chekhov

SUPPLEMENTARY QUESTIONS FOR THE STATISTICAL CENSUS, SUBMITTED BY ANTOSHA CHEKHONTE

16.) Are you a clever person, or are you an idiot?

17.) Are you an honest person? A swindler? A robber? A bastard? A lawyer or . . . ?

18.) Who is your favorite satirist? Suvorin? Bukva? Amicus? Lukin? Yuli Schreier or . . . ?

19.) Are you a Joseph or a Caligula? A Shoshana or a Nana?

20.) Is your wife a blond? A brunette? A starlet? Or a red-head?

21.) Does your wife beat you, or not? Do you beat her, or not?

22.) How much did you weigh in pounds when you were ten years old?

23.) Do you partake of hot drinks—yes or no?

24.) What were you thinking about the night you filled out these census forms?

25.) Did you see Sarah Bernhardt on stage—yes or no?

QUESTIONS AND ANSWERS

QUESTIONS

1.) How can you tell what she's thinking?
2.) What can an illiterate man read?
3.) Does the wife love me?
4.) When can you sit and stand at the same time?

ANSWERS

1.) Search her premises.
2.) A heart.
3.) Whose wife?
4.) When you're sitting in jail.

O WOMEN, WOMEN!

Sergei Kuzmitch Pochitayev, editor-in-chief of the provincial news-paper *Flypaper*, came home from the office tired and worn out, and slumped down on the sofa.

"Thank God I'm finally home! Here I can rest my soul . . . by our warm hearth, with my wife, my darling, the only person in this world who understands me, who can truly sympathize with me!"

"Why are you so pale today?" his wife, Marya Denisovna, asked.

"My soul was in torment, but now—the moment I'm with you—I'm fully relaxed!"

"What happened?"

"So many problems, especially today! Petrov is no longer willing to extend credit to the paper. The secretary has taken to drink . . . I can somehow deal with all these things, but here's the real problem, Marya. There I am, sitting in my office going over something one of my reporters wrote, when suddenly the door opens and my dear old friend Prince Prochukhantsev comes in. You know, the one who always plays the beau in amateur theatricals—he's the one who gave his white horse to that actress, Zryakina, for a single kiss. The moment I saw him I thought: what the hell brings him here, he must want something! But I reckoned he'd probably come to promote Zryakina. So we started chatting about this and that. Finally it turns out that he hadn't come to push Zryakina—he brought some poems for me to print! 'I felt,' he tells me, 'a fiery flame and . . . a flaming fire! I wanted to taste the sweetness of authorship!'

"So he takes a perfumed pink piece of paper out of his pocket and hands it to me.

" 'In my verse,' he continues, 'I am, in actual fact, somewhat sub-jective, but anyway . . . after all, our national poet Nekrassov was deeply subjective, too.'

"I picked up these subjective poems and read them through. It was the most *impossible* drivel I have ever seen! Reading these poems you feel your eyes beginning to pop and your stomach about to burst, as if you'd swallowed a millstone! And he dedicated the poems to Zryakina! I would drag him to court if he dared dedicate such drivel to *me!* In one poem he uses the word 'headlong' five times! And the rhythm! 'Lil*ee*-white' instead of 'lily-white!' He rhymes 'horse' with 'of course!'

" 'I'm sorry!' I tell him. 'You are a very dear friend, but there is no way I can print your poems!'

31

" 'And why, may I ask?'

" 'Because . . . well, for reasons beyond the control of the editorial office, these poems do not fit into the scheme of the newspaper.'

"I went completely red. I started rubbing my eyes, and claimed I had a pounding headache. How could I tell him that his poems were utterly worthless! He saw my embarrassment, and puffed up like a turkey.

" 'You,' he tells me, 'are angry with Zryakina, and that's why you're refusing to print my poems! I understand! I *fully* understand, my dear sir!'

"He accused me of prejudice, called me a Philistine, an ecclesiastical bigot and God knows what else. He went at me for a full two hours. In the end he swore he would get even with me. Then he left without saying another word. That's the long and short of it, darling! And today's the fourth of December no less—St. Barbara's Day— Zryakina's name day! He wanted those poems printed, come wind come rain! As far as printing them goes, that's impossible! My paper would become a laughingstock throughout Russia. But not to print them is impossible too: Prochukhantsev will start plotting against me—and that'll be that! I have to figure out now how to get myself out of this impossible mess!"

"What kind of poems are they? What are they about?" Marya Denisovna asked.

"They're useless, pure twaddle! Do you want to hear one? It starts like this:

> *Through dreamily wafting cigar smoke,*
> *You came scampering into my dreams,*
> *Your love hitting me with one sharp stroke,*
> *Your sweet lips smiling with fiery beams.*

"And then straightaway:

> *Forgive me, O angel pure as a summer song!*
> *Eternal friend, O ideal so very bright!*
> *Forgetting love, I threw myself headlong*
> *Into the jaws of death—O woe, O fright!*

"And on and on. Pure twaddle!"

"What do you mean? These poems are really sweet!" Marya Denisovna exclaimed, clasping her hands together. "They are *extremely* sweet! You're just being churlish, Sergei! . . . 'Through dreamily wafting cigar smoke . . . sweet lips smiling with fiery beams'—you simply don't understand, do you? You don't!"

"It is *you* who don't understand, not I!"

"No, I'm sorry! I may be at sea when it comes to prose, but when it comes to poetry I'm in my element! You just hate him, and that's why you don't want to print his poems!"

The editor sighed and banged his hand first on the table, and then against his forehead.

"Experts!" he muttered, smiling scornfully.

Snatching up his top hat, he shook his head bitterly and went out.

"I will go look for a corner of this world where a shunned man can find some sympathy! O women, women! They are all the same!" he thought, as he marched over to the London Restaurant. He intended to get himself drunk.

DOCTOR'S ADVICE

For a cold, taking extract of *The hair of the dog that bit you* is helpful, on an empty stomach on Saturdays.

Head-spinning can be stopped in the following manner: take two bits of string, tie your right ear to one wall, and your left ear to the wall facing it. As a result, your head's capacity to spin will be inhibited.

For arsenic poisoning, try to induce vomiting, which can be achieved by a sniff of food bought at the Okhotni Ryad market.

For strong and persistent coughing, try not to cough at all for three or four days, and your ailment will disappear on its own.

A NEW ILLNESS AND AN OLD CURE

Operations on the body produce symptoms analogous to bouts of fitful fever (*febris intermutens*). Before making the incision, spasms of the peripheral vessels induce pallor. Pupils dilate. Our general deduction is that the sight of the approaching specialists agitates the vascular motor center and the *nervus oculomotorius*. A chill ensues. During the incision, we note a rise in body temperature and hyperestesia of the skin. After the incision has been performed there is a fever. Sweat breaks out.

On the basis of this analogy, I propose that all medical students dissecting a cadaver take a dose of quinine before coming to school.

FIRST AID

"Make way! Make way! Here comes the sergeant-major with his clerk!"

"The compliments of the season, Gerasim Alpatitch!" the crowd shouts. "Let us pray, Gerasim Alpatitch, that the Lord will bless, not you, not us—but whomever He chooses!"

The tipsy sergeant-major tries to say something, but cannot. He vaguely waves his fingers, goggles his eyes and forcefully puffs out his fat red cheeks as if he were about to blast the highest note on a trumpet. His clerk, a squat little red-nosed man in a peaked jockey cap, assumes an energetic expression and plunges into the crowd.

"Which of you here is the drowned man?" he asks. "Where's the drowned man?"

"Here! Here!"

The peasants have just pulled a gaunt old man in a blue shirt and bast shoes out of the water. The man is soaked from head to toe and sits on the meadow babbling, his arms spread out and his legs apart.

"O Saints in Heaven! O Christian countrymen of the province of Ryzan and the district of Zaraysk. I've given all I own to my two sons, and now I'm working for Prokor Sergeyev . . . as a plasterer! Now, as I was saying, he gives me seven rubles and says, 'You, Fedya,' he says, 'you must now worship me like a father!' May a wolf eat him alive!"

"Where are you from?" Egor Makaritch, the clerk, asks him.

" 'Like a father!' he says. 'May a wolf eat him alive! And that for seven rubles!' "

"He's babbling! He doesn't even know what language he's talking!" Anisim the squadron leader shouts in a cracked voice, soaked to the waist and obviously upset by the event. "Let me tell you what happened, Egor Makaritch! Come on now, let's have some quiet! I want to explain everything to Egor Makaritch. So the old man's walking over from Kurnevo—come on now, boys, quiet!—Well, so there he is walking over from Kurnevo, and the devil made him cross the river, there where it's shallow. The old man, being a bit tipsy and out of his mind, walked, like an idiot, right into the water, and the current knocked him off his feet and he rolls over like a top! Next thing he starts shouting like crazy. So there I am with Lyksander—what the hell's going on? Why is this man shouting? We look—he's drowning! What are we to do! 'Hey, Lyksander!' I shout. 'Holy Mother of God! Dump that goddamn harmonica and let's go save that peasant!' So we both throw ourselves right into the water, and, by God, it's churning and swirling, churning and swirling—O save us, Holy Mother of Heaven! So we get to where it's swirling the most, Lyksander grabs him by the shirt, I by the hair. Then the others here present, who saw what happened, come running up the bank, shouting—all eager to save his soul—what torture, Egor Makaritch! If we hadn't gotten there in time the old man would have drowned completely, never mind the holiday!"

"What's your name?" the clerk asks the drowned man. "And what is your domicile?"

The old man stares dully into the crowd.

"He's out of his mind!" Anisim says. "And how can you expect him not to be! Here he is, his belly full of water! My dear man, what's your name—no answer! He has hardly any life left in him, only a semblance thereof! But half his soul has already left his body! What a calamity, despite the holiday! What do you want us to do now? He'll die, yes he very well might! His mug is all blue!"

"Hey! You!" the clerk shouts, grabbing the drowned man by the shoulders and shaking him. "You! I'm talking to you! Your domicile, I said! Say something! Is your brain waterlogged? Hey!"

"Ha, for seven rubles, can you believe that?" the drowned man mumbles. "So I say to him, 'A dog upon you! We have no wish, thank you very much, no wish . . . !' "

"No wish to do what? Answer clearly!"

The drowned man is silent and begins to shiver with cold, his teeth chattering.

"You can call him alive if you want," says Anisim, "but if you take a good look at him, he doesn't even look like a human being anymore! Maybe some drops might help!"

" 'Drops'?" the clerk mimics in disgust. "What do you mean, 'drops'? The man's drowned and he wants to give him drops! We have to get the water out of him! What are you staring at? You don't have an ounce of compassion, the lot of you! Run over to the village, on the double, and get a rug so we can give him a good shaking!"

A group of men pull themselves away from the crowd and run over to the village to find a rug. The clerk is suddenly filled with inspiration. He rolls up his sleeves, rubs his palms against his sides and does a series of little movements, designed to show his bristling vigor and decisiveness.

"Don't crowd me, don't crowd me!" he mumbles. "All those who are superfluous here, leave! Did anyone go to the village? Good!

"Gerasim Alpatitch," he adds, turning to the sergeant-major. "Why don't you just go home? You're totally soused, and in your delicate condition it's best to stay home!"

The sergeant-major vaguely waves his fingers and, wanting to say something, his face puffs up as if it were about to explode in all directions.

"Put him on it!" the clerk barks as the rug arrives. "Grab him by the arms and legs! Yes, that's right. Now put him on it!"

"And I tell him, 'A dog upon you!'" the drowned man mumbles, without resisting or even noticing that he is being lifted onto the rug. "We have no wish to!"

"There, there! Don't worry!" the clerk tells him. "No need to be frightened! We're only going to shake you a bit, and with the help of God you'll come back to your senses. The constable will be over any minute now, and will draw up an official report according to the regulations. Shake him, and praise be the Lord!"

Eight robust men, among them Anisim the squadron leader, grab hold of the corners of the rug. At first they shake him timidly, as if they are not sure of their own strength. But then, bit by bit, they get a taste for it, their faces taking on an intense, bestial expression as they start shaking him with voracious passion. They stretch, stand on tiptoe and jump up and down as if they want to fly up in the air with the drowned man.

"Heave-ho! Heave-ho! Heave-ho! Heave-ho!"

The squat clerk runs around them, trying with all his might to get hold of the rug, shrieking in a cracked voice: "Harder! Harder! All together now! Keep up the rhythm! Heave-ho! Heave-ho! Anisim! You're lagging! Heave-ho!"

In the split seconds between heaves the old man's tousled head and pale puzzled face, filled with horror and physical pain, bob up from the rug—but immediately disappear again as the rug flies up to the right, plunges straight down and then with a snap flies up to the left. The crowd cheers. "Go for it! Save your soul! Yes!"

"Well done, Egor Makaritch! Save your soul! Yes, go for it!"

"Well, boys, and once he's better he'll have to stay right here! Yes,

36

the moment he can stand on his feet, the moment he comes back to his senses, he'll have to buy us all a bucket of vodka for our trouble!"

"Damn! Harnessed poppies on a shaft! Look over there, brothers! It's the lady from Shmelyovo with her bailiff! Yes, it's him. He's wearing a hat!"

A carriage draws up. In it sits a heavy middle-aged lady wearing a pince-nez and holding a colorful parasol. Sitting next to the driver on the coach box, with his back to her, is Stepan Ivanitch, the bailiff—a young man wearing a straw hat. The lady looks shocked.

"What is going on?" she asks. "What are they doing over there?"

"We're reviving a drowned man! Happy holidays, your Ladyship! He was a bit tipsy, you see; this is what led to it! We were marching all around the village carrying icons! What a feast!"

"Oh my God!" the lady gasps. "Reviving a drowned man? But that's impossible! Étienne," she calls out to Stepan Ivanitch, the bailiff, "for heaven's sake go tell them to stop immediately—they will kill him! Shaking him—this is pure superstition! He must be rubbed and given artificial respiration! Please, go over there immediately!"

Stepan Ivanitch jumps down from the coach box and approaches the shakers. He has a severe look on his face.

"What are you doing!" he shouts at them in a rage. "That's no way to revive a man!"

"So what're we supposed to do?" the clerk asks. "After all, he drowned!"

"So what if he drowned! Individuals unconscious due to drowning are not to be shaken, they are to be rubbed! You'll find it written on every calendar. Put him down immediately!"

Bewildered, the clerk shrugs his shoulders and steps to the side. The shakers put down the rug and look with surprise first at the lady, and then at Stepan Ivanitch. The drowned man, his eyes now closed, is lying on his back, breathing heavily.

"Damn drunkards!" Stepan Ivanitch shouts.

"My dear man!" Anisim says, panting, laying his hand on his heart. "Stepan Ivanitch! Why such words? Are we pigs? Just tell us plain and simple!"

"You can't shake him, you have to rub him! Undress him! On the double! Grab hold of him and start rubbing! Undress him, on the double!"

"Boys! Start rubbing!"

They undress the drowned man, and under the bailiff's supervision start rubbing him. The lady, not wishing to see the naked peasant, has the coachman drive her a little further down the road.

"Étienne!" she calls to Stepan Ivanitch. "Étienne! Come here! Do you know how to administer artificial respiration? You must rock him from side to side and press him in the chest and stomach!"

"Rock him from side to side!" Stepan Ivanitch shouts, returning to the crowd. "And press him in the stomach—not so hard, though!"

The clerk, who, after his feverish spurt of action is standing around not quite himself, also joins the others in rubbing the drowned man. "I beg you, do your best, brothers!" he says. "I beg you!"

"Étienne!" the lady calls out. "Come here! Have him sniff burnt leaves and tickle him! Tickle him! Quickly, for God's sake!"

Five minutes pass, ten minutes. The lady looks over at the crowd and notices a commotion. She hears the peasants panting and the bailiff and the clerk barking out orders. A smell of burnt leaves and alcohol hangs in the air. Ten more minutes pass and the peasants keep on working. But finally the crowd parts and the bailiff comes out, red and covered with sweat. Anisim is right behind him.

"He should have been rubbed from the start," says Stepan Ivanitch. "Now it's too late."

"What could we have done, Stepan Ivanitch?" Anisim sighs. "We got to him too late!"

"What is going on?" the lady asks. "Is he alive?"

"No, he died, may the Lord have mercy upon him," Anisim says, making the sign of the cross. "When we pulled him out of the water there was life in him and his eyes were open, but now he's all stiff."

"What a pity!"

"Well, fate decreed that death would fell him not on dry land but in the water! Could we have a small tip, your Ladyship?"

The bailiff jumps onto the coach box, and the driver, glancing over at the crowd as it backs away from the dead body, whips up the horses. The carriage drives on.

* * *

DATES OF FIRST PUBLICATION IN RUSSIAN PERIODICALS

After the Fair (Yarmochnoye "itovo") *Razvlechenie,* no. 36, September 13, 1884.

Confession—or Olya, Zhenya, Zoya: A Letter (Ispoved' ili Olya, Zhenya, Zoya: Pis'mo) *Budilnik,* no. 2, 1882.

Two Letters (Dva pis'ma) *Oskolki*, March 10, 1884, no. 10, signed "A man without a spleen."

Mayonnaise (Mayonez) *Oskolki*, September 17, 1883, no. 38, signed "A man without a spleen."

A Lawyer's Romance, A Protocol (Roman advokata: protokol) *Oskolki*, no. 6, 1883, signed "A man without a spleen."

A Fool, or The Retired Sea Captain: A Scene from an Unwritten Vaudeville Play (Dura, ili kapitan v ostavke: stsenka iz nesushchestvuyushevo vodevilya) *Oskolki*, September 17, 1883, no. 38, signed "A. Chekhonte."

Questions Posed By a Mad Mathematician (Zadachi sumasshedshevo matematika) *Budilnik*, no. 8, 1882, signed "Antosha Chekhonte."

A Serious Step (Seryozny shag) *Oskolki*, no. 26, June 28, 1886, signed "A. Chekhonte."

Supplementary Questions for the Statistical Census, Submitted by Antosha Chekhonte (Dopolnitel'nye voprosy: k lichnym kartam statisticheskoi perepisi, predlagaemye Antoshei Chekhonte) *Budilnik*, no. 5, 1882.

Questions and Answers (Voprosy i otvety) *Oskolki*, no. 7, February 12, 1883, signed "A man without a spleen."

O Women, Women! (O zhenshchiny, zhenshchiny!) *Novosti Dnya*, February 15, 1884, no. 45, signed "Anche."

Doctor's Advice (Vrachebnye sovety) *Budilnik*, no. 39, 1885, signed "A doctor without patients."

A New Illness and an Old Cure (Novaya bolezn' i staroe sredstvo) *Polnoe Sobranie Sochinenii*, volume 4, 1930–31.

First Aid (Skoraya pomoshch) *Peterburgskaya Gazeta*, no. 168, June 22, signed "A. Chekhonte."

Silence
and
The Boat-Women
A Story and a Dance-Drama
Yasunari Kawabata

—Translated from Japanese by Michael Emmerich

TRANSLATOR'S NOTE

Both "Silence" and "The Boat-Women: A Dance-Drama" come from a single book—a stunning, difficult collection of works in disparate moods and genres, titled beautifully Fuji no Hatsuyuki, First Snow on Fuji. *The book was published in April 1958, ten years before Kawabata received the Nobel Prize, one month before his fifty-ninth birthday, and like his other later works it is concerned with forms of presence and absence, with being, with memory and loss of memory, with not-knowing.*

It happens that "Silence" is the story that made me want to translate all of Fuji no Hatsuyuki—*that "Silence" is what inspired me, a young translator, to start translating. So it's particularly pleasing and appropriate that "Silence" should be the first of the works in the collection to appear in English, or in any other language besides Japanese. (Bradford Morrow and I have an idea that the story echoes in its structure Kawabata's novel* The Master of Go. *The continuing development of a western context for reading Kawabata and other Japanese writers is thus symbolized in this selection.) It is appropriate, too, that "The Boat-Women" be paired here in* Conjunctions *with "Silence." The piece was a first for Kawabata: written in 1954, it was the first of only two works for the stage that Kawabata ever created. Neither "The Boat-Women" nor the second piece, "Sounds of an Old Village," have received the attention of critics in the West. The poetry of "The Boat-Women" is extraordinary, though, and is perhaps in some sense Kawabataian as nothing else is. If Kawabata's style is centered in concentration, "The Boat-Women" is concentrated completely.*

The many "verses" in "The Boat-Women" are neither exactly "poems" nor "songs"—they are instead some combination of the two. Each verse is marked in the text with a vaguely mountain-like symbol, which indicates that the line is to be intoned—or chanted? or sung? Certainly the allusive intricacies of the language call to mind the traditions of the Noh—rather than simply spoken. The verses are divided into blocks of five or seven syllables in the Japanese, as Japanese poetry almost always is, and they are written in "classical" or "pre-modern" language; the rest of the dance-drama is composed in more or less "modern" prose. The battle fought between the enemy Genji and Heike clans at Dan-no-Ura in 1185, the history of which is told in The Tale of the Heike, forms the background of the piece. It is perhaps helpful to know that at this battle the Genji triumphed over the more sophisticated Heike, the courtly Heike, and that the story of Dan-no-Ura is one of the most moving and often-told stories in Japanese literature.

* * *

SILENCE

IT IS SAID that Ōmiya Akifusa will never say a word again. It is said that he will never again write a character—though he is a novelist, and only sixty-six years old. What is meant by this is not simply that he will no longer write novels, but that he will no longer write even a single letter or character.

Akifusa's right hand is paralyzed, is as useless as his tongue. But I have heard that he can move his left hand a little, and I thus find it reasonable to assume that he could write if he wanted to. Even granting that he would find it impossible to write passages of any length, still it seems likely that he could write words in large *katakana* when he wanted to ask that something be done for him. And since he is now unable to speak—since he can neither signal nor gesture with freedom—writing even the most crooked *katakana* would allow him to communicate his thoughts and emotions in a way not otherwise possible. Certainly misunderstandings would be less common.

However ambiguous words may be, they are certainly much easier to understand than clumsy body language or awkward gestures. Even supposing that old Akifusa managed to show by gestures that he wanted something to drink—by pinching his lips into a shape that suggested sucking, for example, or by miming the act of lifting a cup to his mouth—just making it clear whether it was water or tea or milk or medicine that he wanted, which of just these four—even that would prove difficult. How would he distinguish between water and tea? It would be perfectly clear which he meant if he wrote "water" or "tea." Even the single letter "w" or "t" would get the message across.

It is strange, isn't it, that a man who has made his living for forty years using letters and characters to write words should, now that he has almost entirely lost those letters and characters, and consequently come to understand the powers they possess in the most fundamental sense, and with the greatest certainty—now that he has become able to use them with such knowledge—it is strange, is it not, that he should deny himself their use. The single letter "w" or "t" might be worth more than all the flood, the truly tremendous flood of words and letters he has written in his life. That single letter might be a more eloquent statement, a more important work. It might well have more force.

I thought I might try saying this to old Akifusa when I visited him.

Going from Kamakura to Zushi by car one passes through a tunnel, and the road is not very pleasant. There's a crematorium just before the tunnel, and it's rumored that lately a ghost has been appearing there. The ghost of a young woman shows up riding in cars that pass beneath the crematorium at night—so the story goes.

It would still be light when we passed, so there was nothing to worry about, but nonetheless I asked the familiar-looking taxi driver what he knew.

"I haven't encountered her yet myself, no—but there is one fellow in our company who's given her a ride. And it isn't just our company, either—she's ridden in other companies' cabs too. We've got it arranged so we take a helper along if we take this road at night," the driver said. Judging from the way he spoke, he had repeated the story often enough to make him tired of telling it.

"Where does she appear?"

"Where indeed. It's always cars coming back empty from Zushi."

"She doesn't appear when there are people in the car?"

"Well—what I've heard is that it's empty cars coming back. She fades in near the crematorium, I guess. And from what I hear it's not like you stop the car and she gets in, either. You don't know when she gets in. The driver starts feeling a little weird and turns around, and there's this young woman in the cab. But since she's a ghost there's no reflection of her in the rear-view mirror."

"That's bizarre. I guess ghosts don't reflect in mirrors?"

"I guess not. They say she has no reflection. Even if human eyes can see her . . ."

"Yes, but I suppose human eyes would see her, wouldn't they. Mirrors aren't quite so impressionable," I said. But of course the eyes looking at the mirror were human eyes, weren't they?

"But it isn't just one or two people who've seen her," said the driver.

"How far does she ride?"

"Well, you get scared and kind of dazed, and so you start driving really fast, and then when you come into downtown Kamakura you relax, and by then she's already gone."

"She must be from Kamakura, then. She must want to go back to her house in Kamakura. They don't know who she is?"

"Ah, now that I don't know. . . ."

Even if he did know, or if there was some talk among taxi drivers about who she might be and where she might come from, it was doubtful that the driver would be careless enough to say so to a passenger.

"She wears a kimono, the ghost—she's quite a beautiful woman. Not that anyone's looking back over their shoulder at her or anything. You don't exactly ogle a ghost's face."

"Does she ever say anything?"

"I've heard she doesn't speak. It'd be nice if she'd say thank you at least, right? But of course when ghosts talk they're always complaining."

Just before we entered the tunnel, I looked up over my shoulder at the mountain on which the crematorium stood. It was the Kamakura City Crematorium, so it seemed that most of the dead cremated there would want to return to houses in Kamakura. Maybe it would be nice to have a woman as a symbol of all those dead, riding around at night in empty cabs. But I didn't believe the story.

"I wouldn't have thought that a ghost would need to take a cab. Can't they go wherever they like, appear anywhere?"

We arrived at Ōmiya Akifusa's house soon after we exited the tunnel.

The cloudy four-o'clock sky was faintly tinged with peach—a sign that spring was coming. I hesitated for a moment at the gate of the Ōmiya house.

I had only been to visit old Akifusa twice in the eight months since he had himself become a sort of living ghost. The first time was just after his stroke. He was some twenty years my senior, a man I respected, a writer who had been a patron of mine—it was hard for me to see him like that, ugly and miserable as he had become.

But I knew that if Akifusa ever had a second stroke, it was likely to be the end. We lived in neighboring towns—Zushi and Kamakura are no more than a stone's throw apart, as we say—and the fact that I had neglected to visit had begun to trouble my conscience. The number of people who had left this world while I considered visiting them, but somehow never did, was by no means small. It had happened so often I had come to believe that this was simply the way life was. I had been thinking of asking Akifusa to write out something for me on a sheet of *hansetsu* paper, but the idea had come to seem pointless. And the same thing had happened to me several times. Sudden death wasn't the sort of thing I could treat casually. I was perfectly aware that I myself might die at any moment—perhaps one night in a storm—and I did not take good care of myself.

I knew other authors who had died suddenly of cerebral hemorrhages or heart failures, of coronary strictures—but I had never heard of anyone being saved but paralyzed, as old Akifusa had been. If one views death as the greatest misfortune of all, one would have to say that Akifusa was extremely fortunate to go on living, even though he lived as a patient with no hope of recovery—as a disabled man. But that sense of good fortune was rather difficult for most of us to feel. It was also difficult for us to tell whether Akifusa himself felt that he had been fortunate.

Only eight months had passed since Akifusa suffered his stroke, but from what I'd heard the number of people visiting him had already grown quite small. It can be difficult to deal with an old deaf man, but it's no less difficult to deal with a man who is able to hear, but can't speak. He understands what you say to him, though you don't understand what he wants to say to you—it's even stranger than talking to a deaf person.

Akifusa's wife had died early on, but his daughter, Tomiko, had remained with him. There were two daughters, but the younger one had married and moved out—Tomiko, the older daughter, had ended up staying to take care of her father. There was no real necessity for Akifusa to remarry, since Tomiko took care of all the household chores—indeed, he had relished the freedoms of single life—and one might say for this reason that Tomiko had been obliged to make certain sacrifices for her father. The fact that Akifusa remained single, despite having had numerous affairs, suggests too that the power of his will was such that it overcame his emotions—or perhaps something else was going on.

The younger daughter was tall and had exceptionally fine features—she resembled her father somewhat more than her sister did—but this wasn't to say that Tomiko was the kind of young woman one would expect to remain unwed. Of course, she was no longer a young woman—she was approaching forty, so she wore almost no make-up at all—but one sensed a purity in her. She seemed always to have been a quiet sort of person, but she had none of the gloominess and irritability of an old maid. Perhaps her devotion to her father provided some comfort.

People who came to visit always talked to Tomiko instead of Akifusa. She sat beside her father's pillow.

I was startled to see how terribly thin she had become. It seemed odd to me that I was surprised, which meant that it was natural for her to be thin—but even so, seeing Tomiko suddenly grown so old and shriveled depressed me. It occurred to me that the people in that house were suffering.

There was nothing for me to say once I had said the pointless words of a sickbed visitor, so I ended up saying something I shouldn't have said.

"There's a rumor going around that a ghost has been appearing on the other side of the tunnel—have you heard? I asked the driver about it on the way here, as a matter of fact. . . ."

"Is there really? I'm always in the house—I don't hear about anything." It was clear that she wanted to know more, and so—thinking all the while that it would have been better not to mention the matter—I summed up what I knew.

"Well, it's the sort of story one can hardly believe—at least not until one actually sees the ghost. Of course, one might not believe the story even if one did see it. There are always illusions, after all."

"You ought to look for it tonight, Mr. Mita—find out if it really exists," Tomiko said. It was an odd thing for her to say.

"Oh, but you see it doesn't appear when it's light out."

"The sun will have set if you stay for dinner."

"Unfortunately I'm afraid I can't. Besides, it seems that the woman's ghost only rides in empty cars."

"Well if that's the case you have nothing to worry about, do you? My father is saying that he's extremely pleased you've come, and that he hopes you'll make yourself at home. Father—you'll have Mr.

45

Mita to dinner, won't you?"

I looked at old Akifusa. It seemed as though the old man had nodded his head on his pillow. Was he pleased that I had come? The whites of his eyes were clouded and bleary, and there were smudges of yellow even in his pupils—but it seemed that from the depths of those smudges his pupils were glittering. It seemed that he would suffer his second stroke when those glitterings burst into flame—it seemed it might happen at any moment—I felt uneasy.

"I'm afraid I'll tire your father if I stay too long, and that might . . ."

"No. My father doesn't get tired," Tomiko stated clearly. "I realize that it's unpleasant of me to keep you here with a man as sick as my father, but he remembers that he's a writer himself when there's another writer here. . . ."

"He—what?"

I was somewhat surprised by the change that had occurred in Tomiko's tone of voice, but I prepared myself to stay for a while.

"Surely your father is always aware that he's a writer."

"There's a novel of my father's that I've been thinking about a lot since my father became like this. He wrote about this young man who wanted to be a writer—the boy had been sending strange letters to him pretty much every day, and then he went completly mad and was sent off to a sanitorium. Pens and inkpots are dangerous, and they said that pencils were dangerous too, so they wouldn't let him have them. Manuscript paper was the only thing they would let him have in his room. Apparently he was always there in front of that paper, writing . . . at least he thought he was writing. But the paper stayed white. That much was true, the rest is my father's novel. Every time the boy's mother came to visit, he would say—Mom, I wrote it, Mom, will you read it? Mom, will you read it to me? His mother would look at the manuscript he handed her, and there would be nothing written on it at all, and she would feel like crying, but she'd say—Oh, you've written it very well, it's very good, isn't it!—and she would smile. Every single time she went he would pester her to read the manuscript to him, so she starts reading the blank paper to him. It occurs to her to tell him stories of her own, making it seem that she's reading the manuscript. That's the main idea behind my father's novel. The mother tells the boy about his childhood. No doubt the crazy boy thinks he's having his mother read some sort of record of his memories, something that he wrote himself—that's what he thinks he's listening to. His eyes sparkle with pride. His mother has no idea whether or not he understands what she's saying, but every time she comes to see him she repeats the same story, and she gets better and better at telling it—it begins to seem like she's actually reading a story of her son's. She remembers things she had forgotten. And the son's memories grow more beautiful. The son is drawing the mother's story out, helping her, changing the story—there's no way of telling whose novel it is, whether it's the mother's or the son's. When the mother is talking she's so focused she forgets herself. She's able to forget that her son is mad. As long as her son is listening to her with that complete concentration, there's no way of knowing if he's mad or not—he could very well be mad and sane both. And at those times the souls of the mother and the child fuse together—it's like the two of them are living in heaven—the mother and the child are both happy. As she goes on reading to him it begins to seem that her son might get better, and so the mother goes on reading the blank paper."

"That's the one called *What a Mother Can Read*, isn't it?—one of your father's masterpieces. An unforgettable work."

"The book is written in the first person—the son is the 'I'—but some of the things he remembers about his childhood actually happened to my sister and me when we were small. He just had it all happen to a boy. . . ."

"Is that so?"

It was the first time I had heard this.

"I really wonder why my father wrote a novel like that. The book scares me now—now that he's like this. My father isn't mad, and I can't be like that mother and read him a novel that hasn't been written down—but I do wonder if he isn't writing a novel in his head even now."

It struck me that Tomiko was a peculiar person—able to say things like this even though old Akifusa probably heard every word. I didn't know how to respond.

"But your father has already written numerous outstanding works—he and that literary-minded boy are entirely different."

"Do you think so? I think that my father still wants to write."

"Of course, not everyone would agree."

Personally I thought he had written quite enough already, but if I were in old Akifusa's condition—I had no idea what I'd think.

"It's just that I can't write for my father. It would be nice if I could write *What a Daughter Can Read*, but I can't. . . ."

Her voice sounded to me like the voice of a young woman in hell. The fact that Tomiko had turned into the sort of woman who said such things—could it mean that by being in constant attendance on her father, who was a sort of living ghost, she had been possessed by something in him? It occured to me that she might write a book of horrifying memories when Akifusa died. I began to feel a powerful hatred.

"What if you were to try writing about your father . . ."

I refrained from adding—while he's still alive. Suddenly I remembered some words of Marcel Proust's. A certain nobleman has abused lots of people in his memoirs, which are at long last about to be published, so he writes, "I'm on the verge of death. I hope my name doesn't get dragged around in the mud too much, since I'll be unable to answer." Not that it was at all like that with Akifusa and Tomiko. They were by no means strangers—indeed, there may have occurred between them a mysterious or perhaps a perverted emotional interchange, something beyond what most fathers and daughters experience.

I was struck by the strange thought that Tomiko might write about her father as if she had become her father.

Whether it became an empty game or a moving work of art, it seemed that either way it might provide some comfort for both of them. Akifusa might be saved from his absolute silence, from verbal starvation. Verbal starvation is surely not something one can bear.

"Your father would be able to understand what you wrote, and he'd be able to evaluate it—you wouldn't be reading a blank sheet of paper, and if you really wrote about your father, if you had him listen to you read . . ."

"Do you think it would be my father's work? If even a little of it . . ."

"There's no question that some of it would, at least. Anything more—it's up to the gods, and it depends too on how close the two of you are. I have no way of knowing."

But it did seem that a book written in such a way would have more life than a book of memories written after Akifusa was dead. If it went well, even the sort of life he was living now could be preciously literary.

"Even if your father goes on being silent, he could still help you, and he could still fix your mistakes."

"It wouldn't have any meaning if it ended up being my own work. I'll have to talk it over very carefully with my father." Tomiko's voice was lively.

Once more I seemed to have said too much. Wasn't what I was doing like forcing a desperately wounded soldier to return to battle? Wasn't it like violating a sanctuary of silence? It wasn't as though Akifusa was unable to write—he could write letters or characters if he wanted to. Perhaps he had chosen to remain silent, chosen to be wordless because of some deep sorrow, some regret. Hadn't my own experience taught me that no word can say as much as silence?

But if Akifusa were to continue in silence—if his words were to come from Tomiko—wouldn't that be one of the powers of silence, too? If one uses no words oneself, other people speak in one's place. Everything speaks.

"Shall I? My father says that I should give you some saké right away—that at the very least." Tomiko stood.

I looked instinctively at Akifusa, but there was nothing to suggest that the old man had spoken.

The two of us were alone now that Tomiko had left, so Akifusa turned his face in my direction. He looked gloomy—maybe there was something he wanted to say? Or maybe it irked him to be put in a situation where he felt as though he had to say something? I had no choice but to speak myself.

"What are your thoughts regarding what Tomiko was saying just now?"

". . . . ."

I addressed silence.

"I feel sure that you could produce a strange work, really quite different from your *What a Mother Can Read*. I started to feel that way as I was talking with Tomiko."

". . . . ."

"You never wrote an 'I Novel' or an autobiography—perhaps now that you yourself are no longer able to write, by using some other person's hand to produce a work of that sort—perhaps this might allow you to reveal one of the destinies of art. I don't write about myself, and I don't think I could write about myself even if I tried, but if I were silent and if I could write like that . . . I don't know whether I'd feel a sort of joy, as though I had finally realized the truth—if I'd think, Is this who I am?—or if I'd find the whole thing pathetic and give up. But either way, I'm sure it would be interesting."

". . . . ."

Tomiko returned with saké and snacks.

"Can I offer you a drink?"

"Thank you. I hope you'll forgive me for drinking in front of you,

Mr. Ōmiya, but—well, thank you."

"Sick people like him don't make very good conversation, I'm afraid."

"I was continuing our discussion from before, actually."

"Were you? As a matter of fact, I was thinking as I was heating up the saké that it might be interesting if I were to write in my father's place about all the affairs he had in the years after my mother died. He told me everything about them in great detail, and there are even some things which my father has forgotten that I still remember. . . . I'm sure you're aware, Mr. Mita, that there were two women who rushed over here when my father collapsed."

"Yes."

"I don't know whether it's because my father has been in this condition for so long, or whether it's because I'm here, but the two women have stopped coming. I know all about them, though—my father told me all about them."

"But your father doesn't see things in the same way you do." This was self-evident, but even so Tomiko seemed irritated.

"It's impossible for me to believe that my father has told me any lies, and it seems that over time I've come to understand his feelings. . . ." She stood up. "But why don't you ask him yourself. I'll get things ready for our dinner and then I'll be back."

"Please, don't worry about me."

I went along with Tomiko and borrowed a cup. It's best to get the saké in quickly when you're talking to a mute.

"It seems as though your love affairs have become Tomiko's property now. I guess that's the way the past works."

". . . . ."

I may have hesitated to use the word "death"—perhaps that was why I had said "the past."

But surely as long as he was alive the past was old Akifusa's property? Or should one think of it as a sort of joint ownership?

"Maybe if it were possible for us to give our past to someone, we'd just want to go ahead and give it."

". . . . ."

"A past really isn't the sort of thing that belongs to anyone— maybe I'd say that one only owns the words that are used in the present to speak about the past. Not just one's own words—it doesn't matter whose words they are. No, hold on—except that the present instant is usually silent, isn't it? Even when people are talking like I am now, the present instant is just a sound—'I' or 'a' or 'm'—it's still

50

just meaningless silence, isn't it?"

"............"

"No. Silence is certainly not meaningless, as you yourself have . . . I think that sometime before I die I would like to get inside silence, at least for a while."

"............"

"I was thinking about this before I came, but—it seems like you should be able to write out *katakana* at least, and yet you refuse to write even a single letter. Don't you find this at all inconvenient? If there's something that you want done—for example, if you wrote 'w' for water or 't' for tea . . ."

"............"

"Is there some profound reason for your refusal to write?"

"............"

"Oh—I see now. If the single letters 'w' and 't' and so on are enough to get things done, the sounds 'I' and 'a' and 'm' must not be meaningless either. It's the same with baby talk. The baby understands that its mother loves it. That's how it is in your *What a Mother Can Read,* isn't it? Words have their origin in baby talk, thus words have their origin in love. If you were to decide to write 't' every time you wanted to say thank you—and if every once in a while you wrote 't' for Tomiko—just think how happy she would be."

"............"

"That single letter 't' would probably have more love in it than all the novels you've written during the past forty years, and it would probably have more power."

"............"

"Why don't you speak? You could at least say 'aaa'—even if you drool. Why don't you practice writing 'a'?"

"............"

I was at the point of calling into the kitchen to ask Tomiko to bring a pencil and some paper when I suddenly realized what I was doing.

"What am I doing? I'm afraid I've gotten a little drunk—forgive me."

"............"

"Here you'd gone to all the effort of achieving silence, and then I come along and disturb you."

"............"

Even after Tomiko returned I felt as though I had been babbling.

51

All I had done was circle the perimeter of old Akifusa's silence.

Tomiko used the telephone at a nearby fish store to call the driver who had brought me.

"My father is saying that he hopes you'll come talk with him again from time to time."

"Yes, of course."

Having given Tomiko this rather offhand answer, I got into the car.

"Two of you have come, I see."

"It's still early in the evening and we do have a passenger, so I doubt she'll show up—but just in case. . . ."

We came out of the tunnel on the Kamakura side and drove under the crematorium. Suddenly, with a roar, the car began to fly.

"Is she here?"

"She's here. She's sitting next to you."

"What?"

The effects of the alcohol disappeared in a flash. I glanced to the side.

"Don't frighten me like that. I'm in no condition to deal with it."

"She's there. Right there."

"Liar. Slow down, will you—it's dangerous."

"She's sitting right next to you. Can't you see her?"

"No I can't. I am utterly unable to see her," I said. But as I said this I began to feel a chill. I tried to sound brave. "If she's really there—what do you think, shall I say something to her?"

"D—Don't even joke like that. You get cursed if you speak to a ghost. You'll be possessed. It's a terrifying idea—don't. Everything will be fine if we just keep quiet until we've taken her as far as Kamakura."

Yasunari Kawabata

THE BOAT-WOMEN: A DANCE-DRAMA

1. KURETAKE'S HOUSE

KURETAKE, a dancer
MURASAKI, Kuretake's daughter (ten years old)
KAGEKIYO, a man of the Heike clan
FIVE DANCERS
KABŪ, a boy spy (twelve or thirteen years old)
KOSASA, Kuretake's servant, an old woman
ONE OF KAGEKIYO'S ATTENDANTS
ONE OF KAGEKIYO'S RETAINERS

> Kuretake's house. Downtown in the capital. The cherry trees in the garden
> are in full bloom. Dusk approaches.
> The curtain rises as the chorus sings the following verse.

⌐\ Buddha is ever present   but does not ever   really appear
—how sad.

> *(The curtain rises.)*

> Kuretake is teaching the steps of a dance to the five young dancers. They
> blossom like the garden's cherry trees, brilliantly.

⌐\ In the darkness before dawn   no human noise   perhaps you
can see him   dimly in a dream.

FIRST DANCER. Even in a dream in the darkness before dawn—the
figure of Buddha. . . .

SECOND DANCER. I've never been able to see him.

THIRD DANCER. The only thing I see even in my dreams is *his*
face. . . .

> They laugh.

FOURTH DANCER. And yet, they say there is a path to Buddha-
hood. . . .

FIFTH DANCER. Even in the playful games of children.

KURETAKE. The lighthearted games of young children are precious
indeed. I myself am spattered with the dark grime of this world—
and yet when I awake in the middle of the night, dreaming in the
dark, suddenly—the motions of a dance, the melody of a song

53

drifts up in my mind. And this—this is the same as being lit dimly by Buddha's light. . . .

FIRST DANCER. But Kuretake, you're famous as a dancer—known in the capital—people say you're superior even to Gojō-no-Otsumae. . . .

SECOND DANCER. Surely a golden Bodhisattva appears in your dreams, and the two of you sing together, and dance.

KURETAKE. Don't be foolish. . . . Otsumae was one of the greatest dancers of all time. She was summoned to the Imperial Palace after she turned seventy—she passed away in the spring of her eighty-fourth year, contented, listening to a poem intoned by the Emperor, who had come to visit her on her deathbed—how could you compare someone like me to her?

FOURTH DANCER. My goodness! (*Surprised.*) I wonder if we'll still be singing at eighty-four.

SECOND DANCER. Hotokegozen, though dearly loved by Lord Kiyomori, visited Giō in Sagano and became a nun at sixteen. . . .

THIRD DANCER. Giō's place in Lord Kiyomori's heart had been stolen by Hotokegozen, so at twenty she became a nun. . . .

FIRST DANCER. At nineteen her younger sister, Gijo. . . .

KURETAKE. In a hopeless world, wherein lies a woman's happiness?

⌁ Flowers of many kinds blossom   fruit ripens   —how sad.

> Urged on by Kuretake, the dancers dance.

⌁ Wanting to play I was born   wanting to frolic I was born
when I listen to the voices of children playing   I am reminded
of my own spring   will it not scatter   the blossoming
flower   reaching to take it   come let's play.

> Kuretake's daughter, Murasaki, enters the garden as they dance. She frolics with (the young) Kabū.
> Kosasa sees them and gestures to Murasaki to come in.
> Kabū looks into the house.

KURETAKE. (*Turning to face* KABŪ, *speaking firmly.*) Slanderers of the Heike Clan are not permitted to enter this house. We have no use for spies.

KABŪ. It's dangerous with all the commotion in town, so I escorted Murasaki home.

KURETAKE. What commotion . . . ?

> Murasaki takes Kabū's hand, invites him to enter the house.

KABŪ. Heike warriors attacked the parade of the Emperor's Chancellor as it was making its way to the palace. Their violence was extreme. . . .

> The dancers are surprised. Kabū continues, speaking as though what he is saying is perfectly ordinary.

Of course, earlier—Lord Shigemori's son met the Chancellor's carriage on his way home from his flute lessons, and when he didn't greet him, he was whipped. It was terrible. But today, with this revenge—I'm sure the nobles realize only too well what the Chancellor did.

> Murasaki dances innocently by herself.

↖ Standing gathering seaweed on the rocky shore of Koyorogi
    do not wet those young women   waves stay
    offshore   waves stay offshore.

> Kabū frolics, seems to be tangled up in Murasaki's dance.
> Kagekiyo comes into the garden.

KOSASA. Kagekiyo has arrived.

> Kabū sees Kagekiyo and flees.
> The dancers stand and begin to leave.
> Kagekiyo prevents them from leaving, then sits down.

KAGEKIYO. I won't let you go home until you sing a verse.

DANCERS. Yes.

↖ I yearn to see you   my love I yearn to see you   I'd be thrilled
    if we could meet   if only we could meet   if I could see you
    if only we could meet.

> The dancers dance. Murasaki dances playfully in their midst.

KAGEKIYO. Your Murasaki's dancing won't embarrass you . . . she's grown beautiful.

KURETAKE. Well, who can say. . . . She's older than ten already—it seems there are some boys who tease her. It's quite pitiful, as it says in the poem.

KAGEKIYO. What? In this world, with the Heike so rich and powerful—my own bravery more resplendent than ever. . . . Well, Kuretake, shall we have a dance?

KURETAKE. Very well.

> Kagekiyo takes up a biwa and begins to play.
> Kuretake dances in time to Kagekiyo's biwa. Murasaki watches, absorbed.

⌇ Oh how precious   the preciousness of this day   this life the life of a drop of dew yet still I chance to meet   the joy of this day.

> Kagekiyo stands and dances in time with Kuretake.

⌇ The sadness of this day   yesterday a dream   tomorrow an illusion   today in reality here on my lap   the biwa I pluck and make sing   whose child listens   it is my own good child   oh how precious   the preciousness of this day.

> An evening breeze blows up as they sing and dance. The air fills with falling petals. The sun begins to sink.
> Kagekiyo's retainer enters the garden.

RETAINER. Sir—

> Coming out into the garden, the old woman prevents him from speaking.

RETAINER. (*To the old woman.*) Tell his lordship that the troops have all been ordered to gather this evening—we're off to destroy the Genji of the eastern lands. . . . I came as fast as I could. . . .

> The old woman is surprised. She has the retainer leave.
> Looking at Kuretake, who is still dancing with Kagekiyo, the old woman has a premonition. It seems to her that something terrible will happen.
> Murasaki becomes involved in the dance, dances innocently with Kagekiyo.
> Kagekiyo too feels vaguely uneasy. He dances all the more intensely with Kuretake.
> The old woman gazes at the dancers, absorbed in thought.

(*Curtain.*)

2. Kuretake's Rustic Residence

KURETAKE
MURASAKI, *about fifteen years old*
TOKIMARU, *formerly Kabū, now about seventeen years old*
OLD WOMAN KOSASA

> Kuretake's grass hut in the bamboo forest at Saga.
> A summer night. The moon shines brightly, quietly.

⌒ Even if it is not so   in the dew-wet fields of Saga. . . .

(The curtain rises.)

> Murasaki stands by herself.
> Kosasa sets out to fetch water from the well.

⌒ Longing for the past in a grass hut   still faithful this
bamboo   a single drop of dew on a bamboo leaf   holds the
light of the moon   but this life too will fall   —how sad.

> The sound of a flute approaches through the bamboo forest.
> Tokimaru (formerly Kabū) discovers Murasaki as he makes his way through
> the bamboo and runs out into the open.

TOKIMARU. Murasaki *(He calls.)*—it's more difficult for a person
hiding from the world to search for a person hiding from the world
than it was for Kabū to search for people who slandered the Heike.

MURASAKI. *(Walking towards him, nostalgically.)* Tokimaru.

TOKIMARU. Murasaki—I only wanted to meet with you once. The
fighting in town frightened me, so I walked through a village in the
mountains, playing my flute, yearning for you.

MURASAKI. My heart was charmed by the beautiful sound of your
flute.

TOKIMARU. The sound of the flute led me on to this place, where a
person I knew long ago resides. I swore that if I met you I would
stop playing. Here, let me give you this flute as a memento. I have
nothing to regret now—now that I have met you once.

MURASAKI. Why do you keep saying "once" . . . ?

TOKIMARU. The haughty Heike, too, lasted but a moment. . . .

⋏ The mighty must fall   they who are together must part   a
single brief meeting is the same as a bond of fifty years. . . .

> Tokimaru gives the flute to Murasaki and holds her hands, reluctant to part
> with her.

TOKIMARU. I'll climb Mt. Hie tomorrow. I prayed as I played my
flute that the day I met you would be the day I became a priest.

> The old woman returns, having filled a bucket with water. She sees them.
> Murasaki and Tokimaru draw apart.

OLD WOMAN. Murasaki, you mustn't leave your mother's side even
for a moment.

> She goes into the house and arranges gentians, miscanthus and other plants
> in the bucket.

TOKIMARU. How is Kuretake?

MURASAKI. In this life there's no way of knowing what tomorrow
will bring. . . . She's worn out from thinking of Kagekiyo. . . .

TOKIMARU. Is she ill?

MURASAKI. She can't bear to play the biwa, even, linked as it is to
the Heike—she can no longer dance or sing—her life has collapsed
completely. She's shameful to look at.

TOKIMARU. No, I'm the shameful one. Horses and carts moved off
to the side when they passed me, with my hair cut short, dressed
in red *hitatare*—and I thought it was because the way I carried myself gave me an air of authority. I walked proudly about town,
burst into ordinary people's houses, captured people. To undo that
sin. . . .

OLD WOMAN. Murasaki, Murasaki.

> She calls Murasaki into the house. Murasaki enters the house sadly, reluctant
> to part with Tokimaru.

TOKIMARU. Murasaki. . . . I'll be a priest after tomorrow—your face
will be my image of the Bodhisattva. I'll worship it day and night.

> Tokimaru starts to head back in the direction from which he came, but
> Murasaki comes out of the house and goes after him.

⋏ In this ephemeral world   just once I was able to meet   a
person dear to me. . . .

Tokimaru walks off into the bamboo forest. Murasaki follows after him for a while, then returns with the flute tucked into her obi.

OLD WOMAN. Murasaki, Murasaki.

Murasaki returns to the house.
Kosasa removes the screen. She lights the lamps.
Kuretake is lying in her bedding, sick.

〻 I yearn to see you   my love I yearn to see you   I'd be thrilled if we could meet.

KURETAKE. Murasaki! We must be grateful—the light of the Buddha came streaming in. For me, a dancer, the light of the Buddha is the light of art. . . . As long as I keep my eyes focused on that single ray, I have no troubles—I'm not sick. I begin to be able to hear the sound of Kagekiyo's biwa, strains that rise from those four strings.

Kuretake rises and takes up the biwa. It reminds her of the past. She embraces it.

〻 You drift on the waves of the western sea   afloat in a boat when a wind blows. . . .

KURETAKE. I don't know where Kagekiyo has gone.

〻 After he had gone   the rustle of leaves in the clump of bamboo   a lonely orphan's ties should be   with a distant father.

They all cry, heads sunk on their chests.
Kuretake sits up straight.

KURETAKE. When your mother is gone you must search for the sound of your father's music.

MURASAKI. Yes, mother.

KURETAKE. You must dance this dance, as I teach you.

Kuretake takes her fan and stands up straight. She tries with all her heart to remain standing, though her legs are unsteady.

OLD WOMAN. Go on, Murasaki . . . do your best to remember the dance your mother is about to show you—go on, Murasaki.

Murasaki takes her fan and stands ready, concentrating intensely.

⌐\ Oh how precious   the preciousness of this day   this life the
life of a drop of dew yet still I chance to meet   the joy of this
day   the sadness of this day.

> Murasaki collapses. The old woman runs to her and lifts her up.

KURETAKE. I'll be watching you from the Pure Land when you dance
to the music of your father's biwa, Murasaki.

> Murasaki is possessed by her mother's spirit. She dances more and more
> beautifully, more and more desperately.

⌐\ Yesterday a dream   tomorrow an illusion   today in reality
here on my lap   the biwa I pluck and make sing
someone's child listens   it is my own good child.

> Kuretake grows progressively weaker, then stops breathing.
> The old woman clings to her, weeping.
> Murasaki continues to dance all the more desperately.

> *(Curtain.)*

3. AKI-NO-MIYAJIMA

KAGEKIYO, *now* blind *(disguised as a* biwa-hōshi)
MURASAKI, *dressed in travel costume*
THREE GENJI SAMURAI
A PRIESTESS OF ITSUKUSHIMA SHRINE
CROWDS OF MEN AT THE FESTIVAL
CROWDS OF WOMEN AT THE FESTIVAL

> A place along the open corridor which circles Itsukushima Shrine. It is the
> day of the Autumn Festival, the autumn leaves are beautiful. The crowds of
> men and women who have come for the festival are dancing.
> Bugaku music continues for a short time, then the chorus sings this verse.

⌐\ Along a path which drifts on waves across the sea   the sighted
and   the blind   in a single boat   adrift in a single fate.

> *(The curtain rises.)*

⌐\ Yesterday we flourished with flowers in the capital   today
we've come to the autumnal western seas   Aki-no Miyajima
the solemn   Heike palace   though he is blind Kagekiyo
is manly and brave   excellently elegant the notes he plays
the familiar tune   tears fall on this biwa of

mine   harari hararin   harari hararin   the lap on which the
biwa rests has grown old.

> Men and women from the festival pass by.
> The blind Kagekiyo leans alone on the railing of the corridor, his biwa on his
> back. He crouches down and listens to the music without moving.
> The music stops and from the direction from which it had come three Genji
> samurai appear, walking down the corridor.

FIRST SAMURAI. The beautiful priestesses on this beautiful day. . . .

SECOND SAMURAI. Long ago a priestess from Itsukushima was summoned to the capital, and at Lord Kiyomori's mansion. . . .

THIRD SAMURAI. She was so lovely she was permitted to dance even
in the presence of the Cloistered Emperor Goshirakawa.

SECOND SAMURAI. The bugaku today was dedicated to the gods by
Lord Yoritomo. . . .

THIRD SAMURAI. He's going off to fight Yoshitsune in Ōshū, he
prays that he'll win the battle. . . .

> They draw nearer to Kagekiyo, and speak suspiciously.

FIRST SAMURAI. Well, well—*biwa-hōshi.*

SECOND SAMURAI. Why would a *biwa-hōshi* be off by himself, sunk
deep in thought? Vulgar, isn't it—that ferocious expression. . . .

THIRD SAMURAI. A suspicious man . . . is he a Genji or a Heike?

KAGEKIYO. I cannot see the Genji world. . . .

THIRD SAMURAI. What?

KAGEKIYO. You'll notice that I'm blind.

SECOND SAMURAI. What can't you see—say that once more?

KAGEKIYO. I do not listen to the thing they call the Genji biwa.

> During this exchange some of the people from the festival come across the
> corridor from the other side, appearing one at a time, and surround Kagekiyo
> and the samurai.

FIRST MAN. Why, it's a Genji interrogation.

PEOPLE. An interrogation, an interrogation!

FIRST WOMAN. They arrest a blind *biwa-hōshi.* . . .

Yasunari Kawabata

SECOND MAN. He said he hasn't got a Genji biwa.

> Everyone laughs.
> First Samurai looks over the women in the crowd.

FIRST SAMURAI. Are there any Heike women? A woman's better than a blind man.

> The women flee.

THIRD SAMURAI. At a Genji festival anything with a "Heike" in its name pollutes the shrine—get rid of that biwa.

> He pushes Kagekiyo away from the railing.

THIRD MAN. Is there even such a thing as a Genji or a Heike at a festival?

FOURTH MAN. It's the people's festival, they're the people's songs.

PEOPLE. Dance, dance!

SECOND SAMURAI. What?

> The samurai look angry, the people of the festival jeer.
> The people dance, as though mocking the samurai.

⌒ Genji and Heike   aristocrats and warriors   parents and children and brothers and brothers attack one another   war is the people's agony   women and children flee   today the town burns   and the looting. . . .

> As the chorus sings this verse the third samurai takes hold of the front of Kagekiyo's cloak. Kagekiyo automatically assumes a fighting position and twists the samurai's arm. The samurai show signs of fear.
> The people laugh.
> The three samurai become angry and drag Kagekiyo to the center of the stage.
> The people jeer with increasing boisterousness.

FIRST MAN. May you turn into a three-horned devil!

FIRST SAMURAI. What!

SECOND SAMURAI. You dare defy us?

> The samurai chase the people, who scatter. The people laugh, clown about and dance as they scatter.
> The samurai return and address Kagekiyo.

THIRD SAMURAI. If you're really a *biwa-hōshi,* sing for us.

SECOND SAMURAI. Yeah, hurry up. . . .

FIRST SAMURAI. Sing.

> Kagekiyo has no choice, so he plays.

⌃ Here on my lap   the biwa my hand knows so well   I play it
I make it sing   ah what a cheery song   whose child listens
it is my daughter.

> The three samurai and the people from the festival all listen.
> Kagekiyo stops playing and stands.

KAGEKIYO. The biwa has many modes, the heart has many registers,
harari hararin.

> The samurai mimic Kagekiyo.

FIRST SAMURAI. It is my daughter, harari hararin.

> The samurai depart, laughing.
> Kagekiyo goes off in the opposite direction.
> The people watch him leave.

⌃ The morning glory   eaten by insects   the fate of flowers
this too when autumn comes   the sighing of distant
fields   the bank of a river   in my dreams as I sleep
I yearn to meet my father.

> Murasaki comes dressed in travel costume from the direction where the
> music had been earlier, with the flute tucked into her obi. She walks down
> the corridor with the priestess of the shrine, looking sorrowful.

MURASAKI. I won't mind even if I have to travel a thousand miles to
meet my father, the man I search for. But I thought if I became a
priestess here at Miyajima I would certainly meet him—that's
why I came.

PRIESTESS. [*Apparently unable to comfort her.*] How very sad. It
sounds as though you're from the capital—and you're so beautiful.
Even if you hope to dance, it won't be allowed.

MURASAKI. You were kind enough to show me that elegant dance—
even that was a comfort. This journey is so terrible, your dancing
was a positive joy.

> Murasaki fusses with her clothes, as though unwilling to part with the
> priestess.

⌒ Autumn drizzle on a mountain path   snow on a road near
the coast   even these breasts of mine freeze   as I travel
alone. . . .

> The samurai return. Seeing Murasaki, they draw near her.

FIRST SAMURAI. Wow, beautiful. I haven't seen you around here,
young lady—are you a Genji firefly?

SECOND SAMURAI. Or a Heike bell cricket?

PRIESTESS. (*Thrown into confusion, shielding* MURASAKI.) She has
asked to be made a priestess, she's a guest. . . .

FIRST SAMURAI. No, she's not the kind of girl to dance before a god.
She looks like a dancer, like she plays with men. Play your flute
for us.

THIRD SAMURAI. Flute . . . ? First that biwa, now this flute—these
travelers with their musical instruments seem a bit strange. And
she's too beautiful—it's suspicious.

> He moves to catch hold of Murasaki.

FIRST SAMURAI. Hey, hey. Play your flute for us. Sing for us. If you
dance well we'll let you be a priestess at the shrine.

MURASAKI. Will you really?

FIRST SAMURAI. Go on, hurry up and dance.

> Murasaki dances.

⌒ Still I chance to meet   the joy of this day   the sadness of
this day   yesterday a dream   tomorrow an illusion   today
in reality here on my lap.

> People from the festival appear one by one as she sings. They watch.
> The samurai mimic Murasaki as she dances.

FIRST SAMURAI. Yeah, you said it—in reality here on my lap.

MURASAKI. Will you let me be a priestess here?

SECOND WOMAN. That song on the biwa, earlier. . . .

THIRD WOMAN. This one was just like it. . . .

MURASAKI. What? What do you mean, a biwa song just like it. . . .

FOURTH WOMAN. A song a traveler sang earlier.

MURASAKI. That traveler. . . . What kind of person was he? Which way did he go?

WOMAN 1, 5, 6. He went that way just a moment ago.

> Murasaki heads hurriedly in that direction.

⌐ Looking out over the mountain scenery   more beautiful than I had heard   Itsukushima.

> Murasaki hurries on as this verse is sung, until a samurai calls out to her.

FIRST SAMURAI. It was this way—if you're looking for the traveler, go this way.

> He points in the opposite direction, winking at samurai two and three.

SAMURAI 2, 3. Right, this way, this way.

MURASAKI. Was it really?

> Murasaki starts to go in the opposite direction.

PEOPLE. That way, that way.

> Murasaki heads back again.

SECOND SAMURAI. Hey!

SAMURAI 1, 3. This way, we're telling you this way.

> The samurai lead Murasaki forcibly in the direction opposite from the one in which Kagekiyo went.

PEOPLE. But—

> The people start to follow, but the first samurai glowers at them.

SAMURAI 1, 2. Dance!

PEOPLE. Dance!

> The people from the festival dance peacefully.

⌐ So very numerous   the votive tablets   the sound of bells on a priestess dancing a bugaku dance   in the rising tide lanterns   not autumn stars reflect   in the autumn-dyed mountains   a deer cries   I bow my head in prayer   with a quiet heart   I'll go from island to island   I board the boat from the sandbank at the torii   untie the line that strings us

to the shore   and push off   the oars' sweep beats a single
rhythm   a peaceful cheery song.

The dancing people move away as they dance.
Then, as if nothing has happened, Kagekiyo appears on the corridor. He
walks from stage right to stage left. When he reaches the middle of the stage
the lights are extinguished.

(*Curtain.*)

4. TOMO INLET

KAGEKIYO
MURASAKI
TWO BOAT-WOMEN
THREE TRAVELERS
TWO BOYS FROM THE VILLAGE
ONE GIRL FROM THE VILLAGE

An inland sea, the harbor at Tomo. The ocean off in the distance, a strait with
no mouth. A small island closer to shore. The sky is overcast, it looks as if it
might begin to snow at any minute. Shikoku is not visible.
The boat-women's small boat is near the shore.
A light snow starts to fall. Children from the village dance playfully.

へ In the inlet at Tomo   women divers fish for bream   in the
sea at Tomo   women divers draw in their nets   they are so
dear   they are so dear.

へ For their sisters   women divers fish for bream   for their
sisters   women divers draw in their nets   they are so
dear   they are so dear.

(*The curtain rises.*)

へ The fish climb   the wind blows   striking the bucket-drum
striking the bucket-drum   how I wish it would clear
how I wish it would clear.

Kagekiyo walks on stage while the children are dancing, then stands still.

GIRL. Look! A *biwa-hōshi*, a *biwa-hōshi*!

FIRST BOY. Gosh it's sad, isn't it—a blind priest.

66

KAGEKIYO. What's sad? The eyes of my heart see the things I want to see precisely as I want to see them. The flourishing capital, bravery at war, my own vigorous form. . . .

SECOND BOY. Tell us a story about that brave war. . . .

KAGEKIYO. And I can hear the sound of music from heaven.

GIRL. Play your biwa for us.

FIRST BOY. The one that goes beron-beron is the story of the Heike clan. . . .

GIRL/SECOND BOY. Barari-karari, karari-barari. . . .

> The children help Kagekiyo take the biwa from his back. Kagekiyo sits in a formal posture and begins to chant.

KAGEKIYO. I myself am a general of the Heike clan, known by the name Aku Nanahei. . . .

⌒ That name roars too   valiant beyond comparison Kagekiyo. . . .

KAGEKIYO. The Heike's luck ran out at war, it is painful even to remember—in the fourth year of Juei at Dan-no-Ura huge numbers of Genji troops overwhelm the Heike boats. . . .

⌒ A nun of the second rank   the Emperor's grandmother always ready   she holds his majesty in her arms   and steps to the side of the boat.

KAGEKIYO. The Emperor is only eight years old, he asks—Nun where are you taking me?—You were born the leader of ten thousand carriages of war, but now your good fortune has ended. First face the east. . . .

⌒ Bid farewell to the great shrine at Ise. . . .

KAGEKIYO. Then face the west and pray to be carried off to the Western Pure Land, then pray to Amitabha Buddha. The Emperor puts his dear little hands together. . . . (KAGEKIYO *sobs.*) Now at last the nun holds him in her arms, saying—Beneath the waves there is another capital. . . .

⌒ Preparing to enter the sea   a thousand fathoms deep   my eyes   how can they see this.

KAGEKIYO. I cry out and crush my own eyes, my own eyes I . . .

∧ Crush.

> The children are silent and still. They are looking at Kagekiyo's eyes. Kagekiyo forces himself to be calm.

KAGEKIYO. Well then, the story of a brave war. . . . At the Yumi river in Yashima, the reverse oar, the fan target.

> The children look bored. Once more they frolic and dance.

∧ Snow streams down   hail streams down.

CHILDREN. The boat's come, the boat's come!

> The children scatter in the direction of the boat, which is not visible.

∧ It falls and   it falls and   still it falls   how I wish it would clear   how I wish it would clear.

> Kagekiyo walks off, holding the biwa to his chest. Two boat-women pass him. It is clear from their expressions that they are waiting for customers.

∧ The fish climb   the wind blows   striking the bucket-drum striking the bucket-drum.

> Two travelers come from the boat and tease the boat-women.

SECOND CUSTOMER. I've heard that if one passes by Tomo offshore the cypress-wood fans beckon. . . .

FIRST BOAT-WOMAN. Tomo's most famous product—boat-women. . . .

FIRST CUSTOMER. Those cypress-wood fans. . . .

FIRST BOAT-WOMAN. Adorn the cabins on the boats. . . .

FIRST CUSTOMER. The scarlet collars. . . .

SECOND BOAT-WOMAN. Are wrapped around our waists. . . . [*She lifts the hem of her kimono and displays her legs.*]

SECOND CUSTOMER. Boat-women are. . . .

∧ Pillowed on the waves   rocking in a small boat   lovely and swaying.

FIRST CUSTOMER. Out on the sea, in this snow?

∿ Snow does not grow deeper on the sea   only the thoughts of women grow deeper.

FIRST CUSTOMER. Perhaps to see the cypress-wood fans. . . .

SECOND BOAT-WOMAN. Let's go to the boat—it's that one, that boat there.

SECOND CUSTOMER. Oh, it's cold. (*He looks at the boat and shivers.*)

FIRST BOAT-WOMAN. Shall we warm you with our snow-white skin?

SECOND CUSTOMER. Snow-white skin, did you say? It looks like goose-flesh to me, like the skin of a shark come up from the sea. I was amazed when I heard that Heike women had become prostitutes—what a story. . . .

FIRST CUSTOMER. This ugly-faced Heike crab, this spider-prostitute. . . .

SECOND BOAT-WOMAN. Weren't the Heike pinched the way a Heike crab pinches?

FIRST BOAT-WOMAN. Weren't the Heike embraced the way a spider-prostitute embraces?

FIRST, SECOND CUSTOMERS. Oh! How frightening!

∿ The fish climb   the wind blows   striking the bucket-drum
striking the bucket-drum   how I wish it would clear
how I wish it would clear.

> The second customer clowns about with the second boat-woman, and the two of them board the boat. The second boat-woman seems filled with power as she rows out. The first customer draws closer to the first boat-woman, and they walk off stage right.
> Murasaki's clothing is disheveled, but she has not lost her elegant and refined air. She chases the third man onto the stage.

∿ In the inlet at Tomo   women divers fish for bream   in the sea at Tomo women divers draw in their nets   they are so dear   they are so dear.

THIRD MAN. I told you my wife and kids are waiting, and you. . . .

MURASAKI. *(Taking the man's hand in hers.)* Even my breasts are cold in this snow. . . .

THIRD MAN. Which one? *(He puts his hands on* MURASAKI'S *breasts.)*

MURASAKI. Even these breasts sleep in pairs, on this lonely chest of mine. . . . *(She leans coquettishly on him.)*

THIRD MAN. There's nothing odd in that—you've got two.

> The man shakes Murasaki off and starts to go. Murasaki runs after him.

⌒ For their sisters   women divers fish for bream   for their sisters women divers draw in their nets   they are so dear   they are so dear.

MURASAKI. I'm not missing anything. When we're doing it. . . .

THIRD MAN. You certainly aren't missing anything—you're beautiful. *(He clasps her to him suddenly, without thinking, then hesitates.)* You're a Heike prostitute, aren't you?

MURASAKI. Yes. After the Heike clan was defeated at Yashima, when everyone was escaping—I was left behind at the harbor in Tomo. . . .

THIRD MAN. How old were you then?

MURASAKI. Why—I must have been. . . . *(She thinks.)*

THIRD MAN. You can't say, can you. That mouthless strait. . . .

MURASAKI. Won't you stay? Have a little rest in a strait with no mouth, be left with no regrets.

THIRD MAN. Your mouth and your lies have both gotten good. Yes, it seems the women are all Heike throw-aways.

MURASAKI. You think the baby bird is pretty, and it wants to be held by the daddy bird. . . .

> The third man gives Murasaki some money. Murasaki makes a face which shows that she thinks the amount too little. The man starts to go. Murasaki runs after him, surprised.

THIRD MAN. Look, I'm giving it to you.

MURASAKI. No, no—I don't need people's charity. . . .

THIRD MAN. Let me go. . . .

MURASAKI. I may have fallen in the world, but I don't beg.

THIRD MAN. You *are* a beggar, and you're stubborn—it doesn't go well with your face. Watch it—I'll throw you into the sea!

> The man pushes Murasaki down.

MURASAKI. Well, of all the rough. . . . I don't beg. I may sell my body, but I don't beg.

> Murasaki tries once more to stop the man. He shakes her off and pushes her down.

THIRD MAN. Grrh.

> Kagekiyo pushes Murasaki and the third man apart and stands between them.

KAGEKIYO. (*To* THIRD MAN.) Don't be violent.

THIRD MAN. Yeah, which one of us is being violent? My family's seen that the boat has come in.

> The man hurries off.
> Kagekiyo feels for Murasaki with his hands, shields her. . . .

KAGEKIYO. Are you hurt? Have your sleeves come unsewn? Oh, your hands are cold.

MURASAKI. (*Shaking him off, repulsed.*) A blind man will sew up the torn stitches for me?

KAGEKIYO. With a needle of the heart, tears in the heart. I'll sew them.

MURASAKI. The road we walk in this world is a mountain of needles—be very careful where you step.

> Murasaki picks up the money the man gave her earlier and gives it to Kagekiyo.

There was a beggar here earlier.

> Murasaki leaves, making a show of her slovenliness.

⌒ In the inlet at Tomo   women divers fish for bream   in the sea at Tomo women divers draw in their nets   they are so dear   they are so dear.

KAGEKIYO. How strange—that woman seemed. . . . She seemed to be a Heike, one of those left behind. [*He sits.*] The beautiful Heike have died out—I'll play for the wanderers.

> He plays his biwa.

⋏ Oh how precious   the preciousness of this day.

> Murasaki returns, seemingly possessed by the sound of the biwa. Then, feeling as though her heart has been pierced, slowly remembering the last dance her mother taught her, she begins to dance.

⋏ This life the life of a drop of dew   yet still I chance to meet the joy of this day.

> At last Kagekiyo stands and begins to dance. They fall naturally into line.

⋏ The sadness of this day   yesterday a dream   tomorrow an illusion   today in reality here on my lap   the biwa I pluck and make sing   whose child listens   it is my own good child   oh how precious   the preciousness of this day.

> Kagekiyo and Murasaki realize that they are parent and child. The want to tell one another their names, but they are unable to—they go on dancing. Snow falls so heavily that the two figures can no longer be seen.

⋏ I try to tell you who I am   but I am filled with shame   shall I say   shall I not say   oh father   oh daughter   and so together they dance   together they dance   a chance meeting   is itself   the fruit of an eternal bond.

> Kagekiyo moves as if to shake himself free of Murasaki, then clasps the biwa to his chest and cries. Murasaki places her own long cloak over Kagekiyo's shoulders and then continues dancing, seemingly even more possessed than before. She continues to stand in the fiercely falling snow.

(*Curtain.*)

Eighteen Poems
Djuna Barnes

—Edited by Phillip Herring and Osias Stutman

EDITORS' NOTE

The poems by Djuna Barnes included in this selection have never before been published. All but one of these remarkable works were written at 5 Patchin Place in New York's Greenwich Village, where she lived from 1940 until her death in 1982. With the exception of "Portrait of a Lady Walking," which can be dated circa 1924–26, these poems were composed after Barnes published her play The Antiphon *(1958) and* Selected Works *(1962).*

Most of the poems date from 1964–80, and reflect Barnes's ongoing interest in the Elizabethans and Jacobeans, especially John Donne. The poems went through many drafts, since Barnes preferred to start afresh each morning rather than returning to yesterday's corrected version of whatever poem or poetic cycles she was currently working on. For the last twenty years of her life she wrote in this revisionary manner. Some clean and presumably final drafts were typed by Barnes and her friend Hank O'Neal from 1978 to 1981, and all of the originals are now part of the Barnes archive at the University of Maryland, College Park. We have maintained in our transcriptions of the following eighteen poems all of Barnes's original punctuation and spellings.

Known primarily as the author of the lesbian tragic novel Nightwood, *in the latter years of her life she thought of herself as a poet. These highly polished jewels in the hard, intellectual, rhymed language of the Metaphysical poets may finally bring to Djuna Barnes the attention she deserves as a fascinating, if difficult, Modernist poet who took an older tradition and worked it magnificently to her purpose.*

*   *   *

73

Djuna Barnes

PORTRAIT OF A LADY WALKING

In the North birds feather a long wind.
She is beautiful.
The Fall lays ice on the lemon's rind.
Her slow ways are attendant on the dark mind.
The frost sets a brittle stillness on the pool.
Onto the cool short pile of the wet grass
Birds drop like a shower of glass.

LAMENT FOR WRETCHES, EVERY ONE

As whales by dolphins slashed, bring on a school
Of lesser fins to passenger the blood,
So comes my general man, both my priest, and hood
To ask, "who drank baptism down in nothing flat?
Who cut the comb in half to see it quick
With buzzing backsides, quartered out of cells?
And sick
And staggered regents staling pedestals?"
I replied:
"What heard of Darkness oysters in your tide?"

DISCONTENT

Truly, when I pause and stop to think
That with an hempen rope I'll spool to bed,
Aware that tears of mourners on the brink
Are merely spindrift of the shaken head,
Then, as the squirrel quarreling his nut,
I with my winter store am in dispute,
For none will burrow in to share my bread.

WHEN THE KISSING FLESH IS GONE

When the kissing flesh is gone
And tooth to tooth true lovers lie
Idly snarling, bone to bone,
Will you term that ecstasy?

Nay, but love in chancery.
In the last extremity,
Duelling eternity,
Love lies down in clemency,
Compounding rogue fidelity!

DERELICTION

Does the inch-worm on the Atlas mourn
That last acre its not inched upon?
As does the rascal, when to grass he's toed
Thunder in the basket, mowed to measure;
The four last things begun:
Leviathan
Thrashing on the banks of kingdomcome.

DERELICTION (Augusta said)

Augusta said:
"Had I the foresight of the mole
I'd have taken my paps underground
Papp'd and staked like a coachmans coat.
There suckled darkness, and the goat;
As women must,
Who suckle dust."

Djuna Barnes

DERELICTION AND VIRGIN SPRING

ITEM:

Tell where is the kissing-crust
Where three labours met; the trine
Father, Son and Ghost?
Not a crumb.
Who broke the bonding of that loaf apart?
Who drank the wine?
Who took the peel
And turn'd the Host on his own heel?
Who made the sign?
Who is the moocher with the down turn'd thumb?
Who capsized Jehovah in a ditch
At Gath?
Leviathan
Thrashing on the wharf at kingdomcome?

SATIRES (Satires of Don Pasquin)

Man cannot purge his body of its theme,
As does the silk-worm ferry forth her thread,
High Commander, tell me what is man
And what surmise?
Is breastmilk in the lamentation yet?
O predacious victim of the wheel,
St. Catherine of roses, turn your gaze
Where woe is;
Purge the body of its dread,
As does the bombace from her furnace heave
To weave a shroud to metamorphose in?
To re-consider in
What bolt of havoc holds your dread?
On what cast of terror are you fed?

VERSE

Should any ask "what it is to be in love
With one you cannot slough, she being young?"
What should it be, we answer, who can prove
The falling of the milk-tooth on the tongue,
Is autumn in the mouth enough.

LAUGHING LAMENTATIONS OF DAN CORBEAU

Observe where Corbeau hops, touches his fly
With cold, fastidious alarm, and piping forth
Flora, with the sweet sap-sucking cry
"What, kiss the famine of an old man's mouth!"
The party's "game" as mystery is posed in truth
"High" as a partridge on a peg is "high."
"Rather will I eat my fists in youth!"
So let them go, for God's sake; I'd as lief
She get my wisdom on a shorter tooth,
Nor shall I "eat my other hand for grief."

LAUGHING LAMENTATIONS

Lord, what is man, that he was once your brag?
A spawling job of flesh with off-set thumb.
Grown so insolent he lifts his leg
Upon the running sessions of his tomb.
And where's the black purse was his mother's bag?
(It coined his faces, both sides, good and ill,)
Why round his neck it bangs for begging bread,
Her Merry thought? The skipjack of the kill.

Djuna Barnes

THE BO TREE

All children, at some time, and hand in hand
Go to the woods to be un-parented
And ministered in the leaves. The frozen bole
The spirit kicks in spring, will that amend
The winter in the hearse? Pick from his hole
The daub was Caesar? Will the damned
Who rake the sparrows bones the fires burn black,
Find the pilgrim down, a tree stuck in their back?

DISCANT (There should be gardens)

There should be gardens for old men
To twitter in;
Boscage too, for *Madames*, sports
For memory, poor puff-balls of a day;
Soundless virginals laid on to ply
Suet to eat, and herbs to make them spin
Cuttle and costard on a plate, loud hay
To start the gnat—and then
Mulberry, to re-consider in—
Resign? repent?
Observe the *haute* meander of pavan
But never ask the one-foot snail
Which way you went.

DISCANT (His mother said)

His mother said
(Who long since in her mother is been hid)
"I am the birth-place and the dead."
"Indeed" he said
"Let it be done;
Let us give our tigers, each one to the other one."

DISCANT (He said to the Don)

He said to the Don, "My Lord
Your dangling man's not crucified
He's gored."
The picador replied:
"Truth is an handled fruit:
Isn't that your finger in His side?"

AS CRIED

And others ask, "What's it to be possessed
Of one you cannot keep, she being old?"
There is no robin in my eye to build a nest
For any bride who shakes against the cold,
Nor is there a claw that would arrest
—I keep the hoof from stepping on her breath—
The ravelled clue that dangles crock by a thread,
Who hooked her to the underworld. I said in a breath
I keep a woman, as all do, feeding death.

AS CRIED

"If gold falls sick, being stung by mercury"
What then, being stung by treason and surprise?
Will turn its other cheek?
And He replies (who is misquoted ere he speak),
"Why She
Who keeps the minerals of Paradise."

Djuna Barnes

THEREFORE SISTERS

Therefore sisters now begin
With time-locked heel
To mourn the vanishing and mewing;
Taboo becomes obscene from too much wooing:
Glory rots, like any other green.

Therefore daughters of the Gwash
Look not for Orpheus the swan
Nor wash
The Traveller his boot
Both are gone.

Seven Unfinished Poems
C. P. *Cavafy*

—Translated from Greek by John C. Davis

TRANSLATOR'S NOTE

When the Greek Alexandrian C. P. Cavafy died in 1933 at the age of seventy, his published poetic corpus amounted to 154 poems. Most of these poems—printed at his own expense and distributed by him—were produced on a very small scale, and, as scholars have noted, Cavafy thereby succeeded to a large extent in determining his readership and its reaction to his work. E. M. Forster first brought international attention to this extraordinary literary figure who, in Forster's words, stood "at a slight angle to the universe." The English author also described Cavafy in another way that was both pertinent, yet as time was to prove, mistaken: "Such a writer can never be popular. He flies both too slowly and too high." Since then, of course, Cavafy has become perhaps the best-known modern Greek poet outside of Greece, more so perhaps than Odysseus Elytis or George Seferis, both Nobel Prize winners.

The seven poems published here in English translation for the first time comprise a selection from a total of thirty-four unfinished works by the Alexandrian. These were first identified in the poet's papers, long after his death, by the literary scholar George Savidis in 1963. It was not until 1994, however, that the Italian neo-Hellenist Renata Lavagnini finally published all of them in a single volume (K. P. Kavafis, Ateli poiimata 1918–1932, *ed. Renata Lavagnini [Ikaros: Athens 1994]). Her edition contains detailed notes and a typographically elaborate presentation of the works' compositional evolution: the printed page graphically reproduces the layers of revisions and alterations that Cavafy made to his handwritten drafts. These poems, as Evripidis Garandoudis recently commented, constituted—until Lavagnini's edition—the only remaining poetic work of Cavafy still to await publication.*

The draft poems come to complement the other poetical work of Cavafy. He had kept them carefully in his files for the purpose

C. P. Cavafy

*of working into final form and, presumably, publishing them. It is
tempting to speculate on the choices the poet might have made
had he lived longer to devote further time to them. They deal
with themes familiar from Cavafy's other poetry: history ("Never
fail to mention Cynegeirus," "In the wooded glades" and "At
Epiphany"), moral speculation ("Guilt") and love (specifically,
homoeroticism, as in "The news in the paper," "That my soul
would pass through my lips" and "On the seafront"). Some, such
as "Guilt," show a combination of these themes.*

* * *

THE NEWS IN THE PAPER

There was also something about blackmail.
On this point, again, the paper stressed
its utter contempt for such depraved,
shameless and corrupt morals.

"Contempt" . . . while he, grieving inside,
remembered a night last year
they spent together in a room
of a hotel-cum-brothel: but afterwards
they never met—not even in the street.
"Contempt" . . . while he remembered those sweet
lips, and the white, exquisite,
divine flesh which he hadn't kissed enough.

Sadly he read the news while on the tram

The body had been found last night at eleven
down on the seafront. It wasn't certain
if a crime had been committed. The paper
expressed regret, but, ever righteous,
declared its utter contempt
for the depraved life of the victim.

—May 1918

THAT MY SOUL WOULD PASS THROUGH MY LIPS

There was absolutely nothing dramatic
in his tone when he said "Perhaps I shall die."
He said it in jest. In a way that any
twenty-three year old would say it.
And I—twenty-five—took it lightly.
No air (thankfully) of poetic sentimentality
that moves (vacuous) elegant ladies,
who sigh at the sound of mere trivialities.

But when I came up
to the door of his house
the idea came to me that it was no joke.
Perhaps he *had* died. And, filled with alarm,
I ran up the stairs: his was the third floor.
And without so much as saying a word,
I kissed his brow, his eyes, his mouth,
his breast, his hands, and every single limb;
I thought—as the divine verses
of Plato say—that my soul would pass through my lips.

I didn't go to the funeral. I was ill.
Alone, his mother wept for him, quite
innocently, over his white coffin.

—1918?

C. P. Cavafy

NEVER FAIL TO MENTION CYNEGEIRUS

Because he is from a noble Italian family,
and because he is twenty years old,
and because this is the way things are done in high society,
he has come to Smyrna to learn the art of rhetoric
and to perfect his knowledge of the Hellenic tongue.

And today, without paying the slightest
attention, he is listening to the famous sophist
lecture on Athens. Gesticulating,
full of passionate enthusiasm, the sophist tells
of Militiades, and the glorious battle of Marathon.
But he's thinking of the banquet he will attend tonight,
and his imagination conjures up a delicate face,
beloved lips which he is impatient to kiss . . .

He thinks of how much he enjoys himself here.
But his funds are running low. In a few months
he will return to Rome. And he recalls
that there, too, he owes much money. And that once again
he will have to find ways of avoiding payments
and of securing the means to live in a manner fitting
for someone of his station (he is, after all, from a noble Italian
    family).
If only he could set his eyes on the will
of old Fulvius. If only he knew
just what he is to get from that lecherous old goat
(two years, three . . . how much longer will he last!)
Will he leave him half, a third? Admittedly,
he's already paid off his debts twice.

The sophist is in raptures, almost in tears,
as he perorates on Cynegeirus.

—July 1919

ON THE SEAFRONT

An intoxicating night, in the dark, on the seafront.
And later in the small room of a disreputable
hotel—where we wholly unleashed our sweet, sick passion,
we gave ourselves for hours to "our own kind of love"—
until the windows shone with the new day.

Tonight is like that night:
it has revived for me a night from the distant past.

No moon, utter darkness
(this served our plans), when we met
on the seafront, far away
from the cafés and bars.

—April 1920

IN THE WOODED GLADES, OR,
IN THE WOODS NEAR EPHESUS APOLLONIUS OF TYANA
HAS A VISION OF EVENTS IN ROME

Domitian had become quite wild,
and the provinces suffered grievously under him.
In Ephesus, as elsewhere, discontent was rife.
But one day, while Apollonius
was discoursing in the wooded glades, quite suddenly
he appeared abstracted and seemed to speak
mechanically. Then he stopped his speech
and cried out—*"Smite the tyrant!"*—
in the midst of his many amazed listeners.
For at that very moment his soul had perceived
Stephanos in Rome striking with his sword
Domitian, who sought to defend himself with a golden goblet.
And finally he saw the horde of guards enter
and promptly slay the heinous,
half-dead emperor.

—1925

C. P. Cavafy

AT EPIPHANY

When at Epiphany they plotted the same
as they had done at Christmas,
to drag out the rabble again,
hoping to stir up once more
popular support for the child (alas for little Yannis,
son of good Sire Andronicus, who would have been in safer hands
with her and her son);

when at Epiphany they plotted the same,
inciting the rabble once again to obscenities
and vulgar insinuations about her,
she could not bear the strain a second time,
and, inside the wretched room to which she was confined,
Cantacuzene gave up the ghost.

The death of Queen Cantacuzene, so wretched as it was,
I have taken from the History of Nikephoros Gregoras.
Somewhat different, though no less pitiful, is the version
given in Emperor John Cantacuzenus' historical excursus.

—May 1925

GUILT

Tell that feeling of guilt to moderate itself,
for fine though it may be, it is dangerously one-sided.
Do not let yourself be obsessed or tormented so by the past.
Do not attach such importance to yourself.
The wrong you committed was less serious
than you think, far less serious.
The virtue which led you this way now
was, even then, latent within you.
Look, an instance comes
suddenly to mind explaining
an act of yours which then seemed
less than praiseworthy, but now must be excused.
Trust not your memory absolutely;
there is much you've forgotten—insignificant,
trivial things—that vindicated you enough.

And as for the one you wronged, do not think
you knew him so well. He must have had joys
        that you were unaware of.
So little did you really know about his life
that those deep wounds you thought you'd dealt him
may have been no more than mere scratches.

Trust not your feeble memory.
Moderate that feeling of guilt which, always one-sided,
will go to any length to twist the truth against you.

—October 1925

Cavafy's Ithaka
George Seferis

—Translated from Greek by Susan Matthias

TRANSLATOR'S NOTE

The Homeric hero Odysseus—"the man of twists and turns," as Robert Fagles has translated it—remains very much alive for modern Greek poets, and the best-known poem of C. P. Cavafy, at least for English language readers, is certainly "Ithaka." Cavafy reinterprets Odysseus's decade-long search for his homeland after the end of the Trojan War as an end in itself: ". . . hope the voyage is a long one, full of adventure, full of discovery."

In this 1952 essay, written nine years before he won the Nobel Prize and published here for the first time in English, George Seferis identifies Ithaka with Cavafy's birthplace, Alexandria, Egypt. Cavafy rarely traveled outside Alexandria as an adult, and yet as a Greek living abroad (albeit in a primarily Greek community) he felt, understandably, to be somewhat an exile. Seferis sees Cavafy's personal odyssey as the gradual recognition and acceptance of his authentic poetic voice, deeply rooted in Alexandria and symbolized by the "poor" Ithaka that nevertheless offered Odysseus—and Cavafy—their "marvelous journey" of self-discovery.

For his part, Seferis returned again and again in his own poetry to the figure of Odysseus, at times in the guise of a sailor, "A large man, whispering through his whitened beard words in our language spoken as it was three thousand years ago" ("Reflections on a Foreign Line of Verse"), and at other times as the travel-weary man seeking a warm hearth in a harsh world that has "become an endless hotel," as he wrote in Thrush. Seferis was born in Smyrna in 1900 and after the Asia Minor Catastrophe of 1922 he could never return to his birthplace. He was also often away from Greece, serving as part of the Greek government in exile during World War II and in the diplomatic corps (he was ambassador to England from 1957 to 1962).

Cavavy and Seferis, then, two of Greece's greatest poets in the

Modernist tradition, shared similar Odyssean experiences that shaped their lives and work. As Seferis put it in a 1968 interview with translator and scholar Edmund Keeley: "Greece is a continuous process. In English, the expression 'ancient Greece' includes the meaning of 'finished,' whereas for us Greece goes on living. . . ."

This text comes from Dokimes, Volume III. *Citations from "Ithaka" and "Waiting for the Barbarians" are from Edmund Keeley and Philip Sherrard,* C. P. Cavafy: Collected Poems. *Princeton, N.J.: Princeton University Press, 1992.*

* * *

IN THE POEMS OF CAVAFY, we often find the tone of an internal *dialogue*, as if we were hearing the whisper of the poet conversing with himself. This tone is very obvious in poems triggered by personal reminiscences. But I believe it is also present where we would least expect it: in the historical poems or in poems that offer advice.

In one of his earliest poems, for instance, "Waiting for the Barbarians," where—in the form of a dialogue heard among a crowd gathered in the marketplace—he describes for us a town ready to fall, like a ripe fruit, we notice suddenly that the final stanza seems to be uttered by a man who belongs, yet does not belong, to the psychological makeup of the poem's characters: someone who participates in this unfolding event but who is at the same time its despondent eyewitness:

> *And now, what's going to happen to us without barbarians?*
> *They were, those people, a kind of solution.*

This tone, this "monologue to himself," is, I believe, very deserving of notice for the understanding of Cavafy's poetry. It is this very tone which renders so inexplicably alive certain fragments fashioned from forgotten details of old manuscripts. It is the hidden sound which connects them to the life experience of the poet. I believe that those who have not paid attention to this tone, which comes so naturally to a man of solitude, call Cavafy cerebral—an indefinite enough adjective.

The isolation of Greek poets is great, whether the poet be named Kalvos, Palamas or Papadiamantis. But when I contemplate the life of Cavafy, I think that no one's isolation surpassed Cavafy's own. For this reason, I very much like Takis Papatsonis's remark that Cavafy's humor is of the "cloister" variety:

And now, what's going to happen to us without barbarians?

This too is the humor of a monk, the bitter humor of a man enclosed within high walls. One can note such humor elsewhere as well.

Moreover, even in poems that would seem at first glance to be impersonal images taken from a bygone life, the life experience of the poet is nonetheless always present in one form or another, more hidden or more obvious. That is why his works seem so deeply rooted in our contemporary life. This is indeed a very broad subject and today I can do nothing more than barely scratch its surface by offering one or two examples. The main example I have in mind is "Ithaka."

And if you find her poor, Ithaka won't have fooled you.
Wise as you will have become, so full of experience,
you will have understood by then what these Ithakas mean.

But, really, what do these Ithakas mean?

For the Greeks, seamen or expatriates, people of the Nation or of Greek communities scattered throughout the world, the meaning of Ithaka is inexhaustible. Cavafy is the poet of the Greek diaspora. He gave us, I feel, the most epigrammatic verse about the Greek who achieves greatness outside his fatherland:

with the variegated action of adjusted mental processes.

All of expatriate Greece is contained within this phrase: it is fitting that Cavafy wrote about Ithaka. But let us take a closer look at how this poem is connected more deeply to his life. Here we must consider that when it was written, somewhere around 1911, the poet seemed to be completing a great "circumnavigation" that lasted about twenty-five years, namely the long wandering towards a poetic expression faithful to himself and to his world. We are witnessing a veritable Odyssey. From 1886, when he publishes his first verses—verses of a mediocre disciple of Paparrigopoulos—until the moment when we see him now, he has spent more than a third of his life trying out forms, styles, eras, modes of expression, which he ultimately rejects. Had he died at forty, he would be remembered in Greek literature by two or three good poems, about as many "endearing" ones and a great stack of very bad versifications. Among these latter ones, I count of course some fifty poems unknown to most of the reading public, the so-called "rejected" poems. Now, as he is writing his "Ithaka," all this has been left far behind, along with the frequent complaints of the poet who resents his vain labors and realizes with impatience that he is still "on the first step of the ladder of poetry." Cavafy has discovered his true nature as a poet by now, he has found his characteristic voice; and, strange to say, only now, a little before the composition of "Ithaka," has he found the great capital he was seeking all these many years: Alexandria, with "The God Abandons Antony." One is startled at the thought that this man, who was born in this city and has lived in it so tenaciously, only now, in his forty-eighth year, discovers it. The gestures of a blind man, the tyranny of light which we note in poems such as "The Windows," no longer exist: the poet sees and induces others to see:

> *May there be many a summer morning when,*
> *with what pleasure, what joy,*
> *you come into harbors seen for the first time . . .*

At last, he has found his art, his Ithaka: it is *poor.* And in truth we note that in all his previous efforts, whenever he tended towards opulence of expression, towards pompousness, he failed. Cavafy is a very different poet from, say, Sikelianos; words do not spring up from within him. It took him quite a few difficult years to come to terms with this bitter realization, to accept that with his own nature, the only thing left for him was to grab on to something and to express it in as lean a manner as possible, replacing verbal sumptuousness which he lacked with the greatest possible precision, like that of a naked rock in the light, the light of Ithaka. He had encountered along his path the Cyclops and wild Poseidon rendered in false-ringing grandiloquence—to recall the words of Apollonius that Cavafy will later cite. Now he knows they were but phantoms set before him by his own hesitant soul:

> *Laistrygonians and Cyclops,*
> *wild Poseidon—you won't encounter them*
> *unless you bring them along inside your soul,*
> *unless your soul sets them up in front of you.*

George Seferis

This, as well as the entire poem, is not an *a priori* moral injunction; it is a ripe conclusion after a long struggle with monsters. And this besides:

> *as long as a rare excitement*
> *stirs your spirit and your body.*

This last line shows the kind of liberated sensibility that he expresses with such exactness for the first time. Spirit, body, emotion: a combination that reveals the manner in which Cavafy functions as a poet.

Considering the long journey of this poet towards his Ithaka—of which I have given only a faint idea—I note that the surprising phenomenon in this man is that he was able to create the so very individual features of his art, not only through his gifts, but even more so through his weaknesses. This, I think, is the basis of his originality. His poetry is a ceaseless ascent over its own obstacles. The particular genius of Cavafy is his ability to step upon his difficulties and to rise up, retaining them and remaining true to himself. One marvels observing this poet who seems to start out without any talent, except the talent of persistence, gathering little by little the living elements that he can sort out from a scrap pile, then fitting them together, transforming obstacles into stepping stones, and proceeding with the deliberateness of accumulated experience. From the outset until the moment he reaches his Ithaka, we observe him as he consciously or unconsciously, intentionally or instinctively, discards laboriously and ceaselessly those elements that do not correspond to his inner reality. This is for me the meaning of the poor Ithaka of Cavafy. If we now re-read the final lines of the poem, we will hear, I believe, once more the poet's whisper to which I referred at the beginning:

> *And if you find her poor, Ithaka won't have fooled you.*
> *Wise as you will have become, so full of experience,*
> *you will have understood by then what these Ithakas mean.*

Wise and full of experience: that is what Cavafy was indeed. Not long ago, listening to E. M. Forster speak to me about Cavafy, I experienced one of the deepest emotions I have felt recently. This elderly man recounted his memories with so much youthful freshness. We were sitting at a table in a tiny Indian restaurant. "The Greeks resemble the English, my dear Forster," Cavafy had once said

92

to him, "but there exists a slight difference; we Greeks have lost our capital. Pray, my dear Forster, pray that you English never lose your capital." The writer of *A Passage to India*, who had been linked at the outset of his career with John Maynard Keynes, one of the most famous economists of our time, remained silent for a moment, as if he were hearing from afar the words of his friend, who knew how to speak of the "journeys" of men, as well as of places.

94

From Black and White
Eugène Ionesco

—Translated from French by Esther Allen

TRANSLATOR'S NOTE

One Saturday night in late 1982 at a tiny theater in Westwood, my friend Alina and I saw two one-act plays for children that Eugène Ionesco wrote for his daughter, Marie-France, when she was young. There was a reception afterwards in a gallery that was exhibiting some of Ionesco's lithographs, and the man himself was present, though he did not seem to be a person who made any display of being the man himself. Alina is Romanian, and was soon deep in impenetrable conversation with Ionesco's wife, Rodica. Not knowing how else to start a conversation with him, I asked in my hard-won Southern California French if he would please sign a poster of one of his lithographs for me. "Esther," I told him. "Comme dans la Bible." Francophile to the marrow of his bones, as only a Romanian can be, he didn't miss a beat. "Ah no," he replied, "comme dans la pièce de Racine."

There it is: my poster. It has hung on the wall of wherever I happened to be living for the last fifteen years: a large, roughly human form (is it a king?) outlined in thick black lines on a white background, and colored in red, green and orange (he did eventually succumb to color). At right, below, a scrawl: "Pour Esther, l'amitié d'Eugène Ionesco."

A year before that evening in L.A., Ionesco had published Le noir et le blanc *(from which the following words and images are excerpted) in a deluxe limited edition with original lithographs (Editions Erker, 1981). It was reissued in a trade edition by Gallimard in 1985; this is the first time any of it has appeared in English. Translating it has been a way of returning the friendship Ionesco's hasty line bestowed.*

The lithographs were made during a residence of several weeks in a charming provincial town; Ionesco was given an artist's studio and an assistant, and gave himself over to the unfamiliar combat with line, shape and image that he found different from

95

yet akin to his usual grappling with language. He had no illusions about the outcome. "Looking at [these sketches]," he writes, "I ask myself how Salvador Dalí and Leonardo da Vinci were able to draw so well, but the universe goes on, so I believe that anyone, no matter who, can or must speak his piece."

These drawings are the work of a man in his early seventies, and in quite fragile health, though with a decade and a half of his life still to go before his death in 1994. Looking at them, we can ask ourselves if Youth might perhaps be nothing more than a highly effective marketing device.

* * *

TO DRAW, PAINT OR PHOTOGRAPH, you have to know, to be able to see, to perceive: behind the reality that is there for everyone (which, true, is no more than approximately the same for everyone) lies a second reality, more subjective and therefore, paradoxically, more universal and more exact, and then, according to each person's individual capacity, a third reality, a fourth, etc. The farther you go in the successive realities, the more of a realist you are, which is to say, the truer you are, not in the sense of conventional realism, but of true realism. There are several degrees of truth, or several depths. Several heights, I would say. But realism isn't reality! It's a school, a style, a manner. This sense of vision is a necessary but insufficient condition, for skill is also a factor, in other words, the art, the mastery that grows out of apprenticeship, the manual range of each artist. Everyone is an artist; I mean everyone is a spiritual being whose eye and hand are more or less practiced. Language is more or less easy: watch out for those who can't speak, or speak with difficulty.

What is all this around me? Why is something there? I put this fundamental question to myself dozens of years ago in a discussion with Emmanuel, a classmate at my lycée. I didn't yet know that the same question had been clearly formulated by the great philosophers. Once it is given that something exists, a second question arises: why is there evil rather than good? The terrible wars that take place now have no fundamental reason for being. And this despite all the explanations and reasons people give: without any motive, independent nations are swallowed up. The seizure of the economy by hegemony or war is superfluous, since all sorts of exchanges can be made through contracts and treaties. Industrialization can enable us, in the long run, to find a way to give everyone their daily bread. Wars are what prevent the development of greater universal well-being. They drain away all the energy and wealth that could have gone toward useful activities. Not long ago, the President of a Republic received a foreign Head of State. To the question asked by the President—"Why do you and your allies wish to overthrow Afghanistan's social and economic regime, when the Afghan people do not want you to? They are happy as they are."—the idiot Head of State replied, "*Ah non, il faut faire la Revolution.*" Whereas it is obvious that that is precisely what must no longer be done, what no one must ever do again. All the reasons given for political action, historical action, are simply irrational.

This hunger must be appeased, these appetites must be destroyed. I speak only as a sensible man. This simple, sensible language is spoken by no one or by very few people. Because it is banal, people consider it devoid of truth. Whereas the truth is elementary. I've already spoken of all this several times in my books. Maurice Genevoix used to tell me that I had so much good sense I seemed to be out of my senses, mad. Someone else declared that I was abnormally normal. I am a mortal who is more constantly and more sharply aware of his mortality than are many others. I had many friends I would have wanted to show my drawings to. I still have several, far fewer. Where are the rest? C. tells me, "I doubt they're anywhere." My turn to lose my senses: I doubt they're nowhere.

Ate too much at noon, drank too much beer; I no longer feel supple at all, I'm out of sorts. Maybe only for as long as it takes to digest. I start on some other drawings, my therapy.

One cannot keep oneself from thinking, it's been said. All right, then, let's think. And I think, I think, I would like to think only drawing. There is always that other language, my language, the words that overrun me, the words that creep into the drawings, which can often be reduced to words.

This character: is it a King? That thing around his head: is it a crown? He looks quite sad to me and yet I draw him in a state of joy, his advisors surround him. These advisors are unlike any others: their heads are triangles, with the wide base on the bottom. That's one interpretation. I think it's hard to give this drawing any other. No, these are lines on paper, lines and paper. Paper.

From a black spring emerge, explode, several types of black and white creatures. But why only human heads and not plant or animal heads? I'll do that another time, I hope, if Larèse loans me his studio again. Does it turn? A turning composition. I believe that the nucleus in the middle is the dispenser of life, a kind of life. (Not at all, I add, it's a piece of non-thought. Look, there are two ovals, two little ovals, towards the top, at right and left.) But no, it's just a carousel, like the ones at parks and traveling fairs. But the carousel symbolizes, too.

Eugène Ionesco

The tree of evil, which projects its creatures. On the right, above, a triangle, a figure that is trying to escape. This is plausibly the tree or mast of evil; to the left is a devil on his seat. To the right, a triangular figure with tridents or forks for teeth, or serpents' tongues; closer to the tree, a diabolical figure, sad, severe, but to the left of the tree, a grinning head, a second grinning head that looks like Uncle Nicou, poor idiot. Why is that triangular head, a little farther up on the left, so morose? It may be a psychiatrist or a psychoanalyst; he has a kind of black boot to his right, I wanted to make it a form devoid of any sense. (How tiresome, I haven't taken any more tranquilizers.)

In fact, this should be a graphic composition with some black, some white and some geometric forms. I shouldn't have put in those lines that look like noses, eyes, eyebrows. Fortunately, on the far right, a black triangle—which means absolutely nothing—supports, at the end of a chain, another black triangle. One does no more than find nature's forms again, debased. That's what one finds most often: triangles, rectangles, rings and thorns. I haven't gotten to steampowered machines, much less electronic machines. But my objects are not tools: hence their uselessness, of which I approve. I repeat myself in my drawings because nature repeats itself. Still, the inventory of nature's forms is far more numerous, far richer. Once again, I have a plan to do better: to deform other forms. As for inventing nonexistent forms, that's another problem, more difficult. Perhaps impossible. I'm ready for all sorts of undertakings; I will attempt the impossible. For that, I tell myself, you must not have too much science, ingenuity and ignorance of drawing will see you through. This drawing, too, is a composition, for everything starts at a center from which these forms move away. I have the feeling that it's rhythmic. My hope is that this is all that can be said of these shapes, these lines: a rhythmic equilibrium of antagonistic figures or forms. The black part, richer. Once again, I have a plan to do better: in the black areas, you can see the grain of the stone where the pencil has rubbed against it. There is light there. Rhythm and light, as far as I can tell. That's all, that's how one should speak of a graphic composition, but it is imperative to make things no one has seen before, otherwise why draw: to compose the uncomposable or to compose well with the uncomposable, or to make the composable uncomposable. Theories.

There is nothing to do, finally; one always falls back on black and white, on evil, cruelty, however ridiculous they may be. There is no good, in my drawings, or who knows, despite myself, this light that appeared on its own, the top of the bright tree. Are there really so few things that express at least what is somewhat good? If this black holds up in the light, have I nevertheless made a positive work? There is also, at right, a platform that looks like a woman's hat. That's what it looks like to me, but not to other people, who will see something else there. But any one of these drawings is unlikely to be looked at with the particular attention I might want. What will speak is the whole. Maybe.

Eugène Ionesco

The same procedure: a black tree with black branches and black leaves, the branches that emerge from the trunk have heads, or support heads. It strikes me as funny. It may be funny. With my ghosts of Good and Evil, black and white, I will have made no more than some funny drawings, fortunately.

Men's heads and horses' heads emerging from calyxes. Toys for children; it looks, pictorially, as if it's taking flight: is it merry?

There again I didn't know too well what I was going to do, it was the hand that guided me, distracted me, the hand which is the rhythm.

Eugène Ionesco

Too embarrassed to interpret this drawing.

White and black. Hanged white men and hanged black men. Compelled not to admit it. But above all, equilibrium of white and black, equilibrium within antagonism. The figures, pretexts for shapes. Is this true?

I cannot truly affirm that this drawing does not represent a tree. It is even a widower tree, an orphan tree. It bears not a single flower, a single leaf. It is alone, it has no children. No one near it. Sad, abandoned. Its own abandonment is what it offers. It weeps like a willow.

I could put some green, red, pink on it: it would have flowers and leaves. But I can no longer lift its sagging branches.

Yet I find it worthy in its sadness. Is it waiting for spring, even now?

The little white spots on the trunk are the grain of the stone: it is a child of stone. Its branches don't seem frozen to me, it is sad—but not dead or sick. Some movement. Does it want to touch the earth?

This is not an old tree. It is an adult. It is sorrowful but severe, far from being prostrate or dying. It has a soul.

A heart blooming at the foot of a branch that bears flowers and shoots. Beside it, other flowers, another heart, pirouette freely through the air. The light penetrates or surrounds them. A clover, larger than life, or a flower, or a heart is growing out of the central branch. Nor does the branch sink into the earth or into a trunk. The branch itself, detached, pirouettes freely.

Not far, on the right margin, a Saint Anthony's cross. The composition, forms and light, seems to me to be there.

Eugène Ionesco

Conclusion

What you've looked at: it wasn't faces, it wasn't masks, it wasn't monstrous figures, it wasn't caricatures, it wasn't shapes, or signs, it was nothing.

Perhaps semblances of fleeting apparitions. Right now all is calm in the space of this mental universe.

———

Back in Paris we learn that Maurice Genevoix is dead. Two days later, we attend his formal obsequies at the Invalides, for he was a severely disabled war veteran. He was ninety years old, one of the youngest men I've ever known. After having finished writing a book at the age of eighty-nine and a half, he wanted to begin a new career as a painter. I didn't see him often enough, outside of the Académie where I so rarely go. The last time I saw him, we all had to march in a single-file line from the dictionary chamber to the library. I don't remember what ceremony it was all for. He was behind me. He started tickling me. I knew another very young old man, Paul Morand, who also died at close to ninety. He was more than eighty when he wrote one of his best books, *Venise.* He didn't like my habit of wearing a polo-neck sweater to the sessions on the dictionary. He told Simone Gallimard, "Advise him to wear a shirt and tie." Two days later, a Thursday, I went to the Académie wearing a tie, I pointed it out to him with my finger, and he caressed my cheek with such tenderness. He was my sponsor at the Académie, he and Wladimir d'Ormesson, and Genevoix was the secretary in perpetuity. All three of them asked me to present my candidacy at once, while I was very hesitant. Wladimir d'Ormesson is also dead. I've lost three young friends, who were among the best. Because there was a lot of opposition to my candidacy and he wasn't sure I would succeed, Paul Morand went to get Henri Massis, who was very sick, he put him in a car and brought him to vote for me. I was elected on the first round by seventeen votes against sixteen: the decisive vote was cast by Henri Massis, a dying man. Two weeks before Paul Morand's death, my wife called him to tell him we were going to invite him to our house in the country soon. Paul had just written me a letter saying he had no more than a few moments left in front of him. Then he had a heart attack, was taken to the hospital and did not come back.

Back in Paris, I also learn that Soviet forces have massed on the Polish border and are threatening to invade. War, too, between Iraq and Iran, undoubtedly over the oil route.

Late summer, the sky is blue, transparent, God may be looking at me.

The Life Sentence
A Missing Passage from "The House of the Dead"
Fyodor Dostoevsky

—Translated from Russian by Peter Constantine

TRANSLATOR'S NOTE

Fyodor Dostoevsky's Notes from the House of the Dead *is a major work of psychological insight, a rich tapestry of the inner life struggles of a procession of characters banished to the harsh conditions of a nineteenth-century Siberian prison camp. Fiction and memoir are interwoven, insofar as Dostoevsky himself experienced life in such a prison camp from 1850 to 1854.*

"The Life Sentence" was not incorporated in the published text of Notes from the House of the Dead. *It was found among the papers of Alexander Milyukov, a friend of the Dostoevsky family, and was first published in the complete works of Dostoevsky,* Polnoe Sobranie Sochinenii *(Leningrad, 1972). It appears here for the first time in English.*

* * *

IN OUR PRISON barracks, Fyodor Mikhailovitch said, there was a young prisoner, a passive, quiet and uncommunicative man. I kept my distance from him for a long time—I didn't know how long he had been at hard labor, or why he had landed in the special section reserved for men convicted of the worst crimes. He had a good reputation with the prison authorities because of his exemplary conduct, and the convicts liked him for his gentleness and servility. We gradually became closer, and one day, as we were returning from labor, he told me the story behind his exile. He had been a serf in a province near Moscow, and this is how he ended up in Siberia.

"Our village, Fyodor Mikhailovitch," he began, "is big and prosperous. Our squire was a widower, not yet old—I wouldn't say he was evil, but befuddled and debauched with the female sex I would say. We had no love for him. Anyway, I decided to get married: I needed a woman to run my house, and there was a girl I loved. We came to an understanding, we got permission from the manor, and they married us. And as me and my bride left the church and were going home, we went by the squire's estate, and suddenly six or seven of his men came at us, grabbed my wife and dragged her off to the manor. I ran after them, but some men threw themselves on me. I yelled, I fought, but they tied my hands with straps and I couldn't break loose. Well, so they made off with my wife and dragged me to my hut, and threw me all tied up onto my sleeping bench, with two guards outside. I tossed all night, and late next morning they brought my bride back and untied me. I got up, and she threw herself on the table, crying with misery. 'Don't torment yourself!' I tell her. 'It is not your fault that you fell into sin!' From that day on I kept thinking and thinking how I could repay the squire for fondling my wife. I sharpened my ax in the shed, so sharp you could slice bread with it, and carried it hidden so no one would see it. It might well be that the other peasants saw me hanging around the estate and realized I was up to no good, but no one cared. No one had much love for our squire. But for a long time I couldn't get at him—he was with guests or with his lackeys. It was very hard. And I felt a stone in my heart that I couldn't pay him back for his evil deed. The bitterest thing of all was seeing my wife's misery. Well, so one evening I was walking behind the manor garden. I look—and there's the squire, walking down the path all alone, not seeing me. The garden fence was a low balustrade with a trellis. I let the squire walk ahead a ways, and then jumped over it. I pulled out my ax, stepped on the grass so he wouldn't hear me and crept up behind him. I got really close, and grabbed the ax with both hands. I wanted the squire to see who had come for his blood, so I coughed on purpose. He turned, saw it was me, and I threw myself at him, bringing the ax down on his head . . . Wham! Here you go! This is for having loved her! Brains and blood came spattering out. He fell without a gasp. And I went to the police station and declared that this and that had happened. So they grabbed me and beat me and sent me here with a twelve-year sentence."

"But you're in the special section for convicts with life sentences!"

"The life sentence at hard labor, Fyodor Mikhailovitch, is for a completely different matter!"

"What was it?"

"I finished off the captain!"

"What captain?"

"The one in charge of the chain gang. It was clearly his fate. I was

111

marching in a chain gang—that was the summer after I had settled things with the squire. It was in the province of Perm. The chain gang was huge. The day was blistering hot and the march went on and on. We were collapsing in the baking sun, we were worn to death. The soldiers in the convoy were barely moving their feet, while we, who weren't used to the chains, suffered terribly. Not everyone was strong—some were old, others hadn't had a crust of bread in their mouths all day. On this march no villagers came to the roadside to give us even a bite to eat. All we got was some water once or twice. How we made it the Lord only knows. So when we arrived at one of the camps some of the men just fell to the ground. I can't say I was finished, just really hungry. On forced marches in those days the chain gangs were fed. But here, we look and nothing's set up yet. And the prisoners start saying: 'What! They're not going to feed us? We have no more strength, we're skin and bones! We're sitting here, we're lying here, and no one's even throwing us a piece of food!' My feelings were hurt. I was hungry, but felt even worse for the old and the sick. 'Will we be getting some food soon?' we ask the soldiers.—'You have to wait!' they tell us. 'We haven't got the order yet.' So tell me, Fyodor Mikhailovitch, was this fair? A clerk was walking through the barracks and I said to him: 'Why don't they give us food?'—'You can wait!' he answers. 'You won't die!—'But look,' I tell him. 'Everyone is at the end of their rope, marching all day in this heat! Give us something to eat now!'—'We can't!' he says. 'The captain has guests, and they're having breakfast. When they're finished, I guess he'll give the order!'—'Will that be soon?'—'When he's eaten his fill and picked his teeth, then he'll come out!'—'What's this?' I say. 'He's resting, and we're dying like dogs?'—'Hey! How dare you raise your voice to me!'—'I'm not raising my voice to you,' I answer, 'I'm just saying that we have sick men who can barely move!'—'You're trying to start a brawl! I'm going to tell the captain!'—'I'm not trying to start a brawl!' I tell him. 'And you can report to the captain whatever you want!' Some of the prisoners began complaining and someone started swearing at the officers. The clerk flew into a rage. 'You're a troublemaker!' he shouts at me. 'The captain will take care of you!' He left. I was seized by a fury that I cannot describe. I knew this would end badly. I had a pocket knife for which I had traded my overalls with a convict in Nizhni Novgorod, and I don't remember now how I slid it from under my shirt into my sleeve. I look up, and I see an officer come out of the barracks, his mug all red, his eyes looking like they're about to pop—he must have been drinking. And that damn clerk behind him. 'Where's the troublemaker!' the captain shouted, and came right at me. 'So you're the one making trouble?'—'No, sir, I'm not making trouble. It's just that I'm worried for the others—do we have to starve to death? Neither the Lord nor the Czar has decreed it should be so.' He flies at me, shouting: 'How dare you, you nobody! I'll show you what's decreed for scum like you! Call the soldiers!' And I have my pocket knife in my sleeve and hold it ready. 'I'll teach you a lesson!' he shouts.—'Sir, you'll teach *me?* There's nothing *you* can teach *me!* I don't need your teaching to know myself!' I told him that to spite him, to get him even angrier so he would come closer. He won't be able to hold back, I think to myself. Well, I was right. He clenched his fists and ran at me. I jumped and whammed my knife into his belly and slashed it right up to his throat. He keeled over like a log. That was that. His unfairness towards the convicts had really maddened me. It was for this captain, Fyodor Mikhailovitch, that I ended up in this special section for life."

Antonia Pozzi, 1932

Twelve Poems
Antonia Pozzi

*—Translated from Italian with an
afterword by Lawrence Venuti*

LYING

Now the gentle
      annihilation
swimming backwards
sun in the face—brain
steeped in red
      through tight lids—.
That evening in bed
      the same
position the dreamy
      bright pupils
dilated drink
the blanc
      soul
of night.

—Santa Margherita, 19 June 1929

115

Antonia Pozzi

OMEN

The last light fades
on the poplars'
clasped hands—
the shadow
shivers with cold and
     waiting
behind us
slipped around our arms
     making
          us
more alone—

The last light falls
on linden branches—
in the sky
     the poplars'
     fingers
ringed with stars—

Something drops
from above
toward the shivering shadow—
something cuts the dark
a gleam—may be
something not yet—
someone who will be
     tomorrow—
     a creature
     of our grief—

—Milano, 15 November 1930

Antonia Pozzi

SWOON

November didn't
return:
    but at noon
        the sparrows
        cry
on the soaked branches
as if wishing
    night
    to fall.

Somebody forgot
    to fix
    the weights
in the clock:
the bird says
    cuckoo
just twice
    stops on its porch
    to watch
the pendulum
    jerks
    to a halt.

Now
I can't tell
time.

            —21 February 1935

Antonia Pozzi

ABSENCE

I sought your face
behind gates.

But the house
was anchored in a gulf
        of silences
the curtains fell
limp between
empty arcades,
        dead sails.

Offshore
the lake
        fled
debouched
from the unreal mountains,
gray-green waves
on the stairs
        withdrawing
from the stone.

In a slow drift
beneath the rapt
        sky,
the boat
vast
    and pale:
        we eyed
the red circle growing
on the shore
        azaleas,
        mute clusters.

—Monate, 5 May 1935

118

FLIGHT

The narcissus leans
a fresh face
into the breeze.

Child's hands
abrupt
      hedges
grasp at gates.

Breath-blown
in my run:

glimpses of things
      rubbished—useless
bridges—deafening
      abyss
devouring me.

        —*10 May 1935*

THE HEIGHTS

Wisteria bloomed
      slowly
over us.

The last boat
crossed the mountain lake.

At dusk
I gathered purple petals
in my apron
when the gate banged
the way back plunged
into darkness.

        —*11 May 1935*

OCTOBER

This nocturne
        liquid
     over the pebbles
collapse
of a dead season.

Languorous
     coal fires in the mountains
and a weak gleam
freezes
     in the fountain.

Dawn eyes
       the last
      flocks
descending
dogs, horses
a faint dust
over the ridge
      discomposed.

—Pasturo, 30 September 1935

Antonia Pozzi

THAW

Now the voided
                    road
        suspends us
from its lights:

borne by airy graves,

while words
            avoid
distant waters
down below.

Tomorrow
we will reach a sluice:
melting
        wary
of cracks,
                snow.

Easing
down my face
            regains
its warmth:

when
the soft soil flowers
                    in me
        the grace
of your lips.

—10 December 1935

Antonia Pozzi

ENVOI

The crags rose
             winged
   with terror
on the sleigh's
great flight:

and the red sun sank
   in a horse's shadow
over the ridge
of fir trees.
Then faint
guitar chords,
choruses
             soft, broken
beyond the peaks
raced with the sunset
over the hollow
tinkling canter.

At evening
the last pink hand—
a stone—
             beckoned above
saluting:
and pale
in the violet air
prayed to the stars.

Slowly in the night
the rivers
washed me
away.

—Misurina, 11 January 1936

MAY DEATH WISH

A mountain
cloister
    of leaves
    redeems
the laughter
of blue flowers.
Stop, pale
    sun
  nail
to the ground
these temples
      downed
  in moss
translate the weight
to eternal
    vernal.

—*May 1936*

Antonia Pozzi

SEPTEMBER EVENING

Snow   mountain   air

fills the village
          with bells
flings open doors
         to the gaunt
   late
   hay:

when the children
         hang
on the carts
brushing the warm
paths in the valley
transparencies
        of bright
houses.

Then the *winge*
reaches me
from the shadow
        gypsies
camped by the roads.

—Pasturo, 13 September 1937

Antonia Pozzi

PAN

A patch of sun
        danced with me
tepid on the brow,
the wind still rustling
the farthest leaves.

He came later
alone: the foam
of these waves
        blood
and a hammering of bells in the dark
deep in the dark
        through violent whirlpools
        through silent red jabs—
at the ripping.

Afterward
the ants stitched
a living black thread
        in the grass
        near the hair
and on my—
        on your
dewy face
a butterfly
parted
its wings.

—*27 February 1938*

Antonia Pozzi

* * *

Antonia Pozzi was born in Milan in 1912. During the 1930s she was the friend of leading Italian poets and critics, philosophers and publishers. She wrote a thesis on Flaubert, as well as an essay on Aldous Huxley. In 1937 she began teaching, but her fragile health deteriorated. In December of 1938 her body was found on the outskirts of the city, in the snow. She had drugged herself and contracted pneumonia. She died the next day. The official report listed the cause of death as "a sudden attack." Among her papers was found a set of notebooks that contained over three hundred poems. Written between 1929 and 1938, the poems are what she called "my secret diary." Their existence was known only to her closest childhood friends, particularly two women to whom she sent manuscript copies.

———————

Antonia's suicide at twenty-six, as well as her gender, made early critics uncomfortable, reluctant to pronounce her an important contemporary poet. So they decided that the case was moot, her talents unfulfilled. They searched for signs of "femininity" in her poems. Eugenio Montale preferred to read them as *poems*, which everywhere evinced a "desire to reduce the weight of words to the minimum." And he shrewdly observed that "this desire already constitutes Pozzi's departure from the generic feminine gratuity that is the dream of so many male critics."

———————

Between 1939 and 1989 Antonia's poems were published in several substantial selections. Yet they were all based on texts edited by her father, Roberto, who undoubtedly wanted to craft a respectable image of his daughter. Thus he revised the line, *"Tremolano nella mia anima impura"* ("They tremble in my impure soul") by deleting the word *"impura."* He also retitled poems to remove any hint of suicide. *"Fine"* ("End") became *"Imbarco"* ("Embarkation").

———————

Stylistically, the poems are representative of "hermeticism" (*ermetismo*), the powerful combination of precise language, dense

126

imagery and free verse that dominated Italian poetry from the 1920s to the 1950s. Antonia admired the first books of the major hermetic poets: Giuseppe Ungaretti, Montale, Salvatore Quasimodo. She would underline titles and phrases in their work. And she understood it in the context of international Modernist trends. She read Eliot, Pound, Valéry and Rilke in the original languages.

Ermetismo was initially a pejorative label, a swipe at the obscurity created by the Modernist form of the poems, their avoidance of ornate diction and rhetorical tropes, their discontinuities and ellipses, their metaphysical silences. Yet this poetry came to dominance under Mussolini as a defense against fascism, a withdrawal from hopeless political action to evoke deeply personal experiences, at once dramatic and transitory. Antonia's poems are frankly autobiographical, intimately connected to the decisive moments in her life. These moments began at age five, when her parents purchased an eighteenth-century villa in Pasturo, a small village in the mountains of northeastern Lombardy. Then at fifteen she fell in love with a classics professor at her secondary school, a man whom her father forbade her to marry, but who returned her love. Antonia continued the relationship for some years before finally abandoning it.

In 1955 the British publisher John Calder issued a bilingual selection of Antonia's poems rendered by Nora Wydenbruck, a translator of Rilke. Wydenbruck's version was based on texts that Roberto Pozzi had edited. She also tried to efface the Modernist style of the poems. A reviewer for the *Times Literary Supplement* described her translation as "overscrupulous sometimes in its purpose of making the original as intelligible as possible." Wydenbruck herself wrote that "English is perhaps the language best adapted to imitate the terseness and render the delicate overtones of Antonia's diction." But this had little effect on her translation. Where the Italian reads simply "bianca bellezza" (white beauty") or "veste" ("clothes") , the English inflates and exoticizes: "white, dazzling splendour," "veils."

Against the backdrop of British and American poetic traditions, Antonia Pozzi conjures up suggestive resemblances, some more telling than others. Emily Dickinson, Sylvia Plath—an isolated woman whose unsettling poetry is dubiously edited by friends and relatives is now a familiar figure in our literary history. The mark of a compelling translation, however, is its impact on the native traditions it must use to rewrite the foreign work. Antonia offered me an unusual opportunity to make Modernist poetry in English a little less familiar. Relying on a 1989 Italian text that returns to her notebooks and manuscripts, I tried to recreate precisely those features that Wydenbruck perceived in the poems. When I read the Italian, however, I heard the stripped-down classicism of H. D. and the angular but mellifluous rhythms of Lorine Niedecker. I even recalled specific poems, like H. D.'s "Wine Bowl" (1931) and Niedecker's "In Exchange for Haiku" (1959):

> *July—waxwings*
> *on the berries*
> *have dyed red*
> > *the dead*
> *branch*

The sound effects I sought weren't so much in the Italian as inspired by its abrupt musicality, now resonant with Anglo-American Modernism. Yet no reader is likely to confuse the poetries in play here. On the contrary, Antonia's landscape, her personal dramas, her tragic death all ensure that any resemblance to poets living or dead is purely . . . uncanny.

The Indifferent One
Marcel Proust

—Translated from French by Burton Pike

TRANSLATOR'S NOTE

Proust intended this story for Les plaisirs et les jours, *but substituted another for it. It was written in 1893–1894, when Proust was twenty-two, and published in an obscure and ephemeral periodical in 1896. As he was beginning to write* A la recherche du temps perdu *in 1910, Proust tried to find a copy of this story; it is not known whether he succeeded. The many links between the story and the novel are striking. The story was recovered and published in French only in 1978, and was previously available only in a very limited edition in English by another translator.*

*   *   *

I.

MADELEINE DE GOUVRES HAD just arrived in the box of Mme. Lawrence. General de Buivres asked: "Who are your gallants this evening? Avranches? Lepré?"

"Avranches, yes," Mme. Lawrence answered. "Lepré, I didn't dare."

Indicating Madeleine, she added: "She is so difficult, and as it would have been almost like introducing her to a new acquaintance . . ."

Madeleine protested. She had met M. Lepré several times, found him charming; he had even, once, lunched with her.

"In any event," Mme. Lawrence concluded, "you need have no regrets. He is quite nice, but there's nothing remarkable about him, and nothing at all for the most spoiled woman in Paris. I can quite understand that your kind of intimacies makes you difficult."

Lepré was very nice but quite insignificant, that was society's opinion. Madeleine felt that it was not at all hers, and was astonished; but as Lepré's absence did not cause a more lively disappointment in her either, her feelings did not go so far as to worry about it.

Heads in the hall were turned towards her, friends were already

129

coming up to greet and compliment her. This was nothing new, but yet, with the subliminal clairvoyance of a jockey during a race, or an actor during a performance, this evening she felt herself triumphing more easily and more completely than was usual. Without a jewel, her bodice of yellow tulle covered with cattleyas, her black hair was also adorned with cattleyas, which suspended pale garlands of light within this shadowy tower. As fresh as her flowers, and like them pensive, with the Polynesian charm of her hairdo she recalled the Mahenu of Pierre Loti and of Reynaldo Hahn. Soon a regret mixed in with the happy indifference with which she saw her graces mirrored this evening in the dazzled eyes that reflected them with an infallible fidelity, a regret that Lepré had not seen her thus.

"How she loves flowers!" Mme. Lawrence exclaimed, looking at Madeleine's bodice.

She indeed did love them, in the vulgar sense that she knew how beautiful they were and how beautiful they made her. She loved their beauty, their gaiety, their sadness too, but from the outside, as one of the stances of their beauty. When they were no longer fresh, she threw them out like a faded dress.

Suddenly, during the first intermission, Madeleine glimpsed Lepré down in the orchestra, a few instants after General de Buivres and the Duke and Duchess of Aleriouvres had left, leaving her alone with Mme. Lawrence. Madeleine saw that the door of the box was being opened for Lepré.

"Madame Lawrence," she said, "will you authorize me to ask M. Lepré to stay with us, since he is by himself in the orchestra?"

"But the more so, my dear, as I will be obliged to leave in a few moments; you know, you gave me permission; Robert is not feeling well.—Do you want me to ask him?"

"No, I'd rather I did."

During the intermission, Madeleine let Lepré chat with Mme. Lawrence the whole time. Leaning on the edge of the box and looking at the hall, she affected to scarcely pay attention to them, certain of being better able to enjoy his presence when, shortly, she would be alone with him.

Mme. Lawrence went out to put on her cloak.

"I invite you to stay with me for this act," Madeleine said with an indifferent amiability.

"You are very kind, Madame, but I cannot stay, I must leave."

"But I will be all alone," Madeleine said in an urgent tone; then, suddenly, desiring almost unconsciously to apply the maxims of coquetry contained in the celebrated "If I don't love you, you will love me," she caught herself: "But of course you are right, and if you are expected, please don't be late. Adieu, Monsieur."

She sought to compensate by the warmth of her smile for the harshness that seemed to her implied in this permission. But this harshness was only relative to her violent desire to keep him there, and to the bitterness of her disappointment. This advice to leave, given to anyone else, would have been perfectly amiable.

Mme. Lawrence came back. "Well, he's leaving; I'll stay with you so you won't be alone. Did you say tender farewells?"

"Farewells?"

"I believe he's leaving at the end of this week for a long trip to Italy, Greece and Asia Minor."

A child who since its birth breathes without ever having been aware of it does not know how essential to its life is the air that swells its chest so gently that it is not even conscious of it. Will the child, during a fit of fever, or in a convulsion, suffocate? In the desperate efforts of its being, it is almost for its life that it struggles, for the lost tranquility that it can only recover with the air from which it never knew itself inseparable.

In the same fashion, it was only at the moment when Madeleine learned of this departure of Lepré of which she had not remotely dreamed, that she understood, in feeling everything that was tearing itself away from her, what it was that had happened. And she looked at Mme. Lawrence, crushed, disconsolate and yet gently, harboring no more resentment towards her than does the poor suffocating patient against the asthma that is strangling him, who, through eyes filled with tears, smiles at the people who pity him without being able to help him. Suddenly she stood up.

"Let us leave, my dear friend, I don't want to make you get home late."

While she was putting on her cloak she caught sight of Lepré and, in her anguish at letting him leave without seeing her again, she quickly went downstairs.

"It would be a shame, especially if he is leaving, if M. Lepré were to imagine that he did not please me."

"But he never said that," Mme Lawrence answered.

"But yes, since you imagine it, he imagines it as well."

"No, quite the contrary."

"But because I'm telling you," Madeleine answered harshly. And as they had caught up with Lepré: "M. Lepré, I expect you for dinner

131

on Thursday at eight."

"I am not free on Thursday, Madame."

"Then Friday?"

"I am not free then either."

"Saturday?"

"Saturday, agreed."

"But my dear, you forget that you are to dine with the Princess d'Avranches on Saturday."

"So much the worse, I shall cancel."

"Oh, Madame, I would not wish . . . !" said Lepré.

"But *I* wish it!" Madeleine cried, beside herself. "There is no way I will go to Fanny's. I never intended to go."

Returning home, Madeleine undressed slowly, recalling the events of the evening. When she came to the moment that Lepré had refused to stay with her during the last act, she turned red with humiliation. The most elementary coquetry, like the strictest dignity, demanded that after that she observe an extreme coldness towards him. Instead of which, this triple invitation on the stairs. Indignant, she proudly raised her head and glimpsed herself in the depths of the mirror, so beautiful that she no longer doubted that he loved her. Worried and upset solely by his imminent departure, she imagined the tenderness that, for some reason she did not know, he had wanted to conceal from her. He was going to profess his love, perhaps in a letter, very soon, and would doubtless delay his departure, would leave with her . . . How? . . . One mustn't think about it. But she saw his handsome, amorous face drawing close to hers, demanding pardon. "Wicked boy!" she said.

But then perhaps he did not yet love her; he would leave without having had time to fall in love with her. . . . Desolated, she lowered her head, and her glance fell on the still more languishing glances of the faded flowers on her bodice, which beneath their withered pupils seemed about to weep. The thought of how briefly her dream, unconscious of itself, had lasted, how briefly her happiness would last if it were ever realized, associated itself in her mind with the sadness of these flowers which, before dying, languished on this heart that they had felt beating with its first love, its first humiliation, and its first sorrow.

The next day she refused to have any more flowers in her room, which was habitually full and sonorous with the glory of fresh roses.

Mme. Lawrence, when she entered, stopped in front of the vases where the last cattleyas were dying, despoiled of beauty, for eyes without love. "What's this, my dear, you who adore flowers so?"

"It seems to me that it's today that I love them," Madeleine was going to respond; she stopped, annoyed at having to explain herself, and feeling that there are realities that one cannot get across to those who do not already bear them within themselves.

She contented herself with smiling amiably at the reproach. The feeling that this new life was unknown to everyone, and perhaps to Lepré himself, caused her a rare and grieving pride. Letters were brought; not finding any from Lepré, she made a gesture of disappointment. Measuring the distance between the absurdity of a disappointment when there had not been the slightest sustenance for a hope, and the all-too-real and cruel intensity of this disappointment, she understood that she had ceased to live solely the life of events and facts. The veil of lies had begun to unfold before her eyes for a duration impossible to foresee. Only through him did she see things any longer, and more than anything else, perhaps, those things which she had wanted to know and to live most genuinely and most like Lepré, those things which related to him.

But a hope remained that he had lied, that his indifference was a front: she knew from the unanimity of opinion that she was one of the most beautiful women in Paris, that her reputation for intelligence, wit, elegance and her high social station added prestige to her beauty. Lepré, on the other hand, was considered an intelligent and artistic man, very gentle, a very good son, but he was little sought after, had never been successful with women; the attention she was bestowing on him must seem to him something improbable and unhoped-for. She was amazed and hoped. . . .

II.

Even though Madeleine had, in an instant, subordinated all the interests and affections of her life to Lepré, she didn't think less of him, and her opinion was only reinforced by the opinion of everyone else that, without being disagreeable, he was inferior to those remarkable men who, in the four years since the death of the Marquis de Gouvres, consoled her widowhood by visiting her several times a day, and who were the most cherished ornaments of her life.

She was well aware that the inexplicable inclination that made of him a unique being did not raise him to that level in the eyes of others. The reasons for her love were within her, and if they were also, a little, in him, it was neither in his intellectual superiority nor even in his physical superiority. It was precisely because she loved him that no expression, no smile, no walk, were as agreeable to her as his, and it was not because his expression, his smile, his walk were more agreeable than others' that she loved him. She knew men who were more handsome, more charming, and knew it.

And so when on Saturday, at eight fifteen, Lepré entered Madeleine's salon, he was met, without his suspecting it, by a most passionate friend and most clairvoyant adversary. If her beauty was armed to conquer him, her mind was no less armed to judge him; she was prepared to pick like a bitter flower the pleasure of finding him mediocre and ridiculously unequal to the love she bore for him. It was not out of prudence! She felt that she would always be taken up again in the magic net, and that the links of chain mail that her too incisive mind would have broken while Lepré was present would have been repaired by her industrious imagination as soon as he had left.

In fact, when he came in she was suddenly calmed; in giving him her hand, it seemed that she took all his power away from him. He was no longer the sole and absolute despot of her dreams, but nothing more than an agreeable visitor. They chatted; then all her prejudices fell away. In the delicacy of his kindness, the bold accuracy of his wit, she found reasons which, if they did not absolutely justify her love, explained it, at least to some degree, and, in showing her that something in reality corresponded to her love, made it put out roots and gave it more life. She noted, too, that he was much handsomer than she had thought, with a delicate and noble face of the type of Louis XIII.

All the memories of the art associated with the portraits of Louis XIII's time were from then on associated with the thought of her love, bestowing on it a new existence and causing it to enter into the system of her artistic tastes. She ordered from Amsterdam the photograph of a young man's portrait that resembled him.

She met him a few days later. His mother was seriously ill, his voyage postponed. She told him that she now had on her table a portrait that reminded her of him. He seemed touched, but cold. This made her suffer profoundly, but she consoled herself by thinking that he had at least understood, if he had not enjoyed, her attentions. To love a boor who would not have been aware of it would have been even more cruel. Then, reproaching him in her mind for his indifference, she tried seeing again the men who had been infatuated with her and towards whom she had been indifferent and coquettish, in order to practice towards them the adroit and tender pity that she would at least have tried to obtain from him. But when she met them, they all had the horrible defect of not being him, and the sight of them only irritated her. She wrote him; he did not respond for four days, then a letter came which anyone else would have found amicable, but which threw her into despair.

He wrote: "My mother is getting better, I shall leave in three weeks. Until then, my life is quite full, but I shall try to come by once to pay my respects."

Was it jealousy for everything that "filled his life" and that prevented her from penetrating it, disappointment at his departure and that he would only come to see her one more time before then, or was it rather disappointment that he did not feel the need to come see her ten times a day before he left?

She could not stay at home, hastily put on a hat and left on foot, quickly traversing the streets that led to his house, with the absurd hope that, by some miracle she was counting on, he was going, at the turning of a square, to appear to her shining with tenderness and that, in a glance, he would explain everything to her. Suddenly she saw him walking along, gaily chatting with some friends. But then she was ashamed, thought that he would guess that she was looking for him, and abruptly turned and entered a shop. On the following days she no longer went looking for him and avoided the places where she might meet him, keeping up this last bit of coquettishness toward him, this last dignity toward herself.

One morning she was sitting alone in the Tuileries, on the terrace of the Bord de l'Eau. She let her disappointment drift, expand, refresh itself more freely in the broadened horizon, gather flowers, soar with the hollyhocks, the fountains and the columns, gallop in chase of the dragoons who were leaving their Orsay quarters, go drifting about on the Seine and glide with the swallows in the pale sky. It was the fifth day since the friendly letter which had desolated her. Suddenly she glimpsed Lepré's big white poodle, which he let out alone every morning. She had joked with him about it, had told him that one day someone would steal it. The animal recognized her and came up to her. The mad desire to see Lepré that she had repressed for five days completely overcame her. Seizing the animal in her arms, shaking with sobs, she hugged it for a long time with all her strength, then undid the posy of violets she was wearing on her bodice and, attaching it to the dog's collar, let it leave.

But, calmed by this crisis, assuaged as well, feeling better, she felt her rancor fade little by little and some joy and hope returning with the physical well-being, and felt herself valuing life and happiness. Lepré was going to leave in seventeen days, she wrote him to come dine the next day, excusing herself for not having answered him, and spent a fairly pleasant afternoon. In the evening, she dined in town; many men were to be at this dinner, artists and sportsmen who knew Lepré. She wanted to know if he had a mistress, any kind of bond, which would prevent him from approaching her, which would explain his extraordinary conduct. She would suffer greatly if she learned anything, but at least she would know, and perhaps she could hope that given a little time her beauty would transport him. She left her house having made up her mind to ask this immediately, then seized with fear, she didn't dare. At the last moment, what impelled her upon her arrival was less the desire to know the truth than the need to speak of him to others, this sad charm of evoking him in vain wherever she was without him. After dinner, she said to two men who were standing near her, and whose conversation was quite free: "Tell me, do you happen to know Lepré?"

"We've been seeing him every day forever, but we're not very close to him."

"Is he a charming person?"

"He is a charming person."

"Well! Perhaps you could tell me . . . please don't consider yourselves obliged to be too kind, for it concerns something that is truly quite important to me.—There is a young girl whom I love with all my heart and who has shown some inclination for him. Is he someone one could marry without fear?"

Her two interlocutors remained embarrassed for a moment.

"No, that cannot be."

Madeleine, quite courageously, continued, in order to get finished as quickly as possible: "He has a long-standing affair?"

"No, but it's really not possible."

"Tell me why, I assure you, I beg of you."

"No."

But then, after all, it was better to tell her, she might imagine the ugliest or the most ridiculous things.

"Well! All right, and I believe that we are not doing any wrong to Lepré in telling you; first, you must not repeat it, of course all Paris knows it anyway, and as for marriage he is far too honest and delicate to dream of it. Lepré is a charming fellow, but he has one vice. He loves base women that one picks up in the mud, and he loves them madly; sometimes he passes his nights in the suburbs or on remote boulevards, at the risk of getting himself killed someday, and not only does he love them madly, but he loves only them. The most ravishing woman in society, the most ideal girl, leave him absolutely indifferent. He cannot even pay them attentions. His pleasures, his preoccupations, his life, are elsewhere. Those who do not know him well used to say that with his exquisite nature, a great love would draw him out of it. But for that it would take a person capable of feeling such a love, and he is not capable of it. His father was already that way, and if his sons won't be, it's because he won't have any."

The next day at eight o'clock Madeleine was informed that M. Lepré was in the salon. She went in; the windows were open, the lamps had not yet been lit and he was waiting for her on the balcony. Not far from them some houses surrounded by gardens were resting in the softened light of evening, distant, Oriental and religious as if it had been Jerusalem. The sparse and caressing light bestowed on each object a completely new and almost moving meaning. A luminous wheelbarrow in the middle of the dusky street was touching, as was, a little further on, the dark and already nocturnal trunk of a chestnut tree, beneath whose foliage the last rays were still soaking. At the end of the avenue the setting sun was gloriously bending like a triumphal arch paved with celestial golds and verdure. At the neighboring window heads were reading with a simple solemnity. In approaching Lepré, Madeleine felt the pacified sweetness of all these things soften, make languid, pry open her heart, and she had to restrain herself so as not to weep.

He, however, handsomer this evening and more charming, treated her with delicate cordialities that he had not shown up to then. Then they chatted seriously, and she glimpsed for the first time the full extent of his intelligence. If in society he did not please, it was precisely because the truths he was searching for were situated below the visual horizon of witty people, and because the truths of great spirits are ridiculous errors on earth. And then his goodness sometimes lent these truths a charming poetry, as the sun gracefully colors high peaks. And he was so nice to her, he showed himself so grateful for her kindness that, feeling she had never loved so much, and having renounced the hope of seeing her love returned, she suddenly glimpsed with joy the hope of the intimacy of a pure friendship, thanks to which she would see him every day; and she adroitly and happily let him know of her plan. But he, saying that he was very taken up, could scarcely be free for more than one day every two weeks. She had told him enough to let him understand that she loved him, if he had wanted to understand. And he, as diffident as he was, if he had had the shadow of an inclination for her he would have said so in words of friendship, even the most trifling. Her disordered glance was fixed on him so intently that she would have immediately made them out, and would have been greedily sated by them. She wanted to stop Lepré, who was continuing to talk of his time so taken up, of his life that was so filled up, but suddenly her glance plunged into the heart of her adversary, so far that it could have plunged into the infinite horizon of the sky stretching out before her, and she felt the uselessness of her words. She was silent, then she said: "Yes, I understand, you are very busy."

And at the end of the evening, when he was leaving, as he was saying to her: "May I not come to say farewell?" she answered with sweetness: "No, my friend, I have things to do, I think it would be better to leave things as they are."

She was waiting for a word; he didn't say it, and she said to him: "Adieu!"

Then she waited for a letter, in vain. So she wrote him that it was better to be frank, that she could have let him believe that she liked him, that that was not the case, that she would prefer not to see him as often as she had requested with an imprudent cordiality.

He answered that he had in fact never believed in anything more than a cordiality that was celebrated, and which he had never had the intention of abusing to the point of annoying her by coming so often.

Then she wrote him that she loved him, that she had never loved anyone but him. He answered that she was jesting.

She stopped writing to him, but not, at first, thinking of him. Then that happened too. Two years later, tired of her widowhood, she married the Duc de Mortagne, a man of great handsomeness and wit who, until Madeleine's death, that is to say for more than forty years, decorated her life with a glory and an affection to which she did not show herself insensible.

Christmas Vacation
Truman Capote

—Edited by Bradford Morrow

EDITOR'S NOTE

*"Christmas Vacation" is one of the earliest surviving manuscripts
written by Truman Capote, and is by far the most significant and
substantial of his childhood literary efforts. This is its first appearance in print.*

*The young author had originally titled his tale "Old Mrs. Busy-
body" and had conceived it not as a Christmas story, but the
harsh, satiric portrait of a domineering small-minded spinster. A
close inspection of the first page of the original manuscript reveals
that Capote, an eleven-year-old sixth grader at Trinity School in
New York, erased both his original title and chapter heading, having written some pages of his narrative before deciding to recast it
as a Christmas tale. In his first draft, it is apparent that the opening sentence read simply, "Old Mrs. Busybody stood gazing out
the window looking at several young boys and girls smoking cigarettes." If a bit inert, it was grammatically correct: a complete
sentence. Only later, revising the story with a precocious attention to dramatic detail, did he add—with a darker pencil and in
a more slanted hand—the phrase, "Christmas was only a few
days and as," which somewhat mangled his earlier tidy sentence,
but contributed to what he saw as a more promising overture. It
provided, too, a purposeful reason for Lulu Belle and her family's
visit, not to mention the comical exchange of gifts in the final
chapter.*

*Written in 1935–1936, "Christmas Vacation" is clearly juvenile
work. However, it proves abundantly the seriousness of Capote's
decision, made when he was nine or ten years old, to become a
writer. Above all, it displays rare perseverance in one so young,
and has a rounded feel with plots and subplots all developed, and
resolved. Its narrative seldom pauses; its dialogue barrels forward
with many of the characters' voices nicely differentiated by specific catchphrases, mannerisms or accents; its manic slapstick*

139

comedy—sometimes acerbic, sometimes violent—is generally timed with the deftness of a born storyteller. "Christmas Vacation" is also important in that, however highflown its burlesque and caricatures, it plausibly documents autobiographical elements of Capote's childhood. Indeed, Capote's biographer Gerald Clarke, who was kind enough to read the manuscript and consult with me about the work, recalls Capote having claimed to have published in a Mobile, Alabama, newspaper the first part of a similar story with a protagonist named Mrs. Busybody, and that friends and relatives were so scandalized by its thinly disguised, unfavorable characterizations of them that the rest of the work was never published.

The detested Mrs. Busybody—who is present primarily at the beginning and end of the novelette, cast as the grudging host of her balmy relatives—was evidently based on a neighborhood lady whom Capote and his friends disliked. Mrs. Busybody and Lulu Belle would seem to be amalgams, pastiches, of others around him in Alabama at the time as well. Certainly, Capote's neglectful mother, Lillie Mae, who darted in and out of Capote's childhood as whimsy, finances and selfishness dictated, shares Lulu Belle's impatience with children if not her willingness to beget them. The reader can easily imagine that when—in full-blown riotous Katzenjammer Kids style—Lulu Belle and her wacky family arrive at Mrs. Busybody's for the holiday, Capote was inspired by the eccentric, brawling household on Alabama Avenue in Monroeville, where young Truman was raised by an unorthodox clan of relatives after his mother temporarily abandoned him there in 1930. As Gerald Clarke writes in Capote, the boy was taken in by "three quarrelsome sisters in late middle age . . . [in] an atmosphere heavy with small secrets and ancient resentments." Capote's novelette vividly suggests in the character of Lulu Belle the tempestuous Jennie Faulk, Lillie Mae's cousin who ruled the roost in Monroeville, where she was locally famous for her nasty disposition. In pure Lulu Belle fashion, Jennie "once whipped a lazy yardman with a dog chain" and, as Clarke reports, "another time, spotting someone who she thought had cheated her . . . jumped out of her car and attacked him on his own front porch. . . ."

Altercations, anarchy, alcohol (Jennie and her sister, Sook, were particularly fond of their bottle, much like the character Uncle William in Capote's story) were daily a part of life on Alabama

140

Avenue. And the sisters' brother, the meek, soft-spoken, cloistered Bud Faulk, would seem to provide a partial model for Capote's alienated character Uncle William, as well. "Surrounded by contentious, difficult women and half-invalided by asthma," Clarke writes, "Bud . . . kept to himself." Capote's biological father, the jinxed Arch Persons, an ingratiating con artist and dreamer given to failures great and small, prefigures Uncle William, too, when, writing to his brother John about the fact that Lillie Mae was divorcing him so that she could marry Joseph Garcia Capote, he exclaims, "She was just as cruel and heartless about it as possible. Girls are sure a pain." Uncle William, feeling utterly beaten by his wife in the final chapter of "Christmas Vacation," similarly concludes, "I guess a married man just hasn't got a chance."

In agreement with Truman Capote's literary executor, Alan Schwartz, I have edited the original manuscript as lightly as possible, only correcting obvious misspellings and adding punctuation where Capote left it incomplete or in the haste of composition left it out altogether. In the very few places it seemed necessary to add a word for coherence, the insert is bracketed. Although Capote freely alters spellings of the name "Lulu Belle" and "Lulubelle," I have in this transcript maintained "Lulu Belle" throughout, in part because it seems to me consistent with period Southern spelling of the name, and partly because if one sees any of Capote's contemporary feelings toward his mother, Lillie Mae, present in the characterization of Lulu Belle, this spelling seems most fitting. The minor character "Lizzie" is spelled inconsistently (Lizzie, Lissie, Lizzy) and I have used the first spelling since there is no clear reason to prefer one over another, except in the case of "Lissie," which is used in a bit of dialogue and again displays, I believe, Capote's ear for colloquial elocution. I have also kept Capote's spellings, or possibly deliberate misspellings, of generally exclamatory words used in dialogue, such as "scallywags," "raggimuffin," "laggert" and, for instance, "Mothaw" as he attempts to mimic the British accent of the hapless Selby Pifflesniffle. Since we are reproducing the original holograph, which was written in pencil on ruled yellow notebook paper, the edited transcript is meant, as much as anything, to be a guide to reading it in facsimile.

That this fragile manuscript has survived is largely because of two Capote admirers: his English teacher at Trinity, John E. Langford, who kept it for some forty-five years, and Frederick Vanacore, who obtained the document at Charles Hamilton Gallery on April 15, 1982, and has now generously made it available to us for publication. I want to thank Caroline Donner for making the initial transcription of the manuscript, Andreas Brown and Gerald Clarke for kind advice, and Alan Schwartz of the Truman Capote Literary Trust for permissions and magnanimity.

* * *

Christmas Vacation
By Truman Capote

CHAPTER I.
CHRISTMAS GUEST

Christmas was only a few days [away] and old Mrs. Busybody stood gazing out the window looking at several young boys and girls smoking cigarettes.

"Tusk! Tusk! I don't know what this younger generation is getting to be," she mumbled then she hobbled out of the kitchen toward them.

"You young ruffians, stop smoking those cigarettes this minute!" cried Mrs. Busybody as she waved her cane at them.

"Well! Well! if it isn't old Mrs. Busybody herself," hollered one of the boys. "And in person too," cried another. A little girl who was near Mrs. Busybody took a deep draw on her cigarette and blew the smoke right in Mrs. Busybody's face. Still another offered her a cigarette.

"Why! Why! I never. You young scallywags. I should report you to the police," gasped Mrs. Busybody.

She then rushed into the house out of sheer humiliation. Mrs. Busybody was a fat old widow whose only amusement was crocheting and sewing. She was also fond of knitting. She didn't like the movies and took an immediate dislike to anyone who did enjoy them. She also took great delight in reporting children to their mothers over the slightest thing that annoyed her. In other words no one liked her and she was considered a public nuisance and a regular old Busybody.

We now find Mrs. Busybody at the telephone calling up the different parents of the children who she had caught smoking.

After doing this she picked up her crocheting and sat down in a rocking chair with an air of accomplishment.

Just then the doorbell rang and Mrs. Busybody dropped her crocheting and went to answer. "Well! What do you want," she asked.

"Telegram for you," replied the boy.

"Huh! Well what are you standing there for, hand it here."

"Well, er, sign here first please," the boy asked politely. Mrs. Busybody did as she was told but acted very impatient about it.

Finally receiving the telegram Mrs. Busybody sat down comfortably to read it. She looked at it and seemed very pleased at receiving a telegram but when she opened it and read its contents she looked as though she had lost her last friend. The telegram read, Dear Mrs. Busybody, Uncle William and I are coming to visit you for Christmas. The kids are coming too. Will arrive tomorrow.

Love, Lulu Belle

"Heavens," cried Mrs. Busybody, "this is terrible. How will I ever get everything fixed up for tomorrow. I didn't even know they were coming. They are uninvited guests. And bringing all those children too. Let me see, there are seven of them and they all eat like little hogs. OH! gracious me alive what will I ever do. Those people will be the death of me yet."

CHAPTER II.
THE UNINVITED GUEST

Well, Mrs. Busybody *must* have found a way of getting her house cleaned up, for the day had arrived and her house was spic and span. Mrs. Busybody was grumbling, as usual, for she never had a smile on her face. She walked out of the house in her Sunday apparel and started toward the railroad station. "Those people! I declare to goodness!" exclaimed Mrs. Busybody. She was soon at the station, inquiring what time the train would arrive. "In another half hour," replied the station agent. "What! Why these new-fangled things—Now when I was young—!" but she was cut short by a group of young boys running down the gutter splattering muddy water all over the sidewalk, of which she got her share. "Why those young raggimuffins!" she cried. "I shall report you to the police!" And that was just what she did! Seeing an officer across the street she hobbled over to him to report the incident to him. The way she explained to the officer the children had nearly drowned her with mud. "Well," said the officer,

"Let's get this straight. You say that some kids ran by and splattered mud on you." "Yes, that's right, officer," she said. "They nearly drowned me in it! Not to say the least about ruining my best dress." "Well," said the officer, "I guess I'll have to look into this." So doing as he said, he began to follow the boys. The first bit of information he gathered was in a drug store where the boys had bought an ice cream apiece and didn't have sufficient funds to pay for their purchase. And as the druggist said, "He threw them out on their ears." So the officer went around gathering similar odd pieces of information, until he finally came upon the boys themselves. Grabbing them by the back of their necks he dragged them back to the railroad station, where Mrs. Busybody identified them as she said, those "horrible boys who splattered mud on her Sunday dress." "Well," the officer said. "These kids are charged with *more* than just splattering mud on your dress!" "Well, I never!" exclaimed Mrs. Busybody. "What are these charges?" "Well," began the officer. "They bought ice cream without paying for it, and broke several store windows, and sneaked up behind a lady and put a lighted firecracker down her dress." "Why awful terrible children!" exploded Mrs. Busybody. "You should be sent to the reform school!" "That's just what's going to happen to them!" roared the officer. And so he walked away dragging the children behind him.

Mrs. Busybody traveled back to the waiting room and sat down on a bench. She looked at her wrist watch and saw that an hour and a half had passed! "Gracious me alive!!" she said as she got up from the bench and rushed to the station agent and explained to him what had happened. Just as the station agent started his explanation the train roared in! Mrs. Busybody turned around and rushed to the platform! The train stopped to a standstill and the porter stepped down and put the stepper on the platform. There were hideous cries inside the car such as: "Mamma, Mamma! get me some candy!" "Ma! Ma! take me to the movies an' gimme some candy!" "Shut up Willie! Hush, Andrew!" "Baw! Baw!" "Shut up Oswald! Do you want me to bean you!" "Oh me love, can I have just a teenie weenie drink of rum?" "Be quiet, you lope of a dope!" Pow! Pow! "Please don't hit me no more," came Uncle William's wee little tiny voice. Finally the hoodlum procession came down the platform toward Mrs. Busybody. "Pssst, pssst. Lookit that ole dame!" came a whisper through the crowd. "Blah, Blah!" a troupe of tongues came out at Mrs. Busybody! "Well," said Mrs. Busybody, "It's about time you arrived! We'll all go home now." As they tramped through the streets they passed by a candy shop. "Baw! Baw! Gimme some candy Ma!" "Couldn't I have a wee little piece of candy?" spoke Uncle William's small voice. "Shut up!" Pow! Bang! Lulu Belle's umbrella broke over Uncle William's poor head. They finally arrived home and got settled waiting for the further adventures of the following week.

CHAPTER III.
UNCLE WILLIAM MAKES TROUBLE

"William! William! You get up from that bed this minute, you lazy laggert!" "Yes, honey, just a minute," replied Uncle William's small voice. "Well you'd better get up this minute before I lam the daylights out of you!" Uncle William got out of bed and put on his pants. He felt in his pockets and saw that his pockets had been thoroughly gone through the night before. Sneaking up to Lulu Belle he said in a meek voice, "Oh! Precious little darling dumpling you are the apple of my eye, the most pretty rose in the garden couldn't you lend me a quarter so's I could get me just a little booze." "Go away, you lowdown son of Satan. I ought to turn you upside down and shake all the shinny out of you and make [a] cocktail out of it!" Crash! Bang! "Oh! Oh! honey let me up please! Oh! honey, have mercy on my soul!" Just then Lulu Belle looked up on the mantel and grabbed Mrs. Busybody's most prized china vase and hurled it at poor Uncle William. Just then old Mrs. Busybody stomped in. When she saw what had happened she almost fainted! "Oh!" she gasped. "Why did you break my china vase on that drunken minded verminous creature! It was ginuine China, I tell you! *Ginuine!*" Poor Uncle William crouched in a corner in fear! Mrs. Busybody gave Uncle William such a dirty [look] that the poor old man trembled all over in fear. "Come into the next room with me!" said Mrs. Busybody. So poor Uncle William was dragged into the next room and nobody knows what happened then, but it was something terrible!

Night soon came. Uncle William was locked in his room for the night as usual. It was getting late. Uncle William knew that, for Lulu Belle had stopped telling Mrs. Busybody what she would do to him the next day. It was soon midnight. Uncle William quietly raised the window and jumped out. He ran around the house to see that no one was watching him. Then he quietly crept under Lulu Belle's window. He ran around the corner. And guess what he ran into. A crap game! He said in a very little voice, "May I join you all?" "Certainly," said

145

a gruff voice. The game had started. "Come on, seven!" Uncle William's voice could still be heard far down the street. "Shoot 'er in there!" Uncle William's voice could still be heard far down the street.

When the game was over, Uncle William lost everything. "I'm sorry, boys," he said in a small voice. "But I don't have sufficient funds to pay you all." "So you don't, eh!" "Well take this!" Biff! Bang! Ouch! "Let me up! Let me up!" came Uncle William's small voice. Crack! A liquor bottle broke over Uncle William's poor head.

The noise awoke Lulu Belle. She hurried down the street toward them. "You leave my husband alone!" she roared. Bang! Ouch! Stop it! Biff! Pow! Pow!

When the fight was over Lulu Belle dragged Uncle William back to the house where she locked him in his dingy little room. Lulu Belle attacked Uncle William vigorously! She said, "Why you drunken old lope-eared billy goat! The very idea of you sneaking out, you limb of Satan!"

After a good beating Uncle William was locked safely in his room and they all went to bed.

CHAPTER IV.
THE KIDS MAKE TROUBLE

"Ma! Ma!" "I want some candy for breakfast!"
"Well you can't have it, Ulysses! If you don't shut up, I'll knock your block off!" "Mama! Mamma!" "I want a doll!" "Well you can't have it, Lizzie so shut up before I bean you one."

"Ma! Ma! I want some ice cream!" "Ma! please give me some!" "Will you shut up. Lissie!" "Baw! Mamma!" "I don't want to shut up!" "Baw, Mama!" Whang! Whang! Ouch! Mamma! Ouch! "Now if you younguns don't stop this bawling and crying, I'm afraid I'm going to have to whip every one of you!" Immediately the room hushed to silence. "Well, now everybody sit down to this breakfast table and eat their breakfast!"

Mrs. Busybody, who was already at the table, gave them a dirty look as they all sat down, one by one. "Eat your cereal," Lulu Belle commanded. "Baw! Mamma, I don't like cereal!" spoke up Lizzie. "I don't want cereal, I want coffee!" "You can't have coffee, it's not good for you!" "Baw! Mamma you've been reading those advertisements again!" Lulu Belle got up from the table and pointed her finger at

Lizzie. "You eat your cereal, do you hear me! And don't let me hear you mention coffee again! And if you do, I'll crown you one!"

"Ouch! Ma! Tell Oswald to quit pulling my hair!" "Oswald! What do *you mean* pulling your sister's hair?" But he continued to pull his sister's hair. Lulu Belle grasped him by his shoulder and spoke in a sharp voice. "Did you hear me? *Let go your sister's hair!!*" Oswald let go the grip on Lizzie's hair slowly. "Oh! Heck! A fellow can't even pull anybody's hair these days!"

In the meantime, poor Uncle William was eating his breakfast on the mantelpiece, for he was too sore to sit at the table with the rest.

While back at the table, the so-called hideous cries of the children could be heard. The argument about pulling the hair was still on. Lulu Belle was talking. "Now Oswald, if you want to pull anybody's hair, pull your brother Andrew's." "You do," piped up Andrew, "and I'll bust your nose!" "You bust his nose again" (for he had busted Oswald's nose before) "and I'll bust that thick big skull of yours!!" There was much argument over "busting Andrew's skull." However, it ended with both boys, Oswald and Andrew, getting a sound spanking.

After breakfast all the children went out in the yard to play. Oswald spied a little boy riding a tricycle across the street and went over to play with him. After playing with the little boy a while Oswald said, "Say, what about you coming to play with us kids on the other side of the street?" "Well, I will ask Mothaw if I can come," answered the little boy in a British accent. He walked up to a house and rang the door bell. His mother answered it. "What do you want, Selby?" "Mothaw, this little boy wants to know whearther I can come over to Mrs. Busybody's house to play with him." "But, er, I suppose so, Selby, dear, but be careful and don't hurt yourself." So they were off.

"What is your full name?" Oswald asked. "Selby Arnold Pifflesniffle," he answered. "My what a funny name," laughed Oswald. Little Selby looked displeased at his playmate's remark.

They were soon all playing on the lawn. "Let's have a game of hide and go seek," said Oswald. "O.K.!" they all shouted. "Selby, You can be it," said Willie. "I don't want to be it. I *won't* be it!" shouted Selby. "You won't which?" asked Willie. "I repeat," said Selby. "I *won't* be it." "So you won't, eh? Well take this! and this!" Ouch! Bang! Sock! "Let me up! Let me up! Let go my hair! Bloody murder! Ouch! Mothaw! Tell them to let me up!"

Just then Lulu Belle walked out on the lawn. Squinting one eye,

147

she said, "Willie! you let that child up this instant! And if you don't I'll break your bean!" Willie got up off Selby and he ran across the road crying: "Mother! Mother! help I'm dying!"

While back on the lawn Lulu Belle was giving a lecture. "Now you get in this house this instant and don't make any more trouble."

CHAPTER V.
THE HOODLUMS LEAVE

"Now is everything packed?" Lulu Belle was saying. "Yes, me darling, it's all packed," William answered meekly. "Well don't stand there like an idiot, tote those bags out in front of the house." "Yes, me darling." After this task was done, Lulu Belle had something else for him to do.

Finally all the work was completed. Uncle William tiptoed up to Lulu Belle meekly. "Darling," he began, "Don't you think that I ought to have a little booze for all this hard labor?" "All right, this once, I'll let you have it, for your own happiness and enjoyment," said Lulu Belle. Uncle William was very pleased to hear this, for it was the first time Lulu Belle had ever agreed to let him have whiskey. "But first," she continued, "you will have to go down to the station to buy the tickets. And on the way back you can get a quarter's worth of toddy. And here is the $15.00 for the ticket money and here is your quarter for your shinny. Now don't stay long for the train leaves in an hour, and we be on time."

So Uncle William disappeared out the door.

Lulu Belle went upstairs where the children were. "Now you children hurry up with your baths!" "Baw! Ma! It isn't Saturday night yet! And I don't want to take no bath!" "Well you're going to!" shouted Lulu Belle.

So all of the kids got in the bath. They all took their baths and got dressed.

Then Lulu Belle went down to find Uncle William. But Uncle William was nowhere to be found. "William! William! Where are you?" cried Lulu Belle. "Hmm!" she said. "I guess he's already got the tickets and he's probably down at that saloon loitering around. Well I guess I will have to go down to the saloon and get him," she said as she vanished out the door. Arriving at the saloon she said, "Well where are the tickets you big fathead." "Now don't get so excited honey I er," William stammered, "spent five dollars of the

148

money on a wee bit of shinny."

"Why you!" howled Lulu Belle, "You dirty son of a satan. I'll break your backbone you drunken minded verminous creature. I'll brain you." We'll skip what happened then for it was terrible. We now found poor Uncle William in a bed with bandages all over him.

"Well," Lulu Belle was saying, "You've certainly made a fine mess of everything." "Yes honey," came William's ever so small voice. And continued Lulu Belle, "You've spent almost half the ticket money, fortunately though I have enough to get us home through Mrs. Busybody's kind contribution. We've missed the train though but there's a train leaving at 6 o'clock we'll take and if it wasn't for your big thick headedness we wouldn't be in this mess." "Yes honey," answered William meekly. Lulu Belle walked across the room and put something in a spoon and made Uncle William swallow it. After this was done she left the room only to be called back by Uncle William's calling. "Well what is it?" she asked. "Honey," he asked sympathetically, "Will you please send Willie down to the book store and get this book for my Christmas present?" He handed her a slip of paper which had the title of the book on it. "Well alright," she said gruffly, "I'll send him for it." She then went downstairs to send Willie for the book. But before handing him the slip of paper she read it and wrote something down on the piece of paper. She gave Willie the money for the book and he was off. However, he soon returned and gave Lulu Belle two parcels instead of one. She carried them up to Uncle William's room and handed him one of the parcels and sat down in a chair with the other. They both opened them hurriedly. The title of Uncle William's book was "How to Get Around Your Wife," By T. R. Bunk. The title of Lulu Belle's book was "How to Torture Your Husband," By *Mrs. T. R. Bunk*. After several hours of reading, Uncle William happened to glance over in the direction of Lulu Belle. When he saw that she was reading a thick [book], much thicker than his, he strained his eyes which had big black circles around them to see the title of the book she was reading. When he finally did read it the poor fat old man looked very depressed. "Honey," he said, "what are you reading that for?" "Well!" she retorted. "You got a book on how to get around your wife so I got one on how to torture your husband. I believe in the old saying," she said, "A tooth for a tooth and an eye for an eye." Uncle William dropped his book in defeat. "Aw," he said, "I guess a married man just hasn't got a chance." At this point Lulu Belle looked up at the clock and saw it was 5:30. "Eeek!" she screamed. "It's 5:30

and we have to leave at six o'clock. Get up out of there and get dressed. We have to catch the train." "Ohh!" screeched Uncle William as he made an attempt to get out of the bed, "I'm so sore." "Sore or not you get out of that bed before I lam the daylights out of you." So Uncle William got out of bed with much pain. Lulu Belle then went downstairs to get the children ready. When everything was done she called the taxi cab company and told them to send over three cabs (for one or two was not enough to hold them to Main and Chestnut street). When the cabs arrived everyone piled in, including Mrs. Busybody. When they arrived at the station Lulu Belle walked over to the ticket office. "I want nine tickets to 'Slumtown' please." "Nine tickets to where?" "Slumtown," Lulu Belle repeated. "Never heard of the place," retorted the ticket agent. "Well er," Lulu Belle began, "I know it's not a regular stop. It's what's commonly known as the gashouse district." "Oh! I know where that is," the ticket agent laughed. "Here are your tickets. The train will be in any minute now." So Lulu Belle walked over to where the rest were and sat on the waiting bench with them. The seven kids were crying for ice cream and candy as usual. Uncle William was asking for a little snort of whiskey, and Mrs. Busybody was grumbling and mumbling as usual. Just then the train roared in and Lulu Belle, Uncle William and the kids got aboard. They waved goodbye to Mrs. Busybody. As Mrs. Busybody left the platform she said, "Thank heavens those people are gone at last," and so ended her Christmas vacation.

Christmas Vacation
BY TRUMAN CAPOTE
CHAPTER I. Christmas guest

Christmas was only a few days and as Old Mrs. Busybody stood gazing out the window looking at several young boys and girls smoking cigarettes.

"Tush! Tush! I don't know what this younger generation is getting to be like" mumble then she hobbled out of the kitchen toward them.

"You young ruffians stop smoking those cigarettes this minute!" cried Mrs. Busybody as she waved her cane at them.

"Well, well, if it isnt old mrs Busybody herself hollered one of the boys. "And in person too, cried another. A little girl who was near mrs. Busybody took a deep draw on her cigarette and blew the smoke right in mrs Busybodys face, still another offered her a cigarette.

Why! Why! I never. You young really pags. I should report you to the police, gasped mrs Busybody.

She then rushed into the house out of sheer humiliation. Mrs. Busybody was a fat old widow whose only amusement was crocheting and sewing. She was also fond of knitting. She didn't like the movies and books and immediate dislike to any one who did enjoy them. She also took great delight in reporting children to their mothers over the slightest thing that annoyed her. In other words no one liked her and she was considered a public nuisance an also a regular old Busybody.

We now find Mrs. Busybody at the telephone calling up the different parents of the children who she had caught smoking.

After doing this she picked up her crocheting and sat down in a rocking chair with and air of accomplishment.

Just then the doorbell rang and Mrs. Busybody dropped her crocheting and went to answer. Well! what do you want she asked.

Telegram for you replied the boy. Huh! Well what are you standing there for hand it here.

152

well er sign here first please the boy asks
politely. Mrs. Busybody did as she was told
but acted very impatient about it.

Finally recieving the telegram
Mrs. Busybody sat down comftably to read
it. She looked at it and seemed very pleased at
recieving a telegram but when she opened
it and read its contents she looked as
though she had lost her best friend. The
telegram read. Dear Mrs. Busybody,
uncle William and I are coming to
visit you for Christmas . . . The kids are
coming too. We will arive tommorow
                              Love, Zulu Belle

Heaven's cried Mrs. Busybody this is
terrible how will I ever get everything
fixed up for tommorow, I didn't even
now they were coming They are uninvited
guest, And Bringing all those Children
Too. Let me see there are seven of
them and they all eat like little hogs.
OH! gracious me alive what will I ever
do. These people will be the death of me
yet,

ChaptEr
II The Uninvited Guests

Well Mrs Busybody must have
found a way of getting her house
cleaned up, for the day had arrived and her house was spic and
span. Mrs. Busybody was grumbling, as usual, for she never
had a smile on her face. She
walked out of the house in her
Sunday apparel and started
toward the railroad station.
"Those people! I declare to goodness"
exclaimed Mrs. Busybody. She
was soon at the staton, inquiring
what time the train would arrive.
"In another half hour," replied the
station agent. "What! Why these new-
fangled things—" "now when I was
young—" but she was cut short
by a group of young boys running
down the gutter splattering muddy
water all over the sidewalk, of

154

which she got her share. "Why
those young raggimuffins!" she
cried. "I shall report you to the
police!" And that was just what
she did! Seeing an officer across
the street she hobbled over to him
to report the incident to him. The
way she explained to the officer
the children had nearly drowned
her with mud. "Well," said the officer,
"Let's get this straight," "You say
that some kids ran by and
splattered mud on you." "Yes,
Thats right officer," she said. "They
nearly drowned me in it!" "Not
to say the least about ruining
my best dress. "Well," said the
officer, "I guess I'll have to look
in to this." So doing as he
said he began to follow
the boys. The first bit of information he gathered was in
a drug store where the boys
had bought an ice cream

apiece and didn't have
sufficent funds to pay for
thier purchase. And as the
Druggiest said "he threw them
out on thier ears." So the officer
went around gathering simular
odd pieces of information, untill
he finally came upon the
boys themselves. Grabbing
them by the back of thier
necks he dragged them back
to the railroad station, where
Mrs. Busybody identified them
as she said those "horrible
boys who splattered mud on
her Sunday dress." "Well," the
officer said. "These kids are charged with more than just splattering
mud on your dress!" "Well, I
never!" exclaimed Mrs Busybody.
"What are these charges?" "Well,"
began the officer. "They bought
ice creams without paying for
it, and broke several store wind-

ows, and sneaked up behind a
lady and put a lighted firecracker down her dress." "Why
awful terrible children!" exploded
Mrs. Busybody. "You should
be sent to the reform school!"
"That's just what's going to happen
to them!" roared the officer. And
so he walked away dragging
the children behind him.

Mrs. Busybody traveled
back to to the waiting room and
sat down on a bench. She
looked at her wrist watch and
saw that an hour and a half
had passed! "Suchous me
alive!!" she said as she got up
from the bench and rushed
to the station agent and explained to him what had happened.
Just as the station agent started his explanation the train
roared in! Mrs. Busybody
turned around and rushed to

the platform! The train stopped to a stand still and the porter stepped down and put the stepper on the platform. There were hidouse cries inside the car such as: "Mammy, Mamma! get me some candy!" "Ma! Ma! take me to the movies an' gimme some candy!" "Shut up Willie!" "Hush, andrew!" "Baw! Baw!" "Shut up Oswald!" "Do you want me to bean you!" "Oh me love, can I have just a tunie weenie drink of rum?" "Be quiet, you lope of a dope! Pow! Pow!" "Please don't hit me no more came uncle Williams wee little tiny voice. Finally the hoodlum procession came down the platform toward Mrs. Busybody. "Psst, psst, lookit that ole dame!" came a whisper through the crowd. "Blah, Blah!" a troup of tounges came out at Mrs. Busybody!

"Well," said Mrs. Busybody.
'I'ts About time you arrived."
Well all go home now.'"
As they tramped through the
streets they passed by a
candy shop. "Baw! Baw! Gimme
some candy ma!" couldn't I
have a wee little peice of candy
spoke Uncle williams small
voice: Shut up!" Pow! Bang!
Lulu Belles umbrela broke over
Uncle williams poor head.
They finally arived home and got
setteed waiting for the further
adventures of the following week

Chapter III
Uncle William Makes
Trouble

"William! William! you get up from that bed this minute, you lazy laggert!" "Yes, honey, just a minute," replied Uncle William's small voice. "Well you'd better get up this minute before I lam the daylights out of you!" Uncle william got out of bed and put on his pants. He felt in his pockets and saw that his pockets had been thouroly gone through the night before. Sneaking up to Lulu Belle he said in a meek voice "Oh! Precous little darling dumpling you are the apple of my eye, the most pretty rose in the garden couldn't you lend me a quarter so's I could get me just a little booze" "go away, you

lowdown son of Saten!" "I ought
to turn you upside down and
shake all the shinney out of you
and make Cocktail out of it!"
Crash! Bang! Oh! oh! honey
let me up please! Oh! Honey,
have mercy on my soul!"
Just then Lulu Belle looked
up on the mantel and grabbed
Mrs. Busybody's most prized
china vase and hurled it at
poor Uncle William. Just then
old Mrs. Busybody stomped in
When she saw what had happened she almost fainted. "Oh!
she gasped. "Why did you
break my china vase on that
drunken minded verminous
Creature!" "It was genuine China, I
tell you! genuine!" Poor Uncle
William crouched in a corner
in fear! Mrs. Busybody gave
Uncle William such a dirty
that the poor old man

trembled all over in fear.
"Come into the next room with
me!" said Mrs. Busybody.
So poor Uncle William was
dragged into the next room
and nobody knows what happened then, but it was something
terrible!

Night soon came. Uncle
William was locked in his
room for the night as usual.
It was getting late. Uncle
William knew that, for Lulu
Belle had stopped telling
Mrs. Busybody what she would
do to him the next day. It
was soon midnight. Uncle
William quietly raised the
window and jumped out.
He ran around the house
to see that no one was
watching him. Then he quietly
crept under Lulu Belle's window. He ran around the corner.

And guess what he ran into
a craps game! He said in a
very little voice, "may I join
you all?" "certainly" said a
gruff voice. The game had
started. "Come on, seven!" Uncle
Williams voice could be heard
far down the street. "Shoot 'er
in there!" Uncle William's
voice could still be heard
far down the street.

When the game was over
Uncle William lost everything.
"I'm sorry, boys," he said in
a small voice. "But I don't have
sufficent funds to pay you
all." "So you don't, eh!" "Well
take this!" Biff! Bang!
Ouch! "Let me up! Let me
up!" came Uncle William's
small voice. Crack!
A liquor bottle broke over
Uncle Williams poor head.
The noise awoke Sulu

Truman Capote

Belle. She hurried down the street toward them. "You leave my husband alone!" she roared. Bang! ouch! Stop it! Biff! Pow! Pow!

When the fight was over Lulu Belle dragged Uncle William back to the house where she locked him in his dingy little room. Lulu Belle attacked Uncle William vigourisly! She said, Why you drunken old lope-eared billy goat! The very idea of you sneaking out you limb of Satan!"

After a good beating Uncle William was locked safely in his room and they all went to bed.

Chapter IV
The Kids Make Trouble

"Ma! Ma!" "I want some candy for breakfast!" "Well, you cant have it, Ulysses!" "If you don't shut up, I'll knock your block off!" "Mama, Mamma!" "I want a doll!" "Well you can't have it, Lizzie so shut up before I bean you one!"

"Ma! Ma! I want some ice cream!" "Ma! please give me some!" "Will you shut up, Lissie!" "Baw! Mamma!" "I don't want to shut up!" "Baw, Mamma!" "Whang! Whang! Ouch! Mamma! Stick!" "Now if you younguns don't stop this bawling and crying, I'm afraid I'm going to have to whip every one of you!" Immeditly the room

hushed to silence. "Well, now
everybody sit down to this
breakfast table and eat thier
breakfast!"

Mrs. Busybody, who was
already at the table, gave them
a dirty look as they all sat
down, one by one. "Eat your
cereal," Lulu Belle commanded.
"Baw! mamaa, I don't like cereal!"
spoke up Lizzy. "I don't want
cereal, I want coffee!" "You can't
have Coffee, its not good for
you!" "Baw! mamma you've
been reading those advertisment
again!" Lulu Belle got up from
the table and pointed her finger at Lizzy. "You eat your
cereal, do you hear me!" "And
don't let me hear you mention
coffee again!" "And if you do,
Ill crown you one!"

"Ouch! ma!" Tell oswald
to quit pulling my hair!"

"Oswald!" - "What do you mean by pulling your sisters hair?" But he continued to pull his sisters hair. Lulu Belle Grasped him by his shoulder. And spoke in a sharp voice. "Did you hear me?" "Let go your sister's hair!!" Oswald let go the grip on Lizzie's hair slowly. "Oh! Heck." "a fellow can't even pull anybody's hair these days."

In the meantime, poor Uncle William was eating his breakfast on the mantle piece, for he was to sore to sit at the table with the rest.

While back at the table, the so called hidouse crys of the children could be heard. The augerment about pulling the hair was still on. Lulu Belle was talking. "Now Oswald, if you want to pull

anybody's hair, pull your
brother Andrews." "You do,"
piped up Andrew." "And I'll bust
your nose!" "You bust his
nose again (for he had busted
Oswald's nose before) and I'll
bust that thick big skull of yours."
There was much augurment
over "busting Andrews skull."
However it ended with both
boys. Oswald and Andrew
getting a sound spanking.
    After breakfast all the
children went out in the yard
to play. Oswald spied a little
boy riding a trycicle across
the street and went over to
play with him. After playing with the little boy a
while Oswald said, say, what
about you coming to play
with us kids on the other
side of the street?. "Well,
I will ask mother if I can

come," answered the little boy in a British accent. He walked up to a house and rang the door bell. His mother answered it. "What do you want, Selby?" "Mothaw, this little boy wants to know wheather I can come over to mrs. Busybody's house to play with him." "But, er, I suppose so, Selby, dear, but be careful and don't hurt yourself." So they were off.

"What is your full name?" Oswald asked. "Selby Arnold Rifflesniffe," he answered. "My what a funny name," laughed Oswald. Little Selby looked displeased at his playmates remark.

They were soon all playing on the lawn. "Let's have a game of hide and go seek," said Oswald. "O. K." they all shouted. "Selby, you can be

it. said Willie. I don't want
to be it, I won't be it! shouted
Selby. You won't which? asked
Willie. I repeat, said Selby.
I won't be it! So you won't, eh?
Well take this! and this! Ouch!
Bang! Sock! Let me up! Let
me up! Let go my hair!
Bloody murder! Ouch! Mothaw!
Tell them to get me up!

Just then Lulu Belle walked
out on the lawn. Squinting
one eye she said, Willie! you
let that child up this instant!
and if you don't I'll break your
bean! Willie got up off Selby
and he ran across the road
crying: Mother! Mother! help
I'm dieing!

While back on the lawn
Lulu Belle was giving a lecture.
Now you get in this house
this instant and don't make
any more trouble.

Chapter V
The Hoodlums leave

"Now is everything packed?"
Lulu Belle was saying. "Yes,
me darling, it's all packed."
William answered meekly.
"Well don't stand there
like an idiot, tote those
bags out in front of the
house." "Yes, me darling."
After this task was done, Lulu
Belle had something else
for him to do.

Finally all the work
was completed. Uncle William tiptoed up to Lulu
Belle meekly. "Darling," he
began. "Don't you think I
ought to have a little bonus
for all this hard labor?"
"Allright, this once, I'll let
you have it, for your own
happyness and enjoyment."

said Lulu Belle. Uncle William
was very pleased to hear
this, for it was the first time Lulu Belle had ever
agreed to let him have whiskey. "But first," she continued
"you will have to go down to
the station to buy the tickets.
"And on the way back you
can get a quarters worth of
toddy." And here is the 15:00
for the ticket money and
there is your quarter for
your skinny." "Now don't
stay long for the train
leaves in an hour, and we
be on time."
     So Uncle William dis-
appeared out the door.
     Lulu Belle went upstairs
where the children were.
"Now you children hurry up
with your baths!" Baw! Ma
It isn't Saturday night,

yet! and I don't want to take
no bath! "Well youre going
to!" shouted Lulu Belle.
So all of the kids got
in the bath. They all took
their baths and got dressed.
Then Lulu Belle went
down to find uncle William,
But uncle William was
no where to be found, William! William!
where are you cried Lulubelle. Hmmp! she
said I guess he's already got the ticket and
He's probably down at that saloon loitering
around, well I guess I will have to go down
to the saloon and get him she said as
she vanished out the door arriving at
the saloon she said "Well where are the
ticket you big fathead. Now don't get so
excited honey, er "William stammered "spent
five dollars of the money on a wee bit of dinner,
Why you! hollered Lulubelle, you
dirty son of a satan I'll break your backbone
you drunken minded venomous creature; All I own
you. Well this what happened then for it

173

was terrible. We now found poor uncle william in the bed with bandages all over him.

"Will?" Lulubelle was saying, "You've certainly made a fine mess of everything. Yes honey came williams everormall voice. And continued Lulubelle you've spent almost half the ticket money fourteen though I have enough to get us home on through mrs. Busybody's friend contribution were missed the train though but there's a train leaving at 6 o'clock we'll take and if it wasn't for your big thick headedness we wouldn't be in this mess. Yes honey aswered william meekly. Lulubelle walked across the room and put something in a spoon and made uncle william swallow it after this was done she left the room only to be called back by uncle williams calling "Well what is it? she asked Honey he asked sympathetically. Will you please send willie down to the book shop and get this book for my christmas present. handed her a slip of paper which had the title of the book on it well alright she said gruffly I'll send him for it. she then went down stairs to send willie for the book. But before handing him the slip of paper she read it and wrote somthing down on the piece of paper, she gave willie the money for the book's and he was of. However he soon returned and gave lulubele two parcels instead of one. She carried them up to uncle williams room and handed him one of the parcels and sat down in a chair with the other they both apened them hurriedly. the title of uncle williams book was "How to get around your wife" By T. R. Bunk. the title of lulubeles book was "How to torture your husband" By Mrs. T. R. Bunk. After several hours of reading uncle william happened to glance over in the derection of lulubele when he saw that she was reading a thick much thicker than his he trained his eyes which had big black circles around them to see the title of the book she was reading. When he finaly did read it the poor fat old man looked very depressed. honey he said what are you reading that for. Well! she retorted you got a book on how to get around your wife so I got one on how to torture your husband I belive in the old saying she said. a tooth for a tooth and a eye for and eye. Uncle william dropped his book in defeat. aw he said I guess a married

man just hasn't got a chance. At this point
Lulubel looked up at the clock and saw
that it was 5³⁰. Gee! she screamed it's
5³⁰ and we have to leave at six oclock get up out
of there and get dressed we have to catch the train.
Ohh! screeched uncle William as he made an attempt
to get out of the bed. Oh no before. Now or not you get
out of that bed before I beat the daylights out of
you. So uncle William got out of bed with much
pain. Lulubel then went down stairs to get the
children ready. When everything was done she called
the Taxi Cab Company and told them to send over
three cab's (for one or two was not enough to hold them)
to Main and Chestnut street. When the cabs arrived
everyone piled in including Mrs. Bayley. When
they arrived at the station Lulubel walked over to
the ticket office. I want nine tickets to "Slumtown"
please. Nine tickets to what. Slumtown Lulube
repeated. Never heard of the place retorted the
ticket agent. Well then Lulubel began oh know
its not a regular stop it's whats commonly known as
the yo hola district. Oh I know where that is the
ticket agent laughed here your tickets the train
will be in any minute now. So Lulubel walked

over to where the others were and sat on the waiting bench with them. The seven kids were crying for Ice cream and candy as usual. Uncle William was asking for a little snort of whiskey, and Mrs. Busybody was grumbling and mumbling as usual. Just then the train roared in and Suddenly Uncle William and the kids got aboard. They waved goodbye to Mrs. busybody. As Mrs. Busybody left the platform she said thank heavens those people are gone at last, and so ended the Christmas Vacation.

Fumerie

Mary Butts

—Edited by Nathalie Blondel and Camilla Bagg

EDITORS' NOTE

The important contribution of the English Modernist Mary Butts (1890–1937) is now beginning to be properly recognized. Although there have always been avid admirers, until recently the range and power of her writing were pushed aside by anecdotes about her flamboyant personality and dramatic lifestyle. Yet behind this persona, sustaining and driving it, was an impassioned writer whose prolific output includes novels, stories, poetry, essays, an autobiography, reviews and plays. She wrote of the Great War in her story "Speed the Plough" (1921) and her novel Ashe of Rings *(1925). She explored Greek legend, the grail myth and history in works such as "Bellerophon to Anteia" (1923), "The Later Life of Theseus, King of Athens" (1925),* Armed with Madness *(1928),* The Macedonian *(1933) and* Scenes from the Life of Cleopatra *(1935). Her interest in the supernatural led her to write the haunting stories "With and Without Buttons" and "Mappa Mundi" (1938) as well as an in-depth study of the genre, "Ghosties and Ghoulies" (1933). Her concern for ecological issues and the break-down of religious belief are repeatedly discussed in essays and reviews, and her novel* Death of Felicity Taverner *(1932) integrates a modern parable and a dramatic detective story.*

A substantial number of her writings are now back in print (including all those mentioned above). "Fumerie" forms part of that still-too-large body of her work that was never published. In a diary entry in June 1927 Butts asked: "Is there a person among our 'ever widening circle of friends' who is not smoking, wishing to try, about to give up, giving it up, gives it up, starting again, or superciliously denouncing the practice?" "Fumerie" was written by Butts (already a drug user of long standing) during the summer and autumn of 1927 while travelling in Brittany and then in her flat in the Rue de Monttessuy, Paris, a small street dominated by the Eiffel Tower. It defies categorization, moving between essay and fiction, between the careful specifications of a technical manual and the witty, lyrical description of the Art of Opium Taking. While it extols the pleasurable and often disorganized aspects of the magical opium circle, darker elements are only just kept in check as the vulnerability of the opium-eaters in this country beyond the ken of day-to-day reality is powerfully conveyed.

In Paris in September 1927 Butts wrote of the pleasure of being among her friends, who included the French artist Jean Cocteau (who illustrated Butts's work), the American composer Virgil Thomson and the English writer Douglas Goldring. There was "love, friendship, a little work, some cash" and, as she noted: "Much less opium needed" (Butts's emphasis). Indeed, as she completed "Fumerie" she wrote of "the rather easy opium fight, as if we were laughing at one another, pushing an adored friend reluctantly and temporarily out of the house." Towards the end of September she read Baudelaire's Les Paradis Artificiels *from which she quotes in "Fumerie." There is one direct diary reference to this essay-story in early October when she decides to "question if Shakespeare knew what it was, and whether the pepper-trade and its passions were a mask for 'It.'" Yet as her relationship with Virgil Thomson deteriorated, darker moods predominated with only temporary respites such as a day in mid-October when she reminded herself, somewhat shakily, to "remember this day: opium down to seven pipes: all the things done, grief over Virgil put in its proper place . . ."*

Like many addicts, Jean Cocteau tried to convert several of his friends; more than one of her contemporaries testified that Mary Butts, although she believed strongly in the inspirational value of opium for her writing, never felt the need to do so. This was characteristic of her generosity of spirit and the fact that, as with all she did in her life, her motivation was rarely the act in itself, but what it evoked and explained to her. "Fumerie" is an excellent example of her ability to translate this understanding back into writing.

Mary Butts's original spelling and punctuation have been retained in this first publication of "Fumerie." The manuscript of "Fumerie" forms part of the Mary Butts Archive housed at the Beinecke Library, Yale University.

*   *   *

THE DUKE SAID: 'Next Friday evening, wind and weather permitting, I propose to get drunk.' A good statement, but it refers to a liberation of the spirits infinitely rowdy and gross in comparison with the subject of this sketch, which is the inhalation of the poppy-head juice called opium, rightly prepared and worthily received.

'We few, we happy few, we band of brothers.' Shakespeare, in a moment of enthusiasm about something else, has described its supreme social aspect as a uniter of friends, a solvent of prejudice, a gentle sapper working beneath the barriers of race.

The people whose existence will be lightly shewn, Helen and Martin, Charles, André and George might have lived in ignorance of each other, in casual contact or, a friendship once made, in squabbles and misunderstandings; might have passed years stealing the affections of one from the others, or in repeating highly coloured versions of what the others had been seen doing out the night before, in their cups. Some diversion is necessary, and life being what it is, few things should be allowed to stand in the way of a good time. But diversions in 'boites de nuit' are of the nature of costly public spectacles, necessary, from time to time, in this city, as were the classic games; but no alternative to regular hours of vision or repose.

Helen is american, Charles is english, Martin american and André french. George is almost too english to be true. Out each and every night on a spree, how little they would have known each other, how little race-personality would have filtered through race-personality, the french to clarify, the american to be generous, the english to make subtle. They might have drained their healths and their pockets and never discovered each other, or set out on the perspective-opening journey of opium into the secrets of the race and the human heart. What follows is not that story, but some notes it has amused me to make, hints from the Travel Bureau, the opium Baedeker, which, so far as I know, has not been written cheerfully enough in the western world. We have had ecstasy and mystery, descriptions touched with cold fear. De Quincey and Baudelaire. The Halitosis histories America gives us monthly suggest another description of that state which opium can never create but only elicit, the only moments of life whose value remains serene, the hours when man 'se trouve, en même temps, plus artiste et plus juste'.

Elsewhere, Shakespeare calls it a 'drowsy syrup'. Smoked, it is not so particularly, unless you take too much. But what did he mean by syrup? If he meant what we mean, he knew the stuff we use. This touches an enquiry. From the fifteenth century on, the world went mad on pepper and the spices of the far East. They were known in the middle ages, and have passed from an exciting luxury into the commonest of necessities. But did those ships which set out on the dangerous, interminable voyage after nutmeg, cinnamon and cloves return with something extra in the hold? Were the chests of food-and-health-preserving fruits of the earth alternated with such stuff as sacks of poppy-heads packed in clay? Was the spice trade, or what gave it its mysterious energy, a mask for the search after the strongest, least brutalising and most dangerous stimulant known to man?

It seems clear that it was smoked nowhere until the seventeenth century, and then first in China. If Shakespeare knew it as a syrup, he must have drunk it diluted, or, God help him, evaporated and chewed. Did the Doges at Venice throw an opium party? Did a little dinner at the Borgias include it? Subject for a historical enquiry of great human interest. But for such a research the writer must be interested in opium; to be interested, he must have tried it; and having tried it, he must have become a will-less, truth-less victim of morphine. People do not like to be called that. So it is not likely that we shall ever know.

In the sixteenth century, Paracelsus extracted morphia. That most sensible magician also insisted on a supply of pure water for the town whose ruler had made him its medical officer of health. He also restated the practical-mystical theory of 'signatures' or correspondences between the visible and invisible regions of nature. Some day Science will have another Clerk Maxwell to spare, and that business will be looked into. Before that day, she might make an effort, and discover an antitoxin to the prison in the unripe seed of a common flower.

FIX YOUR TRAY!

Invitations to 'come and smoke' are not always a diplomatic passport to the land of heart's desire. The slips between a jar of B____s and his lip only the apprentice smoker knows. There is the tray. The needles. THE LAMP. The moistened rag or piece of sponge. The pipe, its bowl, the vinegar. Tape. The dross-box and palette.

George has a tray, its original lacquer clotted with oil-soaked dross. His favourite needles are bent. The head has fallen off the mother-of-pearl bee that hangs on the lamp-glass and, choking inside in a pool of mixed opium and olive oil, impedes the flame.

Charles enters, saying 'Nien, nien' in what he hopes is chinese for an urgent need to smoke. Helen, Martin and André are sprawled,

181

impatient; drawing fiercely on cigarettes. The lamp sputters, falls to a bead. Is coaxed: shoots up. The pipe on the bent needle bursts into flame, is blown out, skinned and stabbed again on the bowl rough with burnt dross. Falls off: is caught, licked, thrust on again. Crumbles to dust.

Interval.

George rolls over on his back and gives it up, while Charles cleans the bowl: another needle: licks his fingers. The shrill bubble of a perfectly cooked pipe rises agreeably, while Helen, Martin and André turn over, expectant at last.

Thud. Clatter. The heavy clay 'fourneau' drops off the pipe, shatters the lamp-glass (the only one). Charles crushes the opium-ball, which has fallen off the fourneau in its turn and lost itself behind the lamp, in his teeth, and rushes to the bathroom to spit. Like angry dogs, stretched out but not asleep, the party turns on George.

Affairs will probably right themselves in time; but meanwhile temperaments have been exasperated and auras, which had entered George's fumoir all the colours of a healthy rainbow, have now been reduced to a monotony of dingy browns.

Memory-training is the smoker's first obligation.

BE PREPARED.

For insufficient and too sufficient oil.

For waxed or moistened tape, which drying loosens the bowl.

For silver needle-points wrenched off the straight.

For each and every perversity of so-called inanimate matter.

For the live temperament, the diabolic perversity, the ingenious devilry, the highly-strung nature of opium; and each morning in anticipation of your 'deux heures de calme' —

FIX YOUR TRAY.

George's pipes are too large; André's are too small. Through undercooking, Charles' bubble on the bowl like porridge. Helen's fall off because the fourneau is cold. Martin is notorious for his burnt pipes. How human nature repeats itself in our simplest acts! But the underlying fault from which these imperfections arrive is Impatience. It takes a year's practice to make a pipe, and each of the band in his impatience to get down quick to a little peace tries to build up the source of pleasure too fast. 'Sorry,' they say, 'it was the bottom of the pot.' 'My hand shakes.' 'The stuff is too thin.' 'The stuff is too thick.' Such are the common excuses by which pipe after pipe is ruined; the rhythm of your regime perhaps destroyed. Pipes should be rolled on a palette: any piece of jade will do, and at the same time help preserve that atmosphere of the magic east, about which opium is rapidly correcting a number of our most cherished misconceptions.

DAMN THE LAMP!

Is it a subconscious protest, relic of a misapplied sense of sin which so frequently inhibits the purchase of oil and wick? You are in a hotel, and a descent into the salle à manger at midnight to rob a cruet is hardly the best preparation for your bedtime pipe. Nor is a strip cut out of your finest wool sock a convenient and economical substitute for the 'mèche' which should be the smoker's first care.

. . . Unnecessary, on the other hand, to gild the lily, as Helen did in the days of her debut, when a famous smoker called to teach her the necessary arts, and she, instead of common olive oil had lit her silver lamp with Guérlin's Après l'Ondée which burns a pale blue and scented instead of a yellow, vegetable flame, and added to the smokers' anthology an imperishable joke.

Tape.

By tape I should mean tape, preferably waxed tape, to be cut in nicely calculated lengths. In fact I mean almost any piece of material, including lace shoulder straps, strips of handkerchief, shoelaces and string.

I have seen the bowl bound and jammed on the pipe by the stuffing out of a valuable tie, damp rose leaves, a piece of George's braces.

And I have been present at more shattering moments when the heavy fourneau has crashed off the pipe, broken the lamp-glass and upset the drug; known more ruined pipes, and wasted opium caused by inattention to this preliminary measure than by any other smoker's procrastination.

I do not know the french for tape.

I cannot remember it.

I buy mending for my boy-friends' socks and carry the colours in my head: their different kinds of cigarettes, and all shades of ribbon.

I cannot buy tape.

It is good luck to be a woman: you always wear shoulder straps.

I went out the other day and bought a mile of it.

'What Did They Think They Smelt?'

You are in a hotel. Your friends (non-smokers) gather round your bed.

183

'Why haven't you opened the window?'

'They can smell it half way down the corridor.'

The drug just set on your needle bursts into flame, or crumbles as you press it on the bowl. The window is flung open, the night wind rushes in: sets our papers flying—rain follows and the uncontrollable outside world. Emotion will spoil your 'kief'. Spoils it.

And what will the other people in the place, some who are undoubtedly hurrying to their rooms for their daily dose of peace, if they have not smelt what will be most agreeable to them, think they have smelled?

'We are down to twice-cooked dross, and drinking George's bowl washed out with Dubonnet—' You sympathise, perhaps press tighter to your breast the little tin you have ordered and paid for a month past, expected for a fortnight, given up hope of a week ago; and, after a rendez-vous fixed for successive days at your flat, received after a two-hours' wait in a workman's café off the Port St Denis.

Perhaps you will share it with them.

Perhaps the last time they left you to derange your interior with three times distilled burnt morphine. BUT —

IT IS USELESS TO ORDER IN TIME. ANTEDATE NECESSITY AS FAR BACK AS IMAGINATION WILL CARRY.

'I DON'T FEEL WELL.'

'Yes, make me another—It doesn't seem to be doing me any good.'

The novice gasps away at the seventh, seventeenth or twenty-seventh pipe the careless or malicious friend has rolled: while the well-meaning spectator (non-smoker) goes away to prepare black coffee.

Administers it.

DISASTER.

Your pleasure consists not in the number of pipes, but in the attitude, mental and physical, of repose.

OPIUM IS NOT A WHISKEY AND SODA.

KEEP STILL!

How can you expect Nature to do her work if you do not assist her, and frequently outrage her inviolable laws?

Helen is running about making tea for Martin, who has exceeded his ration while he offered battle this time to the french telephone. André has roused himself to argue with a non-invited non-smoker who arrived drunk. George and Charles were late, and could not agree to take turn and turn with the lamp. The interval between tea and dinner was a mere spell of agitation; the meal a discord; the evening devoted to important social obligations, a fiasco.

All this could and should have been avoided.

KEEP STILL.

You are going away for the first time with It. Probably it will not have occurred to you that the problem of packing now presents serious developments.

In default of a travelling set you have followed the usual course in the case of extraneous objects, and your smoker's outfit is secreted in socks, between handkerchiefs, in a shoe.

Lucky for you if you have committed to the sponge bag the bottle, tin, flask or jar on which all depends.

If you have not, on unpacking you may find a morass; chemises, or shirts, toothbrushes, make-up and books gummed together by an inseparable, uncollectable mass of semi-solidified opium.

Useless to repine, you will probably soak each article in your wash-hand basin, bottle the result collected by means of your douche and drink it day by day.

NEXT TIME YOU WILL HAVE LEARNED:

that opium has the qualities of treacle, glue, quicksilver and india rubber.

ALSO:

that liquid, blown to bubbles, cooked to paste, to dust, opium is a living substance, a magic extract. One that knows its own business and who are its own people. If you do not learn its ways, it will leave you, and leave ruin behind it.

The band had brought its dross to be cooked at Helen's flat. Left alone she would be sufficiently competent to deal with it.

In the privacy of her kitchen she assembled a clock, a casserole, fan-folded filter papers. A lawn cloth, a razor blade, a spoon. The stripped wood of more than one matchbox. A slag-heap of volcanic-looking cinders. Tied in a pudding bag, bobbing in a frothy brown sea, the precious extract begins to separate from its ash, when—Martin enters: a minute later Charles and André. Then George, who says, while the others peer:

'I say, are you sure you are doing it right?'

Instead of giving him a piece to suck which would act as a gag, with lovely courtesy Helen stops to explain: to justify. And half an hour later, the clock is ticking frantically, and ascending the corridors above, draft-blown down the stairs to the Concierge's lodge wafts an opium breeze. Over a low flame, in a kitchen littered with debris, a dark surge in the casserole is at the point of thickening. In one minute, five, ten, there will be more opium in the world. But the five midwives are engaged in frantic dispute. Unvarying routine essential to successful delivery sacrificed to conflicting theory.

While Helen, half-stupefied, harassed, aching, stirs and stirs.

God help her if George in a moment of compassion takes her place and, transferring the compassion to himself, raises the flame and finally, in a moment of conviction that André knows nothing whatever about opium-cooking, leaves it to look after itself, in order to persuade him.

Another smell will insinuate itself through the stupefying, vegetable sweetness, a smell of the Pit. Cries, sniffs, a rush to the kitchen to find a split casserole and harsh stinking cinders in place of the honey-smooth black liquid.

But if the final tragedy be averted, there remains still the agitating scene: arguments which continue while the new brew is being tried out, until, overcome by its sheer strength, everyone agrees that everyone else is in the wrong.

There is only one way to prepare opium from dross: convince yourself that it is a bechamel sauce you are making to pour on a fish; and after straining the boiled ash, stir until it thickens over a low flame.

You will stir and stir. Stir and stir and stir and stir: till hope dies and your right arm and your left are attacked by paralysis. One quarter of an hour will succeed another, while black drops, airier than soda water, drip off the spoon. Then, hardly perceptibly, drops which are not so light.

The quality of the brew will alter: fat, gold-skinned bubbles will rise and pop deliberately, like a wink. A wave off the spoon will rise (and try to stick) to the casserole side.

It is over. First lowering the vessel into a bowl of cold water, you can pour, scrape, share, lick it off.

DO IT ALONE.

The room is lit from the low bookshelves by a huge glass wine bottle, filled with water, a piece of the sea at home, topped with an electric bulb, and shaded by a round of lacquered parchment painted with ships. In the open fireplace, a log whistles, another blazes in a level fence of flames while underneath the red-hot wood crumbles ashes charred to a white bloom.

On the black floor-divans are lying Helen and Martin, Charles, André and George. Between them, on the low table topped with a mirror and with dragons for legs, their tools are scattered, the needles and palette, the dross-box and opium-cup. A bamboo pipe bound in ivory smoked to the colour of amber, another of ivory finished with jade. Glass and bronze, silver and enamel, mother-of-pearl and green stone. Objects of virtù and delicate use in their proper employment, lit by the olive oil lamp, the oldest in european use, over whose flame a needle is twirled, redipped and spun again. Bubble clusters blow out, dark, gold skins of opium. They click and whisper, the needle-rod thrills in the hand, the beads enlarge, crisp and trembling. Crushed on the palette, the needle is clipped and blown again. And again. Until—when not too crisp and dry, and not too wet; when no more black drops can be pressed out on the palette, and when no dust powders the jade; when the pipe has been rolled to a perfect cone . . .

André raises the pipe. In the small light he is a shadow to which, in the light-circle, are attached two fine hands. He heats the bowl, the grey clay incised with small gold flowers, gives a last twist and presses the pipe on. It rests over the needle-hole, pierced, shapely. Helen takes the pipe. For thirty seconds a low whistle rises as she smokes, André guiding the drug with his needle-point. She puts the pipe down and lies back. An instant later André's fingers, delicate as the needle, are dipping and turning again.

'Your turn, mon ami.' Helen slips aside into the shadow on outer cushions.

'Shall I make for you now, André? It's going well today.'

Helen says: 'I remember now how that song goes.'

'Sing it to us later,' says Martin, 'I'm altering that poem.'

Charles decides in a flash how an old quarrel which he had not begun should be ended.

André, following Polycrates, and to protect perfection, cuts out a pipe.

George beams and has another.

'My favourite breakfast, opium and strawberries.'

Wake up on a strict and diminishing regime, with a slight chill and a slight ache. Part your hair and wash your face; set your tray and drink your tea; if it is summer, eat your strawberries. Read the paper; smoke a cigarette; listen outside to the morning air, the mysterious

187

plain-chants sung up and down a Paris backstreet.

Imagine a crisis which would turn you out of bed, before you have smoked, to run all day about the city. If you know you can, you are safe.

Smoke three pipes. Lie still and low on your back and let the day fall into its perspective.

Come back at evening to dress. Drink tea with a lemon wheel in it. Smoke what is left of your regime, down to the final sporting event, the scrapings off your palette.

Half an hour for sleep, half an hour for meditation and praise of Paris, preparing for its night's play. Half an hour for bath and make-up; then skip out of the house and into a taxi and over the Place de la Concorde to whatever the night has in its cup, a cup which is usually filled.

'THEY SMOKE OPIUM.'

I think I understand the reaction of the non-smokers when they say that. It is what they would feel if we were known to have killed to obtain the philosopher's stone. And got it.

For well or ill, that is to say for fifty per cent of each, smokers are inside a ring. As near a ring to a magic ring as a man can win by his senses. Equally, non-smokers, the people who have heard about it and are afraid to try it—for the question cancels down to fear and to nothing else—are subtly linked. They are not the people with whom opium disagrees; who have been caught by its derivations and sworn off. Nor are they necessarily, though generally, 'enemies of the rose'. They are, I suspect, people with whom it will have nothing to do. Opium knows its own business. Those it wants, it finds—even out of their ranks.

But I am glad that burning, hanging, drawing and quartering have gone out of the possibilities of fashion.

While, on our side, we have always a card to play. We have excommunication.

Tréboul — Paris 1927

188

The Snowstorm
Robert Musil

—Translated from German by Burton Pike

TRANSLATOR'S NOTE

The Snowstorm *is a kaleidoscopic and disturbing fantasy that jumbles fragments of a rich literary heritage with Modernist techniques in a kind of dramatic Cubism. It has echoes of the medieval mystery play* Everyman, Goethe's Faust, Hofmannsthal's The Fool and Death, Strindberg *and the Viennese folk dramatist* Raimund. *It is a mixture of lyric, satire, parody, morality play and allegory, with disturbing threads of hatred, incest and pedophilia. The relations between mother and son, man and wife, and criminal and society—the subconscious made conscious—are themes that recur in Musil's work, from the story* "The Blackbird" *to* The Man without Qualities.

The Snowstorm *(translator's title) is the prologue, published in 1920, to an unwritten play that was to be called* The Zodiac. *The text is taken from Robert Musil,* Gesammelte Werke in neun Bänden, *ed. Adolf Frisé (Rowohlt, 1978), vol. 6, 453-462, and has never before appeared in English.*

*   *   *

Characters:

MAN	PROFESSOR
WOMAN	SERVANT
NEED	GENERAL
HEAVENLY APPARITION	POLITICIAN
MOTHER	BOY FLAKE
GIRL	GIRL FLAKE
BLACK MARKETEER	COLD
JUDGE	STORM

(*Country road. Snowstorm. Dark evening.* MAN, WOMAN *appear, struggling with great difficulty. They stop, exhausted.*)

MAN. Death, Need! (*He lets a heavy peddler's pack slide off his shoulders and leans on it, exhausted.*)

WOMAN. What are you up to? That nonsense is all you've been muttering for the last hour.

MAN. Half-hour; there must be a reason. It was my heart talking: I ought to have left the damned pack lying where it was. I've abandoned everything I owned, and here I'm having to drag this leftover crap through this weather! Death, Need! Haha, no, I thought I needed to save it!

WOMAN. We'll die if we go on standing here. Give me a hand. (*She can hardly keep from being blown over by the storm.*)

MAN. Yes, we're sure to die.

WOMAN. Come on, let's go! We haven't seen a house for hours, there must be one coming up soon.

MAN. (*Leaning against a tree.*) I can't. It's too much for me.

WOMAN. But what am I supposed to do? Croak here on the road like a horse?

MAN. On!

WOMAN. On!

MAN. No, you go on by yourself.

WOMAN. Oh God, and leave everything lying here?

MAN. Go, go! You'll find a house. Get going, I tell you!

WOMAN. But I'm afraid of the storm!

MAN. Get going, I said! Otherwise you'll croak. (*He beats her with the stick.*)

WOMAN. Oh, you beast!

MAN. Otherwise you'll croak!

WOMAN. God will punish you for chasing me off alone into the night! (*Leaves howling.*) . . . alone into the night . . .

MAN. (*Screaming after her.*) Otherwise you'll croak!

(*The* WOMAN *struggles with great effort through the storm. Exit.*)

MAN. I want to do my dying alone. . . . You can die fifty paces on. (*Again leans against his tree. Takes a half-emptied schnapps flask from his breast pocket, holds it up against the faint trace of light.*) Yes, yes, there's still a little, still a drop. (*Without drinking, throws the bottle down in the snow.*) Death, Need!—since I've got rid of the bitch I don't need the schnapps; drinking only comes from talking.

(*A weak, spreading shimmer of light pours out of the flask, and in the shimmer two words are suddenly standing. Medium figures in dark, hooded mantles, at the start fused together into a single silhouette.*)

MAN. Since when do I know you? You weren't sung to me in my cradle! Damned words! You were the worm in the apple of my life! Yet how beautiful the apple was.

NEED. Didn't you laugh when old people trembled?

MAN. (*Cheered by the idea.*) Yes, yes!

NEED. When you saw a face twisted by grief and illness?

MAN. Yes, yes, and it still makes me laugh when I think of it. It's a stupid, puffed-up way of suffering. People should hold their faces in front of their suffering the way they hold their hats.

NEED. I love you! I have always loved whoever can speak the way you do!

MAN. By God, you only began to love me when I was thirty. And how modestly you insinuated yourself! First a quick visit once or twice every few months, that was nice and fine without tiring me unduly. Then a few hours' company during the day. And suddenly you were lying beside me in bed every night and I couldn't get rid of you.

NEED. If I threw one arm around your chest and the other around your belly, how you resisted, my boy! And yet you yielded yourself up. How your moans cut through me when I was riding on your neck!

191

MAN. You sold my pillow and took away the sheet. Then you had to lie on bare straw yourself!

NEED. And no nightshirt any more, and soon just a shirt. And no bath and no hot water and soon no more soap. How you finally stank, kid, like a rotting carcass. You who used to go around in batiste.

MAN. When I gobbled up the food the dog had left in its bowl, that set me up again. What a genius man is, even on the way down! Let others wear my silk shirts.

NEED. Enough, sweetheart; you're boring me already. I stayed faithful to you for too long, on account of your philosophical notions. I have company.

MAN. Not the pimp?

NEED. Yes, he's going to kill you now. I don't have any more time to bother with you.

MAN. O my little bat, do I deserve this?

NEED. Have you ever deserved anything?

MAN. But surely not such a bold, ceremonious death as your pimp?

NEED. As long as things were going well you spat in the outstretched hands of the poor, but when you had to hold out the beggar's hat you quickly put it on if a rich man passed by. So don't be too slow, nobody's going to help you.

> (*In a flaring up of the light, it looks for a moment as if a pimp and his girl are standing irresolutely before the collapsed man. Then the scene goes dark. The light brightens again, and a beautiful woman is standing beside a wayside shrine as if she had just alighted. Bluish white baroque silk gown, gold crown in her hair. The* MAN *has pulled himself up by his stick, as if he were about to go on.*)

HEAVENLY APPARITION. Stop my child, where are you going? Don't you know I am your mother?

MAN. What trunk did you crawl out of? Huh? There's a smell coming from you ...! And what splendid silk you're wearing; it crackles like thousands of tiny electric sparks. Like the firewood in the oven when the boy was dropping off to sleep. You are

192

electrifying me. You're torturing me. The smell of night came out of the oven. The sleigh tinkled quickly past the courtyard wall. The little girl sat in the bright hollow of my ear, the snowflakes whirled past the lanterns of my eyes, powdering her hair, the horses snorted in my nose, and oh, whenever I cracked the whip the little girl jumped through a hoop, her small apple-blossom-red skirts flew up and the silver stars on her panties blurred. But already, you know, the night was thawing, big drops, then mirror-black puddles—

HEAVENLY APPARITION. Stop, my child, where are you going?

MAN. Oh you're right. It wasn't winter at all. The winter was terrible, with all those surly grownups in a room. It was longing for winter, autumn. Mother opened up the trunks, the sisters' vanity fell upon them. Oh now I know everything. How sweetly you smell of furs and camphor! I've always loved you! Silk remnants came to light. Lingerie. Sweatpads. Winter stockings. Feathers. Sachets. Butterflies. Green birds. Moons . . . Magically the woman stepped out of the trunk.

Where were you later, after I had grown up and could have held you? Is it only now that I get to see you again for the first time? How awful the women were. The sisters like naked cake-dough. And after the second child the Eve who had been officially assigned to me had a pelvis like a goat's behind. Unfaithful? What for? It's always the same spongy soul-dumpling that you stab with a fork.

HEAVENLY APPARITION. Stop, dearest.

MAN. Sure, sure. Just go on shining. (*The light grows brighter. The background emerges: beyond the driving snow a blooming landscape becomes visible, seen as from its high margin.*) What are you doing? What sort of magic are you conjuring up?
Out of an evening like a sprung-open shrine
Thing after thing sways gently into night.

HEAVENLY APPARITION. Beloved, this world is thine and mine!
It's like a dance across a gentle meadow slope
Whose softly twined greens glide away around us
While it points the enchanted foot ever downwards—

MAN. You and I already feel our steps
Around which space opens like ballooning sails!

193

HEAVENLY APPARITION. And now the dance slowly makes us part,
Weaving around us drunken in a thousand places
In our turning—

MAN. That it already strides onwards grand and spectrally
You and I feel, trembling to our core.
The earth sinks down, raising us around each other!

> (*The* MAN *has been performing a lonely, ghostly dance.
> Suddenly he sinks down, and as he falls the stage goes dark.
> When he raises himself up again, his old* MOTHER *is stand-
> ing in a pool of light in front of him.*)

MAN. "Stop, my child!" We know that already! You old devil, do
you see, do you see what you've brought me to!

MOTHER. (*Stretching out her hands.*) My child! My child!

MAN. Oh yes indeed, *your* child! Your little pucker-mouth, your little sugar-puff, your little doll! Your hope! Your will! Your love!
Yours, yours, yours! Damned umbilical cord, you'd all like to play
jump-rope with it and with us our whole lives long! Did you give
me money when I was already reading and buying books?

MOTHER. But I did give you money.

MAN. Yes, but when I married my woman, that Satan, like you, you
sniffed that out right away, then you didn't give me any.

MOTHER. No, she was your misfortune!

MAN. Yes, she was my misfortune!

MOTHER. (*Spreading out her arms to him in pain.*) My child! My
child!

MAN. A good thing that you're not stirring from the spot. And when
I was despised and driven out, did you give me money to restore
my good name?

MOTHER. But I didn't have any more. Your debts had swallowed up
everything.

MAN. And you dare say that? A mother without money, a mother
who can't clear stones from the path, make featherdown snow,
fetch down stars, is a fraud! Get out!

MOTHER. Oh what an evil heart you have!

MAN. It always dupes you. (*He weeps. The vision disappears. A pretty, lively young girl, in the dress of fifty or sixty years ago, appears.*)

MAN. Thanks be to God, this is a pleasant change. What are you up to, child?

GIRL. I'm climbing trees.

MAN. Of course, but watch out for the storm.

GIRL. It carried off my hoop.

MAN. That's not a particularly inventive story, but how enticing your legs are! Go on, climb! No storm can touch you, no, hardly grasp the hem of your skirt. I'm just an old uncle making a little fun of myself. Let's see your teeth. Your breasts are surely just as melting and shimmering. Let me tell you some jokes. I'll pose you riddles.
What's the prettiest thing in all the land?
A pink pink pink silk garter.
And on it, and on it?
A sweet, obedient jumping jack,
A jumping jack, a pumping jack,
A jumping, kicking, pumping jack,
To pull, to pull
For little Miss—
So, you have to rhyme with that. Marie? Stefanie? Melanie? Rosemarie? My mother was also called Rosemarie. So what's your name?

GIRL. Guess!

MAN. Guess, guess! I bet you're only looking for a good-looking man up that tree!

GIRL. A good man and a little baby, a golden baby, that he will make for me.

MAN. And what's the little baby going to become? Something big? Yes, something that brings happiness and freedom. You remind me of something; if I only knew what.
Like the dress of a dead cousin of grandfather's,
Soft chamber, so secret and remote,
You hung in the fragrant closet of the world.

195

Oh childhood glow, divided by darkness,
Oh loneliness under silk skirts placed above us
Shimmeringly lit
By the beloved's body of golden dates.
I must have seen a picture of you once, from my grandparents'
time. Who are you, who awakens such sweet memories?

GIRL. (*In the tone of the earlier scene.*) Don't you know that I'm
your mother?

MAN. What—!

(*The vision disappears. One by one, the enemies become
visible, standing by the trees lining both sides of the road.
All in formal fur coats. The* JUDGE *wearing a beret, the*
PROFESSOR *with uncovered skull, the* BLACK MARKETEER *in
a top hat, the* SERVANT *in a stiff, round hat, the* GENERAL *in
a general's hat, the* POLITICIAN *in a black floppy hat.*)

MAN. Are you here too?

BLACK MARKETEER. I wanted to have a look at you.

MAN. Sure, come freeze along with me.

BLACK MARKETEER. Don't worry, I'm keeping warm.

MAN. If I had on a fur coat like yours, I'd think of something better
than just thinking that I'm warm while others freeze.

BLACK MARKETEER. That's why you don't have a fur coat; don't you
know that, you blockhead?

MAN. Oh! Judge! If I get my rights, you'll come out all right. Tie him
up, wind his bloody guts out of his belly, brand his hide with the
iron of justice! Like you were able to do with me.

JUDGE. Nòt so heavy-handed, my dear fellow. There was a tangle of
paragraphs ready and waiting for you—whenever society can't fit a
person into any category, it finally sticks him safely in the court-
room category! But that person is only an overzealous exaggeration of an indispensable foundation of order, the sense of acquisi-
tion and sticking together.

MAN. Oh? And how you grabbed hold of me for trifles! Shook me
back and forth between the bars for immoral thoughts, revolu-
tionary thoughts, subversive thoughts, bitter thoughts!

JUDGE. Don't start acting up again, malcontent! One can live quite comfortably anywhere in a martyr's clothes! You need to have a right to improve the world!

BLACK MARKETEER. Have money!

PROFESSOR. Be right! This scoundrel had talent. Today he might even have been a professor. But he never had the scientific notion of honor.

MAN. Being a curator in a corner's corner, a lighthouse for shipping on a drop of water, spending decades untying a tiny knot in life's belt while others are yanking it into bed along with the other clothes: what a paragon of human ambition!

PROFESSOR. You weren't pure enough for the abstract exercise of spiritual power: to be right!

JUDGE. (*Interrupting, like a glockenspiel.*) To be right!

BLACK MARKETEER. (*In musical counterpoint.*) To have money!

SERVANT. (*In descant.*) Saved up! Saved up!

MAN. What, you too? You thief! Didn't you steal the money out of my pockets?

SERVANT. Saved up! Saved up! You left it lying around. I used it to start my business, let it flow into the general circulation of goods, contributed it to the people's prosperity! Gentlemen, I call upon you as witnesses!

MAN. Rogue! Swine! Scraped like a mole in broad daylight, and you thought that the moon was a gold coin! You viper! You possum! You preening pheasant! You money-mouse! You vole! (*Laughs.*)

SERVANT. (*Apologetically.*) Saved up!

BLACK MARKETEER. (*Reinforcing him.*) To have money!

JUDGE, PROFESSOR. (*Growling.*) To be right!

SERVANT. Saved up! Saved up!

GENERAL. Pennied up! Pennied up!

MAN. You?

GENERAL. I give orders.

BLACK MARKETEER. (*Waving off the* GENERAL.) He has no money.

JUDGE, PROFESSOR. (*Doing likewise.*) He has no respect for the law.

MAN. (*Mildly.*) He and I were in school together.

GENERAL. (*Rasps at him.*) Stand up straight! Stand at attention! I am power.

PROFESSOR, BLACK MARKETEER, JUDGE. I am! I am! I am!

MAN. Watertight. An honorable burial. Where's the politician?

POLITICIAN. L'état, c'est moi.

MAN. Simply put—and it does you great credit.

GENERAL. None of you knows this man. If he isn't constantly forced to wash himself, to keep things organized, to eat with knife and fork, he'd be running around again on all fours.

MAN. You're half right, on all twos. But you're altogether right. Oh, if only I had had power just one time! Listen! Listen!

ALL. We have no time.

SERVANT. You've always talked, and never worked!

BLACK MARKETEER. A person must act!

GENERAL. That's the way it is.

SERVANT. It's time that people like you disappeared!

GENERAL. That's the way it is.

MAN. I'll live longer than all of you! Me!

ALL. It's time for you to die.

MAN. No, you!

ALL. No, you! You! You!

MAN. You! You! You!

> (*The wind, meanwhile, howls its cheerfully horrifying summons.*)

ALL. (*Like a glockenspiel, swelling stronger and stronger. Under their hats, their hair stands on end, they pull like raging dogs chained to their trees and point their fingers at the man, while he answers with the same gesture.*) It's time for him to lie down and die!

MAN. (*Jubilantly.*) I'm immortal! (*He collapses. The stage is plunged into darkness. The* MAN *crouches, exhausted, at the foot of the tree. The snowflakes come. A youth and a maiden speak. Fantastic costumes. They radiate light.*)

BOY FLAKE. There he's cowering, cover him up!

GIRL FLAKE. It makes me sick. He stinks of schnapps!

BOY FLAKE. Come on, we have orders!

GIRL FLAKE. I wish it were an animal. They make such pretty, clean patterns with their feet.

BOY FLAKE. You should be an icicle! The master has ordered us.

GIRL FLAKE. The wind should ruffle you up; let the master try and catch me!

BOY FLAKE. Come on, be good, do it quickly. Then we can melt together. Please, pretty snowflake!

(*Ballet:* STORM *and* COLD *appear, a shaggy old man in a machinist's outfit and an ugly old crone.*)

STORM. (*Sits down on a pile of gravel and calmly lights his stubby pipe.*) Thank God, a break. The master has been pinching me in all my limbs to make me howl right and lay about me.

COLD. You're not really a storm at all, just a wind.

STORM. Of course. In civilized regions people don't die on the roads any more. Unless by automobile. But sometimes the master has terrific ideas. Thank God that we did manage to carry out his order and blow out the light of this tough fellow's life. Eh, pal? (*He claps his hands encouragingly. The ballet, drooping, whirls around.*)

BOY FLAKE. Come, glider!

GIRL FLAKE. I don't want to any more.

BOY FLAKE. Hey, you have to make storm and cold, otherwise we'll melt.

STORM. I'd much rather do that, play around a little bit with warm smoke.

COLD. I'd like to take a rest too, for once.

GIRL FLAKE. Lazy bones! Oh, how warm you're letting it get; I'm expiring!

COLD. Humans claim that's the highest experience they can have together.

BOY FLAKE. But we're supposed to kill a man!

STORM. It's done already.

[*All go over to the fallen man, whom the snow has covered. Both snowflakes melt together in blissful fatigue on his grave. Beside the surrounding trees, all the figures of the play again become visible.*]

MOTHER. [*Stretching out her arms.*] My child! My child!

BLACK MARKETEER. Gentlemen, I think I express what we all feel when I say: not one more evil word about a dead man!

MOTHER. [*One arm painfully extended, slowly raises her other hand to cover her eyes.*]

ALL. [*With their hats solemnly on their breasts.*] O God, O God, O God, another one dead!

[*Curtain.*]

1944 Journal
[The Liberation of Paris]
Michel Leiris

—Translated from French by Lydia Davis

TRANSLATOR'S NOTE

To know himself, according to Michel Leiris (1901–1990), was to know the other, and to know the world. His life's writings were dominated by the project of exploring himself with the same scrupulous care, curiosity and objectivity he brought to his work as ethnographer. His complete Journal 1922–1989 *(edited by Jean Jamin, Gallimard, 1992), many hundreds of pages and as yet untranslated, constitutes only one form of his autobiographical writing. Some of the material from the following extract was later reworked and incorporated, for instance, in a "diary" of over a hundred short dreams called* Nuits san nuits et jours sans jours *(Nights as Day Days as Night, translated by Richard Sieburth, Eridanos Press, 1987); and in Volumes I, II and IV of his vast "autobiographical essay,"* La Règle du jeu *(Rules of the Game):* Biffures, 1948 *(Scratches, translated by Lydia Davis, Johns Hopkins University Press, 1997);* Fourbis, 1955 *(Scraps, translated by Lydia Davis, Johns Hopkins University Press, 1997); and* Frêle Bruit, 1976. *(The third volume is* Fibrilles, 1966.)

More autobiographical volumes preceded and followed Rules of the Game. *Early ventures into Surrealism and a fascination with the fertile possibilities of language and the unconscious led to a volume of poems and a novel, as well as inventive "glossaries." Participation in the first major ethnological expedition through Africa (Dakar-Dklbouti) in 1931–1933, in order to measure himself against reality, as he said, resulted in the astonishing 1934 "personal chronicle,"* L'Afrique fantôme—*as yet untranslated.*

After serving in Algeria for one year in 1939, Leiris spent most of the war in Paris writing and working as an ethnologist at the Musée de l'Homme at the place Trocadéro, where he would continue to work until 1971. An explanation of some of the names

201

Michel Leiris

mentioned in the extract: Zette, often referred to in the diaries as Z, was Leiris's wife, Louise (née Kahnweiler); Le Castor, "the Beaver," was Sartre's pet name for Simone de Beauvoir, punning on her last name; Jeannette was Jeannette Druy, later to become a secretary at the Galerie Louise Leiris, Leiris's wife's art gallery. The city of Ys, referred to in the May 20 entry, was a legendary city in Brittany said to have been swallowed up by the waves in the fourth or fifth century. The T.C.R.P. is the Paris transport authority. The "Lewitzky-Vildé-Oddon affair" refers to several colleagues of Leiris who were arrested and executed by the Germans in 1942.

One more word of explanation: beginning on September 19 and ending on November 30, Leiris evidently wrote out in more complete form the notes he had taken during the dramatic days of August 15 to 26. The "{ }" brackets indicate insertions he made as he rewrote the notes after the fact. Two instances of interpolations made still later are signalled by regular brackets and the words "Author's Footnotes," as in the original French text.

The entire extract can be regarded as a "true" or "factual" context for the roughly extemporaneous event related as eerie dreamlike or nightmarish fiction or quasi-fiction by Maurice Blanchot that follows in this issue of Conjunctions. But the real or true (as for instance Leiris's image of the turbaned woman directing traffic) is often no less dreamlike than the fictional or the dreamed event, as Leiris was at pains to show most especially in Night as Day   Days as Night but at every point in his oeuvre.

* * *

January 28
I IMAGINE—without intending to make use of it—the following subject for a story: in an oppressed town the inhabitants are finally obliged to make an absolute choice between being part of the firing line and being among those shot; in fact, nothing remains but these two groups confronting each other.

March 20
Tomorrow at eleven o'clock, at the Eglise Saint-Roch, religious service in memory of Max Jacob, who died in the Drancy camp.

May 2
Learned of the death of D[eborah] L[ifchitz] in the Auschwitz camp.

May 6
"Each human reality is at the same time a direct project of meta-morphosing its own For-itself into an In-itself-For-itself and a project of appropriating the world as a totality of being-in-itself, under the guise of a fundamental quality."
(Sartre, *Being and Nothingness*, pp. 707–708.)

May 17
Dream.—I am to be shot. This happens to the accompaniment of a sort of fiesta [. . .]. I say my goodbyes to Z[ette], very harrowing; I say goodbye (or look for her in order to say goodbye?) to Castor. I am not under guard: apparently completely free. In front of my friends, who line the streets as though for the arrival of the Tour de France, I make my way, accompanied by Z (who escorts me as though I were a child in need of reassurance), to a rockface (very irregular and covered with outcrops) that is the execution wall. I press my back against it with all my strength, as though I were trying to embed myself in it, not so much in order to disappear as to draw into myself some of its rigid-ity, not a physical but a moral rigidity, in other words, courage. The hoofbeats of horses are heard and perhaps the sound of troops march-ing; it's the firing squad arriving. I am suddenly sickened with panic, feel my desire to make a good appearance dissolve; then I grow angry and tell Z I will not let myself be killed like this. Now I rush away and plunge, head down, into an alley below street level, parallel to the line of my friends, the spectators. The fall awakens me, or rather sends me into another dream in which I explain to someone this method I have of making my dreams end by deliberately falling. Then I run this dream through my mind again, I redo certain parts of it, with other details. This second version involves, for instance, a rectangle of white paper given to those who are about to be executed, on which they are permitted to write down their last words; this rec-tangle of white paper will be glued to their mouths (like a gag) when the time comes for them to be executed.

May 20
Coming home at 11:40 with Z by bike, after dinner at J.-L. Barrault's, encountered at our doorstep a fellow in a cap 30–35 years old, drunk or a little nuts (or maybe both), who claimed to be a "lad from up north" and asked us the way to "the lost city, the audacious city." All of this in cordial terms.

Z thinks he's a guy from the barges. Moreover, I realize when I mull it over that by "the lost city, audacious city," he must mean the city of Ys. A drunken waterman in search of the sunken city?

May 29
Bataille's lapse, yesterday, in a discussion during which he called me an "idealist" and a "Kantian": "the categorical *aperitif.*"

Characters in disguise, characters not in disguise:
Castor, Lucienne Salacrou, Zette are not women in disguise.
Jeannine, Françoise L, the Kosakiewicz sisters, Pauline are women badly disguised.
Sylvia is a woman cunningly disguised and Dora a woman aesthetically disguised in her portrait by Picasso.
Far greater difficulty in making the same classification for men, no doubt because in their case the disguise is less exterior. However:
Picasso and Reverdy are not men in disguise.
Braque is a man admirably disguised.

Language tic, observed lately in Dora Maar. Under the pretense of making a jest (she began doing this, it seems, in order to imitate—mockingly—Marie-Laure de Nouailles), she inserts into many of her phrases the interjection: "Say I." In reality, she must do this out of a need to refer perpetually to herself.

June 11
"I write so that I will be loved" (said Jean Genet the other evening).

September 19 (and following)
Notes on the Liberation of Paris, written over these recent days and completed today.

Tuesday August 15 (Assumption)
Posters calling upon all able-bodied men to join the F[orces] F[rançaises] de l'I[ntérieur].
{As for me, some time ago I enlisted in the patriotic militia organized by the Comité du Théâtre du F[ront] N[ational], signing up under the name of "Gérard," serial no. 1092, with Salacrou as intermediary. I'm also waiting for a liaison in order to form an F.N. at the Musée de l'Homme.}
Lunch at Salacrou's with Sartre, Castor, Zette and Merleau-Ponty. Zette and I came back home for dinner. Salacrou, apropos of the

uprising: "It should not be done eight days before, but one hour before" {implied: before the arrival of the regular troops (allusion to the situation of the Warsaw patriots, which is becoming disastrous)}. I agree. No policemen in the streets; they have been on strike since this morning.

Wednesday the 16th
Zette tells me about the Ober-Quartier moving out of 29, rue d'Astorg. The spectacle of Paris without policemen, without visible Germans, and still without Allied troops.

Via a telephone call from my niece, I learn that my brother Pierre has left Paris with the youngest of his sons to go join a group of F.F.I. (operating, I will later learn, in the area of Château-Thierry); his other son is to leave the next morning for the same destination. My niece and I go to my mother's home and persuade her to leave her apartment at 102, rue Erlanger (because we think the Allied troops will enter by the porte de Saint-Cloud) and move in with my niece at 23, quai Voltaire.

Thursday the 17th
Accompanied by my niece, I go get my mother in the late afternoon and take her by bicycle, she in a trailer, to 23, quai Voltaire. Numerous German vehicles are moving through the streets. On the bridges, people are looking in the direction of Meudon at the columns of smoke rising from the Germans' destruction of equipment. Explosions and cannonade.

After dinner, Z and I go to see my mother at 23, quai Voltaire. At about the time we are about to leave, a noise of gunfire (volleys from submachine guns). We wait a little, then we leave, for calm seems to have returned. Outdoors, there is still a little shooting, but on the other side of the Seine. As we are going past the rue Guénégaud, a revolver shot, coming from that street; the bullet passes very close to us (a few days after, when the "rooftop army" appears, I will think this shot was fired by a provocateur).

Friday the 18th
Z tells me that her friend Jeanne Chenuet was present at the liquidation of the Gestapo's stocks in the rue des Saussaies; when the crowd became too dense, the Germans fired into the air in order to extricate themselves.

Next door to us, the T.C.R.P. building is occupied by the strikers.

Toward evening, one of them holds forth: "Comrades . . ." (I don't hear it myself, it's little Jeannette who tells us this.)

We have learned that the undertakers' assistants, then the garbage-men, had gone on strike.

Saturday the 19th

The T.C.R.P. is decked with flags. At the corner of the rue Dauphine, posters have been put up announcing that the Comité Parisien de la Libération is assuming command of the national uprising.

Coming out of the Trocadéro, I learn from my colleague Champion (whose arrest we are demanding today because of his attitude at the time of the Lewitzky-Vildé-Oddon affair) that there is gunfire in the area of the Champs-Elysées. Coming back on my bike along my usual route (the quays on the Left Bank, starting from Alma), I find, at the pont des Invalides, an armed German who is redirecting traffic along the Right Bank. Having reached the pont de la Concorde, I start across it in order to regain the Left Bank: on the right-hand sidewalk, just at the entrance to the bridge, there is a large puddle of blood; to my left, a military vehicle, parked, filled with Germans in helmets with guns cocked. Continuing on my way, I see, at the corner of the rue de Solférino, several people gathered around the dead body of a civilian (a man in a gray suit, with a soft gray hat covering his face). A little farther on, a cyclist crossing my path asks if one can get by: without stopping, I answer that the streets are open as far as the pont de la Concorde. Arriving near my house, I see a patrol of helmeted and armed Germans on the other sidewalk going toward the pont Saint-Michel; on my sidewalk, another helmeted and armed German is walking in the same direction; in front of the T.C.R.P., he points to the flags and speaks angrily.

During lunch, a telephone call from Salacrou to summon me to the Comédie-Française (which it was agreed we were to occupy) and to ask me to tell Sartre and Jacques Bost. I go look for Sartre at the Hôtel de la Louisiane, where I find him with Castor and [Nathalie] Sorokine. Sartre, Castor and I come back to the house. Telephone call to Bost to tell him to meet us at the Comédie-Française (he will join us there with Chauffard). Telephone call to Rouget, the fellow from the Trocadéro who is, in principle, part of our little group; thinking that we will do nothing at the Comédie-Française, I tell him there is no point in his disturbing himself (in the following days, after many efforts, he will find something to do in the Saint-Séverin quarter and will take part in attacks on tanks, onto which they hurl

Michel Leiris

flammable bottles from the rooftops). At the Comédie-Française, where Pierre Dux and Julien Bertheau are directing operations, a number of actors are present—among others, Yonnel, whose acquaintance I make in this way and with whom I talk about Raymond Roussel; it is agreed that along with Bertheau and Marie Bell he will recite poems by Max [Jacob] during the radio broadcast planned by [Jean] Lescure for after the Liberation. In the course of the afternoon, there is some vague suggestion that our little team should go in combat formation to fetch some weapons from the place de la République. For weapons, we have only about four revolvers, I think, one of which is jammed, and a number of cartridges (perhaps a half-dozen rounds for each weapon). In a hall adjoining the lobby where we are meeting, a detonation: Bertheau, checking the functioning of one of the weapons, has let off a shot. In place of weapons, there is an abundance of pharmaceutical supplies; packets of bandages and various vials are lined up on an old desk.

Sartre and I made our way from my house to the Comédie-Française without difficulty. Hardly anyone in the streets, because the rumor is going around that people were advised over the radio from London not to leave their homes after three o'clock (and in fact after three o'clock we see, from the Théâtre-Français, only the rare cyclist). In the rue de Rivoli, close to the rue de l'Arbre-Sec, a Red Cross station. From the Théâtre-Français we telephone the house to say we have arrived safely.

Z, Castor and Sorokine are at the house with Jeanne, Jeanne Chenuet and little Jeannette; attacks by German vehicles begin on the quay early in the afternoon. Since Castor and Sorokine would rather be at the Welcome Hotel (at the corner of the rue de Seine and the boulevard Saint-Germain, a calmer spot at the moment than ours), Z is going to accompany them there. This is what I learn when I telephone Jeanne for news; she also tells me that "it's horrible," that the Resistance fighters are installed on the balcony of the house next door (at the time I think she means the T.C.R.P., occupied for political reasons by the strikers, but she is actually talking about the building at the corner of the rue des Grands-Augustins, number 53), that the fighting is violent, that they have "taken hostages" (at least, this is what I think I hear in the flood of words): I tell this to Sartre and we are very worried. A little later, Castor telephones from the Welcome Hotel to advise us not to go back home; we in turn advise her and also Z not to move, but Z declares that she is going to go to the house and see what has become of Jeanne and Jeannette and that then she will return to the Welcome. I telephone 53 *bis* some time after and learn that Z hasn't arrived there yet; I tell Jeanne to advise her not to go back to the Welcome (since that route is dangerous) but to stay at 53 *bis*. Once the telephone is hung up and after thinking about it, I decide that this advice is bad because—if I am to believe what Jeanne told me during our first conversation—there is a risk of German reprisals against our block of houses. For a period of time we are anxious, having found out from a telephone call to Sorokine that Z and Castor left for the quai des Grands-Augustins a long time ago. At last, a telephone call from Z tells us she has arrived safely at 53 *bis* with Castor (after having been trapped for a long time in the rue de Seine), and that they won't move from there between now and tomorrow.

In the late afternoon, Camus lets Sartre know that he will be waiting for him at the place des Victoires that same evening or the next day at eleven o'clock. We think this is part of his famous plan to go and occupy the premises of *L'Intran[sigent]*, a plan that Sartre and I had abandoned when we decided to join the military unit of the Comité du Théâtre of the Front National. I tell Sartre that as far as I'm concerned, I've done my part (participation in the occupation of the Théâtre-Français, while waiting to obtain the liaison I've asked for with the F.N. of the national museums and to be able to organize something at the Musée de l'Homme), and that I don't intend to try my luck elsewhere.

Dinner in a black-market bistro in the rue Montpensier, with Salacrou, Sartre and the movie star Madeleine Robinson. Next to us Bertheau, Lise Delamare, her sister and a young actor [Tony Taffin] are having dinner; Bost and Chauffard have stayed at the Français, from which Bertheau and Dux have decided to send everyone home, requesting they meet again the next morning.

Among others at the Français that day: the movie actor Daniel Mendaille, whom I recall having met when I was staying in Addis Ababa, at the Gleizes Hotel, but to whom I did not identify myself.

After dinner, all four of us go to spend the night at Salacrou's, in her apartment in the rue de Montpensier. Beautiful view over the gardens of the Palais-Royal, completely calm. Gunfire (with tracer bullets) from the direction of the Banque de France. We drink rosé wine. No electricity. In the darkness, Madeleine Robinson sings to us: "On the palace steps. . . ." By now the uprising is no more than a backdrop to a frankly pleasant evening. Concerning a bright glow of fire noticed in the vicinity of my house, I will learn the next day that what was involved was a German truck, full of gas, that was burning against the Notre-Dame Hotel.

Sunday the 20th

At about nine o'clock, return to the Théâtre-Français to receive orders: Bertheau sends everyone back home. Telephone call to the house to see if it's calm: yes. Therefore, return. Bost and Chauffard, who have spent the night in the lobby of the Comédie-Française, leave for the Left Bank with Sartre and me. Passing through the place du Carrousel, we notice, fairly far away from us, a German car; a man and woman, who also see it, are hurrying toward the buildings (which, if things go badly, will be able to offer some shelter). A sort of *minus habens*—no doubt consumed by fear—asks us where we are going and, learning that we are going to the Left Bank, attaches himself to us; we will have great difficulty in ridding ourselves of the little man, rather young, clean-shaven, with a foreign accent (or simply a speech impediment?) and the look of an invalid. At the corner of the rue des Saints-Pères (or the rue Bonaparte) we leave Chauffard (who is returning to his house, near the Sénat). Reaching the Pont-Neuf, we see a group of civilians armed with rifles preparing to cross the bridge, heading toward the Palais de Justice.

Bost comes with us to the house. We haven't been there long before the attacks on German vehicles begin. Very organized: in the street, lookout men signaling the approach of the vehicles with whistle blasts and then instantly hiding; at the windows, snipers; in the building adjoining ours (at the corner of the quay and the rue des Grands-Augustins) a team made up mostly of men from the police has ensconced itself, armed with revolvers, rifles and grenades. The method consists of first trying to hit the tires or, if that doesn't succeed, the driver of the vehicle; when a vehicle is immobilized, they throw grenades into it. When the occupants have stopped reacting, the F.F.I., emerging from their hiding places, surround the vehicle, take the survivors prisoner, then search to see if there are any weapons; if they find any they leap around the vehicle shouting Hurrah! An infinitesimal number of vehicles manages to get past. There seems every reason to believe they will be stopped farther along in any case. After each of these battles and without the firing having ceased altogether, the Red Cross teams come to collect the wounded: men and women running with stretchers and waving a white flag marked with a red cross, the men dressed in white smocks belted at the waist and wearing white caps.

Among the vehicles that we see attacked, there is one car that

209

comes out of the quai Saint-Michel in the midst of heavy gunfire; it passes in front of the pont Saint-Michel and enters the quai des Grands-Augustins; at that moment, the driver having no doubt been hit, we see it swerve and then crash against the storefront of the Librairie Académique Perrin. It catches fire almost immediately. Since it is bearing a large red cross on its roof, I'm surprised—and even shocked—that the F.F.I. have attacked it. The blazing car is quickly surrounded by armed men. We hear the occupants shouting: "Comrades! Mercy!" In front of the right-hand car door, the only one that would allow the occupants to get out, a young man is positioned, one knee on the ground, his revolver aimed, in order to prevent the Germans who are in the car (there are two or three of them) from escaping. A dispute begins among the fighters surrounding the car. Some shout: "Let them fry! Let them fry!" The others: "Finish them off! Finish them off!" Horrified (even though certain aspects of the scene remind me of a bullfight, especially the resemblance of the kneeling young man with his revolver to a *puntillero*, and seem to me full of grandeur and beauty), I leave the window and go off into the kitchen where, mechanically, I wash my hands at the tap in the sink; as soon as I become aware of the significance of my gesture (it's the ritual washing of the hands, similar to Pilate's, that I have just rediscovered), I turn off the tap and go back to the dining room window. With his revolver, the young man finishes off one of the Germans who has gotten out of the car and whose body we see writhing for a moment on the ground. A lull; then a series of powerful detonations that cause the people who were surrounding the car bearing the red cross to run away: [it] was stuffed with grenades, which are now exploding.

Another scene: an authentic Red Cross truck is stopped; aimed at by the attackers, those who occupy it show their armbands with red crosses, raise their arms and are taken prisoner.

Vision: at a fair distance, almost level with the pont Saint-Michel, we see a German lying flat on his face on the pavement, writhing in pain in a brief death throe.

Departure of Sartre, Bost and Castor (who spent the night here with Z).

At the windows of the Dépôt building, armed resisters. Cars stop in front of the door from time to time, and men and women get out, preoccupied, busy. From time to time, the arrival of a vehicle captured from the Germans (greeted with hurrahs) or the arrival of prisoners.

Michel Leiris

Several times in the course of the day, we will hear gunshots that seem to come from the vicinity of Notre-Dame; what is happening (apparently) is that a German infantry gun is firing at the Préfecture de Police.

From the window of one of the houses on the opposite quay (a fourth-floor window), a man wearing a tricolored armband beckons to the team working on the balcony of the house next door to us; lunch is ready.

We have lunch ourselves, in the dining room, but the meal is frequently interrupted by the attacks on vehicles. Sometimes we go to the window to watch; sometimes, if the fighting is too violent and the explosions too powerful, we withdraw to the rooms overlooking the courtyard.

During the afternoon, a moment of extreme emotion. A German patrol, coming from the quai de Conti, is suddenly pointed out. Risking a look out the window, I do indeed see men dressed in gray and armed with submachine guns advancing one at a time with many precautions, taking shelter behind the trees; they have reached the Monnaie. Complete silence: so as not to reveal themselves, the resisters do not fire. Expecting that at any moment a violent battle will break out (since I haven't yet realized that, in this case, there is only one thing the F.F.I. can do, and that is not move), I am painfully distressed: isn't the sending of this patrol the prelude to a siege of our block of houses, a reprisal operation that will end by setting the block on fire, massacring the inhabitants or—the happiest outcome, but one that hardly appeals to me—taking the men hostage? A tank (or a car) carrying a heavy machine gun or a small-caliber gun stops just in front of our door and fires in the direction of the pont Saint-Michel. It makes an infernal racket. Z, Jeanne, Jeannette, Jeanne Chenuet and I leave the large bedroom in the rear, where we had taken refuge, to go down to the ground floor; the concierge, his wife, his son and some friends of theirs are in the courtyard and all seem to be very frightened. For a moment I wonder if I shouldn't go on down to the cellar (a hiding-place in case the Germans should enter the house), but seeing that no one else is thinking of this, I give up the idea. After a while, calm having returned, we go back up to the apartment. We learn from the team at the house next door that the patrol has withdrawn and that it has no doubt gone to get reinforcements. I grow more and more frightened—foreseeing a victorious siege of the block—but I stay here, because there is nothing else to do but wait and see what happens. Our neighbor upstairs (who often

211

uses our telephone since she has none of her own) comes down to our apartment because she was expecting a relative for dinner and wants to tell him it would be more prudent not to come.

The afternoon is already quite far advanced when a police officer in uniform comes out of the Dépôt and, standing against the parapet at the embankment, shouting at the top of his voice in order to be heard over the river, orders the people on our side to cease fire. The order is not heeded, even though he repeats it several times. A truce has been declared, and we feel relieved, thinking that now the fighting will have to stop soon. Not long after, we hear the sound of a bugle from the direction of the pont Saint-Michel giving in its turn the appropriate call to signal a ceasefire. The rifle fire continues nevertheless. From our dining room window, Z asks the F.F.I. on the balcony of the house next door why people are continuing to fire; they answer that it is the Germans who are not observing the truce. After some time, the truce is announced again by a car equipped with a loudspeaker. We also see a car going along the quai des Orfèvres, with a helmeted German on one running board and a French policeman in uniform on the other, both standing. Since the rifle fire is subsiding, Z and I go out. On the quai des Grands-Augustins we meet several of the F.F.I. from next door, who have also come down. We congratulate them on their fine work. One of them, very young (who had been throwing grenades), tells us, laughing: "They said the police were collaborators ... Well! We showed them!" We head toward the Welcome Hotel. At the corner of the quay and the rue Dauphine, the car with the loudspeaker has stopped. I mingle with the listening crowd as it announces the conditions of the truce. What I remember in particular is that the Germans promise to treat the F.F.I. prisoners as prisoners of war. A Negro with a bit of the look of a pimp (some time before the uprising I had noticed him from my window, walking on the quay in a white suit, wearing the same broad felt hat he is wearing again today) addresses me, asking for information. He notes with satisfaction what I tell him about the promise concerning the prisoners and declares that now France is no longer dishonored. I too, like him, consider it satisfying that the Germans have consented to negotiate with the Comité de Libération, that is, to recognize it implicitly as an official authority.

At the Welcome Hotel we find Castor and Sorokine, who tell us what has happened in their part of town. We go back down with Sorokine, to walk around; but after going a little way toward the boulevard Saint-Michel, she leaves us to go back in. There's quite a crowd in the street and everyone looks pleased. We go left on the boulevard Saint-Michel. At the rue Saint-André-des-Arts, a young man wearing the tricolored armband of the F.F.I. tells us it isn't prudent to stay outside: the fighting will resume at any moment, and it would be better for us to go back home. We comply. Sylvia Bataille and Lacan come over to our house after dinner and we drink champagne.

Monday the 21st
Z and I go by bicycle to the gallery, then to the Trocadéro. In the vicinity of the gallery, the entrance to the rue d'Astorg is still guarded by a heavy machine gun: there is an NCO here in country dress spotted (for camouflage), a tall young brute with a thick moustache; also the machine gunner (a little guy, thin and pale, with a pince-nez or spectacles) and two or three armed soldiers. We meet Olga Roux-Delimal. While I wait for Z (who has gone to the gallery to see what new developments there may be), I see some people from the F.F.I. Red Cross go through the place Saint-Augustin carrying a stretcher on which an old lady in a dress and a black hat is lying.

From the gallery we make our way to the Trocadéro witout any difficulty. I go to see Rivière, to whom I say that I'm waiting for a liaison from the F.N. of the national museums. He takes me to the office of the architects of the building, to see one Sigwalt, a member of the "Liberation" group commanding the F.F.I. of the 16th arrondissement who are occupying the Palais de Chaillot as military.

When we return, we see that barricades are beginning to go up in our own neighborhood, especially on the quai de Conti (where a barrier of stones and other materials is being built across the road from the Monnaie).

Toward lunchtime, a telephone call from Sartre letting us know that he is going to move with Castor into his old hotel, the Chaplain (which, since it is situated in Montparnasse, seems to him preferable to the Hôtel de la Louisiane from the point of view of safety). In addition, we learn from a telephone call from Dora Maar that Picasso has left his home and that she herself is going to move into Olga Roux-Delimal's house in the place Malesherbes (in fact, she will return home at the end of the day). Seeing that the *quartier* appears to be changing into a Fort Chabrol and that all our friends are taking off, I decide to send Jeanne and Jeannette to stay with Josette Gris, in the boulevard Montparnasse, while Z and I will go move in with Lucienne Salacrou in the avenue Foch (from which it will be easy for me to go to the Musée de l'Homme).

Telephone call from Lucienne: Salacrou invites me to come, if I have time, to the Comédie-Française, where they are celebrating; since I still believe there is a truce (not yet aware that it has been openly proclaimed to be at an end and, moreover, has never been taken seriously by anyone), I do not feel at all obliged to go there, thinking they will meet there only in order to drink a toast in honor of what quite a few others and myself had taken to be an armistice.[1]

Z and I, with some toilet articles and nightclothes, leave for Lucienne's,[2] whence I go on to the Trocadéro. At my office, I receive a visit from a boy who is coming to see me "on behalf of Jules" and declares that he belongs to the F.N. of the Musée des Arts et Traditions Populaires, where he works as an architect; it is agreed that he will telephone me at the Salacrous' if they need me.

Return to the Salacrous', where Merleau-Ponty (who was with us the first day of the occupation of the Français) comes to dinner.

During dinner, a telephone call from Dalmau (the boy who came to see me that afternoon at the Musée): he tells me the F.N. has decided to go ahead with the occupation of the Musée de l'Homme and that I must therefore come to the Palais de Chaillot to spend the night there, sleeping (as I choose) either at the Musée de l'Homme or at the Musée des Arts et Traditions Populaires with the people from the F.N. of that institution. I finish my dinner quickly and leave on my bike for the Palais de Chaillot, through perfectly calm streets.

At the entrance to the left wing of the Palais de Chaillot, parleys with the F.F.I., who are guarding the door. Because they have orders not to allow any strangers to enter, I enter the Arts et Traditions Populaires by the small door that opens onto the gardens. Here I find Dalmau, who has moved in with several comrades (including Mauss's niece, who is working at the Arts et Traditions Populaires under the name of Melle Maurin); it is agreed that I will sleep in the lecture hall of the Centre de Documentation Folklorique, which

---

[1]It was that day, I think, that the rumor went around that an agreement had been concluded according to which the retreat of the German armies would take place through the northwestern and northern outer boulevards.

[2]On the way—along the rue de l'Universitié, I believe—we buy an issue of *Temoignage chrétien*, the first newspaper we see for sale.

they are using as a guardroom. I go to see Rivière, who has been sleeping in his office for several days in order to be prepared for whatever may happen. I return to see Sigwalt, whom I inform that the F.N. is ordering me to occupy the Musée de l'Homme. Sigwalt tells me that, since the Palais de Chaillot has been classified as a "cultural building," our mission consists of making sure no one fights there and in guaranteeing, if need be, the protection of the structure against looters. He declares, in the conversation, that he could give me command of a detachment of "a hundred men" (*sic*). [. . .]

Return to the Centre de Documentation Folklorique, where I sleep on a table. The F.N. of the Arts et Traditions Populaires has no weapons. Only the F.F.I. guarding the palais de Chaillot have some.

Tuesday the 22nd

I return to the Salacrous' early in the morning to wash up, then go on foot to the Musée de l'Homme. As I am entering the museum, I meet Dr. Vallois, to whom I announce, after a brief bit of conversation, that I am—symbolically—occupying the museum in the name of the F.N. He does not hide from me the fact that this news doesn't surprise him at all. It is agreed that our occupation will remain discreet. [. . .] In the vicinity of 1 *bis* avenue Foch, which is now my home, one hears only rare gunshots. Generally speaking, the appearance of the 16th arrondissement is radically different from that of the 6th: German cars drive about without anyone either making way for them or firing at them. Numbers of people—young men or young women—go about with Red Cross armbands, in order to appear to be doing something or to guarantee immunity for themselves. On the esplanade between the two wings of the Palais de Chaillot, people look anxiously toward the south, hoping to see billows of smoke that would tell them the battle was approaching.

In the evening, while Falck and I are at the museum, a heavy cannonade that shakes all the basement doors. Accompanied by the head caretaker, Billion (who has been sleeping at the museum for several days already), and the concierge's daughter, we go up onto the terrace. In the direction of Villeneuve-Saint-Georges, we notice at fairly long intervals an intense glow with a plume of smoke, followed by a heavy, muffled explosion: a German naval gun must be firing out there. Almost everywhere in Paris: the sound of motor vehicles in motion, gunfire, companies of firemen. Here and there, flares.

Michel Leiris

Wednesday the 23rd

After taking a shower at the museum, I go to meet Zette at avenue Foch. As the idea of abandoning our *quartier* has always revolted her, and I myself am rather disgusted with the 16th, we decide to go for a walk on the quai des Grands-Augustins, where we meet Jeanne and Jeannette on their way back from Josette's. At the same time, I will go let my colleague Baillon know that we have formed an F.N. at the Musée de l'Homme and that we are proceeding to occupy it.

Departure on bikes from Lucienne's (general remark: I feel much calmer when I go about with Z than when I go alone; one of the main reasons—perhaps the main one—I wanted to move close to the Musée de l'Homme is that, had we remained at the quai des Grands-Augustins, I would have had to make that long, rather dangerous trip all alone). Having arrived within sight of the Grand-Palais, we see the building in flames. A little way beyond the Gare des Invalides, the quay is guarded by a detachment of armed Germans. Z wants to continue on her way and ask them for permission to pass. I tell her she is crazy and that we run the risk of being fired at. We therefore make a detour, opting not to go along the quays. In our *quartier*, we marvel at the F.F.I., who are preventing people from going through certain strategic points (certain parts of the quays and certain barricades, for instance). The rue des Grands-Augustins is barricaded, almost at the level of the quay, by an S.I.T.A. truck (in normal times used for removing household trash).

I stop in at Baillon's house, as I intended to, and I tell him that if he has nothing better to do, we are counting on him to guard the Musée de l'Homme. He answers that this is all right with him, and that as soon as he has settled his wife in a quieter part of town, he will go to the museum. He has nothing better to do here: when he offered his services to the local administration of the 6th, they answered him that they had no weapon to give him; even so, he had managed to stand guard at the barricades a few times, relieving fighters while they went off to eat.

I am scarcely back at the house when the alert is given: a German tank is patrolling our neighborhood. Rifle fire and cannonade on the Right Bank. A tank (or heavy-machine-gun car?) passes quickly along the quai des Orfèvres, coming from the Pont-Neuf, and turns in front of the Palais de Justice. Disorderly rifle fire. Some shots, fired against the Resistance, are apparently coming from a house on the quai des Orfèvres (it was the same thing during the truce); they are firing at suspicious windows. The alert continues, so we decide to have lunch

216

here while waiting to be able to leave again. During a lull, the Resistance people set about shifting the S.I.T.A. truck that is obstructing the rue des Grands-Augustins. At first I watch them from the window, then, with Z's agreement, I decide to suggest giving them a hand. I go downstairs and offer my services to a fellow whom I find leaning against the corner of our carriage entrance and who is wearing a Basque beret and a tricolored armband. He answers me that I needn't bother: the truck is now in place. During the conversation that follows, he explains to me that his specialty is attacking tanks, and he shows me his equipment: the bottle of gas that one throws first, the grenade that one hurls next in order to light the gas and lastly the rifle with which one cuts down the Germans when they try to leave the blazing vehicle. All of this in the simplest tone, without any bragging, and as though this sort of work were the easiest thing in the world. I go back up to my apartment. Conversation, out the window, with an F.F.I. who is still on guard on the balcony of the house next door. He is bored, because he no longer has any work to do: in fact, no German vehicles have passed since the barricades have been up. (Addition to the conversation with the fellow of a minute ago: how one attracts tanks, with a skillfully directed gunshot toward the labyrinth of streets where they get caught in the traps, of the mobile barricades.)

The rumor is circulating that a column including no fewer than a hundred (*sic*) tanks has just emerged from the Luxembourg and is heading toward our neighborhood; this news has been given out officially to the command post of the F.F.I. established in the bistro at the corner of the rue Dauphine and the rue de Pont-de-Lodi (just opposite my tobacconist's shop), the command post in whose canteen our friend Jeanne Chenuet works. Hearing rifle fire and cannonade in the direction of Saint-Germain-l'Auxerrois, I telephone Moré (10, quai de la Mégisserie, which is—though I didn't think of this—quite a bit farther to our right than the presumed direction of the fighting) to ask him if they are fighting in his area; he answers me that it is in the area of the Carrousel.

They announce that the expected column has changed direction and the alert is over. Zette and I take advantage of the period of calm to leave. After depositing Z with the Salacrous, I go to the Musée, where Baillon will not arrive until the evening because shortly after our departure a new tank came to patrol, so that he could not leave his home. [. . .]

Return to the Salacrous', where Sartre and Castor come to have

217

dinner with us and spend the night. I learn through Sartre, who went to the Français, that the local administration of the 1st arrondissement sent word asking for volunteers for the barricades there. I tell him I am rather inclined to go; I am available, in fact, because after the meeting of a short time before I realize that there is no question that the people in the Palais de Chaillot will fight, and because I have also learned, through Dalmau, that the upper echelon of the F.N. did not consider the occupation of our respective workplaces to be military work. However, the next morning, I will say to myself that there's no sense in running all over this way, and I will let Sartre know of this reversal of my decision of the evening before.

I am now more reassured than worried by the barricades and feel attached to our *quartier*, to which I finally want, pretty much, to go back.

Thursday the 24th
At the museum, under Falck's escort, inspection by the two F.N. of the underground passageways connecting the Musée des Arts et Traditions Populaires, the Théâtre de Chaillot and the Musée de l'Homme; this with a view to a possible escape should the Germans seize the building or a section of the building, which there is no thought of defending. But it is obvious that if we were to be pursued we would get lost in the labyrinth of underground tunnels.

Lunch at Lucienne's with Castor, who has stayed (whereas Sartre left with Salacrou for the Comédie-Française). Because the radio has announced that Paris (where the fighting is far from over) has been liberated, we decide, Z and I, to go back to the quai des Grands-Augustins to witness the actual liberation in our own neighborhood. Since Castor is afraid to set off by herself, I go with her on foot as far as the place de l'Alma, then continue to the museum by way of the avenue de Tokyo. From the avenue de Tokyo, I hear a fairly brisk fusillade coming from the warehouses of the Ville de Paris (?) located on the other bank. I go first to the folklore museum, then to the Musée de l'Homme, where I announce to Schaeffner that—since there is really no need for me to take night guard duty at the museum again (others, moreover, can now do it in my place)—I am going back to my own neighborhood, eager to see the liberation there. I return to avenue Foch to get Zette, and we leave, after a telephone call to Jeanne to find out if the *quartier* is approachable.

Coming back by bicycle, we cross the rue de Bourgogne, which has been a veritable firing range for some time now. People urge us to cross it on foot, claiming that the Germans are most likely to fire at cyclists. We comply and notice a German soldier with a submachine gun in ambush at a street corner.

The *quartier* is still agitated. Barricades. F.F.I. special service. We meet two young fellows walking like Sioux Indians, slipping along the walls with rifles in hand, who say they are looking for militiamen and Germans who have supposedly infiltrated the blockhouse. [. . .]

From time to time, spoils of war (German vehicles or prisoners) arrive in front of the door of the Dépôt, greeted with cheers. A light gun captured from the Germans is set up in firing position in front of the door of the Dépôt, aimed toward the Pont-Neuf.

Toward the end of the afternoon, the radio announces that the Leclerc division has entered Paris, but in Paris people know the news is premature. In the approaches to the Dépôt, we observe that many policemen have donned their uniforms again to welcome the troops. An airplane passes very low over the Dépôt; submachine guns are fired in volleys (for a time I will think that a German airplane was cut down by the occupants of the Dépôt with submachine guns— because after the volleys one could see the airplane wobble—but upon reflection, and since I do not see the news announced anywhere, I will realize that this was simply an observation plane— probably an Allied one—and that the volleys we heard must have been merely salutes).

Fairly late in the evening (which we have spent expecting to see elements of the Leclerc division cross the pont Saint-Michel any minute, coming from the porte d'Orléans), a series of blue, white and red flares go off from the Palais de Justice; the great bell of Notre-Dame begins to ring (soon followed by the bells of other churches); the people inside the Palais de Justice and the Dépôt sing *La Marseillaise,* then, in a sort of spoken chorus, shout out two or three times, "Liberation!" Telephone calls back and forth to various friends concerning the great news. Coming from the pont Saint-Michel and racing at full speed in the direction of the Pont-Neuf, a cyclist appears, bent over his handlebars and yelling over and over: "The Americans (*sic*) are at the Hôtel-de-Ville!" (The next day, when I see the soldiers of the Leclerc division, I will understand why he made this mistake: given their equipment, it is quite natural that someone seeing these soldiers for the first time should take them for Americans.)

Toward the end of the afternoon, I had seen a large black automobile bearing a British flag arrive at the Dépôt.

219

Michel Leiris

To bed, with the intention of rising early to go see the soldiers of the Leclerc division.

Friday the 25th

Out early with Z and Jeannette to see the Leclerc division. From the people who are outside we learn that we have to go to the Notre-Dame square. We cross the pont Saint-Michel, then proceed along the Préfecture wall: on the sidewalk, quite a lot of glass from panes broken by bullets; numerous holes and scratches in the walls. When we reach the bridge that extends from the rue Saint-Jacques, we come upon a group of armored cars of the Leclerc division, around which a huge number of enthusiastic people are crowding despite the early hour. Sudden fusillade: these are shots (submachine gun or machine gun) fired by Germans or militiamen occupying the tower of the Sorbonne observatory, rue Saint-Jacques. Soldiers of the Leclerc division shout to the crowd: "Stand back! We're going to shoot . . ." The people do stand back, in fact, but—at least most of them—without really taking cover. Small tanks armed with submachine guns and a tank armed with a light gun move into position and open fire on the tower. Shooting with a marvelous precision: we see the shots constantly land, marked by the blossoming of a plume of white dust on the spot on the tower that has just been struck (and this excites cheers). Soon the occupants of the tower are reduced to silence. The vehicles then abandon their positions and, after turning in the square, come to park alongside the Hôtel-Dieu. We follow the current and find ourselves near the narrow garden along the Seine on the side of the square. More gunshots, which produce a certain confusion. They are coming from the other bank (houses close to Saint-Julien-le-Pauvre) and, they say, from Notre-Dame itself. The soldiers shout to us to lie down because they are going to open fire and we will then find ourselves caught between enemy fire and their own, since they are in firing position, backed up against the Hôtel-Dieu. With some other people, we remain crouched behind some cars parked along the square, which protects us against the shooters on the other bank. The din of French shooting (which is as loud as it can be for us, since we are positioned in front of the guns) is deafening. A fellow who happens to be next to me remarks, laughing and blocking his ears, "This is going to scare the little birds." Near us there is also a nurse, who is blocking her ears as well and who screws up her eyes when the noise is too loud. After a few minutes of heavy firing, a commander arrives, shouting: "They're crazy to fire like that! If

220

they go on, there won't be anything left when they need it ..." A moment later, the firing stops. We take advantage of this to go to the Hôtel-Dieu. Some F.F.I. urge people to disperse, go back home. But we don't really know which route to follow, nor where to take refuge temporarily, because we hear gunfire more or less on all sides. While we are near the Hôtel-Dieu, we see two or three wounded civilians brought in, including a woman and a man with a bloody face. We think for a moment of walking around behind the Préfecture, but we give up that plan, since the Leclerc vehicles have gone in that direction to continue their cleanup operations; besides, we instinctively prefer not to deviate from a known route. Taking advantage of a lull, we therefore go back home, retracing the route we took when we came.

Leclerc vehicles are parked all along the quai des Grands-Augustins, and their occupants are naturally thickly surrounded and feted by the people of the neighborhood. What is immediately striking is the cosmopolitan appearance of this group: pure Frenchmen side by side with Spaniards and people from North Africa. One of the first whom we engage in conversation is a Spaniard, who has already fought in the war against Franco in the Republican army; he offers me a glass of wine (from a bottle that has just been given him), a courtesy I finally accept, not without a little shame at allowing myself, a civilian, to be regaled by one of the soldiers who has just liberated me. Another fellow (who will embrace Z and Jeannette and whom I will also embrace, like a brother) is a native of Aveyron. A third—whose birthplace I don't know—repeats jovially to the people, who are, in their emotion, rather taciturn: "Well, talk to me ... Come now, talk to me!" A fourth, of a distinctly Berber type, tells me he is from Oran. A fifth person (the first to whom we say anything) is a rather large fellow and well proportioned, with regular and slightly worn features; on the side of his face, he has a scar; he is blond, with light eyes, and his skin is very tanned; he has the good looks of a convict or outlaw in a movie; we give him a bottle of champagne, which he wants to drink with us, but we refuse, wanting him to enjoy it with his companions. Of all those with whom we speak, this one is the least loquacious, the saddest; when we ask him what life is like in the division, he answers: "Fighting ... Nothing but fighting ..." I have no idea what either his background or his social situation might be.

Back up in our apartment, from the windows we watch the picturesque sight of vehicles with soldiers who are beginning to settle

221

in all around us and are surrounded by people. On the hood of each vehicle, a broad band of oilcloth the color of currants (intended, it appears, to let the Allied aircraft know the vehicle belongs to an Allied division).

The attack on the Sénat by Leclerc and F.F.I. elements is planned for the beginning of the afternoon. Since yesterday, people have been dreading the explosion of twenty tons of cheddite that has apparently been stored in the Sénat.

After lunch, Sartre, Bost and Castor come looking for us to go for a walk and we leave, taking Jeanne and Jeannette with us. Along the quai Saint-Michel, American vehicles are parked, all driven by Negroes. We cross the pont Saint-Michel and reach the boulevard du Palais. There is a quite a crowd in front of the entrance to the Préfecture de Police, where official personages are expected (or are already there, just as at the Hôtel de Ville). Many tanks and armored cars of the Leclerc division, all heavily surrounded. We then go up the boulevard Saint-Michel and see there, among other soldiers of the armored division, a fellow with a thick moustache who is saying to the people that he was previously the director of a bank in the Cameroons. Encounter with Pancho Picabia's brother, who tells us how, that morning, he had to stay flat on his face for a very long time near the Belfort Lion to protect himself from the rifle fire. Sartre suggests going up the boulevard Saint-Michel as far as we can, to see what is happening around the Luxembourg, where the fighting has begun; I agree, even though it scarcely appeals to me. But we have hardly reached the boulevard Saint-Germain when we are urged not to proceed further. We therefore go back home and separate, arranging to meet that evening, since we have planned to have dinner at the home of Olga Kosackiewicz and Jacques Bost, in the Chaplain Hotel, then stroll through Montparnasse, where people were dancing around bonfires the evening before.

Visit from Moré, whom we then accompany back to his house, where he wants to show us the marks of bullets that entered his living room. A few houses away, we are stopped by some F.F.I. getting out of a car: they are offering to share some war booty with the passersby, namely a bottle of vermouth. The concierge of the house in front of which their car is stopped brings some glasses and we pass the bottle around.

Going with Castor to Olga K's, we learn that the Sénat has just surrendered. Consequently we decide to stop in at the home of Jean and Zanie Aubier (who live at 1, rue de Fleurus) to see how they have endured the emotions of the battle. We find them at home; they have come up only a few minutes before from the basement, where they have had to stay for some hours with their young child. While we are there, a group of German prisoners comes out of the Luxembourg, their hands crossed above their heads. From the Aubiers', I telephone the Adrians (enthusiasts of Kermadec who live on the boulevard Saint-Michel opposite the Ecole des Mines and the Luxembourg greenhouses). I want to hear their news and tell them the Sénat has just surrendered; but I'm forced to give up on this telephone conversation: on their end, the fighting is still so violent that the explosions hurt my ears just hearing them over the telephone.

Castor, Z and I set off again in the direction of Olga's. Having arrived there, we learn and we see for ourselves that there are many rooftop snipers (or people under cover in the windows of the houses) at the Vavin intersection and they are systematically firing on everyone who passes in front of the Dôme and the Coupole; thus, at regular intervals, or almost, we see two or three wounded persons being carried away on stretchers.

Dinner as arranged, but instead of walking around Montparnasse as we had planned, we come back to our own neighborhood, joined by Wanda, Olga's sister. In the rue Vavin we come upon a French broadcasting van painted entirely black, with its inscriptions in large white letters; a flood of music is pouring out of it. Crossing the rue Auguste-Comte, we see, among other traces of the fighting (a burnt German tank, small blockhouses destroyed by French tanks, etc.) the windows of the Lycée Montaigne with all their panes broken. (At the corner of the Luxembourg Gardens at the intersection of the boulevard Saint-Michel and the rue Auguste-Comte, flowers will be placed (I no longer recall exactly if it was this same day or only afterward that I saw them) for F.F.I. or soldiers who fell at that spot.) Going down the boulevard Saint-Michel, we see, near the Médicis Fountain, a woman collecting wooden paving blocks that were used to make a barricade; an F.F.I. stops her from providing herself with fuel this way. Farther down, tanks from the Leclerc division are lined up on the sidewalks for the night; one of them is parked halfway in the entrance to a movie theater. Among the fellows we talk to, one is very friendly (average size, robust, sunburnt and wearing glasses); he's probably a cultivated boy; he tells us that at the Sénat they tried to do as little damage to the building as possible, but it was inevitably chipped a little, even so; he explains how distressing it is to fight in Paris, since one doesn't want to damage its monuments too much.

Michel Leiris

At the end of our walk we are in the Saint-Séverin *quartier,* which is swarming with people: people from the barricades, people from North Africa or colored people, white and black Americans, etc. Impossible to find a spot in a bistro. From the sidewalk in front of our house, when we get back, we see figures leaning out of the window, figures that (in the darkness) we don't recognize. Jeanne's voice shouts to us to come quick, because "an American is here." Z and I immediately think of Waldberg and we take the steps four at a time. It is in fact Waldberg, captain in a special service, who has come by car from Normandy with an architect from Granville (who was working in liaison with his service) and an old Belgian garage mechanic (now in the American army and W's driver). Effusions; introductions to all our friends, who come upstairs behind us. Exchange of news, etc.

Waldberg and his two companions sleep here.

Saturday the 26th

In the morning, departure in Waldberg's car to visit Mauss, whose student he was, like me. Everywhere we go, the sight of the American W excites enthusiasm: when we happen to be out of the car for the various errands he has to do, people will come up and shake his hand, saying, "Thank you!"; they will lead children up to him, etc. Others, less discreet, will beg for cigarettes or biscuits. Mauss tells us that that very morning his wife was nearly killed by a rooftop gunman: a bullet entered the window of their ground floor apartment and lodged in the wall just above the bed in which Mme. Mauss was lying. On our way back, as we reach place Saint-Michel, we see the traffic being directed, spectacularly, by an attractive woman with makeup, wearing blue pants and a white shirt and sporting a broad belt and a red turban.

Lunch, before going to the Salacrous', who have invited us, along with a number of others, to come watch from their balcony the ceremony that is supposed to take place at the Arc de Triomphe in honor of the arrival of General de Gaulle.

[It was shortly before or after this lunch, I think, that we saw, from our balcony, a woman with shaved head and no shoes being walked along the quai des Grands-Augustins. Armed insurgents surrounded her, jeering at her but not touching her; the woman ceaselessly moved her head from left to right and from right to left with an obsessed air, as though saying "No." (A sight almost as painful as that of the first yellow stars, during the German occupation; in any case, it appeared to be a sort of reply to that.)}

Z and I go off to the Salacrous' by bicycle; we are to meet Castor and Sorokine there. On the way, an enormous crowd, traffic diverted in spots. Place de la Concorde, enormous rose of a crowd covering the famous fountains written about in *Fantomas*. When we arrive at Lucienne's, we quickly realize that we will see nothing: everything is going to take place on the side of the Arc de Triomphe facing the Champs-Elysées. On the rooftops, firemen armed with rifles, to spot possible snipers. Swarming crowd down below: regular troops, policemen in uniform (who are cheered as they parade past), trucks loaded with armed F.F.I. waving tricolored flags, etc. From time to time, a stretcher carried by two medical orderlies in white smocks crosses the square; these are most likely people who have fainted because of the excessively large crowd and who are being transported to a first-aid station. All that we perceive of the ceremony itself is the clamor of the crowd. We quickly decide to go back, thinking that, all things considered, we will see more by mingling with this crowd than by staying on a balcony so unfortunately situated. When we reach the corner of the avenue des Champs-Elysées and the rue de Presbourg, we decide to stop for a little while and wait for the crowd to become less dense so that it will be easier to move about walking our bicycles. Suddenly, shots ring out, and we see people begin to scatter. At first, we are very frightened that this will degenerate into a deadly panic, but happily nothing of the sort happens. Since the crowd is no longer too thick, there is no jostling. Following the stream, we go down the rue de Presbourg, then the rue Vernet on the left; Sorokine and Castor have gone off on their own. In the rue Vernet, we lay our bikes down on the ground and take cover, Z crouching behind a car, I lying prone along the wall, face to face with a gentleman lying prone like me. The rifle fire, at first fairly heavy, is soon sparser, and we concern ourselves with going back to the quai des Grands-Augustins. We manage this after a rather long time and after various delays and detours, because whereas we thought that once we left the main streets we would have no trouble, we see that people are firing desultorily everywhere, even in very small streets.

Back in the house, from the balcony we see a soldier of the Leclerc division (or the Larminat?—because he is wearing a red garrison cap) performing elegant and perilous acrobatics on the roofs of the houses across the street as he chases—though without success—the rooftop snipers.

Dinner at home with Waldberg, Sartre, Castor, Chavy (at whose house W spent the morning and whom we agreed he should invite). During the course of the evening, bombing, several blasts quite close: to our right, a big fire (involving, as we will find out the next day, the Halle-aux-Vins); we hear airplanes, we see flares. We all go down to the cellar. As I am about to cross the threshold of the apartment (waiting for Jeannette, who was in bed, had to dress and is lagging behind the others), a rather heavy strike from which I feel the wind, which reminds me unpleasantly of the bombing of Boulogne-Billancourt. Waldberg—who witnessed a few other raids in Normandy!—laughs to see us all go down into the cellar. Once we come back up, we continue talking for quite a long time in the darkness (while watching, from the dining room windows, the Halle-aux-Vins in flames), then separate.

(Writing finished November 30)
Addition to Friday the 25th. — Leaving our house with Moré on our way to his home, we encounter a German prisoner on the quai de la Mégisserie flanked by two F.F.I.: he walks peacefully, almost smiling, with the look of someone for whom it's over at last. His two guards flank him, but are not holding him. Z and I notice that this prisoner is a pleasant exception: those we have seen up to now (especially the officers, pale with rage) never had this nonchalant bearing and offered no opening for the least possibility of fraternizing.

December 7
Have relapsed, with the coming of the Liberation, into my former depression. Must believe those who say that neurotics were in better health during the four years of the Occupation.

* * *

AFTERWORD

The Instant of My Death
Maurice Blanchot

—Translated from French by Jeff Fort

TRANSLATOR'S NOTE

The following work was published in French in 1994 and this is its first appearance in English. It is, more than any other narrative work by Blanchot, an autobiographical text. This is clear from its many concrete historical references: Blanchot writes of himself as a young man, of his family, of the large house that remains stand-ing in Burgundy and of historical events of World War II. There is no reason to believe that the experience it relates did not actually occur. Blanchot himself attests to this in a letter (cited by its recipient, Jacques Derrida, in Demeure, *1998), which begins: "20 July [1994]. Fifty years ago I had the good fortune* [le bonheur] *of almost being shot to death." The autobiographical dimension of the story is nevertheless far from straightforward. Blanchot even seems to have deliberately signaled this by including certain inaccurate dates among those that he mentions: 1807 instead of 1809 (the facade) and 1806 (Napoleon). (This is pointed out both by Derrida and by Blanchot's biographer, Christophe Bident.) These slight displacements mark the way in which this text, like the moment of* bonheur *at its center, hovers uncannily between literature and history, fiction and testimony.*

Blanchot's career is marked by many shifts and ruptures, both political and aesthetic, involving the relation of writing to politics and history, and one of the most important of these occurred around the time at which this story takes place. Before the war, Blanchot wrote political essays for right-wing journals in which, from a nationalist and anti-German position, and with a shrill and incendiary style, he called for quick and radical solutions to France's political problems. After the surrender of France in 1940, Blanchot, apparently disgusted and demoralized, turned away from any overtly political writing and concentrated on his novels and literary criticism, eventually withdrawing to the house

depicted here. But this activity, too, was not without its com-
promises, for the critical writing appeared in a literary journal
supported by the Vichy government and subject to German cen-
sorship, the Journal des débats, by whom Blanchot was paid for his
work. (Some of these essays were collected in **Faux Pas**, published
in 1943 by Gallimard.) At the same time, it is known that he had
ties to the Resistance and helped transport Jews and others in
danger across the border to Switzerland. (After the war, Blanchot's political stance was decidedly leftist.) The following piece
is heavily charged with many of the associations surrounding this
complex wartime situation.

 There are two significant translation problems worth pointing
out. First, "Le pas au-delà," which means both "the step beyond"
and, by a play on words, "the not beyond," is the title of one of
Blanchot's previous books. Second, the final words of the text
read: ". . . l'instant de ma mort, désormais toujours en instance."
The phrase en instance carries a range of meanings which no
English expression can cover. By itself, instance can mean "the
site of administrative or juridical authority, the site of a judgment or verdict . . . such as a court of justice . . . , but also [in
expressions with en instance] the imminence or the reprieve, the
supplementary delay before the "thing" . . . that is just about to
occur" (Derrida). It is the condition of waiting indefinitely for an
event that is already well on its way. In a legal context, en
instance can mean "pending," but it can also be applied, for
example, to a letter about to be posted. But instance can also
mean "insistence," one form of which I have chosen in order to
maintain the literal association with "instant" (both derive from
the Latin instare), and in order to underline the constant urgency
of such an instant—which Blanchot, born in 1907 and now one of
the last living authors of his generation, relates here, across a
breach of fifty years, to his own impending death, and thus to all
the writing in between.

I REMEMBER a young man (a man who was still young) prevented
from dying by death itself—and perhaps the error of injustice.

 The Allies had succeeded in gaining a foothold in French territory.
The Germans, already beaten, were struggling in vain with a useless
ferocity.

 In a large house ("the Castle," it was called), there came a rather
timid knock at the door. I know that the young man went to open

up for the guests who were no doubt asking for help.

This time there was screaming: "Everybody out!"

A Nazi lieutenant, in a shamefully perfect French, ordered the oldest to come out first, then two young women.

"Out, out!" This time he was screaming. The young man, however, did not try to run away, but slowly stepped forward, in an almost priestly manner. The lieutenant shook him, showed him some cartridges, some bullets. Manifestly, there had been combat, the land was a land at war.

The lieutenant choked on a bizarre language, and brandishing the cartridges, the bullets and a grenade under the nose of the young man, already less young (one grew old quickly), he shouted distinctly: "See what you've come to now."

The Nazi lined up his men, in order to hit the human target according to the rules. The young man said: "Send my family back inside, at least." So be it: his aunt (94 years old), his mother, who was younger, his sister and his sister-in-law, a long, slow procession, silent, as if everything were already finished.

I know—do I know it—that the one at whom the Germans were aiming, awaiting only the final order, experienced at that moment an extraordinary feeling of lightness, a sort of beatitude (though it was in no way cheerful)—a sovereign elation? The encounter of death and of death?

In his place, I will not attempt to analyze this feeling of lightness. Perhaps he was suddenly invincible. Dead—immortal. Ecstasy perhaps. Rather the feeling of compassion for humanity in its suffering, the happiness of being neither immortal nor eternal. From now on he was bound to death by a surreptitious friendship.

At that instant—an abrupt return to the world—there burst forth the considerable noise of a nearby battle. The comrades of the *maquis* were trying to bring help to someone they knew was in danger. The lieutenant went away to find out what was happening. The Germans still stood at attention, prepared to remain thus in an immobility that stopped time.

But at this point one of them approached and said, in a firm voice: "We, not Germans. Russians," and, with a sort of laugh: "Vlassov army," and he signaled to him to disappear.

I believe that he went far away, still with the feeling of lightness, until he found himself in some distant woods, called "Bois des bruyères," where he remained sheltered by the trees he knew well. It is in these dense woods that suddenly, and after how much time,

he regained a sense of reality. There were fires everywhere, a continuous series of fires, all the farms were burning. A little later he
learned that three young men, farmers' sons, complete strangers to
all combat and whose only fault was their youth, had been slain.

Even the bloated horses, on the road and in the fields, attested to a
war that had lasted long. In reality, how much time had been flowing away? When the lieutenant returned to discover that the young
castle-dweller had disappeared, why wasn't he driven by anger and
rage to burn the Castle (immobile and majestic)? Because it was the
Castle. On its facade was inscribed, like an indestructible memory,
the date 1807. Was he cultivated enough to know that this was the
famous year of Jena, when Napoleon, on his small gray horse, passed
beneath the windows of Hegel, who recognized in him "the soul of
the world," as he wrote to a friend? A lie and a truth, for, as Hegel
wrote to another friend, the French pillaged and ransacked his
dwelling. But Hegel knew how to distinguish the empirical from the
essential. In that year, 1944, the Nazi lieutenant had a respect and
consideration for the Castle that the farms did not inspire. Nevertheless, they rummaged through everything. They took some money; in
a room set apart, "the high chamber," the lieutenant found some
papers and a sort of thick manuscript—containing war plans perhaps.
Finally he left. Everything was burning, except the Castle. The Lords
of the land had been spared.

This was no doubt when there began, for the young man, the torment of injustice. No more ecstasy; rather the feeling that he was
alive only because, even in the eyes of the Russians, he belonged to
a noble class.

That's what war was: for some, life, for others the cruelty of
assassination.

There remained, however, in the moment when the gunshot was
suspended and could only be awaited, that feeling of lightness which
I could never interpret: liberation from life? the opening of infinity?
Neither happiness nor sorrow. Nor the absence of fear and perhaps
already the step beyond—the not-beyond. I know, I imagine, that this
irreducible feeling changed whatever existence remained for him. As
if the death outside of him could only, from now on, come up against
the death within him. "I am alive. No, you are dead."

Later, after returning to Paris, he met with Malraux. The latter recounted to him that he had been taken prisoner (without being
recognized), had succeeded in escaping, but had lost a manuscript in

the process. "It was only some reflections on art, easily reconstructed, whereas a manuscript couldn't be." With the help of Paulhan he carried out investigations which could only come up empty.

What does it matter. There remains simply the feeling of lightness, which is death itself, or, to say it more precisely: the instant of my death, insisting always from now on.

Claus Peymann and Hermann Beil on Sulzwiese

Thomas Bernhard

—Translated from German by Gitta Honegger

TRANSLATOR'S NOTE

I hate the theater with every fiber of my being
I despise it like nothing else
nothing is more repulsive to me
but this is why I am totally consumed by it

—*Thomas Bernhard*, Claus Peymann
Buys Himself a Pair of Pants
and Takes Me to Lunch

Poet, playwright, novelist, Thomas Bernhard was first and foremost a theater person, a Theaternarr *with all the resonances of the German term: a theater fan, theater nut and a theatrical fool. Growing up in Salzburg, he couldn't help but absorb from an early age the best and worst that the lavish summer festival had to offer: the absurd histrionics of an entire city turning itself into a stage; the selling of Mozart as* Mozartkugel, *or "Mozart-balls," little chocolate balls with the composer's profile on the wrapper; the annual spectacle of Hugo von Hofmannsthal's adaptation of* Everyman *in front of the historic cathedral on* Domplatz *or Cathedral Square, framed by exquisite baroque facades from where Death's repeated calls for the dying Everyman would echo across the city in sync with the setting sun. Above all, there were the climactic experiences of legendary performances by the world's greatest opera singers and actors. Their voices carried from the open-air festival theater up to the slopes of Mönchsberg where the adolescent Bernhard could listen free of charge.*

The unsparing repetitive drill of rehearsals driven by insatiable ambitions to reach superhuman levels of perfection against the terrifying odds of failure is the leitmotif throughout Bernhard's writing. It also makes for the intrinsically performative structure of Bernhard's texts. All his work is theatrical, including his prose in which Bernhard stages (and observes) himself in the act of writing. He is the consummate actor of his craft, the performer of his stand-in narrators who in turn reconstruct another character, usually a dead person, from his journal entries and remembered utterances. In the process of quoting, the first-person narrator also becomes the deceased's impersonator.

When read as texts in performance, the much-discussed (if not dreaded) darkness of Bernhard's prose is animated, like Beckett's, by the antics of human survival strategies in the face of death, strategies that are always rooted in performance.

Claus Peymann and Hermann Beil on Sulzwiese *is the third work in a trilogy of* Dramolette *("dramalettes" being a term Bernhard coined for his ten-minute or so one-act plays) about his long association with director Claus Peymann. The first,* Claus Peymann Leaves Bochum and Goes to Vienna as Artistic Director of the Burgtheater, *was commissioned by Peymann, then in his last season as artistic director of the Bochum Theater, for their staged farewell party. It shows Peymann and his secretary, Christiane Schneider, packing his suitcases with Bochum dramaturgs and actors, discarding others (some of them dead) and unpacking them at the Vienna Burgtheater. The second,* Claus Peymann Buys Himself a Pair of Pants and Takes Me to Lunch, *was written for the 1986 special edition of* Theater Heute, *the leading German-language theater magazine. It highlights Peymann's triumphant, if highly controversial, initial season at the Burgtheater. Peymann's challenge to Bernhard that he write a "Welthammer"—a play that says it all, as it were—seems to foreshadow the public spectacle surrounding the opening of Bernhard's last play,* Heldenplatz, *in 1988. The first publication in German of* Claus Peymann and Hermann Beil on Sulzweise *in 1987 in the German weekly* Die Zeit *took both Peymann and Beil by surprise. It marks the high point of their tenure in Vienna.*

The Peymann trilogy, published and produced under the general title of Claus Peymann kauft sich eine Hose und geht mit mir essen (Suhrkamp Verlag, 1993), Claus Peymann Buys Himself a Pair of Pants and Takes me to Lunch, *offers unique glimpses of Bernhard's sense of humor at its most relaxed and affectionate. It is one of Bernhard's rare public tributes to their long artistic relationship. This is the first appearance in English of any of the trilogy's plays.*

In 1970, Peymann, then thirty-three, staged Bernhard's first

233

Thomas Bernhard

full-length play, Ein Fest für Boris (A Party for Boris), *at the Deutsches Schauspielhaus in Hamburg, one of Germany's preeminent theaters. It was the beginning of a historic collaboration that was marked by public controversy, political scandals and definitive productions of Bernhard's plays. Peymann went on to direct the world premieres of most of Bernhard's plays, at the Salzburg festival (*Der Ignorant under der Wahnsinnige, *1972;* Am Ziel, *1981;* Über allen Gipfeln ist Ruh, *1982;* Der Theatermacher, *1985;* Ritter, Dene, Voss, *1986) and in Stuttgart, where Peymann was artistic director from 1974–1980 (*Der Präsident, *1975;* Minetti, *1976;* Immanuel Kant, *1978;* Vor dem Ruhestand, *1979). He also directed* Die Jagdgesellschaft *for the Vienna Burgtheater in 1974. Stuttgart marked also the beginning of his long, continuous collaboration with dramaturg Hermann Beil who accompanied Peymann to Bochum. During their tenure at the Schauspielhaus Bochum (1979–1986) they developed what* Theater Heute *termed "das Modell eines Deutschen Stadttheaters"—the model of German city-theater (as opposed to the Nazi ideal of a National Theater). Peymann's company and Peter Stein's Berlin* Schaubühne *ensemble were the pathbreaking institutions that defined West German, if not German, language theater of the seventies and eighties. When Peymann became artistic director of Vienna's Burgtheater in Fall 1986, with Hermann Beil as co-director, he brought with him some of their signature Bernhard productions and enshrined Bernhard as national playwright, much to the chagrin of his arch-enemies among Austria's leading politicians. The hate campaign against Bernhard reached its climax in 1988 with Peymann's production of* Heldenplatz. *The tide has meantime turned. Nearly ten years after his death, Bernhard has become an official, government-approved myth and national treasure.*

A final note. In Bernhard's will, he prohibited all new productions of any of his plays in Austria. Understandable in view of his ambivalent relationship with Austria and his treatment by Austrian politicians, but unduly harsh toward Peymann, Bernhard's characteristically contradictory final gesture might have anticipated the Austrian's notorious finesse in besting legal obstacles. The Peymann trilogy had its successful premiere at the Akademietheater, the Burgtheater's more intimate space, on September 30, 1998. The performance marked another farewell for Claus Peymann who is leaving the Burgtheater at the end of this season to begin his tenure as artistic director of the Berlin Ensemble.

* * *

Music by Schubert from far away
CLAUS PEYMANN, the artistic director of the Vienna Burgtheater,
sits under a blooming linden tree and bites into a big cold Wiener
schnitzel
HERMANN BEIL, his associate artistic director and dramaturg, sits
next to him. He unwraps an even bigger cold Wiener schnitzel and
takes a bite
The air is still

BEIL (*looks across the Danube all the way to Slovakia*)

PEYMANN (*after a second bite from his schnitzel*)
The Tempest is what counts

BEIL (*after a second bite from his schnitzel*)
Naturally

PEYMANN Don't always say naturally Beil
Nothing is *natural*
The Tempest is the most unnatural
all of Shakespeare is unnatural

(*suddenly agitated*)

and The Tempest is Shakespeare at his most unnatural
Artificial all of it Beil
all of Shakespeare's artificial

(*bites into his schnitzel*)

More than anything I'd love to direct all of Shakespeare all at once
and present it all in one evening
one grand Shakespearean concentration Beil
why not a total Shakespearean concentration
if we squeeze all the plays of Shakespeare
into one you understand what I am saying Beil
take all of Shakespeare and make it one you understand
squeeze all the characters of all of Shakespeare's plays
into one evening
turn all the settings of Shakespeare's plays

into one single Shakespeare setting
that would make a grand evening in the theater
don't you think so Beil
The Tempest Richard III and II The Winter's Tale, Macbeth
etcetera etcetera
that would be it

(bites into his schnitzel)

that's what I envision

BEIL *(bites into his schnitzel and takes a sip from a bottle of Gum-
poldskirchner which he has brought along)*
That's what you envision

PEYMANN Yes that's what I envision
this is not insanity Beil
I can assure you
I am dead serious
all of Shakespeare in one evening
and we'll do the sonnets too
the real drama is the sonnets
The Tempest and Hamlet all at once
and everything together no longer than five hours
that would be the climax Beil
You think this is an absurdity
You don't really think that this is an absurdity
all of Shakespeare in one evening
we've got the technology
why do we have all this hi-tech equipment

(bites into his schnitzel)

The theater leads into one single dead end
that's where they all end up
who've been looking for a way out all their lives
the theater offers no way out
except

BEIL except

PEYMANN except if we *present all of Shakespeare
in one evening*
now granted that this would mean
one thousand eight hundred thirty-four

people
and needless to say only the top actors
as performers Beil
and as many sets as plays
but built into each other Beil built into each other
and we'll perform this Shakespeare in all the languages
in which Shakespeare's been performed
and one Viennese and one Prussian version
and a National Socialist
as well as a Zionist variant
and don't forget that there were
Shakespeare productions even in Greenland
and in Kirghiz dialect
and also in Tyrolian Beil

   (bites into his schnitzel)

If only I could stun the world even more
stun the world stun the world stun the world that's what it's
                         all about
the theater is not going anywhere it is walking in place
we've got to make something of the Burgtheater
that no one else before us has ever made of it
Thomas Bernhard thinks that the Burgtheater should be shut
                         down for good
on the next possible Ash Wednesday
and on the following Good Thursday
it should be encased in concrete as solemnly as possible
for all eternity with all its actors
directors and dramaturgs
Thomas Bernhard thinks that the Burgtheater
should be *starved out*
in the most charming Austrian manner
but he didn't say what he meant exactly
The Burgtheater could also be wrapped up
and sent to Mongolia Federal Express
with no return address of course
He also said he could well imagine himself
singlehandedly without another helping hand
armed only with a basic twelve-point pickaxe
hacking it into the ground
so that all that's left is a stinking pile of rubble

with all its actors sitting on top of it
naked and exposed
reciting Shakespeare and Nestroy
with such unbelievable dilettantism
that eventually they would become such a public nuisance
that all the psychiatrists in Vienna would issue an order
to have them committed to a speech class for beginners
where they'd be stuck for the rest of their lives
because of their incompetence
He could also imagine
that in an instant the Burgtheater could become
a national mental institution
for those who have proved themselves incurable
so that overnight Vienna would have
its only mental institution on Ringstrasse
right across from City Hall
and the Director of this mental institution
where no one can be cured
would be Vienna's mayor Mr. Zilk
who as we all know
resides right across from our Burgtheater
Vienna's mayor will simply be appointed director
of the only government-approved mental institution for the
                                        performing arts
that's really very simple
the Burgtheater could also be left as is and turned into
a theater museum and instead of the actors
there could be wax figures on stage
and wax figures in the audience
and every two hours the curtain would rise
and the wax figures on stage would bow
and the wax figures in the audience would applaud
and then the curtain would fall again

  (*he bites into his schnitzel*)

that would be Bernhard's ideal theater
Bernhard also said
that the Burgtheater would make an ideal
coffee-processing factory
and that the Austrian government should make the
                                        appropriate offer

238

to its most popular coffee firm Meinl
the Burgtheater even looks like an old-fashioned
coffee-processing factory
with its two fireplaces
where the coffee could be roasted
don't ever listen to Bernhard Beil
don't listen to Bernhard
that arrogant theater monster
Shakespeare
as he's never been done before
the way I've just indicated Beil
the way I actually have him in mind Beil
the way I'll stage him Beil
you hear me Beil
do you hear me

BEIL *(who has just taken a bite from his schnitzel)*
Naturally

PEYMANN All I ever get from you is your
naturally
if for once you'd say *artificially*
artificially Beil *artificially* Beil *artificially*
everything in this world is *artificial* Beil
artificial artificial Beil *artificial*
while with you everything is always *natural*
it drives me crazy
I really needed this
climbing up here on this hill
to discuss The Tempest with you
and all I get is your *naturally*
all I ever get from anybody is this
naturally
everyone around me keeps saying *naturally*
while what they should be saying all the time is *artificially*

   (bites into his schnizel)

That's why I had to come up here
to eat my schnitzel
and to hear you say nothing but *naturally*
For Christ's sake Beil
say *artificially* for once

and say it a million times every day if you must
but stop saying *naturally*
there's nothing left that's natural
and in Vienna least of all
I wanted to do The Tempest
and I'm going to do all of Shakespeare
all of Shakespeare
that's too much for dramaturgy Beil
too much for dramaturgy
dramaturgy is not equipped for the theater
I envision
it's not for the theater I want to do
let's just say
that for that kind of theater dramaturgy *per se* is too simplistic
if not to say
that it simply is *too stupid*
for that kind of theater
all dramaturgs wherever they may be
simply are *too stupid*

    (bites into his schnitzel)

When I watch you *how* you bite into your schnitzel
I think
that this won't do for *all of* Shakespeare
and in fact it certainly won't do for *all of* Shakespeare
for one Shakespeare yes for The Tempest yes
even for Macbeth if you insist
but not for *all of* Shakespeare

    (bites into his schnitzel)

Shakespeare the way he's always been done
can't be done that way anymore
everywhere they're doing Shakespeare these days
the way he can't be done anymore
theater all over the world is megalomaniac hack theater
hack dramaturgs hack directors hack actors
If theater can still be done at all
it's the kind of theater
I want to do
It's nauseating
what they're doing these days

and especially what they're doing with Shakespeare these days
for decades now the theaters are doing
the oldest kind of stock
it is an unbearable situation Beil
and this unbearable situation has to end
Is that so hard to understand
don't you understand me Beil

BEIL *(who has taken a bite from his schnitzel and at the same
time has been shaking with fear of ticks, because he knows that
on this hill there are millions of ticks which can inject menin-
gitis and Lyme disease into the body)*
Naturally
I understand you
naturally

PEYMANN *(disappointed by* BEIL *he has taken the bottle of Gum-
poldskirchner and does not intend to share it anymore)*
We only have one way
to do theater
the way it's *never* ever been done before
he has thought about it all his life
how to do theater
the way it's never been done before
that's what Bernhard said
I've been thinking *all year*
how one could do theater the way
it's never been *done* before

BEIL *(taking in the view of Vienna and biting into his schnitzel)*
That's absolutely horrifying Peymann

PEYMANN That's not horrifying at all
now that I know exactly
what I have to do
what I have to perform
all of Shakespeare everything by Shakespeare
in one evening
in five hours
all of world theater which is to say the entire Shakespeare
as one single five-hour concentration

Thomas Bernhard

> *(his head drops on his chest, he is almost finished with his*
> *schnitzel*
> *then he raises his head again)*

I think I've got it

BEIL What

PEYMANN The objective the action

BEIL What objective what action

PEYMANN *My* theater
my Shakespeare
my future
my goal
my cosmic theater

BEIL *(after he has polished off his schnitzel)*
Delicious schnitzel

PEYMANN *(after he has polished off his schnitzel)*
I will stage all of Shakespeare
in one evening
that won't last longer than
five hours
with the best actors in the world
with the best designers in the world
with the best audience in the world
at the Burgtheater of course

BEIL Naturally
at the Burgtheater Peymann
where else

PEYMANN Where else where else where else

> *(gets up and looks down at Vienna)*

BEIL *(also gets up and looks down at Vienna)*

PEYMANN We'll never find a beautiful city like this again
you hear me Beil
never again
And never again such a good audience
you hear Beil do you hear me

BEIL Naturally
I hear you

PEYMANN Come on
let's go down to the city

(*he goes down to the city*)

BEIL (*follows him, after he has picked up the pieces of paper in
which the schnitzels had been wrapped and put them in the
pockets of his trousers*)

PEYMANN (*stops at a picturesque viewing point*)
To be honest my dear Beil
This whole year we've been in Vienna now
I haven't slept a single night

BEIL Neither have I

PEYMANN I don't know how long one can take this kind
of sleeplessness
It's a phenomenon
as far as I'm concerned

BEIL Same here

PEYMANN It seems to me the Viennese are full of hate
where others love
and where others are full of hate
they love
We haven't quite got the knack of it my dear Beil
Last night I dreamed
Chancellor Vranitzky threw himself on me
and strangled me
and Mrs. Havlicek our Minister of Culture
smashed my head
with a brick
and Mayor Zilk kicked me in the ass
and before I lost consciousness
all the actors ridiculed me
And you my dear Beil
you closed my eyes
and shut my mouth
You brutally forced my jaws together

Thomas Bernhard

I've been dreaming all year
that I'm getting killed
the Viennese approach me from behind
they call my name and kill me
they lie in ambush everywhere
and hit me on the head
They trip me everywhere I turn
and hit me on the head
I am received by Chancellor Vranitzky
it is a trap
I am received by Minister of Culture Havlicek
it is a trap
I am received by the President of Actors' Union
it is a trap
wherever I went
I walked into a trap
I came to Austria
and walked into a trap
I walked into the Burgtheater trap Beil
Don't you ever dream such dreams Beil
aren't *you* ever killed by the Viennese

BEIL *(polishing his glasses and humming the Trout Quintet)*
Naturally

PEYMANN What do you mean naturally
naturally
or naturally no
naturally yes
or naturally no
Christ you always use such dramaturg language Beil
talk to me normally for once
Do you have such dreams or not
doesn't anybody kill you in your dreams
are you able to sleep calmly
as if this Viennese hell is none of your business

BEIL *(after he has put his glasses back on and has been searching
for the Burgtheater in the distance)* My dear Peymann
My dreams are much more horrible than yours
I am followed by whole armies of playwrights
and actors during the night

armies of writing and acting dilettantes
armies of imbeciles
Because we've always aimed for the highest standards
and because we brought these standards with us to Vienna
I wake up every night screaming with terror

PEYMANN *(questioning)*
Screaming with terror

BEIL Every night I accept new plays
eight or nine plays a night
that's what I accept every single night
we'd have to perform twelve plays every evening
if we were to perform all the plays
I accept every night

PEYMANN No kidding

BEIL And I audition eight thousand actors
and hire four thousand

PEYMANN No kidding

BEIL For Richard III I have looked at twenty-one portfolios
and bought forty-six set designs

PEYMANN What a nightmare

BEIL Pigheaded I shut down the Burgtheater for two weeks during
the winter
and rented it out to a pedigree dog club from the suburbs
I told the actors
every single Burgtheater actor
to put a muzzle on you
and drive you that way with that muzzle through the center of
the city

PEYMANN No kidding

BEIL I put a bowl of poisoned pea soup
in front of you
you ate it all
but you didn't die
I forced you
to have Hamlet played by a monkey
I sold you the Burgtheater for seventy-three cents

Thomas Bernhard

because I thought it was mine
I climbed the pyramids of Giza with our actors
and I sent you a postcard from Giza
I have stirred the Burgtheater as if it were a pot of soup
I recast your Richard III completely different from what
                                        you wanted
I completely changed the casts of all the plays in the Burgtheater's
                                        current repertoire
You walked toward an abyss
and I screamed *turn back Peymann*
but you kept walking
and you didn't fall into the abyss
you walked on like Jesus Christ
you could walk through the air
Christ once I showed you my teeth
and you slapped my face in return
Suddenly there were only dramaturgs all over the stage
and only actors in all the dramaturgs' offices
once I jumped on you and strangled you
you liked that
you didn't even reprimand me
I am not leaving this place
you once screamed pathetically from the stage of the Burgtheater
I am going to die right here
then I said the word *disgusting* several times
but that didn't faze you at all
You are a shameless bastard Mister Peymann
I yelled in your face several times
You are a megalomaniac
You are a theatrical abomination
that's when you called me an *intellectual hack*
and you ordered me
to take Bernhard's new play and throw it
in his face

PEYMANN No kidding

BEIL *I'm coming with you wherever you go*
    until you'll have destroyed yourself Peymann
    I yelled at you from the balcony
    during a rehearsal of Richard
    In the end it still is just coffee-table theater art

that's what I told you
a theatrical perversity
a dumbfounded theater nightmare
Once you threw your buttered bread at my feet and
I picked it up
but I knew why I picked it up
You kept saying
brilliance brilliance brilliance
but I didn't hear it
I kept cutting all the plays
until nothing was left of them
I cut the entire dramatic world literature
and all you did was laugh at me
scornfully
I'll never forget that laugh

PEYMANN Mrs. Havlicek our Minister of Culture
split my head with an ax
and Mayor Zilk kicked me in the ass
and at the same time he drove a stiletto into my back
and the Burgtheater actors
our own actors laughed at me
and you my dear Beil my dramaturgical friend
you closed my eyes
the night before last I dreamed
that I was chased
through the center of Vienna Beil
dressed only in my underwear
the Viennese whipped me in front of the opera
and I escaped down Kaerntnerstrasse
to St. Stephen's Cathedral where they hit me
even more brutally
I am only human
I am also only human I screamed desperately
that didn't impress them
I ducked under their fists
and finally I managed to run into the cathedral
Wherever I went the Viennese were booing me
I don't want to go back to Germany
I don't want to go back to Germany I whimpered
that's when they drove their knives into my back

Thomas Bernhard

I am the Finance Minister one of them said pathetically
and drove his knife into my back
my dear Beil
I too have dreams as you can see
but I am sure that your dreams
could never be compared to mine
A director's dreams are not a dramturg's dreams

(looks back up the hill)

A hilltop picnic once a week Beil
under the linden tree Beil
for our salvation
for our survival
We have underestimated the Viennese
they are much more malicious and much more malignant
than we thought
but they also know more about art than we thought
we always thought they knew nothing about art
and they would not be as malicious and malignant
but they are the most malicious and malignant species in
the universe
I would've thought of everything but not
that I would ever be doing theater in Vienna
Had you ever thought of doing theater in Vienna

BEIL No

PEYMANN So now we've walked into the trap
the trap of our life
the trap of our existence

(they walk faster)

The dramaturg accuses the director
The director accuses the dramaturg

(they walk almost breathlessly)

But now that we are trapped
in the Burgtheater trap
we have to make the best of it
Everything by Shakespeare in one evening Beil
You remember now
take me at my word

248

and the sonnets as the center
as the center
we've been able to deal with every situation
we'll be able to deal with Vienna my dear Beil
You closed my eyes
excellent dramaturgy you closed them Beil
They buried me in a mausoleum
and there was nothing I could do about it
but before that they gave me many honorary titles and
doctoral degrees
and they made me Honorary President of the Vienna
Horticulturist Association
and there was nothing I could do about that
and I went to the Opera ball
and I went to the Heurigen with our National Socialist President
I had performances for refugee children from the Philippines
and for Catholic charities
and I also did special performances
for the Socialist Save The Children Organization
and I bought a mansion in the most fashionable suburb of Vienna
and there was nothing I could do about that either
and finally I even let them make me an honorary member
of the Vienna Burgtheater
and there was nothing I could do about that
and I hired the daughter of the president of the Association
of Industrialists
and there was nothing I could do about it
and the Viennese critics had only raves for me
and there was nothing I could do about that Beil
and except for our President who came riding in on his horse in
full Wehrmacht uniform
no one came to my funeral
only the critics in gravedigger costumes were there
and our President astride his Macedonian horse in full
Wehrmacht uniform
but the papers reported
all of Vienna was at my grave

> *(suddenly with agitation in his voice, from a vehement urge
> for an espresso)*

Directing means losing one's way

Thomas Bernhard

A German directing in Austria
means having completely lost one's way

(heads quickly down toward Grinzing valley leaving BEIL
behind
running he screams with even more agitation in his voice)

I am telling you
directing is losing one's way
and the theater is the height of insanity
don't you think so Beil

(shouts down into the Grinzing valley)

If I didn't have you
and The Tempest

(after a pause, with a sigh)

The Tempest alone isn't enough
Richard and The Tempest aren't enough
it's all wrong all deadly
Shakespeare forgery Shakespeare forgery
it has to be *all of Shakespeare* Beil
the complete works of Shakespeare in one evening
the sonnets too Beil
Sonnet dramaturgy Beil sonnet dramaturgy
the sonnets as the center the core
all of it all of it all of it
Do you think I am capable of doing that Beil
Beil Beil

BEIL *(after he has discovered a cafe where they can have their
espresso)*
Naturally

PEYMANN *(exhausted, thoughtfully)*
Naturally

*(they enter the cafe and drink their espressos, then they go
directly to the Burgtheater where Hamlet is playing the
way it has been done for decades, by itself, rather than all
of Shakespeare all at once)*

(Curtain.)

Hollow Haven

Paul Van Ostaijen

—Translated from Dutch with an
afterword by Duncan Dobbelmann

Hollow haven
hollow bulging swells
always   the same time
splashing pier dyke
play empty waters
                    and
so far
hollow   haven   hollow   halls

Trembling skeleton rattling pier
Hoofchatter
The one - single - echoing
        That
        Aimless falling
cell wall heaven
always that marching of the one person
                    the one wagon

Did the walls move slightly glowing tale of **Poe**'s

Paul Van Ostaijen

Abandoned tombs

    stuffed mammoth

        sudden desert

            sudden

P o m p e i   **H e r c u l a n u m**

a few are still missing   the all too modern modes of
transportation   to replace you

in the museum of **A r t a n d C r a f t s**

A r t s e t M é t i e r s

hollow haven founded in the year 1914   *O. H. I. C.*

ANNO   MCMIV

simulate the business with some wax puppets

the plague-ridden the watchman the quay-guard

with blue jacket and silver trimmings

PANOPTICUM   glassnumber

and   better variations on the galley slaves of Cayenne

annual fair years of youth fascinated by galley slaves NR 3 and NR 7

and by   the Galley Warden

hollow haven thou hast been nicely replaced as attraction by the
upcoming

! W O R L D ' S F A I R ! in   **M I L W A u K e E**

(il faut exclure les Boches)

252

YOU don't have the lyrical dynamic of tentacular memory anymore
Those born in a seaport want to die there only

                                    they say
(the painter Dupuys left Paris longing for le HÂVRE)

Carcass   Caulking   Hammer-blow on the so finely
arched hull elegant breast
                  much flatter than a halved orange
The   H   ollow   sound
                 though
                 absorbed in the Loud soundvibrations all around
thousandfold e————chó / under   metallic   dome
           lesson from french dictation

leurs
       lourds marteaux
tombent en cadence et domptent les métaux
                      (that's very good for the occasion)

Carcass caulking
        hammer-blow
            metallic dome
                upside down kettle
                    clear clattering of many Bowling Pins
Transatlantichull halfhaven
Opposingbalance : the Other
brown hoBBysoBByhorse lost house slanted wheels harbortrain

Paul Van Ostaijen

sail close-by and dock in the wings

this   transatlantic halfhaven

                Floris Jespers saw correctly

but

        the brown hobbysobbyhorse

is the coloristically precise one

until   transition

the caulkingtarpigment

and   the entire odor   mal

                      a   gam

    most freshly streaming caulking-tar

and the bales

biting sharpness wool skins

    hou

(s   *is written*   FARWEST   cowboy   )

    es fall   cinematrick

A
P
L
A
N
D

oil   PeaNuts   cocoNuts   bodyOil

    national   t s

our }   product   a   m   g

                          o   a   a

    colonial   l   l l

                          f   l f

Ivory   Ivorymarket

and all the things with their reminiscences in

                       sudden little clouds

                      guano

CapetowN   CongO   **CairO**   PATAG ON

                                 I   A

the large shields

the english words and the english accent of the harborpatois

D I S P A C H E

NO_RD^DE_UTSC^{HE}R_LL_O^YD

LORELEY

ZUM HALBEN KILO

NORDISK FLACKE

Tabaxos
Themistokles
Chyriadis

Shed 68

Steels & Iron

hangar

housing

Kattendijk Z W

petroleum tank 7

Uruguay

R. S. L. **Rio Janeiro** LIEBIG

LAPLAND   Tinto   Great EAstern **R**

First class with al the modern comfort

ANTWERP- HARWICH-
Liverpool-   MUSIC
DANCING   G
I
R
NEW YORK L
S

255

Paul Van Ostaijen

SHIPPINGMASTER

good bye

    full

        barrels of freedom

Floris Jespers has gotten a hold of this

and given it a painterly equivalence

which calls up the sensation of smell

        from the caulkingtar to skinbales

earth-colors which cut straight through all senses

I have seen how from the full haven cobblestones moved in all
      directions

and sprang

stroke of the havenheart

gray strip

magic staff

stands bareiy housing all the things

Very   H   ollo·v   H   aven

      from the busy ɛhipping of the past

upside down tub

        all the Fu

           l

            l

               ness Fa

                  l

                   l

                    s

Stand Slouching Slums along the haven

Paul Van Ostaijen

empty

CLatters the shield   *The City of New-York*

disappeared
BLACK JACK

Still-lives of broken signboards

Zum **HALB MAXI**   oncert   *estam*   ELEY   Shippi

KI   café c   **M**   ng

LO

master   *inet*

electric piano whinnying erotically

                                                    band
                                        a   one
                                                    d

PA   *spirits*
        LE - ALE

slouching slums surround   h o l l o w

                           h a v e n

Paul Van Ostaijen

Transatlantic surrogate lighter

CfRiB

abandoned steamercarcass

G N E I S E N

A U

Es ist verboten zu betreten

die   Hafenkommandantur

CARTHAGE

still

Bull and   it's my father and   i'm going

Missisippiriver

Museum castle state centrum

these antiquities

haven Carthage folklore

OLD CURIOSITY SHOP

Hook boats

        splashing of water

             and   rocking

Elvire
   Anna
      Marguerite
         Dinamo
            Mobile
               Ma poupoule

Hook boats small rigging

seen very close-up and flattened out

          current and boats asymmetrical relation

Paul Joostens has painted the boats and the surfaces of their hulls

small full corner of hollow haven

think together   haven

                to paint

haven pure forms

Sudden suspended iron construction

the no-longer-thundering

loud crying of empty cranes and   soundless

      bu   c
       r e d   i
        i   t
              y

               stammering lone li   ness prayer

               aimless tall skeletons

pretentious   rocks   small cruiser on water

         dumb thing

Paul Van Ostaijen

broken carcass
    staring harborwhores hopeless
        Soldiers hardly surrogate for noble seamen
            what happened to the good old days
Hopeless   cranes
    Crying   Whinnying
            falls infertile

Screeching ruSSted locks
wild CAW CAWing birds of prey
endless distance hoarse cranes
        quays
        docks
        slums
        hull

Piano off
   HalT! "Hier is't zum Sammelpunkt der tapferen Feldgrauen"
        poor fallen slums
        irony
        former princess
        nordisk city
        or dutch Betty
whores don't put beautiful flowers next to the Christ of the dyke
        Desert with wilted cranes

B omb   centrum replaced for
        a few boulevard cafés cinemas
        Cries Trembles Hollow Haven

H

        PALE=ALE sleeping
            beauty

Paul Van Ostaijen

* * *

AFTERWORD
BIOGRAPHY AND "SELFBIOGRAPHY"

Paul Van Ostaijen's hometown of Antwerpen is the subject of *Occupied City*, the book of poems from which "Hollow Haven" is drawn. None of *Occupied City* has appeared in English before. Published in 1921 in an edition of 540 copies (with drawings and woodcuts by his friend Oscar Jespers), *Occupied City* shows Van Ostaijen exploiting techniques he learned from Mallarmé, Apollinaire and his Dadaist contemporaries in order to dissect the terrifying contest of commercial, national and military powers he witnessed while Antwerpen was occupied by the Germans during World War I. But Van Ostaijen was no mere mimic: his work traversed poetic styles with a speed and intensity available only to those whose relationship to language is both desperate and passionate. Over a period of twelve years he transformed from expressionist to nihilist to aestheticist—each alteration, not incidentally, marking an equally radical shift in politics. Van Ostaijen's so-called nihilist stage began, predictably, after the war when he moved to a wracked Berlin to avoid jail time for audaciously supporting the Flemings (Dutch-speaking Belgians) at a time when the Walloons (French-speaking Belgians) were ascendant. Ironically, it was in Berlin that he first used his "rhythmic-typographic" technique in writing *Occupied City*, a book which should certainly be considered one of the most stunning and comprehensive critiques of modern "progress"—in all of its guises—among the work of the avant-garde at the time.

What follows is Van Ostaijen's caricature of literary autobiography; it is much more revealing of his personality than it is of his actual biography. What his "Selfbiography" does not reveal, for instance, is that Van Ostaijen was, at various times, a dropout, an art critic, a dandy, an exile, a writer of grotesques, a clerk, a cocaine user, an activist, a sportswriter, a draftee and a bookseller—among other things. As "Hollow Haven" amply demonstrates, Van Ostaijen's cosmopolitan experiences also make themselves known through an array of linguistic appropriations; "Selfbiography" follows suit: the phrase "struggle for life," which is repeated twice, for example, did not need to be translated—it was taken straight from English. Several German words are also consciously used to further help set the reader adrift in Van Ostaijen's imagination: *Alpdruck*=nightmare; *Unfähigkeit*=incompetence; *Wonne*=Bliss. In 1928, Van

Paul Van Ostaijen

Ostaijen died from tuberculosis at the age of thirty-two.

SELFBIOGRAPHY

I was born. This needs to be accepted, though absolute-objective proof is unavailable. Axiom in the domain of subjective experience. Objectively it's only conjecture. Therefore: are we born? To see. To touch. Just laugh at this hardly convincing evidence. I ask: who is actually born?

Nevertheless: I have been born. Despite well-founded doubt, I must also doubt this doubt. The human function appears to have been determined by the doubting of doubt from the beginning.

At two years of age: train wreck. Terror without knowledge left behind, no bad consequences. In the serious struggle for life, meditated on this with bitterness. My life began with derailment. So understandable that I always view life from this angle: how do I derail in the most advantageous manner. For that a person exists in order to derail, I, derailed early, cannot doubt. Did this train wreck actually happen? Is it possibly only a localization of a prematurely ripened desire for derailment? Or else: unclear memory of a very early "*Alpdruck*"?

My family dreamt: musical prodigy. No talent, however. —But circumstances most favorable. Only played soccer once. Enough to retain a 10x2 centimeter scar. I don't play soccer any*more*. Gentlemen, I am a victim of the sport.

After carefree living, struggled to survive in Berlin, Potsdam and Spandau. Not romantic. Fantasy has it that I made it from lift boy to owner of a night-club. Am much too primitive to occupy a prominent position in society. Despite longing very much to reach the level of the Flemish decadents, I realize my "*Unfähigkeit.*" At the point of being named teacher of rhythmic-typographic poetry, I had to decline because not in possession of a frock-coat. If only I had a frock-coat. In the crux of the struggle f.1. cigarette peddler, errand boy (Schlepper) in the service of a night-club with nude dancing. Finally a decent position by recommendation of a prominent art critic: salesman in a shoe store, women's department. By which heavily influenced. See: "Bowlegs," "Sidereal Swagger" = influence shoe store department W.

Very happy with this good situation, although gazing Westward with melancholy. *Le bonheur est fait d'un je-ne-sais-quoi mélancolique.* Brussels. O to see this luxurious city once more. What

262

wealth to die with a Brussels' bar in view. *O Wonne.*

Published three books: *Music-Hall, The Signal, Occupied City.* Maybe this too is only mass-hypnosis. Who can prove that he has read these books? Let alone: understood. God beware: understood. I haven't understood them myself.

Anna Akhmatova, 1910s

Poems and Fragments 1909–1964
Anna Akhmatova

—Translated from Russian by
Roberta Reeder with Volodymyr Dibrova,
with an afterword by Roberta Reeder

UNTITLED POEM

I.

Heaven's coat of arms is curved and ancient.
You barely can make out what's on it.
I told the little girl sitting by the inn
To please wait for me today.

And she gazed at the vernal meadow,
Peeling an orange with her fingers.
She smiled: "Is it true you're not from here?!"
And left, after granting me a single glance.

Neither roads are visible, nor lanes.
I will stop the carriage here.
Never in my life have I loved blondes,
And now I will never love them.

Past midnight we played a game of dice.
I was devilishly lucky that day . . .
And while the guests were still saying goodbye
Outside the window a shadow grew thin.

Humming "Rendezvous in May," I walked
Down an uneven, rickety staircase.
The innkeeper lit my way, repeating:
"Not a sound! In the house are many fine ladies!"

Anna Akhmatova

II.

On the floor moon rays splashed.
My heart at once began to sink, to catch fire,
And blissfully my fingers sank
Into waves of hair fair as flaxen.

Lightning flashed, like a match,
And in the dim sky it died.
In a white dress a sweet little bird
Was sleeping on my very own bed.

She shuddered and folded her arms,
After whispering: "O God, where are You?"
The captivating sounds of her voice
I remember, remember, how pure they were.

—Before 1909

FROM THE UNFINISHED AND "FORGOTTEN"

FROM THE WILL AND TESTAMENT OF A CORNFLOWER

And my princess, wherever she wants to live
Let her have her wish.
And I'm not going to follow this from the grave.
From the grave in the middle of the bare field.
I bequeath her all my silver

. . . .

—1909(?)

A shadow lay on the two-horned moon . . .
. . . . fear.
And there down the curved roads they trotted
Big old men on small donkeys.

—1942

266

FROM A POEMA THAT PERISHED

1.

The Hague dove hovered over the universe
And in its beak carried an olive branch.
And grandpas then with peace did play
Like grandsons now—not with peace . . .

2.

The beauties of that time to me seem
Monstrous . . .
. . . .
O, this sea of cut-off flounces
And hats, like ducks . . . or roosters.
It seemed like the lady was about to quack or crow
Cock-a-doodle-doo . . .

3.

. . . Excerpts of dusty operas
And angelic voices from death:
Caruso, Tito Ruffo and Chaliapin.

4.

And the woman with the mirror eyes
Of an adolescent beggar-girl—sovereign of the stage
And the queen of the Russian Moderne.
. . . .

5.

That century which no longer believes in itself . . .
And in horror snatches at a third,
Where everything is so clear, simple and dignified:
War, divorces, long novels—
Virgin Soil, Resurrection, Rudin, and *Nana.*

6.

At that time we cherished such emotions.
But the future in the next room
Still hung around like a crowd of extras,
Whispering among themselves and yawning
And knowing everything . . . ahead of time.

—*1940s, Tashkent-Leningrad*

267

Anna Akhmatova

FROM *GLORY TO PEACE!*

I. THE GREAT PATRIOTIC WAR

We have truly something to be proud of and to cherish—
A charter of rights, and the speech of our motherland,
And the peace which we guard with great care.
And the valor of the people, and the valor of the one
Who is also closer and dearer to us than anyone,
Who—is our triumphant banner!

———————

To greet the banners, to greet the troops
Of our returning army
Let a song of victory fly toward the skies,
Let glasses clink with joy.

And an awesome pledge we now give
And to the children we bequeath it,
That heavenly peace obtained by fire
Become our only paradise.

—1944-1945

THE FALL OF BERLIN

For two hours I lived through
The four long years again. Holding my breath,
I saw,
            O my Native Land,
How your freedom was saved
By the hand of your most courageous sons
And by the invincible wisdom of the leader . . .
How the best of cherished dreams came true.
. . . And our tanks sped along, like fate,
Crossing alien plains,
And like a Russian song the swanlike voice
            Floated in music.
Everything, everything that appeared like a mirage in the fog
That we heard on the loudspeaker in the night
Everything was illuminated by new rays—
Everything came alive before us on the screen:

268

Anna Akhmatova

The days saturated with history
Are stifling,
    no longer days, but dates—
In the smoke of Berlin—soldiers on their way to the assault.
The last assault—
    and fires broke out.
And with the echo of the last explosions
Blissful silence has finally come.
    Peace—to the world . . .

                          —Excerpt, October 1949, Moscow

II. GLORY TO PEACE

21 DECEMBER 1949

Let the world be reminded of this day forever,
Let this hour be cherished for eternity.
Legend speaks about the wise man,
Who saved each of us from a terrible death.

All the land rejoices in the rays of amber dawn,
And there are no limits to pure joy—
Ancient Samarkand, and polar Murmansk,
And Leningrad twice saved by Stalin.

On the day of the birthday of our teacher and friend
A song of shining gratitude is sung—
Let the blizzard rage
Or the mountain violets blossom.

And a refrain is sung to the cities of the Soviet Union
By the cities of all friendly republics
And by those toilers choked by bonds,
But whose speech is free and whose soul is proud.

And their thoughts fly freely to the capital of glory,
To the Kremlin on high—to the champion of eternal light,
From where a magnificent hymn is carried at midnight
And rings out to the whole world like welcome and support.

———————

Where the desert slumbers, now there are gardens,
Fields and a lake's smooth surface.
Once and for all we will erase the traces
Of war in order to create life.

If we wish, the Pamirs will be moved
Every river will change its course,
But for happiness and prosperity we need peace,
And the ages will be proud of us.

And we will not fear the foreign lie—
We are strong in our truth.
It has already been created—the great plan
Of the future of our land.

———

And in our great fatherland
Before our very eyes a man became
A true sovereign of life,
Lord of mountains and rivers.

And on his lips a wise word,
A radiant word—peace,
Which rings out like the ringing of new bells
Flying over simple people,

Which shines like a guiding star
Amidst the darkness of foreign lands
And encounters the response of all nations:
"Peace is what we seek and thirst for!"
—1950

MOSCOW

How you get better and better day by day
But remain always unchanged.
Preserving your inviolable virtue,
Ardent heart of the universe!

Smooth is your speech, pale blue your dawn,
The arrival of your spring seasons!
A sunny holiday for us—is our meeting with you,
A rejuvenation of our thoughts and feelings.

In the factories the whistle of factory sirens is heard
Echoes of Muscovite glory . . .
Gorky taught young people the truth here,
Mayakovsky glorified life.

Everywhere, where still on the planet Earth
Nations suffer in shackles and chains,
The crimson stars on the Kremlin towers
Appear in dreams to all thirsting for peace.

—1950

POEMS FROM HER LATER YEARS

Glass air above the bonfire
Flows and trembles.
And through it I see a house
. . . .
It does not belong to me.

—1958

———————

. . . Snowdrop flowers turn white,
Having forgiven me long, long ago.

—1950s

———————

Neither treacherous husband nor trembling groom,
. . . . a third,
Who preferred another's nets to mine,
I haven't dreamt of any of them for so long.

Passed over long ago, all the bridges are burnt
And the mortal gates are ready to accept me.

—1960

———————

If only then a stray bullet
Like the light path of July
Had led me somewhere . . .

—1962

It's not with people such as you I parted,
It's not people such as you I sent into the darkness,
Why does burning pity
Cling to my black heart?
There is little left for us to suffer . . .
Give me . . . . and prison

—1963

FRAGMENTS FOR THE CYCLE "THE MENORAH"

1.

Over my shoulder, where the menorah is burning,
Where there's the shadow of the Wailing Wall,
An invisible sinner summons
The subsconscious awareness of original sin.

Polygamist, poet and beginning
Of all beginnings and end of all ends.

2.

The nut tree, shedding, rustles.
Where the diamond menorah shone
There what shines on me—is only darkness.
We are unworthy of seeing each other
. . . .
We are from that meadow preserve.

3.

Along the burning meadow
Where the water is seething
Nothing threw us together.

—1964

* * *

AFTERWORD
AKHMATOVA REDISCOVERED

The life of Anna Akhmatova spans one of the most brilliant and at the same time most horrifying periods in Russian history—brilliant in its art, but horrible in the terror that loomed over the lives of poets and ordinary people. She grew up in a country ruled by an emperor whose weakness brought down a whole dynasty. He was succeeded by the strong, cruel tyrants of the Soviet regime, who in the end brought down the system they helped create. Born in 1889 in Ukraine, Akhmatova spent most of her life in the Russian cities of Petersburg (which became Soviet Leningrad) and Moscow. Having begun as the voice of women experiencing the ecstasy and agony of love, Akhmatova became the voice of her people, crying out against the threats of external enemies and internal tyrants.

Not only have none of these poems been previously published in English but many of them were unavailable even in Russia until 1990, when they were published by a devoted Akhmatova scholar, Mikhail Kralin. The most controversial of the poems are from her cycle "Glory to Peace." Many lovers of Akhmatova's works feel that since these poems in praise of Stalin were written under duress in order to free her son from the Siberian camps, it would be doing her a disservice to publish or translate these verses. However, Kralin disagrees and says in its own way, this cycle is a document of the epoch, no less convincing than her *Requiem*, and the contemporary reader should become acquainted with this tragic page in the biography of the poet. Not to publish them would be equivalent to leaving out works by Shostakovich or Prokofiev that were written as paeans to the homeland and its leader in a patriotic, rhetorical musical style, or similar poems by Mandelstam and Pasternak. In discussing Mandelstam's "Ode to Stalin" in her book *Hope against Hope*, his wife (by that time, his widow) Nadezhda says, "Many people now advise me not to speak of it at all, as though it had never existed. But I cannot agree to this, because the truth would then be incomplete: leading a double life was an absolute fact of our age, and nobody was exempt. The only difference was that while others wrote their odes in their apartments and country villas and were rewarded for them, M. wrote his with a rope around his neck. Akhmatova did the same, as they drew the noose tighter around the neck of her son. Who can blame either her or M."

273

Anna Akhmatova

After a series of earlier arrests and time incarcerated in the camps, Akhmatova's son was arrested again in November 1949. They put him in prison in Moscow, then condemned him to ten years in a Siberian camp. Akhmatova went to Moscow every month to bring him packages, and then continued to keep in contact with him when he was in the camps. Not only did she write letters and visit various authorities in person, but she finally decided to use the only weapon she had to set him free—her poetry. Her friend Nina Olshevskaya, a Moscow actress, contacted Alexey Surkov, editor of the popular magazine *Ogonyok* (Little Light). By this time Akhmatova had been expelled from the Writers' Union because of alleged contacts with foreigners. She had been visited by the famous Oxford professor Sir Isaiah Berlin at the end of 1945 and again at the beginning of 1946 on his way back to London after serving in the Soviet Union during the war on behalf of Britain. Stalin had resumed his xenophobia and broken with his former WWII allies right after the war, as the iron curtain came down. Apparently, he found out about Akhmatova's visit by the famous foreign gentleman and in 1946 punished her for it by including her in a condemnation of various writers and journals which published their works. After this it was impossible for Akhmatova to get anything published. However, Surkov, who himself had no qualms about writing anything to please the authorities and who had written many songs of praise to Stalin and patriotic poetry before, during and after the war, respected Akhmatova and risked his own career by allowing her to publish the poems in his magazine *Ogonyok*.

The war decimated the Soviet Union and millions died. Until the last years the Allies refused to set up a second front and invade France, sending arms instead of men to help the Soviets fight. Stalin remained in Moscow in the embattled capital throughout the war. As Adam Ulam shows in his biography of Stalin, during the war, forgetting for a moment the horrors they suffered under the Terror during the thirties, many people looked on Stalin as a great national leader, the first to deal a military setback to the Fascists. The war ended with a Soviet flag over Berlin and an increase in territorial domain. However, by the time Akhmatova began writing these poems, the situation had changed dramatically. She had been reduced to utter poverty, since expulsion from the Writers' Union meant the impossibility of being published, and her ration card had been taken from her. Only through the help of friends, including Pasternak, did she survive. She was not alone in her suffering. Not only writers, but Shostakovich, Prokofiev and film director Sergei Eisenstein had also been publicly condemned, and thousands of innocent people were arrested or rearrested after the war, as was the case with her son, who had been freed from the camps in order to fight and had participated in the liberation of Berlin.

Thus, there is no question that Akhmatova's cycle of poems in praise of Stalin were not written in the afterglow of the euphoric feeling felt by the Russian people, when the Soviets had just beaten the enemy, and that Akhmatova just might have felt some genuine admiration for the Soviet leader. On the contrary, the poems were written after several years of a horrible replay of the years of Terror, and what is expressed in these poems is the obligatory feelings that were required to be displayed toward Stalin, which had already appeared in so many poems by second-rate poets in the previous decades of the Soviet regime.

Some of her friends were not sure how to react to the work. In 1952 Georgy Makogonenko came to see her and she asked him, "How did you like my Derzhavin imitation?" Stalin was not the first despotic ruler of the Russian people to require panegyrics. Like other poets living in the reign of Catherine II, the poet Derzhavin was required to praise a tyrant. In his 1765 Accession Day Ode to Catherine, Alexander Perpchin writes: "Your power, O monarch, has a beauty like the summer days; Russia, its glory renewed, is flowering like a lily of paradise . . . We live in the midst of a Garden of Eden." Thus Akhmatova was carrying on a long tradition in Russian poetry of using a ready-made repertoire of poetic tropes to praise a ruler who was more famous for misdeeds than noble actions.

As Volodymyr Dibrova has pointed out while working on these translations with me, these poems are brilliant pseudo-imitations of the numerous poems written in praise of Stalin both before and after the war by poets whose aim was to please. What Akhmatova has done is to use the phrases and hackneyed clichés employed in these poems in such a way that they come close to parody. They are reminiscent of musical analogues by Prokofiev and Shostakovich, who were very familiar with the musical rhetoric typical of patriotic hymns and music for marching military bands. They used stereotypical musical phrases and techniques easily recognizable by the people of the Soviet Union in the pieces they wrote to please the authorities.

One who best exemplifies a poet who "writes to please" is Surkov himself. In 1951 he published a collection of poems written before, during and right after the war called *Miru—mir!* (*To the World—Peace*, playing on the word *mir*, which means both "world" and "peace" in Russian). The title is taken from his poem "The Spring of Mankind" written in 1949 about a first of May spring breeze bringing hope to the workers of the world at the same time adding machines, like machine guns, hammer away "in the jungles of New York, in banker's offices." Many of the poems in this collection had been published before, and surely Akhmatova was familiar with them. In fact, in one of her incomplete poems, included here, "The Fall of Berlin," first printed in the Kralin edition, she ends the fragment with "Mir—miru . . ." (Peace—to the world), echoing the phrase in the Surkov poem.

However, often where Surkov is explicit, Akhmatova is more universal. Both write poems against the threat of an external enemy. Yet she never identifies the enemy or specific events, but warns any future foe: "In vain with a bloody shroud/ You are striving to cover our land." After confirming that life now flows on peacefully in her land, she ends the poem with the words: "So with shameful slander do not dare threaten us!"

In continuation of her battle to save her son, Akhmatova delivered a manuscript of an anthology of poems entitled *Glory to Peace!* to the publisher *Soviet pisatel'* (Soviet Writer). It included thirty-nine original poems, including the "Glory to Peace" cycle, and seven translations. She began the collection with the section "The Great Patriotic War," which included popular poems published during World War II. The editorial board all approved the poems praising Stalin, but rejected others for being too rhetorical or incomprehensible. Over four hundred lines were deleted by the editors. However, one of them, Vera Inber, suggested the collection should be published to show readers an example of "the *perestorika* (restructuring) of consciousness" in the development of a poet like Akhmatova. Other editors understood there was a subtext in these poems criticizing the regime and were afraid to publish the text. The manuscript remained with the publisher for three years. In February 1953, Surkov wrote the director of the *Soviet pisatel'*, urging that the manuscript be published, but without any results. However, Stalin died in March 1953, and that put an end to any publication of this collection.

Some of Akhmatova's very early poems, written before 1909, are translated here for the first time. They were written before she was twenty and already show embryonic intimations of the famous Akhmatova style: simple everyday language spoken by the upper classes by a poet thoroughly familiar with and reacting against the often bombastic, opaque and heavily metaphoric poetry of the Symbolists writing at the turn of the century. Until World War I Akhmatova was the voice of women in love, and she describes all the nuances in a romantic relationship: the initial ecstasy of infatuation to the boredom or hatred aroused by an affair that spoils from too much familiarity. Her later poems show the maturity of a woman who has experienced great suffering at the hands of the political system, and she then becomes the voice of her people.

In the section of Kralin's collection called "From the Unfinished and Forgotten" it is sometimes difficult to discern which are unfinished, which are complete poems but "forgotten" and which are purposely fragmentary but appear to be unfinished, a device that goes back to antiquity. For example, a 1930s poem "Fragment from Destroyed Poems" seems to be a deliberate "pseudo-fragment" and in typical Akhmatova conciseness, it expresses a deep and profound thought with a complex subtext.

> ... Because we'll all go
> Down the Tagantsev, the Yesenin,
> Or the great Mayakovsky road.

Tagantsev was accused of being the leader of a group planning counterrevolutionary activity, and Gumilyov was arrested at the beginning of August 1921 for allegedly participating in this affair and, after futile attempts by his friends to get him released, was shot at the end of the month. The latest evidence shows that Gumilyov's only crime was not informing the government of the plot. The poet Sergey Yesenin hoped the October Revolution would bring a peaceful peasant utopia instead of an industrial world ruled by the proletariat. His disillusionment with the new Soviet state in combination with his self-destructive alcoholism resulted in his suicide in 1925. Ironically, Mayakovsky wrote a poem in response to Yesenin's last poem full of despair: "To die—/ in life/ is not so difficult/ To create life—/ is indeed more difficult." However, in the end Mayakovsky also lost his will to create and succumbed to the same despair as Yesenin. In 1930, the combination of intense criticism of his works and a bad love affair resulted in his suicide. In his last note he says: "Mother, sisters, friends, forgive me—this is not the way (I do not recommend it to others, but there is no other way out for me").

This was not Akhmatova's way, however. She was a survivor and had a strong inner core that enabled her to sustain the hardships of the Stalinist Terror. In fact, in her 1963 one-line poem published here, she writes: "I will not go out of my mind and won't even die," implying that such alternatives had indeed presented themselves to her. The poem here predicts that she, too, at least psychologically, walked down the "Tagantsev, Yesenin, Mayakovsky road," for so many of those beloved by her suffered either arrest, death or suicide.

"The Fall of Berlin" refers to a popular film made soon after World War II with the same title, directed by Peter Pavlenko, with music by Shostakovich and the subject of a poem by that name. It depicts the historic capture of Berlin by the Soviet troops through the eyes of one of the soldiers. There is one amazing scene showing a grotesque version of Hitler's last days, including the marriage ceremony when he weds Eva Braun and his subsequent suicide. At the end of the film Stalin arrives by plane in conquered Berlin. He appears dressed in a dazzling white uniform, and the masses greet him with a rousing song: "We will follow you to wondrous times/ We tread the path of victory." By watching the film, Akhmatova lives once again a condensed version of both the heroism of the Russian people as well as their suffering during this time.

In 1949 when her son was arrested, Akhmatova burned her archive, which included many valuable works in progress, and this is probably when she destroyed stanzas from "From a Poema that Perished," which she initially entitled "Poema about the Beginning of the Century." It was written in the 1940s, both in Tashkent, where she was living during the war, and upon her return to Leningrad. The term *poema* is used by Russians for a long narrative poem. In the last years of her life Akhmatova was able to recreate some fragments of the poem. The work alludes to famous events and people at a time in Russian history when the threat of imminent revolution hung in the air. It begins with a reference to two peace conferences at The Hague called by Tsar Nicholas II, contrasting that period to when the poem was being written, during the Second World War. The "sovereign of the stage/ queen of the Russian Moderne" is the famous actress Vera Komissarzhevskaya, whose theatrical productions in collaboration with Meyerhold changed the nature of modern stage performance.

As we can see from the above, the poems presented here include a broad range of themes. They also reflect the complexity of the poet herself as well as the times in which she lived.

From Cahiers
E. M. *Cioran*

—Selected with an afterword by Norman Manea,
and translated from French by Richard Howard

Friday April 24 1959
I would give all the poets for Emily Dickinson.

I am a Mongol laid waste by melancholy.

September 27 1959
Evil is as much a creative force as Good. Yet of the two, it is the more active. For too often Good loafs.

January 6 1960
The story of the Fall may be the profoundest thing ever written. Here everything is told of what we were to experience and suffer. All of history in one page.

"And they heard the sound of the Lord God walking in the garden in the cool of the day . . ." Reading that, one feels, one *shares* Adam's fear. "Who told you that you were naked?" God gave Adam and Eve happiness on condition they neither aspire nor attain to *knowledge* and to *power*.

January 20 1960
That terrible proverb: "While the sage reflects, the fool reflects too."

July 20 1960
Since my old enthusiasm (now very much a thing of the past) for Rilke, I have never been so attached to a poet as to Emily Dickinson. Familiar as her world is to me, it would be still more so had I had the audacity and the energy to wed my solitude completely. But I have failed to do so too often, out of inertia, frivolity or else fear. I have dodged more than one abyss, by a combination of calculation and

279

instinct. For I lack the courage to be a poet. Is it because I have brooded too much over my grievances? My ratiocinations have made me lose the best of myself.

September 1 1960
    God, "our old neighbor," as Emily Dickinson calls him.

September 1 1960
    Adam was just a beginner, it is Cain who remains our universal sovereign, the true ancestor of our race.

April 4 1962
    My strength: to have found no answer to anything.

October 11 1962
    To live is to be capable of indignation. The sage is a man who no longer protests. Hence he is not above but *alongside* life.

October 22 1962
    When I think that in my youth I regarded the anarchist as humanity's fulfillment! Is it progress or is it decline to have arrived at a resignation which makes me consider any act of rebellion as a sign of infantilism?
    And yet, if I no longer rebel, I continue to be indignant (which perhaps comes down to the same thing). This is because *life* and *indignation* are virtually equivalent terms. Nothing that is alive is *neutral*. Neutrality is a victory *over* life, not life.

October 26 1962
    Proust's system of three adjectives which seem to cancel each other out and which actually complete each other. One example among hundreds, among thousands. Charlus' irony is characterized as: "bitter, dogmatic, and exasperated."

November 13 1962
    "Sadness will last forever." These seem to have been Van Gogh's last words. I could have spoken them at any moment of my life.

November 13 1962
    I am part Slav, and part Magyar, not Latin at all.

December 19 1962
I, I, I—how tiring!

December 31 1962
The moment I am well, inspiration abandons me, even *subjects* founder. With good reason have I been crucially influenced by Pascal's answer to his sister when she urged him to seek medical attention: "For you do not know the disadvantages of health and the advantages of disease."

How well I remember reading that, in the library of the Carol Foundation in Bucharest—I had to struggle to keep from crying out.

December 31 1962
No friend ever tells us the truth. That is why only the silent dialogue with our enemies is fruitful.

February 1 1963
The role of insomnia in history. From Caligula to Hitler. Is the inability to sleep the cause or the consequence of cruelty? The tryant *lies awake:* that is what defines him as such.

April 7 1963
I hate the young, those who remind me of my past enthusiasms.

April 7 1963
A defense of France: a nation of misers cannot be superficial.

June 1963
My cowardice in the face of life is congenital: I have always had a horror of any responsibility, any task—an instinctive horror of whatever did not immediately concern me. The contrary of a "leader." And if, when young, I often envied God, was it not because God, being over all, seemed to me Irresponsibility itself?

October 1963
Insomnia.
"When the bird of sleep sought to nest in the pupil of my eye, he saw my lashes and feared the net." (Ben al-Hammara, twelfth-century Andalusian poet.)

E. M. Cioran

November 5 1963
Terrible night, like so many others. I take too many pills; my system no longer endures them. I should leave my ills in peace.

December 1963
Reread a few poems by Emily Dickinson. Moved to tears. Everything that comes from her has the capacity to overwhelm me.

February 1964
Yesterday evening, at the Church of Saint-Roch, *The Messiah.* Two hours of *jubilation.* I am ashamed of having put so much stock in depression for so many years. True, I do so effortlessly (and daily), whereas I could count on my fingers the times I have really known jubilation. But then I was the Soul of the World.

February 1964
The melancholy of being understood—for a writer, there is none greater.

March 21 1964
"A polymorphous pervert"—Freud's admirable definition of the child.

April 1 1964
A fit of melancholy which the Devil himself would envy.

April 1964
During my peregrinations in the Jura I saw a cat hit by a car, which flung it high in the air. It uttered an *unforgettable* cry; then lay there motionless beside the road staring into space; that stare, too, was unforgettable.

January 1 1965
The Jews, because ill-treated by the Gothic kings, "collaborated" with the Arabs when they invaded and occupied Spain. When the occupation began, they took over police functions in the towns. Seven centuries later, the Catholic kings ordered their expulsion. (And it's the Jews who are accused of having too good a memory, unable to forgive or forget!) Impossible not to discover constants in history. What the eighteenth century called "fanaticism," "superstition." But these flaws are not the appanage of religion, since one

discovers them in any form of faith, wherever there is any kind of *enthusiasm.*

January 4 1965
  I am *metaphysically* Jewish.

January 4 1965
  Job—my patron.

January 4 1965
  I shall never console myself for the mediocrity of my enemies.

April 5 1965
  The antidote to boredom is fear. The remedy must be stronger than the disease. My whole life will have been nothing but a vacillation between the two.

June 23 1965
  Sleepless night.
  Insomnia dries up my veins and strips me of what little substance is left in my bones. Hours tossing in bed with no hope of ever losing consciousness, of drifting off into sleep. A real pillage of body and mind.

June 25 1965
  The enormous sadness in the eyes of a gorilla. An elegiac animal. It is from this stare that I am descended.

  Insomnia, insomnia.
  What is odd about these nights is how one manages to be reconciled with death. For such reconciliation is, or should be, the supreme goal of humanity.

October 1965
  I have almost always ended by adopting the opinions of those I most opposed. (The Iron Guard [the Romanian extreme-right movement], which I had detested at the start, became for me a phobic obsession.) Having attacked Joseph de Maistre, I suffered his contagion. The enemy insidiously triumphs over a man without character. By dint of thinking against someone or something, you become its prisoner, and reach the point of loving that servitude.

E. M. Cioran

October 27 1965
The ultimate simplification—Death.

October 27 1965
The sick humor of the vanquished.

October 27 1965
There is something worse than anti-Semitism: anti-anti-Semitism.

November 22 1965
"Nature is a haunted house, art a house that tries to be haunted" (Emily Dickinson).

November 29 1965
Someone telephones to ask if I know a Romanian writer named Mihail Sebastian, whose mother happens to be in Paris . . . I was *stirred*. Sebastian had just been appointed Cultural Attaché to Paris when he was run over by a truck during the Liberation. He would have had a great career, for it is hard to imagine a Romanian more French than he. What a fine mind; what an admirable, distraught man! And he is unknown. And here I am complaining all day long and cursing my fate, what a lesson! One must get used to thinking about the injustices others suffer in order to be able to forget one's own. I shouldn't complain, I'm not entitled to; on the other hand, I can hardly utter hosannas. I must find the right tone between horror and jubilation.

January 5 1966
I learned at a dinner last night that Paul Celan has just been confined to a sanitarium after having tried to kill his wife. Coming home late that night, I was overcome by a real fit of terror and had a terrible time falling asleep. Waking this morning, I encountered the same fear (or anguish, if you like), which never slept at all. He had great charm, this impossible man. So complicated and difficult to know, but whom one forgave everything once one forgot his unfair, senseless grievances against everyone.

January 5 1966
Around 1934 I happened to be in Munich. I was living under a tension which even now, when I think about it, makes me shudder. It seemed to me then that it wouldn't take much for me to found a

religion, and that possibility filled me with the greatest terror. . . . Since then I have calmed down . . . dangerously so.

February 12 1966
Romanians. Upon contact with us, everything turns frivolous, even our Jews. We have sterilized them, we have made them lose their genius, especially their religious genius. No miraculous rabbis among us, no Hasidism. The visceral skepticism of our race has been deadly. Their sojourn among us more pernicious than an assimilation. We have made them almost as *superficial* as ourselves; anything more, and we might have assimilated them altogether.

May 19 1966
For some, the prospect of dying (Proust, Hitler . . .) impels them to a frenzy of activity: they want to conclude *everything*, complete their work, and thereby become eternal; not a moment to lose, they are stimulated by the notion of their end—for others, the same prospect paralyzes them, leads them to a sterile *sagesse*, and keeps them from working: what's the use? The idea of their end flatters their apathy, instead of disturbing it; whereas among the first group, it rouses every energy, good as well as bad.

Who is right here, where is reason? It is hard to say, especially since both reactions are justified. Everything depends on our inclinations, on our nature. In order to really know someone, you have to know what the thought of his end *releases* in him: is it exciting or benumbing? Lucky those who set to work because they think they're going to die, who in this idea find a truly dynamic impulse! Less fortunate those who lay down their arms and wait, for they have *too much* time to envisage their conclusion. They die during all the moments they dedicate to the idea of death: moribund in the full sense of the word, *inexhaustibly* moribund.

June 10 1966
My cowardice in the face of the authorities. I lose all my powers in front of anyone in an official position. Whereby I am indeed a descendant of a nation of slaves, defeated and humiliated for centuries. As soon as I am dealing with a uniform, I feel I am in the wrong. How well I understand the Jews! Always living in the margins of the State! Their drama is my own. In truth, descended from a nation whose curse is ordinary, but a curse all the same—I was made to understand a curse *par excellence.*

285

E. M. Cioran

How I hate my timidity, my hereditary lack of dignity.—This afternoon I suffered spasms of self-disgust, I actually loathed myself to the point of a murderous frenzy. I wonder sometimes by what miracle I still manage to endure myself. Self-hatred bordering on shrieks or tears.

Whatever I do, I shall never take root in this world.

June 19 1966

Jakob Taubes told me an upsetting thing: the recent ordeals of the Jews have produced no *original* prayer capable of being adopted by the community and recited in the synagogues.

June 26 1966

How correct Simone Weil's observation, that Christianity was to Judaism what Catharism must have been with regard to Christianity . . .

September 2 1966

All nations are accursed. The Jewish people more so than the rest. Its malediction is automatic, obvious, entire. Self-evident.

The Romanian Jew is anti-Romanian; the American Jew anti-American, and so on. But the French Jew is not anti-French. He doesn't *dare*. Why?

France has—or rather, has had—a *prestige* monopoly, creating a prejudice favorable to itself, by which everyone aims to benefit.

October 18 1966

One in the morning—Death of my mother.

I learned about it from a telegram which arrived tonight. She had lived her life. For several months she had betrayed disturbing signs of extreme old age, yet even this morning I received a postcard from her dated October 8th which revealed no mental weakening. She wrote that she was suffering from a depression which she was told, she added, was merely that of old age. —Tonight, J. M. came over. We were celebrating his birthday. Someone rang; I did not go to the door. A few minutes later I went to see if there was a message, or something. Nothing. An hour later, having gone to look for a book, I saw a telegram had been slipped under the door. I already knew what was in it before I opened it. I came back into the room without a word about what had happened. But around eleven o'clock J. M. said he was leaving, that I must be tired, that I was pale. Nonetheless, I concealed my distress as best I could, and I think I was quite *gay* the whole time. But a secret struggle must have been going on within me, which appeared in my face.

Everything good and bad in me, everything I am, I get from my mother. I have inherited her illnesses, her depression, her contradictions, everything. Physically I resemble her, feature for feature. Everything she was is aggravated and exacerbated in me. I am her success and her defeat.

November 3 1966

It is snowing. The city is completely white, buried. How well I understand the Russian abulia, the *aciaïnya*, Oblomov, Katorga and the Orthodox Church!

November 30 1966

Types I resemble: Oblomov, Kirilov, Adolphe and . . . Only more cowardly, more hopeless.

November 7 1966

Paul Bourget (c. 1910?): "Four barriers separate us from barbarism: the German General Staff, the English House of Lords, the French Institute and the Vatican."

December 14 1966

Brooding over the years 1933/34/35, I remember the madness which came over me, my excessive ambitions, my "political" delirium, my positively demented aims—what vitality in derangement! I was tirelessly crazy. Now I am crazy and tired. To tell the truth, I am not even crazy, I merely preserve the residue of my old madness. Fatigue, of course, far from having withdrawn, is on the contrary expanding, in full swing. Where it will take me, I have no idea.

December 17 , 1966

Hitler's marriage with Eva Braun took place a few hours before their suicide. An official was hurriedly summoned, and asked each of them separately the obligatory question: "Are you Aryan?" They answered in the affirmative. If Hitler had said: "No," that would have been the most extraordinary answer in History.

December 29 1966

I have read a book about *Treblinka*. Fantastic nightmare, scarcely imaginable. Absolute, mechanical horror; the *system*. All these books are alike. The executioners are puppets, bureaucrats; conventional genre: poor bastard; the officers always "handsome" with the inevitable sarcastic smile; academicism of the horrible; equal forfeiture of the torturers and their victims. Nonetheless, always intense, one's astonishment at the *impenetrable* fate of the Jews. All other nations have a history; they alone a *destiny.*

January 5 1967

My affinities with the Jewish mind. A taste for mockery, a certain tendency toward self-destruction, unhealthy obsessions; aggressiveness; depression tempered or aggravated by sarcasm, depending on the hour; weakness for prophecy, the sense of always being a victim, even in moments of happiness.

February 4 1967

The scapegoat. We cannot do without it, its existence is required by our biological constitution. Someone must pay for our faults and our failures; if we consider ourselves as alone responsible, what complications, what additional tortures! To have a *good conscience,* is all that we ask: the scapegoat serves that function. It takes an almost superhuman effort to be able to assume the blame ourselves for *everything.* But when we have made the effort we have the distinct sensation that we are approaching the truth. Alas! This does not make us more modest, only more vainglorious.

(In fact, today R. J. told me something disagreeable: I came very close to losing my temper. Yet she was right. I made an effort and overcame my angry impulse. To acknowledge oneself as guilty, at fault, sincerely to confess one's wrongs, to accept every just criticism—that is a rare thing, an event. We are *dans le vrai* only when we understand our enemies or, harder still, our friends, severer judges.)

February 6 1967

There is a rumor that Paul Celan has committed suicide. This unconfirmed news stirs me more than I can say. For months I too have been *agitated* by this "problem." Not having to solve it, I try to decipher its meaning.

March 13 1967

Progress is a Judeo-Christian idea. The Prophets and the *corrected,* amended, emasculated Apocalypse are chiefly to blame. The Last Judgement as fulfillment, as crowning achievement: the Last Judgement *en rose.*

March 28 1967
What the Germans and the Jews have in common: they inspire violent feelings, for or against; never or almost never *normal* feelings.

March 28 1967
What can be held against the Jews: each of them tends to occupy too much room; nothing satisfies him; and he keeps spreading, *manifesting* himself. Jews know no *limit* in anything. That is their strength and their weakness. They go too far in everything, and inevitably they collide with others, those who also seek to advance, but who lack the means.

May 12 1967
The other day at the Collins, I said that all Romanians were imposters. Mounir Hafez asked me: "And do you consider yourself one?"—"In a sense I do," I answered, without being able to make my point more explicit. What I would have liked to say is that the ordinary imposter, in an excess of lucidity or for some other reason, cannot manage to identify himself with anything at all. To my mind, an imposter is not someone who deliberately claims to be what he is not, but someone who cannot be the expression of anything, who keeps too great a distance from whatever he does to be able to embody an idea or an attitude. He is the man of simulacra, not deliberately but fatally. It should be added that, in everyday speech, this is not what is meant by imposture, which always signifies an intention to deceive.

June 2 1967
Telephone discussion with Ionesco about prospects for the State of Israel, whose viability I question after the recent events [the Six Day War, June 5–June 10]. "Everything must be done but there is nothing to do," I concluded, since there is a "curse."

October 30 1967
My love of Bach has overwhelmed me again. I love to listen to him in the dark. I turn off the light and take my pleasure in a tomb. Sometimes it's as if I were listening to music *after* my death.

E. M. Cioran

December 5 1967
In her preface to the American edition of *The Temptation to Exist,* Susan Sontag writes that my essay on the Jews is the most superficial, the most cursory chapter in the book. On the contrary, I believe it is the best, and by far. How lacking in instinct these critics are! Can a text so impassioned be "cursory"? I carried it within myself for years. And what an idea, to declare a thing superficial because one doesn't like it!

December 14 1967
The Jew the extremely successful synthesis of a Frenchman and a German: vivacity and tenacity mingled and combined.
The Frenchman has this in common with the Jew: he believes everything is his due.

January 3 1968
I have just seen Celan for the first time in a year; he has spent several months in a psychiatric hospital, but doesn't mention it. This is a mistake, for if he talked about it, he wouldn't have that *embarrassed* expression (which one always has when one conceals something crucial which *everyone is supposed to know*).
True, it's never easy to discuss one's crises. And what crises!

March 14 1968
Every *noble* attitude is false. Insults are unforgivable, except those from strangers; never if they come from a friend or an acquaintance.

One can forget, one cannot forgive a low blow. All forgiveness is no more than a posturing. What we are made of fails to mix with forgiveness; we are physically unsuited to forgiveness.

Never hurt anyone: how to manage this? By not *manifesting* yourself. For every action hurts someone. By abstaining, one spares everyone. But perhaps death is even better than abstention.

What an extraordinary sensation, for a writer, to be *forgotten!* To be posthumous in one's own lifetime, no longer to see one's name anywhere. For all literature is a question of names and of nothing else. *To have a name,* the expression speaks volumes (*sic*). Well then, no longer having a name, if one has ever had such a thing, may be better than having one. Such is the price of freedom. Freedom, and even more: deliverance. A *name*—all that remains of a being. It's stupefying that one can toil and torment oneself for such a trifle.

April 13 1968

At noon today I observed to Mounir Hafez that Jews and Germans had this in common: that they couldn't realize themselves, no, couldn't *establish themselves* in history. This was apropos of the State of Israel, whose destruction Mounir foresees in the immediate future (three years, he says; I answer that it will last much longer).

September 9 1968

The other day I caught sight of Beckett on a side-path of the Luxembourg; he was reading a newspaper more or less the way one of his characters would do it. He was sitting there on a chair, looking engrossed and absent, the way he usually does. A little sickly too. I didn't dare approach him. What could I have said? I am very fond of him but it's better that we don't speak to each other. He is so *discreet!* And conversation, being a *game,* requires a minimum of posturing and unconstraint. But Sam is incapable of that. Everything about him betrays the man of silent monologue.

November 22 1968

To understand other people, you must be obsessed by yourself to the point of disgust, such disgust being a symptom of health, a necessary condition in order to look beyond your own troubles.

November 26 1968

What I like about Christianity is its morbid side, its institutionalized maladjustment.

December 13 1968

Sleepless night.

Incredible how, in the middle of the night, suicide seems the most normal thing in the world.

The truth is in neither revolution nor in reaction. It resides in the questioning both of society and of those who attack it.

After a sleepless night one is almost always a victim of the need to prophesy.

E. M. Cioran

Health, like freedom, has no positive content, since you don't consciously enjoy it when you possess it. It contributes nothing to you, it can enrich no one. So it would be absurd to say that someone made some discovery or had some vision because he was feeling well. It is when you feel ill that you discover something new, health being a state of *absence,* since you are not conscious of it. You would have to be able to tell yourself at any moment at all: *I am feeling well,* and from this derive a real, *conscious* well-being. But such consciousness would be in contradiction with health and would merely prove that health is or is about to be compromised. Any conscious health is a threatened health. Health is a good, certainly, but those who possess it have been denied the opportunity of knowing their happiness. And one might speak without exaggeration of a *just* punishment of the healthy.

December 20 1968
Glanced at a book about Saint Paul. Always the same antipathy to this sinister, terrifying figure—*whom I understand so well.*

December 29 1968
My profound interest in the Jews and in everything Jewish. *Cases,* every one of them. Simone Weil, Kafka. Figures from a world *elsewhere.* They alone are mysterious. Non-Jews are too *obvious.*

"Democracy" is a phenomenon of ageing, let's say, of maturity, of instinctual apathy (!), of exhaustion. France was ripe for a parliamentary regime *after* Napoleon. Democracy is possible only if a nation is exhausted by its adventures, if it has lost the taste for provocation and conquest. This is true for many countries, except England. An important qualification, for England is the only country which can allow itself the luxury of conquest and debate. (And the Roman Senate?)

January 2 1969
"My life is the hesitation before birth." (Kafka)
. . . As I have always felt.

January 4 1969
Kafka: Jewish and ill, hence doubly Jewish or doubly ill.

January 7 1969
An historian aptly remarks that the first Christians were not sorry to be taken for Jews, since the religion of the Hebrews was acknowledged by the laws of the Roman Empire. But at the same time, the historian notes, the Christians suffered the effects of the great unpopularity attached to everything Jewish.

It was during Nero's persecutions that the division between Christians and Jews became very clear. Nero persecuted only the Christians.

January 30 1969
I have just glanced at Kafka's biography (youth). The pictures of Prague and customs they evoke remind me of Hermannstadt. I lived at the other end of the Austro-Hungarian Empire.

February 9 1969
All my life I wanted to be something else: Spanish, Russian, German, cannibal—anything but what I was. In permanent revolt against fate, against my birth. That madness of wanting to be other than what you are, to embrace in theory every condition but your own.

There is only one word to describe the nation I come from and to which I remain loyal since I recognize in myself all its defects: *minor.* Not an "inferior" nation, but a nation in which everything occurs in miniature (not to say in caricature), even disaster.

February 13 1969
Life is extraordinary, in the sense that the sexual act is extraordinary: *during,* and not after. Once you position yourself outside of life and consider it from an external point of view, everything collapses, everything seems deception, as after the sexual performance.
All pleasure is extraordinary and unreal, as is the case for every act of life.

February 17 1969
Colette is supposed to have said of Bach: "A sublime sewing-machine."
There is nothing worse than Parisian wit.

Bach's library included Josephus's *History of the Jews.* Understandable for such a great reader of the Bible. And then the Jews are present in his *Passions.*

February 21 1969

At all costs one must free oneself of one's origins. Loyalty to a tribe must not degenerate into idolatry (the Jews). Nationalism is a sin against the mind—a universal sin, unfortunately.

The Stoics were not so bad as that, and no one has improved on their conception of man as a citizen of the cosmos.

However ridiculous we find the notion of progress, Christianity represents an enormous step beyond Judaism: the whole distance from a tribe to humanity.

Nazism is the spirit of the Old Testament applied to the Germans; Nazism is the German Jehovah.

February 28 1969

People reproach me for certain pages of *Schimbarea la faţă a României* [Transfiguration of Romania], a book written thirty-five years ago! I was twenty-three years old, and crazier than anyone. I glanced at this book yesterday; it seemed to me that I wrote it in a previous existence; in any case, my present self does not recognize itself as the author. Inextricable, one discovers, the problem of responsibility.

How many things I was able to believe in my youth!

For twenty years now—no, for thirty—I have been slandered and pilloried as a reprobate. The strong taste of injustice. In a certain sense, I should not like people to be fair to me. It is much more *fruitful* to be rejected, and even forgotten, than *accepted.* I hold no brief for being *well regarded* by my kind.

March 1 1969

You have to let people say what they will. Eventually the truth will be reestablished. Anything is better than humiliation. Injustice is necessary to the mind; it fortifies, cleanses it. A victim is always, with regard to lucidity, *above* his persecutors. To be a victim is *to understand.*

Ionesco, with whom I had a long telephone conversation about the Iron Guard, and to whom I said that I feel a sort of *intellectual shame* at having allowed myself to be seduced by it, answered very aptly that I "went along" because the movement was "completely crazy."

Just met Lucien Goldmann at Gabriel Marcel's, and afterwards we walked together and then went into a café. He walked me home. A man of certain charm. For twenty years he has given me a reputation of being an anti-Semite, and made enormous difficulties for me. In an hour, we have become *friends.* How strange life is!

A Marxist cannot understand boredom as such, anxiety as such. I spoke of this to Goldmann, quoting Pascal. He maintains that the economic and social conditions Pascal lived in have changed, that there is no reason to cling to "anguish."

April 2 1969
Certainly we are marked by the "cultural" (?) space we come from. Transylvania retains a strong Hungarian, "Asiatic" stamp. I am Transylvanian, hence . . . The older I grow, the more I realize that I belong not only by my origins but also by my temperament to Central Europe. Thirty years' residence in Paris will not erase the fact of having been born on the periphery of the Austro-Hungarian Empire.

April 11 1969
What I owe to the Iron Guard. The consequences I have had to draw from a simple youthful enthusiasm were and are so disproportionate that subsequently it has become impossible for me to make myself the champion of any cause whatever, however harmless or noble or God knows what.
It is good to have paid very dear for a youthful folly; afterwards, you are spared more than one disappointment.
Nationalism is a sin of the mind. To belong to a specific people has no profound meaning (except perhaps for the Jews). The only true community is the one based on the "spiritual family" and not on the national or ideological one. I feel solidarity only with those who understand me and whom I understand, with those we believe in certain values inaccessible to the mob. All the rest is a lie. A people is doubtless a reality—an historical, not an essential reality. When I think of how excited I was in my youth on account of my tribe! What madness, good God! One must wrest oneself free of one's origins, or at least forget them. I have a tendency to refer back to mine, probably

out of masochism, a taste for slavery, for "chains," for humiliation.

The superficial moments in my life, the hysterical moments were those in which History counted more than anything—that was the period of my aberrations.

April 28 1969
Attachment is the origin of all servitudes. The more you want to be free, the less you tie yourself to beings and things. But once you are tied to them, what a drama it is to be released!

We begin living by creating ties for ourselves; the older we grow, the stronger they become. A moment comes when we understand that they represent so many chains, that it is too late to shake them off, for we are too used to them.

May 7 1969
Only Bach can reconcile me to death.

The funereal note is always there in Bach, even in joy. A funereal and seraphic note. To die *above* life, and death, a victory beyond being.

To transcend life—and death—at the center, at the heart of death.

A dying man weeping for joy—Bach is often that.

May 30 1969
The Wrong Demiurge—work of a melancholic viper. As much could be said of all I have written.

June 5 1969
On the usefulness of the enemy.

Only he who creates the void around us does us a service.

My gratitude to those who have made me more alone, who—in spite of themselves, but no matter—have contributed to my spiritual consolation.

July 2 1969
"Life is a perpetual deviation which does not even allow us to become conscious of the meaning from which it deviates" (Kafka).

Enesco, speaking of Bach, called him "the soul of my soul." This simple and apparently naïve expression precisely translates how I feel about the Cantor.

October 1969

Samuel Beckett. Nobel Prize. What a humiliation for such a proud man! The sadness of being understood!

Beckett or the anti-Zarathustra.

The vision of post-humanity (as one says post-Christianity).

Beckett or the apotheosis of the infra-man.

October 24 1969

O. C. said to me that Sorin Pavel was a "failure." I told him that the only interesting Romanians I have known were failures, that what people call by that name is the authentic mode, the true way in which a Romanian can *give his utmost*, that in this fashion the true genius of the nation is manifested.

All the Romanians who have mattered in my life: Sorin Pavel himself, Țuțea, Zaprațan, Crăciunel and the greatest of all, Nae Ionescu, were "failures," which is to say that they realized themselves in "life" without rising or sinking to an "oeuvre."

November 28 1969

Two things which have mattered a great deal in my life: music and mysticism (hence *ecstasy*)—and which are growing distant . . .

Between twenty and twenty-five, an *orgy* of both. My passionate desire for them was linked to my insomnia. Incandescent nerves, constantly swollen to the point of bursting, desire to weep because of an intolerable unhappiness . . .

December 8 1969

Listening to Ruggiero Ricci today on the radio, playing Bach's first Partita, I felt that one must not give up, that one has no right to surrender, and that, as far as I am concerned, it is my duty to get a grip on myself.

January 4 1970

Among the sons of Bach, one feels the will to distinguish themselves from their father, not by deepening but by multiplying the obvious differences. Originality is always easier than profundity. *Invention* is an escape; and it is achieved following any sort of disorder, to descend into the intimacy of things or of oneself supposes a concentration, an extreme exertion not so much of the mind as of the soul.

E. M. Cioran

I get along better with Romanian Jews than with Romanians "strictly speaking." This was already the case thirty-five years ago, before the misunderstanding created by the Iron Guard. With the Jews, everything is more complex, more dramatic and more mysterious than with those shepherds and peasants sunk in their wretched, yet nondescript destiny.

January 23 1970
Yesterday, Ionesco was elected to the Academy. He told me, in terror: "It's forever, for eternity." I reassured him: "No, not at all, think of Pétain, of Maurras, of Abel Hermant and some of the others. They were driven out. You too may have the occasion to commit some act of treason." Ionesco: "So there's hope."

February 19 1970
Ionesco telephoned yesterday, a little drunk. He told me he keeps being amazed, when he thinks about his career, from a schoolteacher in Romania, then a workman at Ripolin, then a proofreader at the Hôtel de Ville: to end up, finally, in the Academy. I replied that there was no essential difference between his new status as an academician and his old semi-*clochard* situation, and that he should pay no attention to such promotions, which are best forgotten.

March 8 1970
The moment of supreme lucidity for an author is the one when he perceives without illusion the precise value of his work. He behaves toward it as would *an honorable enemy.*

March 11 1970
Yesterday evening, *Waiting for Godot.* A very great play. After fifteen years, not a single wrinkle.

April 26 1970
French people who have known Romanians do not like them. Understandable: they have neighboring defects.

May 7 1970
Paul Celan has drowned himself in the Seine. His body was found last Monday.
I cared for this charming and impossible man, so fierce yet with sudden fits of gentleness, and I avoided him lest I wound him, for

everything wounded him. Each time I encountered him, I was on my guard and kept such a close watch on myself that after half an hour I was exhausted.

May 11 1970
Terrible night. Dreamed of Celan's wise solution.
(Celan went to the end, exhausted his possibilities of resisting destruction. In a certain sense, there is nothing fragmentary or unsuccessful about his existence: he completely fulfilled himself.
As a poet, he could go no further: in his last poems, he was perilously close to *Wortspielerei* [playing with words]. I know of no death more touching or less sad.)

Klee liked to quote: "the art of drawing is the art of omission" (Liebermann). Which is how one might define the art of the aphorism.
For me, to write is *to omit*. That is the secret of laconicism, and of the essay as a genre.

May 12 1970
Thiais Cemetery. Funeral of Paul Celan.
In the bus, from the Porte d'Italie to the cemetery, the ugliness of the suburbs seemed so dreadful to me that once we reached the cemetery, which is beautiful, I had feeling of deliverance.

June 26 1970
The ancient Greeks and the Jews—the most gifted of all peoples.

July 8 1970
A long discussion yesterday evening with a Hungarian poet (Pildusky) about Simone Weil, whom he considers a saint. I said I admired her too, but that she wasn't a saint, that she had too much of that passion in her, that intolerance she hated in the Old Testament from which she emerged and which she resembles in spite of her contempt for it. A female Ezekiel or Isaiah. Without faith and the reservations which faith implies and imposes, she would have been fiercely ambitious. What stands out in her is the will to force acceptance of her point of view at all costs, by overwhelming or even doing violence to her interlocutor. I also told the Magyar poet that she had as much will and energy and determination as a Hitler . . . Whereupon my poet opened his eyes wide and stared hard at me, as if he had just had an illumination. To my astonishment, he said: "You're right."

E. M. Cioran

August 1 1970
Bad night. I tried to ponder serious subjects and failed altogether. Nonetheless, as soon as sleep *desisted*, I realized that I was *conscious*, that I had just emerged from a state of *plenitude* and of *nothingness:* for sleep is nothing but that very contradiction. One is *torn* from sleep, one is banished from it: consciousness is in exile. Only unconsciousness is a homeland.

People accept without excessive terror the notion of eternal sleep; on the other hand, an *eternal* waking (which is what immortality would be, if such a thing were conceivable) is unbearable, in thought as in fact: it gives you the shivers.

August 31 1970
The French were a great nation so long as they had strong prejudices, which they expressed intensely and accumulated grandly. In them avarice was a sign of greatness. They hoarded money and, simultaneously, virtues.

The French peasantry is disappearing. A fatal blow to France, which is thereby losing her reserves, her *capital.* She will never recover from this.

Avarice was a safeguard for France.

September 5 1970
Christianity will be lost unless it undergoes terrible persecutions from now to the end of the century. The Church ought to work in secret for atheists to come to power: only they could still save it.

November 16 1970
Skepticism: delight in the dead end.

In the Absolute, it matters little whether one is a saint or a swindler.

November 18 1970
I am a pupil of Job but a disloyal pupil, for I have not been able to acquire the Master's certainties, I have followed him only in his lamentations. . . .

November 20 1970
This afternoon Celan will be honored at the German Institute. He was a charming man, no doubt about it. And yet what an impossible man too! After an evening with him, you were exhausted, for the

300

necessity to control yourself, to say nothing which might wound him (and everything wounded him) ultimately left you weak and quite dissatisfied with both him and yourself. You were annoyed with yourself for having been so cowardly, for having humored him to such a degree, and for not having ultimately exploded.

Homage to Celan, at the German Center. The actor who read his poems—if only the actors who read poems in France were there to hear how poetry should be read.

(A French poet who read three pages in his own way, as an introduction to the event, thought fit to repeat the word *exorbitant* three times, applying it to the attention with which Celan must be read. I almost hissed him, but neither the moment nor the solemnity of the occasion lent themselves.)

Even Celan, who had something to say, was haunted to an astonishing degree by questions of language. The *word* was an obsession for him—and, a just punishment, what is least real in his poetry derives from that verbal acrobatics he ended with.

Poetry at present is perishing from language, from the excessive attention it pays to it, from this fatal idolatry.

Reflection on language would have killed even Shakespeare.

Love of words, yes; but not this eternal dwelling upon them. The former passion generates poems; the second, parodies of poems.

November 20 1970

A splendid, divine morning in the Luxembourg. I saw people walking up and down, and I said to myself that we the living (the living!) are here only to graze the surface of the earth for a while. Instead of looking at people's faces, I looked at their feet, and for me all these beings were merely footsteps, footsteps going in all directions, a chaotic dance over which it would be pointless to linger ... I had reached that point in my reflections when, looking up, I caught sight of Beckett, that exquisite man, whose presence has something singularly beneficial about it. His cataract operation, made on just one eye for the moment, was entirely successful. He is beginning to see at a distance, which he could not do previously. "I'll end up an extrovert!" he told me. Let future commentators discover the reason, I added.

E. M. Cioran

December 7 1970
The Torah, Mosaic law, has been nicknamed a "portable father-land."

May 22 1970
Every form of attachment is a sin against perspicacity.

June 6 1971
Liberation, liberation—
To suppress prohibitions, to free yourself is all very well, but don't you risk, thereby, coming to a time when you will have nothing left to free yourself from.

October 23 1971
Without failure, no spiritual fulfillment.

November 17 1971
The disaster of being Romanian.
The drama of insignificance.

March 30 1972
I have always dreaded, and admired, people who sleep badly.

I have just read that Lenin suffered from insomnia. Now I have a better understanding of his excesses, his obsessions, his intolerance.

June 19 1972
To turn from Romanian to French is like turning from a *prayer* to a *contract*.

September 1 1972
Non-consent to death is the greatest drama of mortals.

At twenty, all I could think about was the extermination of the old; I persist in believing such a thing urgent, but now I would add to it that of the young; with age one has a more complete vision of things.

October 21 1972
My compatriots—elegiac swindlers.

November 14 1972
Without the notion of a failed universe, the spectacle of injustice under every regime would put even an indifferent man in a straitjacket.

*   *   *

AFTERWORD
CIORAN

In the spring of 1990, I was invited to attend the Salon du Livre in Paris, on the occasion of Albin Michel's publication of my first volume in French, *Le thé de Proust.*

The year before my trip there, I had got to know a friend of Cioran's, Edouard Roditi, a fabled pilgrim of letters. It seems he had written to Cioran about me. One day he showed me a surprising message that had come from Cioran, in French, dated 25 September 1989.

"Mon cher ami,

"Thank you for your letter, which has come at just the right moment. Just a few days ago I was struck, or rather deeply shaken, by Norman Manea's piece. It is the best thing I have read on the Romanian nightmare . . . I left Romania fifty years ago, and it is mainly out of masochism that I take an interest in my origins. How can one explain that the shallowest of all nations should have such a destiny?"

Cioran was referring to my essay "Rumänien in 3 (kommentierten) Sätze" ("Romania—Three Lines with Commentary"), which had just appeared in the German magazine *Akzente.* The same issue had also carried a piece by Cioran entitled *"Begegnungen mit Paul Celan"* ("Encounters with Paul Celan"), a coincidence which probably prompted what he wrote to Roditi regarding "the right moment."

Naturally, I wrote Cioran. I always considered him a great writer, even if I had some doubts about his philosophy. He answered with an extremely cordial letter in which he did not forget to stress that his leaving Romania had been the most intelligent act of his life. (*"C'est de loin l'acte le plus intelligent que j'aie jamais commis"*). And, of course, he advised me to come to live in Paris, too ("the ideal place to bungle one's life").

When I telephoned him upon arriving in Paris, he invited me and my wife over to 21 rue l'Odeon, for dinner.

This fierce cynic, who delighted in overturning axioms and

303

canons, values and virtues, was a short, thin, frail man, both amiable and courteous. He who had once written that he would commit suicide if he were a Jew, and who rejected God while admiring the Führer and the Romanian Fascist "Captain," came across as modest, gentle, polite. The sharpshooter so adulated by French literati lived in a student garret. He told us that until a lift was installed a few years earlier he had heroically scrambled up the stairs several times a day—even after midnight when he returned from his long solitary walks that were well known to the district policeman.

My intention was not to ask him anything but to leave him at the mercy of his own nature and words. Still, if the opportunity had arisen, I should have been happy for us to discuss, for instance, the "barbarity of enthusiasm," one of his many striking phrases in *Le mauvais demiurge.* I thought that, even for a nihilistic prophet of the apocalypse, it might have been interesting to consider the relationship between his youthful enthusiasm for barbarism and his later determined skepticism towards civilization, progress and democracy. But we did not come to such complicated and important matters. He seemed to have prepared himself for a relaxed Mozartian evening, drugged with beauty like the Parisian spring. His gaze and gestures, seeking and bestowing admiration, were directed with a delicate touch of gallantry towards my wife, Cella. . . .

Yet, his conversation did not lack in sarcasm. Although he was briefly exhilarated by the anti-Ceausescu "revolution" of 1989, Romania still remained to Cioran "the space of failure, where things were ruined for good"—comments he repeated with visible pleasure. Less expected, given that this was our first meeting, were his caustic remarks about old friends—especially the Romanian philosopher Noica. With excitement in his voice, he enjoyed describing the servility and grotesque flattery in the Maestro's dealings with fellow professors, students and friends; nor did he hold back from telling us, virtual strangers, about some embarrassing visits that the author of *The Romanian Sense of Being* used to make in his way around Paris. According to Cioran, who seemed more condescending than disgusted, the "transcendental" thinker Noica played the role of a loyal defender of the "Greatest Son" of Communist Romania. "What is this you've got against Ceausescu, eh?" Noica (in fact, Cioran's old comrade) is supposed to have asked with almost pious astonishment. Apparently, Noica also kept a little notebook in which he jotted down the names of everyone he met and talked to in Paris, so that later, returning to Romania, he showed gratitude to his connections in the Secret Police who gave him a passport to travel abroad.

The evening continued after midnight, amid anecdotes and para-doxes, under the spell of a host who was not stinting on verve. "What you need now are some literary prizes. Awards! In Paris you arrange literary glory over dinners. At restaurants, the best restau-rants." He could not possibly accept, as he saw it, the scandalous slipshoddedness of a publisher who failed to arrange fancy promo-tional lunch and dinner parties for an author who had come all the way across the ocean. His physical frailty seemed offset by a robust high-born suppleness. He had an open, welcoming air and was enam-ored of Paris and his local *quartier*, happy to enjoy the benefits of a civilization that he never ceased to mock.

Nevertheless, the French publishing house did something for its guest. The next day, Albin Michel had arranged a photo session with Mme. Giles Rolle, a well-known professional. "I know your fellow countryman, Emil Cioran. I have photographed him, too," she cheer-fully told me. "Some of the pictures came out really well—disas-trously well." Cioran had looked at them with delight in his eyes, continued Mme. Rolle, and then torn them all up. "Forbidden! Prohibited! Me, Cioran, smiling? No one should ever see Cioran smiling."

Unfortunately, I wasn't in touch with Cioran after that trip to Paris. Some years later I heard of his long slow agony, the senility in which the former iconoclast and cynic was peacefully slumbering. The exile who had learned perfect French, becoming France's most brilliant contemporary stylist, had suddenly lost his linguistic refuge and started to speak again in Romanian, the language he had been so happy to abandon half a century ago. Was it a new form of Alzheimer's disease? It certainly was, as the Romanian writer Ion Vartic acutely remarked, a "successful regression," about which Cioran had always dreamt. A way of regressing to the state of the unborn and, in the same time, a way of unknowingly returning from exile, coming home to his pre-birth homeland. "Unconsciousness is a homeland," Cioran himself had written.

Then, in a kind of irony of fate, the world's major newspapers announced the death of this skeptic who had always stressed his in-difference to glory and his boredom with the paradoxes of posterity.

In a *New York Times* obituary Susan Sontag—one of the first in America to write about Cioran—observed that he had practiced "a new kind of philosophizing: personal, aphoristic, lyrical, antisys-tematic." She illustrated this with a characteristic Cioran quote:

E. M. Cioran

"However much I have frequented the mystic, deep down I have always sided with the Devil; unable to equal him in power, I have tried to be worthy of him, at least, in insolence, acrimony, arbitrariness and caprice." It was a quotation that combined his rebellious vitality with the provocative mirage of his phrases, their twisted glowing spikes, the antilethargical shudder, the icy irradiation of his ever-youthful prose, his gnomic solitary thought.

I, too, was asked to characterize Cioran. I recalled that one evening we spent together, and the question I did not manage to ask him. In a few sentences, I tried to relate Cioran's evolution to the evolution of our contemporary world, to the watershed represented by World War II. In the issue of the *New York Times* dated 22 June 1993, my comment appeared as a laconic statement: "He was a brilliant rebel and a challenging misanthrope who tried again and again to awaken us to the nothingness of human existence."

Soon after his death, a stormy controversy (called by some participants "Cioran's second death," although it might have been seen rather as a rebirth) arose in the French and Romanian press. It focused on the political extremism of his youthful misanthropy and rebellion, his involvement with Romanian fascism, his outrageous statements about Hitler and Zelea Codreanu, the "Captain" of the infamous Iron Guard, that extreme right-wing Romanian movement of the 1930s, that claimed to be "Christian-Orthodox."

Readers were reminded that he wrote in 1937, "No other politician of today inspires a greater sympathy than Hitler . . . Hitler's merit consists in depriving his nation of its critical spirit," or what he said, in 1940, at the commemoration of his beloved "Captain," whom he saw as a kind of new Messiah: "With exception of Jesus, no other dead figure was more present among the living."

In 1995, Gallimard published *Cioran, l'heretique,* Patrice Bollon's balanced critical analysis of Cioran's life and work. The book provoked a violent debate in the French newspapers. Jean-Paul Enthoven wrote that "the second death of Cioran promises his orphans a vast loneliness"; Bernard-Henry Levy described a meeting, in 1989, at which Cioran seemed very cautious in talking about his past and quite uncomfortable when asked about his extreme right-wing militantism of the thirties and forties. Cioran was passionately defended by Edgar Morin, Andre Comte-Sponville and Francois Furet. The latter wrote: "Cioran is a great writer and a great moralist, whatever his ephemeral commitment to the Iron Guard was." Finally, Alain Etchegoyen explained, on a French television program, without any trace of irony, that "Cioran's main regret was well and nicely expressed through his silence and his pessimism. Opposite to the penitent Stalinists, he had the merit of discretion. The Stalinists maintained their arrogance, which isn't necessarily a philosophical habit."

In Romania the debate was enhanced by the publication, after the collapse of communism, of Cioran's entire work, including a part of his yet unknown correspondence. And the appearance, after his death, in France, of two posthumous books, *Mon Pays* (Gallimard, 1996), and *Cahiers, 1957–1972* (Gallimard, 1997) was, of course, extensively commented on in both countries. These books show that, unlike his fellow Romanian intellectuals with whom he was associated in the right-wing political movement (Eliade, Noica), Cioran was, after the war, continuously obsessed with his "guilty" youth. He viewed his political commitment to the extreme right-wing "Revolution" as a mixture of craziness and stupidity, due to the suffocating environment of his mediocre and apathetic homeland, an oppressive dead end, without past or future. "My Country! I wanted, by hook or by crook, to cavil at her but she wasn't even there for me to cavil to," he wrote in the early 1950s. Thinking again and again about his country, his countrymen and himself, Cioran concludes, in obvious disgust: "I hated my country, I hated everybody and the entire universe: so that, in the end, nothing was left to hate but myself: which I did, in the devious way of desperation." And he adds: "When I look back . . . it is another man whom I abjure now, everything that means 'Me' is now elsewhere, at two thousand leagues from what I was."

As ambiguous or superficial as his statements may still sometimes be (he thinks, for instance, that the "error" of the Iron Guard was "to conceive a future for a place without one," transferring their guilt onto the country and its people, even while he still believes the Iron Guard's martyrs "achieved for themselves a destiny which exempted their country from having one"), it's obvious that, after the war, Cioran was ashamed and burdened by his past political commitment, and that he kept a distance, in fact, from any politial connections.

Yet, what still proved to be a never-ending, complicated and troubled process was the impossibility of taming his genuine, innate nihilism. For better or worse, his nihilism remained the energetic spiritual force behind his creative writing, behind his originality and style. He kept his lonely struggle alive, as a writer, as a performer, a clownish philosopher mocking philosophy, I would say, a solitary *apatride* with a Buster Keaton mask, and as a seducer, of course, even if the seduction was rarely obtained through virtuous means. He was ever the Devil's advocate.

The Romanian writer Marta Petreu remarked recently, in a rigorous, brilliant essay, *"Doctrina legionara si intelighentia interbelica"* (Apostrof, 1998), that Cioran was a heretic even as he was a supporter of the Iron Guard. Knowing too well that the political project of the Iron Guard meant, in the end, a total suppression of freedom, he still wanted to be a "free man." Claiming for *himself* the right to rebel, to be different, unique, above the mob. His "elitism" seemed to be, as Marta Petreu emphasizes, the essential reason for his ultra-reactionary political views of the 1930s and 1940s. "An epoch of boundless liberties, of 'sincere' and extreme democracy, lingering indefinitely, would mean an inevitable collapse of humankind. The mob wants to be ordered about," Cioran wrote in 1937.

The reader of these fragments I selected for *Conjunctions* from *Cahiers* will recognize the obvious separation and also the lasting connection between the young and the old Cioran. Already aging, he seems, at the time of writing these "notes," more sensitive to human suffering, more vulnerable and even more tolerant. His loneliness and lucidity still play with negation, even in some frivolous form, but his melancholy runs deeper as the consequence of a painful knowledge that the end of his earthly, pagan adventure was near. He seems, indeed, "more inclined to accept even the liberal democratic Western world with its quintessential injustice, with its vermin of businessmen and shopkeepers, with its freedoms," as Matei Calinescu wrote in an excellent study, "Reading Cioran" (*Salmagundi*). And yet, Cioran still thinks, in 1960, in *History of Utopia* that: "'Freedoms' prosper only in a sick body politic: tolerance and impotence are synonymous."

As a master of paradox and, therefore, an "anti" type of thinker, a fighter of banality, canons and standards, common sense and common taste, Cioran always followed his stubborn "anti"-ness, even when the result was not necessarily of real spiritual relevance. "Being paradoxical—embracing ideas and opinions that go against the grain, that are shocking to the common sense or to what is more or less generally accepted—becomes an imperative, a categorical aesthetic (and implicitly amoral) imperative, as it were. A certain kind of (theoretical) extremism is always involved," proposed Matei Calinescu.

This may be also a key for reading some of the fragments in our selection from *Cahiers*. It may contribute, in a way, even to the understanding of the most scandalous statement, such as "There is something worse than anti-Semitism: it is anti-anti-Semitism." What exactly does Cioran mean by this? Does he equate anti-Semitism with the gas chambers? Does he see anti-anti-Semitism as a profitable "show," a false rhetoric and demagogical militantism? And can these two be compared? He doesn't qualify the terms with any adjective: neither dark or frivolous or boring anti-Semitism, nor cheap or vigorous or inflated or boring anti-anti-Semitism. The reader should be reminded, at this point, that Cioran's relationship with Jews and their fate was never simple. He never wrote about the Jews in the consistently harsh way he wrote about his fellow Romanians, and we, probably, cannot ask for more from a zealous nihilist and a heretic. Yet, his statements about Jews were always ambiguous and often held double meanings.

In 1937, when Romanian anti-Semitism was booming and the generic iconoclastic Rebel-Cioran already was a supporter of the extreme right-wing political movement, he proved ready to adopt the "banal" view that the Jewish "antinational spirit" was, of course, a threat to the country. He added, however, that another threat was Jewish "superiority." This was a quite daring "paradoxical" statement, at a time when anti-Semitic laws were based on the assumption of the *inferiority* of the "Jewish race," but it was not necessarily a statement of sympathy or solidarity towards the "enemies" of his country. Similarly, he wrote, then, that anti-Semitism was "the greatest tribute paid to the Jews."

During and after the war, Cioran was, it seems, shocked by the Jewish tragedy, by what happened to his Jewish friends (the novelist Mihail Sebastian, who remained in Bucharest; the Romanian-French poet Benjamin Fondane, killed at Auschwitz; the Romanian-German poet Paul Celan, who committed suicide in Paris). In his postwar essay dedicated to the Jews ("A People of Solitaries"), which Susan Sontag considered "surprisingly cursory and high-handed" (a reference to this statement can be found in this *Cahiers* selection), Cioran attempted a kind of codified dialogue with his prewar texts on the same topic. "I found myself loathing them with the fury of a love turned to hate . . . I had only a bookish commiseration for their suffering, and could not divine what was in store for them."

We may assume, perhaps, that after stating in *Cahiers* "I am metaphysically Jewish," he thought he might allow himself the kind of statement with which some real Jews, well known for their bitter-sweet humor and sarcastic self-criticism, would have agreed. So, gambling with negativity, playing tricks on himself and on the entire world . . . equating anti-Semitism with anti-anti-Semitism (and, hard to believe, *even less* than equating) seemed, probably, simply too easy for that promoter of any and all "anti" impulses. He had forgotten, however, that he also introduced himself, in the same notes, as a Mongol, a Hungarian, a Slav, a Central-European, people not known as great friends of the Jews or of "anti-anti-Semites. . . ."

This and other outrageous quotes mix in a very personal way ("implicitly amoral," as Matei Calinescu emphasizes) right and wrong, and also enter into a dialogue with many opposite, contradictory, stimulating thoughts, original ideas, acute questions, in a challenging miscellany of original stylish bravura.

From a nearly one-thousand-page book, different readers would choose different excerpts. Our selection from Cioran's notebooks tries to offer a diverse image of his preoccupations, pleasures and pain in the period covered by the *Cahiers*. The reader will find references to his reading and writing, to his friends and dilemmas, his connection to music and poetry, his productive insomnia and anxiety, his obsessions with Romanians and Jews and Europeans, with belonging and estrangement. This is a fragmented account of the daily and nightly life of a restless soul, a troubled and troubling mind: the thinker as a blasphemous troublemaker, as an uninnocent child of a tragic century.

I would like to express my gratitude to Patrick Camiller, who translated from Romanian my essay "Meeting Cioran," which is partially incorporated in this afterword; and to Bradford Morrow for his generous help and advice with the entire project. Also I thank Richard Howard, Cioran's brilliant translator, for his deft work here, done on short notice.

Three Stories
Mikhail Bulgakov

—Translated from Russian by Anneta Greenlee

TRANSLATOR'S NOTE

Thirty-year-old Mikhail Bulgakov arrived in 1921 in Moscow where he was to live for the rest of his life. Unaware of the troubles that lay ahead for him, he looked forward to life in the capital, where he thought he would earn his living during the day, and write his books and plays late into the night. "A single wish made me rush about this vast and strange capital," Bulgakov wrote in his diary, May 27, 1924. "To find work that would feed me. And I was always able to find it . . . work most fantastical and brief, like galloping consumption. . . ."

In 1925 Bulgakov began working for Gudok *(A Horn), a newspaper published by the Union of Railroad Workers, where he started out as an editor, and later became a writer of short satirical stories which he based on letters sent in by* Gudok *journalists.*

The three stories in this issue of Conjunctions *first appeared in* Gudok *in 1925, and have never before been translated into English. They remained uncollected in Russia, and for all intents and purposes were unavailable to scholars until a few years ago. Extant copies of* Gudok *are extremely rare. Indeed, before Glasnost, special permits were required to gain access to the archives they were kept in. These stories conjure themes and images found in the author's later work. The séance in "Mademoiselle Janna" reminds us of the variété show in* The Master and Margarita, *where the audience is also mercilessly duped. The hilarious dialogue in "Jumping the Line," defying logic and yet so real, is mirrored in the descriptions of the Soviet bureaucrats and the half-educated bores in works such as* The Heart of a Dog *and* The Fatal Eggs. *The spine-chilling joke of a dream in "The Conductor and the Member of the Imperial Family" becomes phantasmagoric reality in Bulgakov's play* Flight.

Bulgakov's stories constitute an entire Theater of Satire. A great lover of the stage, he writes as if the action were unfolding before

311

his eyes. *This theatrical quality is particularly striking in "Jumping the Line," which consists entirely of dialogue. Descriptions are external, very much like stage directions; characters and situations are highly stylized. These stories puzzled Soviet critics, who often could not make up their minds whether or not Bulgakov was criticizing the "New Man" of Soviet society. There is a universal quality in Bulgakov's social types—they are mirrors of human foibles and paradoxes of existence.*

* * *

MADEMOISELLE JANNA

> We had a performance at our club at the train station in the town of Z, with a clairvoyant called Mademoiselle Janna. She read people's minds and made 150 rubles in a single evening.
>
> —*A Reporter of the People*

THE AUDIENCE FROZE. A lady in a purple dress and red stockings appeared on stage with anxious, made-up eyes, and behind her a perky, moth-eaten-looking impresario in striped pants with a chrysanthemum in his buttonhole. The impresario darted his eyes left and then right, bent over and whispered into Mademoiselle Janna's ear:

"In the first row, the bald one with the paper collar—he's the second deputy station master. He recently proposed, she turned him down. A certain Nourotchka. (*To the audience, loudly*): Greetings, Ladies and Gentlemen! I have the great honor to introduce the famous clairvoyant and medium, Mamselle Janna of Paris and Sicily. She can see the past, the present and the future, and on top of that, our most intimate family secrets!"

The audience went pale.

(*To Mademoiselle Janna*): "Make your face mysterious, you idiot. (*To the audience*): However, you must not think that here we have some kind of witchcraft or other miracle or something. Not at all, for miracles do not exist. (*To Mademoiselle Janna*): Didn't I tell you a thousand times to wear a bracelet for the show? (*To the audience*): Everything, with the permission of the Local Party Committee and the Commission for Culture and Education, is based exclusively on the powers of nature. It consists of vitalopathy based on hypnotism, as it is taught by India's fakirs, who are oppressed by English imperialism. (*To Mademoiselle Janna, in a whisper*): The woman under the poster, to the side, the one with the tiny purse! Her husband is having an affair at the next train station. (*To the audience*): If anybody should wish to know deep family secrets, please direct your questions to me, and I will transmit them by means of hypnotism, having put the famous Mademoiselle Janna to sleep . . . please, Mademoiselle, take a seat . . . one at a time, citizens! One, two, three—Yes! You are beginning to feel sleepy. (*He makes a gesture with his hands as if he were about to stick his fingers in Mademoiselle Janna's eyes.*) Ladies and Gentlemen! You have before you a most extraordinary example of occult science! (*To Mademoiselle Janna, in a whisper*): Fall alseep already! How long are you going to keep staring at me? (*To the audience*): So, she's asleep. Let's begin!"

In the dead silence the station master stood up, went purple, then white, and then asked in a voice wild with fear: "What is the most important event in my life right now?"

(*The impresario to Mademoiselle Janna*): "Keep looking at my fingers, you idiot!" ·

The impresario twirled his index finger under his chrysanthemum buttonhole, then made some mysterious signs with his fingers which spelled out "bro-ken."

"Your heart has been broken by a perfidious woman!" Mademoiselle Janna spoke in a graveyard voice, as if in a dream.

The impresario blinked approvingly. The audience moaned and turned its eyes on the miserable deputy station master.

"What is her name?" the rejected deputy station master asked in a hoarse voice.

"Nou-ro-tch-ka," the impresario's fingers spelled out near his jacket's lapel.

"Nourotchka!" Mademoiselle Janna answered firmly.

The deputy station master rose from his seat, his face all green. He looked gloomily in all directions, and, dropping his hat and a pack of cigarettes, marched out.

"Will I ever marry?" a hysterical woman's voice suddenly shouted from the audience. "Please tell me, my dear Mamselle Janna!"

The impresario appraised the woman with the eye of a connoisseur. He eyed the pimple on her nose, her thin yellow hair and her crooked back. He stuck his thumb between his index and middle finger next to his chrysanthemum buttonhole.

"No, you won't!" Mademoiselle Janna said.

The audience thundered like a squadron crossing a bridge, and the mortified woman scuttled out.

The woman with the tiny purse moved away from the posters by the wall and sneaked up to Mademoiselle Janna.

"Dasha darling, don't!" a man's hoarse whisper came from the crowd.

"No! I will! I'm going to find out all about your tricks and treachery!" the owner of the tiny purse shouted. "Tell me, Mademoiselle! Is my husband cheating on me?"

The impresario eyed the husband, glanced into his embarrassed little eyes, considered the deep crimson of his face and crossed his fingers, which meant yes.

"He is cheating!" Mademoiselle Janna answered with a sigh.

"With whom?" Dasha asked in an ominous voice.

"What the hell is her name?" the impresario thought. "Damn it! . . . Oh, yes, yes, yes, the wife of that . . . damn! . . . Yes! Anna!"

"Dear J . . . anna, please tell us, J . . . anna, with whom the lady's husband is cheating?"

"With Anna," Mademoiselle Janna said with aplomb.

"I knew it! I knew it!" Dasha sobbed. "I've had my suspicions for some time now! You bastard!"

With these words she slammed the tiny purse on her husband's right well-shaven cheek.

The audience roared with laughter.

JUMPING THE LINE

There was a line outside the Moscow Criminal Investigations Department.

"Oh . . . Geez . . . all this waiting and waiting!"

"Even here there's a line!"

"What can you do? Do you happen to be a bookkeeper, if you don't mind my asking?"

"Nope, I'm a cashier."

"Did you come to get arrested?"

"Yeah, what else!"

"That's good. So how much were you caught with, if you don't mind my asking?"

"Three thousand smackers."

"That's nothing, young man. You'll just get a year. But if you take your heartfelt repentance into consideration . . . and the fact that the Bolshevik Anniversary is coming up . . . so, all in all, you'll do three months, and then, the sweet bird of freedom!"

"You sure? You're comforting me no end. I was already real desperate. Yesterday I went to see a lawyer, and he scared the living daylights out of me—the article, he tells me, is such that you won't get away with less than two years' hard labor."

"Pure twaddle, young man! Trust my experience. Hey, you there! Where do you think you're going? Get back in line!"

"Citizens! Let me pass! I filched some official money! My conscience is biting me!"

"Everyone's conscience is biting them! You're not the only one!"

"I squandered the entire holdings of the Moscow Agrarian Industry Store in drink!" a low voice kept mumbling.

"Quite a fellow, aren't you! You'll pay for it now! You'll never see the light of day again!"

"That's not true! What if I'm ignorant? And not educated? And there are hereditary social conditions, huh? And my previous conviction? And being an alcoholic?"

"How come they put you, an alcoholic, in charge of the wine store?"

"I did warn them!"

"Hey you! Where do you think you're going?"

"Citizen Officer! I am tortured by remorse!"

"Hey, stop pushing! I'm tortured too!"

"Excuse me! I've been waiting here since ten in the morning to get arrested!"

"Just give me your last name, place of employment, amount!"

"Fioletov, Misha, tortured by remorseful conscience!"

"How much?"

"In Makrettrest—two hundred smackers."

"Sidorchuk! Process this Fioletov!"

"May I take my toothbrush with me?"

"You may! And you, what was the amount?"

"Seven people."

"A family?"

"Exactly."

"And how much was it you took?"

"Two hundred in cash, a robe, a watch and some candlesticks."

"I don't get it. An official's robe?"

"What do you mean? Us guys don't deal with officials. It was a private family. Shtippelman."

"You're Shtippelman?"

"Me? No!"

"Then what's Shtippelman got to do with it?"

"What he's got to do with it is we knifed him. I'm reporting seven people: his wife, five children and their granny."

"Sidorchuk! Kakhrushin! Take preventive measures! Now!"

"Excuse me, Citizen Officer! Why is this man getting preferential treatment?"

"Please, citizens! Be conscientious! This man is a murderer!"

"Big deal! You're telling us he's a big shot or something? For all you know *I* might have blown up a state institution!"

"This is an outrage! Bureaucracy! We will complain!"

THE CONDUCTOR AND THE
MEMBER OF THE IMPERIAL FAMILY

> Conductors on the Moscow-Byelorussian-Baltic Railroad have been issued Ordinance No. 85, printed in the prerevolutionary days of the Ministry of Transportation, requiring them to provide deferential treatment to members of the Imperial Family.
>
> —*A Reporter of the People*

The conductors were completely bewildered.

The paper that had arrived from the regional center was shiny, thick and official. And on the paper was printed: "He who comes upon a member of the Railroad Workers Union must greet him with a polite bow of the head and with the following words: 'Greetings, comrade!' You may add the name, if the latter is known.

"And if it should so happen that a Member of the Imperial Family appears, you will salute him according to Ordinance No. 85 with the following words: 'Long live your Imperial Highness!'

"And if, beyond all expectations, it should turn out to be the Emperor himself, replace the word 'Highness' with the word 'Majesty.' "

Having received this paper, Khvostikov went home, and was so aggravated that he immediately fell asleep. And as soon as he fell asleep, he found himself on the platform of the railway station. Then the train came.

"What a beautiful train," Khvostikov thought, "I'd love to know what kind of person would arrive on a train like this!"

And no sooner had he thought these words than the plate-glass windows blazed with electricity, the doors opened and out of the blue car stepped the Emperor in person. A shining crown sat rakishly on his head, and a white ermine fur with tails was wrapped around his shoulders. His retinue, spurs clicking and medals glittering, came shuffling along behind him.

"Goodness gracious, what is going on here?" Khvostikov thought, and froze.

"I say! What a surprise!" the Emperor said, staring right at Khvostikov. "If my eyes do not deceive me, we have here my former loyal subject, currently Comrade Conductor Khvostikov! Greetings, my dear fellow!"

"Help . . . Long live . . . Good grief . . . Your . . . I'm finished, and my little children too . . . Imperial Majesty!" Khvostikov uttered, his lips turning completely blue.

"Look cheerful, you swine, when you address the Emperor!" a voice from the retinue hissed.

Khvostikov tried to put on a cheerful face. The cheerfulness looked rather bizarre. His mouth twisted to the right, and his left eye closed of its own volition.

"So, how have things been with you, my dear Khvostikov?" the Emperor inquired.

"My very humblest thanks," Khvostikov, half dead, answered soundlessly.

"Is everything all right?" the Emperor continued. "How is the Mutual Help Fund doing? Lots of general meetings?"

"Everything in order!" Khvostikov reported.

"Haven't you joined the Party yet?" the Emperor asked.

"Definitely not."

"But you do sympathize, don't you?" the Emperor inquired with a smile that touched Khvostikov's spine with a frost of at least five below zero.

"Answer without stammering, you swine!" a voice from behind the Emperor suggested.

"I do, but just a little," Khvostikov said.

"Aha! Just a little! So tell me, if you could, my dear Khvostikov. Whose portrait is that pinned to your breast?"

"This is . . . this is, to some extent, Comrade Kamenev," Khvostikov answered, covering Kamenev's pin with his palm.

"I see!" the Emperor said. "Very nice indeed. By the way, do you have any luggage ropes?"

"Most certainly," Khvostikov answered, feeling the chill in his stomach now.

"Well then! Take this son of a bitch and hang him on the train brake with the luggage rope!" the Emperor ordered.

"But why, Comrade Emperor?" Khvostikov asked, and all his thoughts turned topsy-turvy.

"For everything!" the Emperor replied with gusto. "For the Trade Union, for 'Rise all you accursed . . . ,'" for the Mutual Help Fund, for 'The world of oppression we will destroy,' for the pin, for 'To the very foundation' and . . . for all the rest. Seize him!"

"But I have a wife and small children, Your Comeraderie!" Khvostikov pleaded.

"Don't worry about your children and your wife," the Emperor consoled him, "we'll hang them, too. I have a strong feeling, and I can see it just by looking at you, that your children are Young Pioneers. Aren't they?"

"Pi . . . ," Khvostikov answered like a telephone receiver.

Ten hands grabbed him.

"Help!" Khvostikov screamed, as if his throat were being cut.

And then he woke up.

Bathed in cold sweat.

Frana
Hermann Broch

—*Translated from German by Susan Gillespie*

TRANSLATOR'S NOTE

The great Viennese writer Hermann Broch did not publish his first novel, The Sleepwalkers, *until he was forty-four, after selling the family textile mill where he had worked for twenty-four years. He was a prodigious writer on philosophy, culture, ethics and politics and considered these activities more important than his epochal novels, including* The Death of Virgil *(1945). "Frana," which was conceived in 1907 during a three-month study tour of cotton markets in the southern United States, belies his comment that he "learned nothing" on the trip. Broch, who was the son of wealthy Jewish parents with their roots in Moravia (hence the Czech grandmother), was a convert to Catholicism. He was jailed during the* Anschluss, *but was able to emigrate to America, where he spent the remainder of his life in Princeton, New Jersey, and New Haven, Connecticut.*

"Frana" was published in 1980 as part of the Suhrkamp Kommentierte Werkausgabe. *It appears here for the first time in English.*

* * *

"OH LITTLE BIRD so swift, my little bird of parting . . ." Grandmother sang in Czech, and it sounded the way it did at home in Koniggratz.

Home? Home was here in Alabama, home was this house, where you have been living for half a year, differently constructed from the houses in Koniggratz, with a different smell.

Frana looks out the window. A horse-drawn tram with an open green car ambles past in the direction of town. Between the tracks are little dunes of yellow sand into which the horse's hooves sink with every step, the soft dust rises to the dappled belly, which has already turned quite yellow.

At home there was no horse-drawn tram. But no, home is here.

And here you don't have to go to school. And many things still recall the circus that came to Koniggratz two years before, black men and yellow *manège* dust and a music that is in the air even when you don't hear anything. Like during the pauses in the circus. Too bad that all this is slowly fading.

"Frana, Franischku!" Grandmother is calling.

"Yes, Grandma," Frana replies in Czech and once again he is surprised at this language, which begins to feel uncomfortable in your mouth. There were some things Grandmother had to say twice before you understood them.

1901, September, nine years, two months and six days old; six months in a new domicile.

Grandmother asks Frana to fetch her some vinegar and salt from the store, and Frana asks for money with which to do so. This is not so simple, for Grandmother still reckons in guilders, although this coin long ago fell into disuse in Austria and Koniggratz, Grandmother's private currency. To be sure, she has taught it to Frana; but here you have to pay for your purchases in dollars and cents.

Finally Frana clutches two dimes and a few pennies tight in his fist and sets off, down along the dusty road, whose opposite side has no sidewalk, but instead the tram track running along the ditch. Beyond the ditch stretches the barbed-wire fence of the factory. To the left, the sidewalk is flanked by a thorny hedge; there are some breaks in the latter, so you can observe the various sights of nature and culture, a grovelike plot of cleared land dotted with transparent trees of a kind not commonly found in Koniggratz, and scattered among them, although keeping somewhat closer to the road, were houses, tin-roofed shacks, wagon sheds, stalls, all strewn about in disorderly fashion without fence or enclosure. Frana notices this because his own house lies next to the road, neat and proper; if he had made his home here this would have become his natural, not mysterious stomping ground.

Far below, a tram appears, going in the opposite direction to the one that has just driven off down the hill. Frana crosses the street and lies down flat and long in the ditch. In the factory the spindles are humming, the setup machines drone dully, the flyers click brightly, from time to time one or several looms clatter, all against a background of rustling, rolling transmission belts. These are sounds that Frana can distinguish quite easily, he is familiar with them from Koniggratz, and since the mill began operating a few weeks ago—in the last few days a couple of looms have even started up—it seems to Frana as if his hometown were at the point of gradually taking shape here, like a stage set, and as if his father had been entrusted with this mission, for his father was the foreman at the spinning mill, and his mother was supposed to teach the black girls Bohemian weaving. That is a serious thing, and Frana in the ditch pricks his ears toward the factory and waits. Waits for the horse-drawn tram. This takes a fairly long time, even if only exactly six minutes pass before the horse brings the tram up to where he lies, but they are minutes filled with tension: ear to the ground to monitor the tram's approach, first you hear the soft tap-tapping of the hooves, then the rolling of the iron wheels on the rails, their rhythmic beat as they strike the rails, then the muffled sound in the earth mingles with the open sound that travels through the air, with the squeaking and rasping of the springs, and now it is here, rattling—, the horse snorts, you see the hooves and the slightly matted legs, you wait for it to make a false step and strike you dead, the gray running boards of the tram glide away over you, you hear the voices of the passengers, one more especially hair-raising screech of the entire iron carriage, and then the whole exciting business is over, borne off toward East Hill, which lies in immeasurable distance, where the tramway turn-around is, a place only adventurers go. Frana lies there still for a few moments more before he crawls out of the ditch and sets off for town and the store.

The store is on the left side of the street, near the end of the grove of trees, a big shed with barrels and sacks lying out front, open barrels with tomatoes and others with apples, on the veranda hang the big bunches of bananas, six for ten cents, and in the store you get chewing gum. In Koniggratz there were neither bananas nor chewing gum, on the other hand there were people like Vilim Knize and Arne Skrensky, and there was Milena Zlinova, and not one of the three of them had ever heard of chewing gum or bananas. When Frana is rich, he will send Milena chewing gum and along with it he will write her a letter in English.

Here, at least, there is Charley Buckle. He is the son of the proprietor and wears brown overalls; there are others too, above all a bunch of pickininnies, who, if you are seeing them for the first time, are hard to tell apart and although they are friendly and always ready to play—this Frana had already figured out—must be treated with disdain. A couple of them are forever standing in front of the store, and when they have money they buy sugar cane, whose availability is another charm of this circus country. And when Buckle the father steps out of the store they run away, for they have often stolen apples from the barrels, and the elder Buckle has set up a kind of standing criminal court for them; whenever he finds one of the black boys by the barrels, he boxes his ears.

From all of them Frana has learned English, not a beautiful English, certainly no Oxford English, but a regular Southern drawl that he further embellishes with his singsong Czech accent and, when a word fails him, he patches with scraps of Czech expressions. But his reputation is none the worse for this, here people are accustomed to such things, and besides, fists are more important than language.

Charley stands on the counter of the store arranging the whips that hang from the ceiling. This is an enviable activity, hence he turns a blind eye to the newcomer. Frana goes over to the man behind the counter, the greenish Thomas O'Donnors, whose breath usually smells, and makes his purchases. When he has paid, he gives the dignified Charles a good sharp pinch in the calves, just because they are so invitingly within reach there on the counter, hears with satisfaction the shout of rage, evades the kicking foot, and with as much dignity and as little acknowledgment as Charley had paid him before, he leaves behind the site of his mercantile and social activities, with the bottle of vinegar and the packet of salt in his hand.

Three Poems
Elizabeth Bishop

—Edited by Alice Quinn

EDITOR'S NOTE

These previously unpublished poems are among the many to be found in the author's notebooks and papers bequeathed to the Vassar College Library.

Bishop jotted "Seville, 1936" beside the title "In a Room," dating it to a trip she and her friend Louise Crane took to Spain just three months before the Civil War was declared. (She wrote to a friend, "The prettiest Baroque chapel in Seville has just been saved from burning up—the ceiling all scorched.")

Around this time, she had begun translating Rimbaud. Her poem "The Man-Moth" had been accepted by Bryher's new quarterly in London, Life and Letters Today. She was reading stories by Henry James, poems by D. H. Lawrence and Wallace Stevens's new book, Ideas of Order. The two shorter poems here are undated, but Bishop's longtime editor, Robert Giroux, says that "eye-fee" would be the local pronunciation of "hi-fi" in Brazil, where Bishop lived with her companion, Lota de Macedo Soares.

"A Lovely Finish" is, most likely, a love poem to Lota written in Brazil in the 1950s.

* * *

FOREIGN-DOMESTIC

I listen to the sweet "eye-fee."
From where I'm sitting I can see
across the hallway in your room
two bare feet upon the bed,
arranged as if someone were dead
—a non-crusader on a tomb.
I get up, take a further look.
You're reading a "detective book,"

so that's all right. I settle back.
The needle in its destined track
stands true and from the daedal plate
an oboe starts to celebrate
escape from the violin's traps
a bit too easily perhaps
for twentieth-century taste, but then
Vivaldi pulls him down again.
Said Blake, "And mutual fear brings peace,
Till the selfish loves increase . . ."

A LOVELY FINISH

A lovely finish I have seen
upon a sand flat glassed with sky,
or with a gold-leaf film of sea
re-brushed, re-grained by random cloud.
Can one accuse of artifice
such finishes and surfaces?

When in the dawn you turned to speak
and waited for my teeth to touch
the sugared coolness on that cheek
—the other cheek—I found in such
deliberation of caress
the utmost of your worldliness.

324

IN A ROOM

There was a stain on the ceiling
        Over the bed
        Shaped like a rhinoceros head
With a jagged horn and a trumpet in his mouth.
        The trumpet had blown, without "feeling,"

All the gilt plaster-work, hoarsely
        From his jaw.
        In the morning I saw
Over my head the brilliant results of his music:
        A molding, constructed as coarsely

As an opera-house balustrade.
        Off-center because
        What was one room now was
Three or four rooms of unequal sizes,
        The big chandelier displayed

Its large branched star, snow-flake plan.
        Brassy-gold,
        But with no lamp to hold.
Under the molding the two rusted pipes
        Of the plumbing arrangements ran

To the closet in the corner and bored
        Within it.
        Several times every minute
The hobgoblin toilet trickled and splashed,
        Flushed of its own accord.

The floor was dark red stone, damp and uneven.
        Near one wall
        For no reason at all
A heavy iron chain hung halfway down from the ceiling,
        Giving a medieval sensation of heaven.

One electric light bulb alone was provided.
        Under the light

Elizabeth Bishop

Perpetually, day and night,
All the time I lived there, five flies held a dance.
In unhurried orbits they glided

Like five planets, only both back and forwards:
On the track
They let themselves drift back.
Then began again. Their sound was a boring sentence
Emphasized over and over on the wrong words.

I dried my stockings on the balcony and kept
Untidy piles
Of newspapers on the red tiles
In the beautiful white marble fireplace, with its shelf
Upheld on scallop shells. At night I slept

On the great lumpy bed, in a range of mountains.
And had
The most remarkably bad
Dreams of my whole life, while from the water-closet
Came sounds of far-off squalls and fountains.

When not sleeping, I observed that
All night
Fine gold whiskers of light
Converged on the ceiling from the next room, pricking out
That molding, like a curious cat.

A man and his wife sat up late in there; I could hear
Them fighting
In low voices, and a continuous writing,
"Scratch-scratch-scratch," going on, while they drank
Bottle after bottle of beer.

In the darkness the five flies spoke
Of Revelations
In their hopeless conversations,
Of the gilded beauties of heaven, and the blackness of hell, too,
till thinking
"But here I am in my room," I awoke.

—Seville, 1936

Of Monotony
Louis *Couperus*

—*Translated from Dutch by Duncan Dobbelmann*

TRANSLATOR'S NOTE

Born in The Hague, Louis Marie Anne Couperus (1863–1923) can fittingly be seen as the (only slightly delayed) Dutch answer to Oscar Wilde. Like Wilde, Couperus was well known as a dandy. Couperus also spent much time abroad: as a teenager he lived for a few years in the Dutch East Indies, as an adult he made frequent voyages to the Far East and lived in France and Italy for more than ten years. The most important—and striking—similarity between the two writers is their delightful ability to ironize philosophy by foregrounding the fascinating idiosyncrasies of character to be found in their narrator(s). Such is the case with "Of Monotony," a piece which, like many which Couperus wrote in serial form for Dutch newspapers, mixes autobiography with armchair philosophy. After reading only a few of the serials, however, a certain coyness quickly becomes apparent: the biographical references suddenly seem less reliable, and the philosophy accordingly less casual. Many of Couperus's novels and travelogues were skillfully and generously translated into English during the first quarter of the twentieth century, while his short stories, arabesques and serials—among which some of his best work is to be found—prove much more scarce. This is "Of Monotony"'s first appearance in English.

* * *

THIS IS ABOUT the monotony of hours and days, of people and things, of souls and their emotions. This is about gruesome monotony which the gods, just as people after them, have invented and arranged, in order to make our lives unbearable with regularity and natural laws and such.

This is about the monotony of the seasons, which alternate with the most unrelenting monotony. Never does spring suddenly blossom, like a wonder, in the month of December. Never does the beauty of a landscape of ice surprise us just after we have eaten a peach. The seasons follow on the heels of one another as they have done throughout the ages since the earth has orbited the sun. Never has the sun orbited the earth, for instance, or so it is alleged. . . .

The seasons bring neither wonder nor surprise. They bring the monotonous days which pile up on us. Every day begins with morning, and each morning I am compelled to take my shower and put on my clothes. . . .

Monotony paralyzes every spontaneous flight of my soul in the morning. How then to give her flight during the remainder of the day? Like a slave, my corporality, already often stronger than my soul, has bathed and clothed itself. A breakfast awaits me every morning, at the same hour—just about—. If only, for once, a supper awaited me, with oysters, game and champagne! Oh well, it probably wouldn't appeal to me anyway. . . .

I am monotony's slave. Monotony is the gray, shrouded matron who regulates my entire life with boredom. She allows me, once I have dressed myself—and not before—to go out into the street. The street rises around me like yesterday. Never once has the street become an enchanted wood, and why after all doesn't the street turn into an enchanted wood? Hoogstraat always remains Hoogstraat and Scheveningsche Weg never leads to any other surprise than the sea. The sea is never monotonic—she is always different—but how monotonous she is in her changeability! Her changeability is monotony: she never does anything but change in tint and tone. I can't stand her these days because of this repetitive whimsicality. . . .

My hours revolve with monotonous occupations, activities and recreations. If my lunch isn't ready at one o'clock, I'm unsatisfied with that breach of monotony in my life, and if it is ready, the undisturbed regularity of monotony irritates me. We have divided the day into columns of mornings, afternoons, evenings, nights. The nights are always dark. At twelve o'clock it is always twelve o'clock.

I am always myself. It's hopelessly monotonous always to be myself. Why don't I live a hundred existences? If only I were someone else every day! If only tomorrow morning were presently to become a party, a night of orgy, and if, for once, as soon as I opened my eyes in the morning, I were to find myself a Roman emperior being worshipped, with incense burning, or . . . a young goat-herder who lets his goats graze along the ancient coasts of Laconia. . . . Or a bird in flight, a flower blooming, a waterdrop . . . Good heavens, I would even like to be a cricket, a normal cricket chirping in the garden, or, if necessary, Lucrezia Borgia in an imaginary Renaissance. But I am always myself. The same chains bind me: every day, every hour. I even have a fairly enviable existence, but I find it hopelessly monotonous. Every once in a while I can get up a bit earlier or go to bed a bit later, but that changes nothing about the monotony which tyrannically rules and regulates my poor life. I also bear my name for my entire life. I have sometimes taken on another name on my travels, in order to put up some resistance to the unrelenting monotony of my name, but . . . then I couldn't pick up my letters at the post office. That was very annoying, and I cursed my infringement upon monotony. . . .

Actually, I've always inhabited the same body. It has grown somewhat since childhood and changed slightly over the years, but, closely inspected, it has remained the same. In this body I have always dragged along the same soul.

I wouldn't want to trade my body-and-soul for some other physical-psychic combination. But I would want to adopt thousands of other appearances and still remain myself. I'm so used to my body-and-soul-monotony that I would take on the variousness of existence-and-being as if it were just a masquerade. I am the servant, the slave of my monotony.

I am, monotonously and unchangeably, always a man, a Dutchman, a writer, someone from a good family, and I always have the same vices and virtues. Sometimes they bore me very much with their monotony. They sound in me again and again with the same tone; they never change in tint. Now, today, for once I would like not to be a man, a Dutchman, a writer or from a good family. . . . But I am such a servant and slave to my monotony that I cannot now say what I would want to be and how I would want my vices and virtues changed in tint and tone.

I think I would most like to be a magician. If I only knew where magic is studied! I would sell my soul to devil or demon to get magical powers. To become invisible now and then by a flick of the wrist. . . . To conjure up a sudden Moorish palace in the clouds in which only myself and my love of the moment would be allowed to live. To disallow the pillars to stand immovable in monotonous rows but, with a gesture of my staff, to make them dance a cracking tango around us. To have stiff pillars bend and turn with agile voluptuousness. To transform the rational monotony of life and world, with a

329

magic word, into the glorious madness of ceaseless metamorphosis. To make waves out of clouds, and to make a crystal palace floor out of the unbearable sea, over which the true, varying choruses of multiplicity and thousandtonality would float. To bathe my tired soul filled with spleen—a spleen resulting from monotony—in the prismatic-colored bath of endless change.

The tiresomeness, the boredom of being what one is on the day after yesterday, to go down the unrelenting road and have to be thankful, one's whole life, for monotony, for it usually demands thankfulness. It rings the monotonous bell of our small prosperity, our minimal luck; it doesn't want the wonder and the various ecstasies, and if we dare not to be thankful, it breaks its baker's melody, its nursery rhyme—which is supposed to make us drowsy in our shrill longings—off, with a false tone, and leaves us standing in desperation and cowardly nostalgia for it and its oppressive gifts and goodnesses. Oh, to break with monotony forever!

Come with me; I am the magician! Come with me, you tired and bored! I have now sold my soul: I know the magic which will conjure up eternal change for you, the change of tint, the change of tone, the luxury of eternal surprise. Together we will be who we want to be, we will have what we will have, repeatedly; our loves and our desires will change, repeatedly; our magic castles will flow in and through each other, repeatedly; we will pick grapes among the Northern Lights on icebergs which float in the Mediterranean Sea; we will be mad with changing moods; the stars will rain through each other, and the sea will celebrate her ascension and drift among the clouds. The moon will lie down at our feet like a pale mirror and reflect every metamorphosis of our selves and our being. We will have reached what we longed for: we will be various and powerful through my magic: mornings will shine fantastically with thick masses of clouds and nights will be luxurious with the darkness of thousands of shining suns; every change that you desire I will conjure up for you! I will change you from prince to beggar and from beggar to fakir, from man to woman and woman to man, I will make rubies bloom from lotus stems, and in your feelings, passions and emotions you won't recognize your own soul! I will make the universe, the world, life, change, alter, swarm and transform for you until Monotony itself shall resound with millions of tones and glitter with billions of tints.

*

However, I will not be able to make this variation in your soul, which will after all still remain your own:

I will not be able to give you Satisfaction and Luck. And you will still continue, as will I, who was your magician, to long for the one inaccessible change—in air, in light, in yourself or in whom, or whatever—which would give you, not the magic dazzle, but true happiness and contentment.

You tired and bored, I have deceived you: I was a powerless magician. Tomorrow, along with me, you will get out of your bed a little earlier or later than today, you will have breakfast as always and clothe yourself as always and your occupations and recreations will await you as always and it will be summer if it is summer and it will become evening when evening must come and the air and the sea and the clouds and the waves will surely change, but your soul will feel the same as it always has and it will, after the dazzlement with which I deceived you, be piously, cowardly thankful to Monotony, that matron in her makeshift cloak who cannot be dispelled, for returning and taking you by the hand to the gray path of days and hours which unfurls before you—to the pale, vague Unknown, which you cannot know or see through, to the End, to the mysterious End. . . .

Eugenia onegini

моей душенька

The House Was There
Vladimir Nabokov

—With an afterword by Sarah Funke

The house was there. Right there. I never
imagined the place would have changed so
completely. ~~Was it seventeen~~ How dread-
ful--I don't recognize a thing. No use walking
any farther. Sorry, Hopkinson, to have made you
come such a long way. I had been looking forward
to a perfect orgy of nostalgia and recognition!
That man over there seems to be growing suspicious,
Speak to him. Turisti'. Amerikantsi'. Oh, wait a
minute. Tell him I am a ghost. You surely know
the Russian for "ghost"? Mechta. Prizrak. Metafizicheskiy kapitalist. Run, Hopkinson!

Vladimir Nabokov
1951

---

*The house was there. Right there. I never imagined the place
would have changed so completely. How dreadful—I don't recognize a thing. No use walking any farther. Sorry, Hopkinson, to
have made you come such a long way. I had been looking forward
to a perfect orgy of nostalgia and recognition! That man over there
seems to be growing suspicious. Speak to him. Turisti'. Amerikantsi'. Oh, wait a minute. Tell him I am a ghost. You surely
know the Russian for "ghost"? Mechta. Prizrak. Metafizicheskiy
kapitalist. Run, Hopkinson!*

Vladimir Nabokov

* * *

The typescript of this never-before published introduction to *Conclusive Evidence* (1951) was found clipped to the title page of the dedication copy of that book, in the Nabokov family library. *Conclusive Evidence* was first serialized in various periodicals, primarily the *New Yorker*. This series of articles provided the foundation for what grew to be a series of memoirs; each new installment confirmed Nabokov as the foremost mnemaniac writing in English. A revised and translated Russian version, *Drugie Berega [Other Shores]* followed in 1954, with a foreword in Russian. *Speak, Memory: An Autobiography Revisited*, retranslated and further revised, appeared in 1966 with a new foreword explaining the work's evolution. Nabokov planned a sequel, *Speak On, Memory*, to cover his twenty-year sojourn in the States, but at his death in 1977 he had completed only jottings on note cards, now in the archive at the Berg Collection at the New York Public Library. The original poetic introduction, published here for the first time in English, is unlike the explanatory forewords he would write for many subsequent works, and projects a return to Russia that Nabokov never undertook.

The "house" was the Nabokovs' country retreat at Vyra, fifty miles outside St. Petersburg, vividly described in *Conclusive Evidence* as Nabokov remembered it and depicted by his sketched map on the endpapers of the 1966 revision. The estate was converted into an orphanage and school after Nabokov and his family joined the Russian emigration. During World War II the Germans commandeered it for their headquarters, and burned it to the ground when they abandoned it in 1944. Brian Boyd writes, "Today where Vyra stood there is nothing but a scraggly clump of trees" (*The Russian Years*).

"The House Was There" was just one among many potential titles Nabokov proposed to Victor Gollancz, who planned to bring out the first English edition of *Conclusive Evidence* under a new title that same year. Nabokov had titled the first edition as "conclusive evidence of my having existed"; he admitted to a Gollancz representative that "none of my friends liked 'Conclusive Evidence,'" and offered the following new suggestions: "Clues"; "The Rainbow Edge"; "The Prismatic Edge"; "The Moulted Feather"; "Nabokov's

Opening"; "Emblemata"; and Nabokov's own favorite, "Speak, Mnemosyne!," which was ultimately rejected on the grounds that readers wouldn't buy what they couldn't pronounce.

Nabokov inscribed to his wife, Véra, the copy of *Conclusive Evidence* to which this typescript was affixed. Like many of the scores of books he inscribed to Véra, this copy bears a hand-drawn butterfly, reproduced here. The unique species is named "Eugenia onegini," for Pushkin's classic, and betrays Nabokov's life-long study of lepidoptera as well as his attachment to the father of Russian literature: after spending nearly a decade preparing his first controversial translation of *Eugene Onegin* (1964), he had to wait ten more years to see his revised edition in print, enduring interminable publication delays each time.

Words Nabokov underlined in his "discarded introduction" have been italicized here. While the Russian words "Turisti' " and "Amerikantsi' " need no translation, "Mechta. Prizrak. Metafizicheskiy kapitalist" may be translated, "A dream. A spector. A metaphysical capitalist."

Three Stories
Federigo Tozzi

—Translated from Italian with an
afterword by Minna Proctor

THE IDIOT

FIOCCO, THE IDIOT—thirty years old and still fighting with the other children because they wouldn't leave him alone in the courtyard to cut figures out of playing cards with a pair of scissors—fell into a deep sleep.

It was two in the afternoon. None of the residents of the five-story apartment building were peering out their windows, and Fiocco's parents weren't home. Most of the men were still at work in their stores or offices, and the children and women were napping on account of the heat. Sounds of servants working in the kitchens drifted through the windows left open just a crack. That was all.

Fiocco dreamed and even believed that the King of Spades had married the Queen of Hearts. They had always been his two favorite cards.

So he asked permission to enter their domain and tell them how happy he was for them.

—I know you love each other very much! But I've known that for a long time. Whenever I shuffled the deck and you two were next to each other, I was sure I saw some kind of movement, and I'd even stop playing. Now, here I find you alone together in this pile of trash? Tell me everything. What are you doing in there?

The two cards had been rained on and then dried by the sun. Fiocco loved them no matter how faded they were. Although he would rather have spoken with the Queen, the King was more willing to talk to humans. Looking right into Fiocco's eyes, the King of Spades began to speak. "The only card games you know how to play are gin rummy, slap-jack and *briscola,* so let me tell you a little about what happens when you go off to bed and your family plays without you. Then you'll see what a great memory I have. Cecilia and Laura are your sisters, Arturo is Laura's fiancé, Matilde is your mama, Ugo is your father, Enrico and Giulio are friends of the family. And I'll tell you something else that you should know but would never figure out on your own: the Ace of Clubs was in love with Cecilia. The Ace of Hearts, one of my own subjects, was in love with Laura. The Three of Diamonds was Arturo's good friend, and the Queen of Clubs was in love with Arturo. The Jack of Hearts and the Jack of Diamonds both liked Matilde. Neither the Three of Clubs nor the Three of Spades liked your father much, and none of the cards ever wanted to be in his hand. The Queen of Diamonds was crazy about Enrico. Pay attention, so you don't get confused. We cards know more about what's going on during a game than the people who are playing. It would be quite impossible for me to explain what lengths we go to in order to help our patrons. But in the end we have no control over the luck of the draw, and if we wind up together, we must refrain from expressing either joy or disappointment. You humans have no idea! And for what it's worth, neither my esteemed wife nor I have ever taken sides against anyone. When we are placed face down in the dark, all we can do is try to sneak an embrace. How could you possibly understand our love? Not even the moths dancing in the light know about us!

"Once, convinced she was doing the Three of Diamonds a favor, the Queen of Clubs desperately tried to help Arturo win. Oh, what tension this created every time Arturo and Laura—your sister, Arturo's fiancé—touched. The Queen was so jealous of Laura! The Queen kept slipping from Laura's grasp and finally fell face-up on the table so that the other players could see her. The Three of Diamonds called in all his debts from the other cards in order to please the Queen, and even won the assistance of my esteemed consort. On the third round, the Queen of Clubs fell to Cecilia, your other sister. And throughout the entire game, Cecilia nibbled on her cards—you know how people do that when they are deep in thought, waiting for their turn. The Queen of Clubs was so caught up in the game her heart was racing. And Cecilia is always such a careless player. She puts all her energy into building up points. Very well. The card understood right away that both she and Cecilia were rooting for Arturo. Fortunately, the Ace of Clubs, who I've explained was in love with Cecilia, hadn't been played yet. And so the Queen still had a chance to be useful. But Arturo loves Laura, and he wasn't paying attention to these goings on.

"Maybe it was intuition on Cecilia's part, but she figured out that Arturo needed the Queen of Clubs, and so she played the Queen. The

Ace of Clubs was in Matilde's hand and was doing everything in his power to get away. Matilde stared at him, still undecided about which card to put down, when, as if obeying an order, she played the Ace. Cecilia jumped in her seat with joy! Arturo called *briscola*, racked up the most points and won the game.

"Not only is Arturo a nice boy and one of the best automobile mechanics around, but in your home he's the only chance to keep your father from completely destroying the family. Laura and Arturo's wedding gives your parents some hope for the future, otherwise there would be no reason for them to stay together. You know, sometimes it's better for families like yours to just break up and let everyone go their separate ways in the world. It would mean so much less fighting and less pain—much more serenity and spiritual strength. And you barely understand what I'm telling you. I certainly don't know what miracle is working on you today so that your brain can process all this information. Of course, it's only when you have those scissors in your hands that you really have fun. Oh! Then, your eyes—how your eyes shine! How you must suffer from being barely able to think!

"If I were to tell you to kill yourself, you would do it without a second thought. It's strange how you only understand things that please you or things you'd like to do. Anything else, you think with satisfaction, isn't a comment worthy of one of your paper cut-outs!

"You also want revenge on Laura because her shoes aren't made of gray leather like yours. You look at her shoes with such hatred. You spy on her through the keyhole while she's dressing. You know all of your family's biggest secrets. They don't have the slightest idea how much you know. If you were able to talk, you could even tell them how many times your mother has darned her secondhand stockings.

"And yet you are surprised when you mother kneels by your side and prays for you to get better? Don't you have any idea why you grind your teeth and get suspicious of anyone who comes to comfort her when she cries? Even if that person is Cecilia? Every time you're the slightest bit happy, you want to talk about the number of bricks there are in the walls of each room in the apartment. You counted them! And no one knew what you were doing! After ten years you gave Cecilia the first little bunch of hair she ever left in the teeth of her comb. You found the hair in the courtyard. And you drool for an entire day over the leftover ends of thread your mother throws out after sewing. You stuff your finger in your mouth and then let your anger build up for over a month.

"So why am I telling you all this? Because I know you want Arturo to marry Cecilia instead of Laura. Cecilia loves you and is a good sister to you. But Laura has betrayed you. She never dries the spit from your mouth when you moan because you're feeling even worse and you don't understand anything anymore. Cecilia would always stay by your side, and she never wanted them to put you into the asylum.

"Do you know where you are now? You're in my kingdom. Watch that you don't step on the feet of my beloved wife. It is true though, my dear Fiocco, that once you tried to throw Laura into the well! If she hadn't dropped the bucket and grabbed on to the pulley, you would have drowned her. Do you remember? You can't even speak, and yet you're so strong, you could have won that fight. You delight in reminding her about it. Why is that? Especially when you are all at the table. You'll raise your hand and wave in the direction of the well. You laugh and gesture again, to show her how easy it would be to finish her off. Honestly, you don't think she'd last a day if they left you alone with her! You plucked the feathers off the two turtledoves while they were still alive. Did you do that because they were her birds? Is that why you stabbed Arturo with a knife? Fortunately, you only pricked the palm of his hand. Now Laura has gone and asked Cecilia why she defends you. Your sisters wouldn't even be sharing a bed anymore if Laura wasn't going to be married soon. But you still want to kill her. I know how much you hate her. And I'll tell you another thing: if you do manage to kill her, it will be because you figured out where to hide behind the living room doors. You figured out you must surprise her before she has time to turn on the lights. But Arturo will never marry Cecilia. Then you are going to start beating Cecilia in order to punish yourself. It will go on like that until your parents' friends, Enrico and Giulio, have you locked up with all the other sick people.

"It's inevitable because your drunkard father secretly thinks it's funny. He wants you to kill your mother. But it isn't important what he wants. One glance from her and you fall to your knees. If you did kill Matilde—just like that, for no reason and without any goading from him—he would steal a million lire and give it to you to make you rich. Does that make you laugh? Be careful you don't drool all over my wife's dress. Get a hold of yourself! Then Enrico and Giulio would make your father marry the woman they are both in love with, and they would never leave his side.

"Storms are the only thing that frighten you now. You'd even go to Laura during a storm, and then abuse her once the thunder stops. But you should keep in mind that the Queen of Hearts is observing you with her steely eyes. Prepare a lamb for slaughter, indeed not! She will do anything to protect Laura. You're crazy! Don't you realize that you think her crown is made of gold, and her dress is silk? You think of her the way others think of God. But the mere sight of my black beard disheartens you.

"Do you know what people say about Laura and Cecilia? They call them 'the sisters of that idiot.' Your sisters have heard them. At first, they thought they were being unjustly offended. They were hurt by how mean people could be, how shameless and cynical. That nickname made them feel like the whole family shared some kind of deformity. They had the feeling that everyone knew about them, no matter where they went. At first, they thought maybe they were idiots too somehow. And don't forget that you resemble each other physically. Neither of them were ever able to explain that. They feel chained to your sickness, and that will certainly make them age prematurely.

"Your mother loves you because she blames herself for your unhappiness; every day it gets worse. You are part of her and she feels responsible for everything you do—such is motherhood. Your sisters avoid you because you smell so bad it's almost nauseating. You horrify them. They even teased you themselves when they were younger. The more you didn't act like the other children at school, the more your own sisters would tease you. Every so often, they decide you are more animal than human, and try to pretend you aren't their brother.

"Now you have foolish dreams. Do you really think you're going to be a millionaire someday, a billionaire even? Tell me you don't believe that! Do you know what makes Cecilia's heart race? She is going to be Arturo's sister-in-law and she is in love with him. She knows he will be unhappy and won't love her once Laura dies. I have no idea how she knows all that, but it torments her. She even weeps for your mother, because Ugo makes her suffer.

"You had already gone to bed, or rather, they had sent you to bed, and Cecilia had been in to help you off with your shoes. Ugo came home and punched his wife. His two friends, who never say a word, stood back, pretending they hadn't seen anything. Arturo and Laura were in front of the window, behind the curtains. Cecilia had work as a sales clerk in a clothing store back then. She was in the kitchen. Matilde cowered and buried her head in the crook of her arm. Arturo stepped forward. Naturally, Laura was begging him to defend your mother. When Ugo is drunk he laughs just like you and walks just like you. He takes your mother and shoves her into the kitchen knocking her against Cecilia, making Cecilia spill boiling water all over her hands. Her hands still haven't healed. Arturo grabs your father and tries to hold him back against the wall. Laura cries. Your father is infuriated, and takes a knife from the table and hits her over the head with the handle. Arturo uses all his strength to hold him back. But the friends are on your father's side, and they set him free.

"The party lasted until morning. They drank five more bottles of wine and then, having finished the game, threw all the cards, along with the table and chairs, out of the window into the courtyard where you found us. Arturo and the women locked themselves in the kitchen to tend to their wounds.

"Your father wanted to drag you from your sound sleep and set you up on a kind of throne on the sofa in the living room. Instead, he and his friends came in to gawk at you, and they poured wine all over you and your sheets, trying to get you drunk, too. It wouldn't have taken much for your bed to go up in flames.

"Whatever you do, don't think that your father loves you. When you were twenty years old he tried to hack off your fingers with those very same scissors you're holding now. And don't you remember what he did to you when you were a little boy? You were all living in the country then, and hadn't moved into this house yet. You fell into a fountain, so he put you into the oven that was still hot from baking bread to dry you out. And he laughed so hard! They had to drag him away and explain to him that you might die and he would be condemned for murder. In the meantime, your mother sneaked you out of the oven and saved you. But he never did believe there was any real danger. And even though you don't understand people when they talk, you know he bragged about the whole affair and insisted that cooking in the oven would have done you good. You make him laugh when he's drunk. That's all there is to it.

"The next morning, your father didn't have the guts to show his face. That's why he still hasn't come home. Arturo is too good to abandon Laura. Now, leave us cards in peace."

But Fiocco answered, —Since I can talk to you without saying anything and without needing the usual words, I beg you to do something to keep me from killing my sister. Would I really do something like that? It's true that I feel very clever, and have no need for revenge, but my cleverness is very tempting. It would give me great pleasure to kill her. But if the Queen of Hearts doesn't want me to kill her, you'll have to turn her into a card and tell her not to hate me anymore. You said this is all inevitable and has nothing to do with me. And I confess that when I am around her . . . But why does she have to be my sister?

The Queen of Hearts responded, "I hope a roof falls on your head before you have a chance to commit this crime."

Fiocco started moaning, and he moaned for a long time. Eventually, his mother looked out into the courtyard and saw him. She came down and called his name right into his ear, over and over, trying to make him stop crying. Fiocco finally stood up, but he wanted to bring the two playing cards with him and cut them up into little pieces.

Through the kitchen window of another apartment came the sound of a maid, laughing.

L'AMORE

The cloudy morning brightened, but the sea remained pale.

Virginia Secci had already begun her morning walk, and was moving slowly out toward the far end of the pier made from wooden planks and posts. I watched her from the window of my house, only a few yards from the beach. The sails on the nearby boats were yellow and orange, whereas the boats in the distance seemed to take on the color of the sea itself; almost white.

I never once took my eyes off Virginia because I was in love with her, and I was so very sad. I didn't even feel like leaving the house. Every time I looked at her, I became sad like that—maybe because I loved her too much. I would have liked to whisper dear and innocent words to her, although I did need to keep an eye out for her husband. But I loved her despite him, and was unable to renounce this long-held desire.

That's why I waited for her to return from her walk. In the meantime, I liked to reflect on the naive, sweet, tender things I never said to her.

When she walked close to me—as she was forced to, because I had planted myself on the front stoop of my house, and she lived in the house next to mine—I was overcome by a familiar, ecstatic sensation and didn't even acknowledge her as she passed, although I watched her. I felt myself turn white and, after having met her eyes, shifted my gaze out to the sand. I listened to her footsteps fade.

If I had a voice equal to my thoughts, I would never be afraid to speak. But I don't have an everyday voice, a voice I use with everyone, to speak about anything.

As usual, after having seen her, I locked myself inside the house.

Through the half-closed shutters, light reflections off the waves beat brightly across the wall and down to the floor—like mobile, weightless mirrors.

I looked out the window again in the afternoon, though I was almost certain I wouldn't see Virginia a second time, and the pain I felt was surly and vague like the face of her husband.

While I was standing there, the sea turned an even deeper turquoise, rendering the sky more pale than the water.

Long strips that were almost white ran across the water, reaching all the way to the beach; then they disappeared.

I couldn't remember how long I'd been in the town of Cattolica. Maybe I was convinced that I'd only just arrived. If Virginia had talked to me, I would have told her I loved her.

The sky was entirely gray the next day and it had rained those last hours before dawn. The sea was green at the shore, and purple toward the horizon. I didn't see Virginia. I don't know why, I almost believed I would be able to forget her. But that evening, I couldn't settle down because I hadn't seen her that day.

I was prepared to invent any sort of excuse that would take me to her house—because even finding out she had suddenly died would torment me less than this. But a storm came; a mighty gale blew through Rimini. Many of the fishing boats returned to the harbor, moving painfully, in single file, up the winding stream called Tavollo.

That night I couldn't sleep and I promised myself, not knowing whether I was dreaming or really thinking, that I would see Virginia the next day—even if I had to go find her myself.

But when I woke up, I realized there was no way I could keep that promise to myself. And so I stood in the doorway of my house, waiting for her walk along the pier. But she never left her house.

After noon, the sky became bright, almost serene, then the sea was a splendid turquoise.

The bath houses cast small, oblong shadows.

Not seeing Virginia seemed the most insane cruelty. And, in the meantime, I was convinced her husband, the lawyer Germano Secci, had taken to circling my house with increasing frequency. If he did want to address me, as I first imagined, he might have found some way to do so. But of course, it was he who behaved as though I should notice him. So I avoided him, not because I was frightened, but because there was something very sad about him. He was too tall, pale and thin. He always wore black, and the hems of his trousers blew in the slightest breeze. He carried a large stick in his hand and I often had the impression that his walking stick was more alive than he was. The man left me with a sense of anguish, and meanwhile my yearning for Virginia just grew more intense.

The sea glowed blue toward evening, its dark pools extending in every direction. The boats' sails seemed made out of gold, and there was a hint of pink in the sky at the edge of the horizon.

I remember it all well, because Virginia passed before me at that very moment. I hadn't even noticed her until she was only a few feet from me, and then I only had time to glance up at her face. I looked around, to make sure her husband wasn't there, then took the risk of following her. I was thinking quite seriously about talking to her this time—once evening had fallen. She went down to the pier and sat. I did the same, but I didn't sit. I stood, watching the water between the railing of the pier, hands clasped behind my back. And I listened carefully without looking at her. The wind almost made me cry. The more intense my feelings were, the more impossible it seemed to talk to her. The idea of falling into the water attracted me. The crashing of the waves seemed like chiming bells—at least to my ears.

Meanwhile the fishing boats moved out to the open water. They limped across the horizon, disappearing completely within the half hour despite their snail's pace.

I took note of the fishermen sailing up close to the pier where I stood. They were looking behind me—that's how I knew Virginia was still seated there—and I blushed, so embarrassed it made my head hurt.

It was as if a bell were clanging in the midst of the frothy waves, rippling and raising the surface of the water, never stopping. Every so often the planks creaked, like a voice about to speak, and then fell silent again suddenly. I was outside of myself. What was Virginia doing? Was she thinking of me? Had she even noticed I was there? Finally, I heard her turn back and I wanted to do the same; but, after standing still for so long, I didn't seem to know how to walk anymore. I tripped on a loose board. The distance between the sea and my house seemed to have doubled. Sometimes solitude extends space into the infinite.

The next day, while I was walking around in front of my house and smoking a cigarette, I felt a hand on my shoulder. I turned and the lawyer Secci said to me, "You are in love with my wife."

I felt bad about lying, but I answered, "That's not true."

"Why don't you tell the truth? You're different from other men, so it shouldn't seem strange that I want to talk to you. Hear me out, and you won't be laughing then—I'm sure of it. I'm in love with my wife, too. I love her more than all of her lovers. I'm convinced of that. Every year she betrays me with a new lover. No one who has seen her can help but fall in love with her. She's beautiful. She is beauty itself. There is no other woman like her. When I want to caress her, she tells me I'm a hedonist and the only reason I love her is because I want to possess her. She taunts her lovers with those very same words. They all want her beauty—her beauty alone. We've been married five years, and in all this time she has only grown more beautiful."

Something like a shiver took me, but Secci persisted, clinging to my hand, "Be a friend, try to share my friendship. Don't be misled by me and don't judge me as another man would. You must help me. Become her lover and take her away with you. Don't ever leave her. I want to be certain I'll never see her again. I can't ever forget her, but I'll suffer less this way. You take her."

So this man—who before had given me the impression of being underhanded or even stupid—now planted this unexpected feeling inside me. And I wanted to assure him that we could be friends, so we walked in silence together by the sea.

The wind was mighty, almost thunderous. The sea roared. Lightning burst out from the blackest cloud and flashed all the way from where we stood to Rimini.

He said to me, "Let's go into your house in case she comes out. She mustn't see us together."

We went inside, but it was impossible to speak and so we stood looking out the open window. I was troubled and he tried to calm me with his eyes and a kind expression. But I would not be calmed—after all, he had said that Virginia might be coming.

The water grew more restless, and it was getting dark. Bolts of lightning lit up the entire sea, a sudden, gloomy turquoise, sliced by white streaks of foam; the sea almost gleamed.

Trembling, Secci said to me, "There she is!"

I turned towards Virginia, anxiety coursing through my soul. She passed under my window, tall and soft with long legs; her breasts like those of the most sublime Grecian statue. I realized that the moment had arrived in which I must speak, yet I was terrorized by voluptuous anticipation. I fell to my knees.

Secci smiled and handed me a glass of water.

HOUSE FOR SALE

I knew the three men had come to see me about my house, which was for sale, but I was still pleased to overhear them asking for me. From my room, I could hear that the maid didn't want to let them in. She tried to tell them I wasn't home, but I flung open my door and came out. My voice trembled when I greeted them, then my body followed suit. They laughed as they answered me, winking to each other, and making a joke out of my foolishness. They probably thought I didn't notice. They didn't seem to care one way or another, anyway. I knew very well what was going on, but didn't intend to let it dampen my spirits. I jumped right in, wringing my hands, "Have you come to see the house? You'll be glad you came."

First, I led them through my apartment, which was the smallest in the house. They examined everything. They even paused in front of a loose brick. The one with the cane, Signor Achille, tapped the walls, trying to determine how thick they were. They picked up objects off the tops of the furniture, they felt the curtains. One of the other gentlemen, Signor Leandro, leaned out the window to spit. Then we moved on to the other apartments, where my boarders lived. The boarders welcomed me with hostility and amazement. But since I was happy to pretend I wasn't listening, they began to say nasty things about me to the three buyers. Plans were already being made for when they would take over as landlords. No one gave me any respect. I walked at the back of the group. They all stood and talked as long as they pleased, while I looked at the walls of my house, maybe for the last time ever. Then I stopped looking at the walls. I went in and out of rooms as if I didn't know what I was doing or why I was even there.

When we returned to my apartment, the third gentleman let me know his nickname was Piombo—for lead. He said, "We have already wasted too much time. What are you asking, Signor Torquato?"

I wanted to remove myself from the entire affair. I didn't even want to consult anyone else. I could have asked ten thousand, but I said eight thousand. I was worried even that would be too much, and the men would leave without making a counteroffer.

Signor Achille chided me severely. "Which one of us do you want to sell to? There are three of us."

I responded, "I thought you all wanted to buy it, the three of you together."

Piombo answered, "I wouldn't even give you three thousand for it."

I was confused and risked commenting, "That wouldn't be enough to cover the mortgage, which is seven thousand. I was asking eight thousand so I could have at least one thousand left over for me." Smiling, I turned red.

"And what would you do with a thousand lire?"

"I . . . I don't have anything else. I could live a few months on that."

"One month more or less, what does it matter?"

"That's true," I answered.

"But you can't make a deal with all three of us at the same time."

"I agree."

"So you should keep quiet."

Then Signor Leandro proposed, "I'll give you seven thousand. That will take care of the mortgage."

"And for me?"

"That's not my problem."

I felt very sympathetic toward Signor Leandro. Meanwhile, the other two men were putting on a show of being upset that I had figured out there was only one real buyer in the group. The other two had come along to pretend they were interested in buying the house, to offer less and bring the price down. I understood perfectly well, but didn't mind. Actually, I was offended that they thought they needed to resort to such tactics—as if I weren't honest, and as if I would try to get more money than I would need to cover the mortgage. I didn't want anything anyway. I wanted to be left with nothing.

Signor Leandro, the real buyer, was a merchant, though I don't know what he sold—maybe grain. He had a red face and a black mustache. Signor Achille was blond, and Piombo was old with gray hair. While we were busy having this discussion, I told Tecla, the maid, to make us all some coffee. They couldn't have cared less. The real buyer said impatiently, "Enough chatter! Let's get this over with.

347

Do you accept or not? We don't need to drink your coffee, we can afford to buy coffee for ourselves elsewhere."

I answered, "I only asked her to make coffee because I was trying to be friendly. I wanted to make you feel welcome."

"Who cares!"

So the old man said, "Rather than making coffee, you could give me the chance to make an offer. I wouldn't give you more than six thousand for this house."

The blond man shook his head, as if he pitied the other two men for their stupidity, offering me all that money. It seemed I had set them against each other. This made me feel so embarrassed and humiliated I wanted to just give them the house, but there was still the mortgage to think of. Now I was ashamed of my mortgage because it didn't leave me free to act as I would have liked under the circumstances.

Signor Leandro continued, "If you are satisfied with my first offer, even though I already regret it, we can draw up the contract today at my lawyer's office."

I couldn't have possibly refused. Hoping he hadn't noticed how fragile I was feeling, I proposed, "I can come before lunch, if that would be better for you?"

But he was offended. "I have other, much more important things than this to take care of!"

In order to stop him from speaking to me so rudely, I said, "Forgive me. I had no idea."

"Let's stop the small talk, okay? Two o'clock, no later, I'll meet you at my lawyer's office."

I was embarrassed I didn't know who his lawyer was, but I had to take the risk of asking him. He told me his lawyer was Sig. Bianchi, Esquire—"Do you know where his office is?"

"If I could just have his address—I wouldn't want to make any mistakes."

Tecla had brought the coffee in the meantime. But it had absolutely no flavor and was burnt, so I was at an utter loss for words and very concerned they would notice how awful it was.

Signor Achille, the blond man, said: "Now that you have forced your coffee on us, don't you think we should discuss the brokerage fee for me and him?" He pointed to Piombo with his cane.

As if I had just begun to wake up, I answered, "The brokerage fee?"

"Of course! Do you think we came along for fresh air?"

"But I don't have a cent!"

Now I didn't know if they were ever going to forgive me. Indeed, Signor Achille raised his cane as though he were going to crack me over the head.

"Do you think so little of us?" He grabbed my arm. I wanted to tell them they should get the fee from the buyer, but I was too worried about how Piombo would react. I looked around and, pale with emotion, I said, "If you please, I could give you this wardrobe . . ."

"Is that all you have?"

I responded quickly, hoping to make everything seem more friendly, "There's my bed over there. And the copper pans in the kitchen."

"Are they still good?"

"It's all still good," and I asked the maid to bring some pans in to show.

"I thought we were going to do serious business here!" said the old man Piombo with a look of indulgence.

Which made my heart ache. But I just didn't have anything else to give them. I even scanned the ceiling for something, but there was really nothing left at all.

They drank the coffee and finished the sugar, eating whole chunks of it at a time. I preferred not to fill my cup, hoping they would realize I had made the coffee especially for them. I really wanted them to know that. But they didn't so much as thank me. Piombo suggested, "Why don't you add these cups to the brokerage fee, Signor Torquato?" At that, Signor Achille landed him a blow on the neck. "And which one of us should he give them to?"

In order to calm Signor Achille down, I said, "I don't use those cups anymore."

The buyer picked his nose. He was already immersed in making plans for the house. To that end he asked me, "When can the rooms be vacated?"

I had been thinking about staying on for another few days, but since he had asked so directly, I answered, "I can be out today, as soon as we've drawn up the contract."

"Good. Good!"

"I'm sorry I can't leave sooner."

"It is a shame."

At this point, I began to feel as if my heart were being wrenched from my body. And he seemed to notice my mood immediately; he asked in a threatening tone, "You haven't changed your mind, have you?"

349

I responded with some effort, "No no! Quite the opposite! I was thinking of something else."

"That's all we need now, for you to have second thoughts! We're all adults here, not children! You probably haven't thought about the fact that these two men here witnessed our agreement."

"I assure you," I said, "I was thinking about something else!"

"God willing, you seem to have your wits about you." He walked over to a wall and said, "Tomorrow I'm sending someone over to clean up all these rooms and reinforce the cross beams. I'm going to have him check the roof, too, because the boarders on the top floor told me there's a drip when it rains."

"Yes, it's true, there's a broken tile. I haven't fixed it, because I didn't want to spend the money."

"Then I'm going to have him redo the facade and paint the shutters. The whole thing is going to cost me another thousand. Doesn't that seem like a lot of money to you?"

I was impressed by all this work he was planning, and offered, "Then you'll see what a beautiful house this can be!"

"Did you think we were going to let it go to ruin the way you did?"

It was thoughtless the way he talked to me. His tone suggested I had done something wrong. I was left without an answer for him. No matter how hard I concentrated, I couldn't seem to come up with any words that would express my feelings. All I wanted to do was to stop him from talking to me like that. But he was blaming everything on me and I was hurt. I couldn't think straight, so I said, "I'll leave my family pictures on the walls, I don't know where else to put them . . ."

"You can throw those out."

"Are they in your way?"

"Didn't I just get finished telling you I'm going to clean this place up!"

Then he took Signor Achille's cane and knocked down almost the entire row of pictures, the ones without frames. I would have liked to pick them up, but decided to wait until after they had left. I really did want them to know that those pictures were of my mother and sister, who were both dead now. Maybe then they would understand how I felt. But I didn't dare say anything. Signor Leandro was the new landlord and it was he who had knocked everything down. I didn't want to do anything to upset them. There was a photograph of my father still hanging on the wall above where the others had been, so I said, "Knock that one down, too!"

But he wasn't interested in such nonsense, and shrugged his shoulders. What he did, instead, was to grab hold of an old flower vase I'd been keeping. It was a memento of my sister. When he realized that the dust on the vase had dirtied his fingers, he said, "I shouldn't have touched it."

"Would you like to wash up?" I offered.

Signor Leandro decided to use his handkerchief instead, even though soiling it appeared to anger him greatly. I had become terrified that something else would happen as a result of his curiosity. So I suggested, "We can go down now, if you think it's best."

But one of the others asked, "Do you know if your maid steals things? Keep in mind that she's responsible for this stuff and it's all ours now."

My hand at my heart, I answered, "I swear that not a crumb will be missing!"

"Well, just to be sure, it would be better if you gave us the keys now. That way the maid can leave with us and we'll lock up."

"If you are at all concerned, we must do just as you say. Tecla, come! We're all leaving together."

The maid, who was an old widow, said, "And when will I get the chance to collect a bundle of my things?"

The buyer answered, "I'll let you in, if you come back tonight."

"But what about my pay for this past month?"

The three of them burst out laughing. I was so embarrassed I didn't know what to say.

"We'll talk about it outside."

Signor Achille said, "Wouldn't that be something if you couldn't sell your house because of a maid!"

I told him, "She doesn't understand all this. She is not well educated. But she'll leave with me. I'll make sure she obeys."

The five of us all left together. Tecla was the last out, and she closed the door.

The only thing I could do then was go to lunch. At two o'clock on the dot I was at the lawyer's. Actually, I was the first to arrive. I signed the deed, which had been written on official paper, and I wrote my name as beautifully as I knew how, even though my hand was trembling. I tried to figure out if they were happy with me and whether I might have said something to contradict the impression I would have liked them to have of me. I waited to see if they wanted anything else. But the lawyer said, "You're all set!" And he put a red stamp on the contract.

Federigo Tozzi

Signor Leandro dismissed me, saying, "You may leave now, Signor Torquato."

I said goodbye, as I always do, with respect. Nobody answered. They were already talking amongst themselves by the time I reached the door.

I climbed down the stairs from the lawyer's office, walking as if a weight had been lifted from off me. I don't remember what I did next, or how I spent the rest of the day. By evening I had nothing to eat and nowhere to sleep. I was exhausted, but did everything I could to be strong. It started pouring rain as night fell. So I went to find shelter under the drainpipes of my house that was sold now. I was so sad. I wanted to be happy, or at least as happy as I had been that morning, for I knew this was the hour when my boarders ate supper and the people down in the neighborhood usually played the piano. Those neighbors were always playing some new polka.

* * *

AFTERWORD
THE MYSTERIOUS ACTS OF AN UNSUNG MASTER

Pirandello and Borgese encouraged him. Bilenchi and Moravia celebrated him. Virtually anonymous during his lifetime, ignored for half a century after his death, Federigo Tozzi (1883–1920) has come now to be recognized as one of the masters of modern Italian letters. Tozzi was a prolific writer, producing an extraordinary bulk of work—novels, essays, histories, plays, poetry, book-length aphorisms—before he died at thirty-seven. His more than one hundred short stories are stylized, structured, personal and disarmingly complex. Employing an unassuming form of realism, yet fascinated by the preoccupations of psychology, Tozzi's work offers innovations in form, allegory, private symbolism, and navigates the cardinal directions of Modernist narrative. Through him, we come to a deeper understanding of twentieth-century Italian literature. Tozzi remains the quintessential, yet delicate voice of an antihero; a man who struggled to find a form with which to portray his own tormented life experiences at the dawn of the age of the memoir. The intimate fictions of his short stories never once, however, abandon artifice. Tozzi juggles words like a poet, depicts landscapes expressively like a symbolist, nudges meaning out of connotation and parable.

Tozzi's biography reveals a difficult and bewildering character—somewhat more akin to the gloomy, awkward antiheroes of his stories than one might want to think. While his colleagues tended to represent the neuroses of their protagonists as metaphors for the crises of modernity, Tozzi, rather, seems to have authored his own crisis. Divorcing himself from his father's world as property owner and restaurateur in Siena, Federigo was staunchly a *literato*. He did, however, inherit his father's violent temperament. Expelled from four schools for bad behavior, he finally educated himself in classical and Italian literature, art history, socialism and psychology at the public library. A social misfit, he spent several years in self-imposed seclusion, leaving the house only at night, which earned him the local nickname of *il pazzo* (the madman). His doting mother died when he was twelve and his relationship with his father was riddled with antagonism—the two argued about religion, politics, management of the family estate and women, especially his father's flagrant womanizing. Federigo's own relations with women were similarly tempestuous; he was abusive, jealous and unfaithful. His eventual marriage seemed to function best when the couple was separated, communicating via letter—the mode of their early courtship. His fiction often portrays irreconcilable marriages, and many of his protagonists fall hopelessly and inarticulately in love with intelligent prostitutes, fallen or married women—unattainable figures.

Professionally, Tozzi was a loose cannon. He criticized the mainstream Futurists and *crepuscolari*, openly attacking the powerful editors Papini and Prezzolini. He founded his own (short-lived) magazine *La Torre* in defiance of them, and finally panned a late work by Gabrielle d'Annunzio—one of his early influences—risking publication of his own novel out of the same house. The success he did realize was due in large part to Borgese and Pirandello, who were faithful admirers, and without whose support and editorship, Tozzi would not have published during his lifetime or after.

Why has Tozzi's work, even in Italy, only recently started receiving the popular and critical attention commensurate with his extraordinary innovation? In 1923, Italian literary critic Domenico Giuliotti assessed Tozzi's work in the following way: "Tozzi is not a fun writer—not 'entertaining,' as we used to say. That is why he has not had many readers. He is among those writers who dig into the sadness of life, who digs very deeply; one of those writers who is ignored by his contemporaries and left to be discovered much later." Indeed, it would seem that we have needed almost a century of successors—those who assimilated and embellished the vision of Modernism—as well as the context of his more widely read contemporaries, in order to understand the mechanics and scope of Tozzi's oeuvre.

Where Pirandello was interested in self-conscious form, and Italo Svevo in dramatizing psychology, Tozzi reflected on the layer of significance beneath the surface of daily life, to identify and speculate upon what he termed the "mysterious acts of man." In his aesthetic manifesto "Reading My Way," Tozzi explains that a mysterious act might be a man pausing along his journey to pick up a pebble. The writer's task is to present a perspective on such a moment—a perspective, not merely observation, phrased in such a way that it leads us toward an understanding of the simple gesture. Why does the "idiot" fixate on playing cards? Why is a love-hungry man whelmed by a glass of water? Why does a man selling his house give away his dignity? These short stories lay bare the explicable—yet still somehow inexcusable—emotional justification behind our weakest moments and cruelest whims: betrayal, violence, intoxication, intolerance, rape, suicide, judgment and murder. Alberto Moravia, a fellow speculator of Freud, said that Tozzi might very well have been "the first Italian writer, who, without meaning to, was an existentialist."

Echoing the then current interest in form, Tozzi would say that mere content has no life or even purpose outside of the form in which it is expressed. Here the influence of Edgar Allan Poe can be seen. Poe's writing certainly gave him permission to explore the darker side of man's character. But perhaps more significantly, Tozzi practiced the rigorous stylistic architecture articulated in Poe's "Philosophy of Composition," even paraphrasing the following in his own essay: "In the whole composition there should be no word written, of which the tendency, direct or indirect, is not to the one pre-established design. And by such means, with such care and skill, a picture is at length painted which leaves in the mind of him who contemplates it with a kindred art, a sense of the fullest satisfaction."

Tozzi's short stories challenge traditional reversals, in which illumination or resolution comes through the reversal itself, performing instead a heightened mock reversal that leads dramatically back to the status quo. In "The Idiot" we have a man whose mental disability keeps him from even fantasizing an escape—the recognition, sadly, belongs to the reader only. In "L'Amore," in which our hero is offered the chance to confront the object of his desire and realizes that he is capable only of pining, nothing more—his pining, mirror of the mighty ocean, is reduced suddenly to an impotent glass of water. In "House for Sale," a man's desperate supplication before three heartless men only leads to further abuse; his inability to act against what he recognizes clearly as his own weakness is the tragedy.

As Henry James wrote: "What is character but the determination of incident? What is incident but the illustration of character?" Tozzi's characters operate within the parameters of delusion and that is, perhaps, the key to his place in the twentieth-century canon. By continually encouraging the reader to hope for defiance of tragic destiny—traditional narrative form, Tozzi indoctrinated his readers into the next level of a Modernist sensibility—the inexplicable human character; the mysterious nature of the mundane; the intrigue of plotlessness. It is the unfulfilled promise that Tozzi's characters, thus his stories, are going to defy classical boundaries that gives them their edge. Through a liberal use of Modernist tropes, lyricism, dialect and the fantastic, Tozzi repeatedly deludes the reader into imagining a narrative world free of formal strictures—liberated into a new literature, where destiny is indeterminate, and a happy ending, or at least a merited one, would be possible.

Three Poems
Zinaida Gippius

—Translated from Russian by Anneta Greenlee

TRANSLATOR'S NOTE

Zinaida Gippius is Russia's foremost female symbolist writer. She was born in 1869 in the province of Tula, and died in 1945, as an exile in Paris. By the turn of the century, Gippius had become the leading Russian woman writer, and her poetic innovations opened the way for later poets such as Anna Akhmatova. Her writing was unavailable in Russia until recently; since the fall of the Communist regime, her work is being rediscovered.

As the Russian poet Valery Bryusov said of Gippius's work: "Each poem brings in something new, something that has never before existed in Russian poetry." Gippius's poetry has a disquieting quality, reflecting an anxious inner struggle to reconcile the opposing forces of love and hate, faith and disbelief, hope and despair. Gippius herself wrote in her poem "Song" in 1893: "I want that which does not exist."

The three poems, appearing here for the first time in English, are from Zinaida Gippius: Stikhi, Vospominania, Dokumentalnaya proza *(Nashe Naslediye, Moscow, 1991).*

* * *

MIRRORS

Have you ever seen them?

In the garden, or in the park—I don't know.

Mirrors shone everywhere.

Down below, in the clearing, on the edge,

up above, in the birch, in the fir-tree.

Where soft squirrels leaped,

where rich branches bent,

mirrors shone everywhere.

In the upper mirror—the grass swayed,

in the lower one a cloud passed . . .

But each of them was too sly,

not happy with just the earth or just the sky,—

They each repeated the other,

they each reflected the other . . .

In both, the pink of dawn

blended with the grassy green;

The earthly and the heavenly were equal

in this brief mirroring moment.

Zinaida Gippius

SPIDERS

I am in a narrow cell in this world,
the cell has a low ceiling.
In the four corners I see
four spiders who never tire.
They are dexterous, fat and dirty.
They weave and weave, and never stop.
It is frightening, their ceaseless
and never changing work.
They have woven four spider webs
into one enormous web.
I look and see their moving backs
in the dusty, foul-smelling dusk.
The spider web covers my eyes.
The web is gray, soft and sticky.
And the four spiders are glad
with the gladness of feral beasts.

COMPLEXITIES

Why should we return to simplicity?

Well, I know the reason why.

But not everyone is able.

People like me just can't.

I'm walking through thorn bushes,

they grab at me, I cannot get through.

But even though I fall,

and never reach a higher simplicity,

I simply cannot return.

From The Unknown Fourth Notebook
The Diary of Vaslav Nijinsky: Unexpurgated Edition
Vaslav Nijinsky

—Edited by Joan Acocella, with a
translator's note by Kyril FitzLyon

EDITOR'S NOTE

The diary of Vaslav Nijinsky was written in early 1919, shortly before the great dancer was diagnosed as schizophrenic. Nijinsky wrote this diary in four school notebooks, the first three giving an account, in journal form—and in Russian—of his thoughts at the time, the fourth containing sixteen letters that he wrote in French, Russian and Polish to various people while he was at work on the rest of the diary. When Nijinsky's wife, Romola, finally decided to publish the diary in 1936, she deleted most of the fourth notebook. Of the sixteen letters, she kept only six, inserting them into the main body of the diary. Since its publication, Romola's version has been the only English edition of the diary, and until recently it was the basis of all other translations. Thus the fourth notebook has remained largely unknown.

The following five letters from the fourth notebook, selected from the upcoming unexpurgated Diary of Vaslav Nijinsky *(Farrar, Straus & Giroux), are being printed here in their entirety for the first time. Three of them—those to the President of the Council of Allied Forces, to Eleanora Nijinsky (Nijinsky's mother) and to Serge Diaghilev—were included in Romola's edition, but in heavily bowdlerized form. Romola knew, when she published the diary, that her husband would appear insane to the book's readers, but she didn't want him to appear* too *insane, or insane in the wrong way. To her, he was not so much a madman as a prophet, a humanitarian, who, as she wrote in her preface to the diary, "could not escape . . . the fate of all great humanitarians—to be sacrificed," and it was to this pattern that she cut Nijinsky's manuscript. She deleted parts that might seem improper, including copious material on sex. She also deleted parts that could seem bizarre or tedious, including all the poems in the diary. A case in point is the letter to Diaghilev. She retained Nijinsky's recriminations against his former lover and employer, but as for the 171-line poem that came in the middle of this outburst—a poem of love, wrath, obsession and complicated word-weaving (together with a little obscenity)—the entire thing was dropped. Romola was not going to allow Nijinsky to be represented by lines such as "I am the Prick, I am the Prick/ I am God in my Prick." In fairness, it should be said most wives of the period would have made the same decision.*

In the five letters reproduced below, one can track the developing logic of the fourth notebook, its progression from prose to a kind of vatic poetry. In the first two letters Nijinsky writes plainly enough, and with practical goals in mind. He makes requests, gives instructions. But gradually prose becomes verse, and as in the letter to Diaghilev, Nijinsky yields increasingly to the seductions of wordplay, taking the syllables of his words apart, fashioning new words, and again and again juxtaposing words on the basis of sound, or "clanging."

None of the letters is dated, but the main text of the diary strongly suggests that they were all written in one day. Indeed, they may well have been written in one sitting, in a single burst of energy. This would explain their increasingly manic character: the forced jocularity, the insistent rhythm, the rush and excitement. By the final letters, what we have, much of the time, is simply a sequence of sounds. Even in these letters, however, Nijinsky is not out of control. Many apparent nonsense lines seem to contain elaborate puns. However difficult they are to read, these letters are very careful sound constructions, something like scat singing.

The wordplay poses serious translation problems. The last two letters reproduced here, one to Jean Cocteau and one to Jesus, are not translatable. They are given in the original French, much of it spelled phonetically.

*   *   *

TRANSLATOR'S NOTE

The English version of Nijinsky's Diary *published by his wife, Romola, in 1936, and subsequently translated into many other languages, enjoyed a considerable success. It showed the famous dancer to have been a subtle and original thinker, capable of stimulating observations on life, God and man, which, for those who knew him, were quite unexpected. Some forty years later, however, this version of the diary was found to have been the product of very heavy revision. In 1979, shortly after Romola Nijinsky's death, the diary notebooks were put up for sale, and I was hastily commissioned to translate them for the use of the auction house in describing the notebooks to prospective buyers. From my draft translation, the first attempt at a faithful reproduction of the original, one could see at last the extent of Romola's editing, including the deletion of about two-fifths of Nijinsky's text. Because of copyright restrictions, my translation could not be published, though over the years it was apparently made available to scholars, including Peter Ostwald, who quoted from it in his 1991* Nijinsky: A Leap into Madness. *Only since the recent release of the copyright have full translations of Nijinsky's diary begun appearing, including, now, my own.*

I have tried, in my version, to preserve Nijinsky's highly individual use of words, phrases and syntax. If the translation occasionally appears awkward as a result, it does no more than reflect the awkwardness of the original Russian. One source of difficulty is Nijinsky's bilingualism, the fact that he was a Pole educated in Russia. Though he thought he was more at home in Russian than in Polish, the diary contains numerous "polonisms." Occasionally, his turns of phrase and use of words, while perfectly correct in Polish, make little sense in Russian, even if the meaning can be guessed at. At other points, he has difficulties with his Russian vocabulary, confusing one word with another and making the meaning difficult or impossible to discover unless the reader happens to know what word he has in mind.

If Nijinsky's vocabulary is sometimes faulty, more often it is simply idiosyncratic. A good example is the meaning he attaches to "feeling" (chuvstvo), a central concept in the diary. To him "feeling" means intuitive perception, the ability to understand something—a person, a situation—by merging with it emotionally. Such understanding, which in his mind can be akin to a spiritual experience, is seldom achieved deliberately, and never by means of what he calls "thinking" or "intellect." Nijinsky regards thinking, with some contempt, as the antithesis of feeling: a purely cerebral and almost artificial activity, which never penetrates beneath the surface of things. People who merely think are incapable of knowing the truth or conducting intimate relationships. "Thinking" and "intellect" must not, however, be confused with "reason," which Nijinsky sees as a faculty emanating from God and not subservient to logic.

Another Nijinskian concept is that of "dryness." He speaks of people being dried out, but he does not explain what this means. Presumably it means that they have been deprived of the ability to "feel." Yet another peculiarity is his use of the word "habit." To have a habit means to be a slave to an artificially acquired (and invariably bad) mode of behavior. To have no habits is to be free of all prejudice.

Very seldom does Nijinsky refer to something as being "good" or "bad," but almost always as being "a good thing" or "a bad thing." (The expression "a terrible thing" is a great favorite of his.) This turn of phrase has been preserved in the translation in spite of stylistic disadvantages.

I have also chosen not to interfere with Nijinsky's violations of logic, including his reversals of causal relationships. Though they may be due in part to his linguistic difficulties, these curiosities are more probably a reflection of his disturbed state of mind.

I have dealt similarly with layout. To Nijinsky his narrative was a flow of consciousness, governed not by logic ("thinking"), but by the association of ideas. One result of this is the scarcity of paragraphing. To introduce additional paragraphing in the translation would certainly help the reader, but it would also impose an order and shape which are lacking in the original, and would therefore misrepresent both his state of mind and his vision of reality as a single, unbroken whole. Likewise, I have followed Nijinsky in his shuttling choices regarding capitalization, a matter of great importance to him.

Nijinsky's concern with the use of capital and lowercase letters forms part of his interest in the physical aspect of writing, to which he seems to attribute more than a merely artificial or cosmetic significance. The very tools of writing—ink, pens, pencils—are to him a source of curiosity and wonder. He pays close attention to spelling and accuses himself unjustly of being a bad speller. He worries about his handwriting—which is actually quite neat and regular—and makes sporadic attempts to change it. He feels the sheer effort of writing to be such that writers (including himself, presumably) may be called "martyrs," "similar to the crucified Christ." Self-identification with Christ and

Vaslav Nijinsky

with God is never far from his thoughts. In one way or another, it is a constant theme of the diary.

One feature of Nijinsky's writing that could not be reproduced in the translation is the very strong rhythms which mark his poems, and to which he adheres irrespective of any meaning the poetry might or might not possess. These insistent rhythms may be a verbal expression of his experience as a dancer.

—Kyril FitzLyon

*   *   *

To the President of the Council of the Allied Forces

Romola Nijinsky, in her edition of the diary, identifies the addressee of this letter as the president of the Council of the Allied Forces. It was because of the revolution and civil war in Russia that Nijinsky had not communicated with his mother in a year and a half.

—J.A.

Dear sir, I am a Polish subject. I want nothing from you. I want to ask you to forward this letter. I love my mother, and I want her to know that I am alive. I know that you have a great deal of business to do, but I know that you are a man. You will understand me if you have seen my dances. I know that dancers do not understand business. I understand very well. I am very rich, because I understand business. I ask you to be so kind as to send this letter to my mother under your protection. I know very well that this depends on you. I know very well that you have to show this letter to other authorities. I ask you once again to give me the happiness of sending this letter to my mother. My mother is a sick woman. She has lost one son. She suffers because she cannot see me. She is not a Bolshevik. She is almost 70 years old. She loves me very much. She knows that I am very famous. She knows that I am loved everywhere. She knows that I have very grand connections. She thinks that I am dead because I have not written to her in 1½ years. She thinks that I am dancing in England. She is afraid that people will harm me, thinking that I am a Bolshevik. My mother knows very well that I am not a Bolshevik. She knows my love for people. She knows that I do not like violence. She knows that I do not like this fighting with schoolboys. She raised me, and therefore she knows me. I am a man, not a savage animal. I do not like savagery. I do not like Bolsheviks. They can kill me, but I am not afraid. They wanted to kill my mother

364

because she is a bourgeois. I am not a bourgeois. I am a man. I love everyone. I do not want people to die. I love my wife. She is a Hungarian. I traveled with her during the war. I was in France. The French authorities allowed us through. I went through several times. I love France. I wish France very well. I love England. I love Poland. I love Russia. I love Italy. I love the whole world. I am a man, not a savage animal.

I thank you in advance.

Vaslav Nijinsky.

—Translated from French
by Joan Acocella

TO ELEANORA NIJINSKY

This is the letter that Nijinsky asked the president of the Council of the Allied Forces to forward. Nijinsky's mother, Eleanora, was living in Russia with her daughter, Bronislava, and Bronislava's husband, Alexander (Sasha) Kochetovsky. "Wacio" and "Brońcia" are the Polish diminutives of Nijinsky's and his sister's first names.

—J.A.

My dear Mother, I love you always. I am in perfect health. I did not have any news from you. I wrote to you but received no reply. They sent my letters back. I am happy. I am unhappy, because I cannot see you. I love you and ask you to come to me. I am renting a house where I have installed myself. I have this house for you. I love you because you brought me up. I have a daughter, and I want you to bring her up. I know you have God in you, and I want you to give Him to my daughter. My daughter is a wonderful child, because she listens to those who love her, and therefore I know that she will listen to you. God wants you to be with my daughter. I want you to be with me. I am asking you to come right away. I will send you money for your trip. I do not want politics, I am not politics. I am man of God. I like everyone. I do not want murders. I am young and strong. I work a lot. I do not have a lot of money, but I have enough to give you for your whole life. I want to see Brońcia and Sasha. They are with you. I know they love you. I know it is very difficult for them to get money. They are tired. I want to help them. I love everyone. I do not want money for myself. My wife loves you and wants you to come here. I too want you to come. Please write to me through the English authorities. My address is the English authorities. I know they will love you when they see you. I want you to go to them alone, without Sasha. They are afraid of bolsheviks, and that is why they do not want young boys. I do not know Sasha, because I have not seen him for a long time. I am young, and I do not want bolsheviks, because they kill people. I love Kerensky, because he did not want people's death. Today I do not know him, because he does not reveal his thoughts. I reveal my thoughts because I want people to know me. I do not like partisanship. I am without a party. I know God likes people and does not want their death. The bolsheviks did not understand Tolstoy. Tolstoy is not a bolshevik. I often read Tolstoy. I can see that he loves everyone. Tolstoy loves God, not the party. I love God, and not the party. God is my party. God is with me, and I am with Him.

I kiss you, my mother, and ask you to kiss everybody who loves me.

Your son, Wacio.

—Translated from Polish
by Jaroslaw Anders

TO SERGE DIAGHILEV

From 1908 to 1913 Nijinsky was the lover and protégé of Serge Diaghilev, founder/director of the Ballets Russes. He was also the leading male dancer of that company until 1913, when he suddenly married and Diaghilev, in consequence, fired him. The following letter, written more than five years later, reflects Nijinsky's continuing bitterness over their rupture. It may be the pressure of that emotion that sets off the complicated wordplay in the letter. Often, Nijinsky's choice of words proceeds by association. When he speaks of "declining" in the grammatical sense, as one declines a noun, this makes him think of related words, such as "inclining" or "bowing down," and he takes off in that direction. Elsewhere the association is of sound rather than sense. When he writes of Diaghilev's organizing *truppa*, or troupes, this puts him in mind of *trup*, or corpse, so the next sentence is "I am not a corpse." Often he will use nonsense words, sometimes chaining them off real words. (Thus *muzhay*, or "manhood," in one line produces *vmuzhay*, an invented word, in the next line.) Conversely, invented words, such as *porosh*, *chuy* and *khul*, will lead him back to real words: *poroshok* ("powder"), *cheshuya* ("scaly skin"), *khuy* ("prick"). In such instances, one is uncertain whether to translate the word, thus tearing it out of its phonic context, or leave it in Russian, thus suppressing a meaning that it may have had for him beyond its sound. Decisions have been made case by case.

Poroshok, for example, has been left in Russian, since Nijinsky seems to use it primarily for its sound value. *Cheshuya*, on the other hand, seems to have been chosen not just for its sound—he arrived at it from *khuy* to *chuy* to *chushuya* to *cheshuya*—but also for some lateral sense. It has therefore been translated. As for *khuy*, it will come as no surprise that in a letter to his former lover this word does have a meaning for him beyond its sound. In several instances he writes the word large and bold, and capitalizes it.

—*K.F.*

To Man,

I cannot call you by name, because you cannot be called by your name. I am not writing to you quickly, because I don't want you to think that I am nervous. I am not a nervous man. I am able to write calmly. I like writing. I do not like writing fine phrases. I never learned to write fine phrases. I want to write down thoughts. I need thought. I am not afraid of you. I know you hate me. I love you as a human being. I do not want to work with you. I want to tell you one thing. I work a lot. I am not dead. I am alive. Within me lives God. I live in God. God lives in me. I am very busy working on dances. My dances are making progress. I write well, but do not know how to write fine phrases. You like fine phrases. You organize troupes. I do not organize troupes. I am not a corpse. I am a living person. You are a dead person because your aims are dead. I have not called you friend, because I know that you are my enemy. I am not your enemy. An enemy is not God. God is not an enemy. Enemies seek death. I seek life. I have love. You have spite. I am not a predatory beast. You are a predatory beast. Predatory beasts do not like people. I like people. Dostoevsky liked people. I am not an idiot. I am a human being. I am an idiot. Dostoevsky is an idiot. You thought I was stupid. I thought you were stupid. We thought we were stupid. I don't want to decline. I don't like declensions. You like people bowing down to you. I like people bowing down to me. You revile those who bow down. I like those who bow down. I call for declensions. You frighten declensions. My declension is a declension. I don't want your smile, for it smells of death. I am not death and I don't smile. I don't write in order to have a laugh. I write in order to weep. I am a man with feeling and reason. You are a man with intelligence and without feeling. Your feeling is evil. My feeling is good. You want to destroy me. I want to save you. I like you. You don't like me. I wish you well. You wish me ill. I know your tricks. I pretended to be nervous. I pretended to be stupid. I was not a kid. I was God. I am

Vaslav Nijinsky

God within yourself. You are a beast, but I am love. You do not love those people now. I love those people, everyone, now. Don't think I don't listen. I am not yours. You are not mine. I love you now. I love you always. I am yours. I am my own. You are mine. I like declining you. I like declining myself. I am yours. I am my own.

You are mine. I am God.
You have forgotten that God is.
I have forgotten that God is.
You are within me, and I am within you.
You are mine, and I am yours.
You are the one who wants death.
You are the one who loves death.
I love love love.
I am love but you are death.
You are afraid of death, of death
I love, I love, I love
You are death, but I am blood.
Your blood is not love.
I love you, you—
I am not blood, but I am the spirit
I am the blood and the spirit in you.
I am love, I am love.
You do not want to live with me.
I wish you well.
You are mine, you are mine.
I am yours, I am yours.
I love writing with a pen.
I write, I write
You do not write you tele-write
You are a telegram, I am a letter.
You are a machine. I am love.
You are a woodpecker. I am a woodpecker.
You reach manhood, I reach manhood,
You are a *vmuzhay*, I am a *vmuzhay*
We are *vmuzhai*, you are *vmuzhai*
You are a male, I am a male
We are males, you are males
Your *muzhay* is not my *muzhay*
You are a *vmuzhay*, I am a *vmuzhay*.
You are a male, I am not yours

Yours is he, but mine is not you,
You are yours, but I am He
He is mine, he is not yours.
I want to tell you that you cannot be so.
I want to tell you that you cannot be so.
I am yours, you are mine,
We are we, we are not you—
We are we, we are not you
You are the one who calls for death
You are the one who calls for death
I am yours, but you are not mine
Mine is one's own, but one's own is not yours
You are a woodpecker, I am not a woodpecker,
You knock and I knock
Your knock is your knock, but mine is a knock
Knock-knock, knock, in a knock there is a knock
I am a knock, but I do not knock
You knock, knock, knock
I knock, knock knock
I am knocking in your soul
You knock in your brain.
I love you my knock
I am a knock, a knock, but you are not a knock,
I want to knock within the knock
You knock in the brain, in the brain.
I want to knock for you, knock, knock, knock
A knock is a cockerel
I am a cockerel, but not a cockerel
You are a cockerel, but not a cockerel
I sing, sing, sing
You sing sing, sing
I drink drink drink
You drink drink drink
I am a cockerel a cockerel a cockerel
I am a cockerel a cockerel a cockerel
My cockerel sings sings
Your cockerel drinks drinks
I am a cockerel but you are not mine.
I am a cockerel but you are not yours.
We sing in the cockerel.
I sing without the cockerel.

Vaslav Nijinsky

We sing of the cockerel.
I sing without the cockerel.
Sing cockerel, sing cockerel.
Your cockerel will die, will die
I sing, I sing, I will die, I will die
I sing, I sing, I will die, I will die
You will die without the Cockerel
I will die with the Cockerel
Your cockerel is death, is death
My cockerel is life, is life.
I love you cockerel.
I love you cockerel.
You sing and I sing.
We sing, but I am not yours
I sing well.
You sing badly
I sing, sing, sing
You sing, sing, sing
We sing, but I am not yours
You are not mine and I am not yours,
You do not love me, one's own
I love you not one's own.
You are not mine and I am not yours
We are Yours, you are not theirs
I am Yours, but you are not mine
Mine is Yours, mine is Yours
Poro, poro, poro, tok
I *poro*, I *poro*
I *poro, poro, poro*
You *porosh*, you *porosh*
I *porosh*, you *porosh*
I am *tok* but you are *tok*
Tok, tok, tok, poroshok
I am *porosh* but you are *oshok*
I am *poshok* but you are *dushok*
I am *toshok*, but you are *tushok*
We in *prokh* are *poroshok*
I am *porosh*, but you are *oshok*.
We make a noise, we make a noise
You are not noise, but I am noise
I am young, but you are old.

We are death, but I am young.
Lolod is life, but not a sledge hammer
I am a sledgehammer not a hammer
You are *tok* and I am *tok*
I am *tok, tok, tok.*
Tok, tok, tok, and not *tok.*
We are *tok, tok, tok*
You are not *tok,* but I am *tok*
I am *tok, tok, tok*
I wish you *tok, tok*
You are not *tok,* you are not *tok*
I am *tok,* I am *tok*
I *tok* every day
You *tok* every day
We *tok,* we *tok*
You *tok,* I am not *toch*
We are *toch,* but not *chech*
Chech is *toch,* I am not *toch*
We *chech* and I *chech* I *chech*
Chech, chech, chech is not *chech*
I *chech ul khul*
I *chech* I am *ul khul*
Chul chul you are their *chul*
Mul chul you are *khul*
I am a prick, but not yours
You are mine, but I am not yours
Mine is a prick because the Prick
I am the Prick, I am the Prick
I am God in my prick
I am God in my prick.
Yours is a prick, not mine not mine
I am a prick in His prick.
I prick, prick, prick
You are a prick, but not the Prick
I can prick, prick
You cannot prick a prick
I am not a prick in your prick
I am a prick in His prick.
Chuyu, chuy, I am not *chuy*
You are *chuy* not mine in *chuy.*
I am *chuy, chuy,* you are not *chuy.*

Vaslav Nijinsky

We are *chuy*, not not *chuy*
Chuy, chuy, chuy, not *chushuya.*
I am not a *chuy* in a scaly skin
I am a *chuy*, I am a *chuy chuy*
Chuy chuy chuy, but not *uy*
Uy is intelligence, but not mine
I am intelligencing I love
Mine is the intelligence in the *chuy* intelligence
I am *chuy*. I love.
Chuy, chuy, chuy not scaly skin.
I am God not in a scaly skin.
A scaly skin is intelligence in *chuy*
I am *chuy*, I am *chuy*.

I want to write a lot to you, but I cannot work with you, for your aims are different. I know that you know how to pretend. I don't like pretending. I like pretense when a person wants the good of others. You are a spiteful man. You are not king. But I am. You are not my king, but I am your king. You wish me harm, I do not wish harm. You are a spiteful man, but I am a lullabyer. Rockabye, bye, bye, bye. Sleep in peace, rockabye, bye. Bye. Bye. Bye.

Man to man

Vaslav Nijinsky.

—*Translated from Russian
by Kyril FitzLyon*

TO JEAN COCTEAU

In 1909, during the Ballets Russes' first season in Paris, the nineteen-year-old Jean Cocteau became a fan and friend of the company. Soon he was working for it as well. With Frédéric de Madrazo, he composed the libretto for *Le Dieu Bleu* (1912), which starred Nijinsky. He was also the librettist for *Parade* (1917) and *Le Train Bleu* (1924). Cocteau, then, was part of the Ballets Russes circle from which Nijinsky in 1919 saw himself as banished, and his resentment surfaces in this letter. He describes Cocteau as a man "without light." He then takes off on a long flight of associations. Near the end of the letter he says, "I write very badly but I want to tell you that I love you. I love you, my dear Cocto." Then the sound *coc* (Fr., *coq*, rooster) launches him on another flight of associations, including Russian words. He brings in *mia* and *tia*, Church Slavonic for "me" and "thee," respectively. *Mia* becomes *miaou* (Fr., meow), which then takes him to *chat* (Fr., cat). He ends, "With friendship for a man but not Cocto, Vaslav Nijinsky."

—*J.A.*

Homme.

Je suis un homme
Je suis un homme
Vous ette un homme
Vous ette un homme
Votre homme est une home
Votre home est un homme
Je suis homme
Je suis homme
Vous ette homme mes pas un homme
Je suis homme mes pas un home
Vous ette home mes pas un homme
Homme ne home me home me home
Home un homme mes pas un homme
Vous ette home, je suis un home
Vous ette home sens lumièr
Je suis home avec lumièr
Je suis homme avec un coeur
Vous ette home sens lumièr
Je suis home avec lumièr
Votre home ne pas un homme
Hom est homme ne pas un pomme,
Pomme est pomme est pomme est pomme
Pomme est pomme est pomme est pomme
Pomme est pomme ne pas un pont
Pont est pont pas un pomme
Pomme pomme pone pone pone
Ponee nonee nonee ponee
Lonee ponee nonee ponee
Ronee ronee ronee ronee
Ronee ponee ponee ponee
Monee ponee ponee monee
Jonee jonee ioyonee
Jonee jonee iouonee

Vaslav Nijinsky

Jy iy ioudonee
Donee jonee ioydonee
Monee jonee ioudonee
Donee jonee ioudonee
Ronee ponee ioudonee
Monee tonee ioudonee
Tonee tonee monotonee
Monotonee, monotonee
Ponee, tonee, ponee, tonee
Jonee tonee ioudonee
Joydonee jonee honee
Honee, Honee mojodonee
Mojodonee ioudonee
Donee, donee ioudonee
Ioudonee, ioudonee
Ioudonee monotonee
Ponee pontee pontee piousse
Ponte piousse mono piousse
Piousse, piousse, piousse, piousse
Piousee, piousse, piousse, piousse
Jiousse, iousse, piousse piousse
Piousse iousse ioudonesse
Ioudonesse ponte piousse
Piousse tiousse miousse iousse
Miousse iousse tiousse piousse
Piousse tiousse ioudonesse
Ioudonesse tiousse piousse
Miousse tiousse pontee piousse
Pontee piousse tiousse iousse
Miousse iousse, iousse, iousse
Tiousse piousse miousse iousse
Iousse miousse pontee iousse
Ponte tiousse, ponte piousse
Piousse, piousse, piousse, piousse.
Piousse, piousse, piousse, piousse.
Je suis iousse mes pas piousse
Iousse, iousse, iousse, iousse
Miousse, miousse, miousse, miousse
Je suis iousse, je suis iousse
Je suis miousse, je suis miousse
Je ecris tres malle mais je veux vous dire que je vous aime. Je vous

aime mon chere Cocto. Coc, coc, to, ne pas le coc. Je suis coc vous
ette un coc. Ne pas coc, ne pas coc coc, coc, coc ne pas un coc. Je suis
coc, je suis coc. Coc, coc, coc, je suis un coc. Coc, coc, coc, je suis un
coc. Mon coc et ton coc tu un coc mais pas un coc. Je suis coc tu un
coc. Nous ommes coc, vous ette un coc. Coc, coc, coc, cet un coc.
Coc iyage ne pas un coc. Coc, coc, coc, ne pas un coc. Coc, coc, coc,
cette un coc. Je suis coc mes pas un coc. Pas un coc est un moge.
Mogi, cogi, togi, jogi. Migi, gigi, gi gi, rigi. Tchigi, tchigi, tchigi, rigi.
Tchigi, rigi, rigi, tchigi. Migi, tigi, tigi, tigi. Jagi, jagi, jagi, jagi. Je suis
russe pour ça je dis que je suis ja. Ja, moi, moi est ja. Iia, jia, jia, jia.
Tia, tia, tia, tia. Mia, mia, mia, mia. Mia, mia ne pas miou. Miou,
tiou, miou, tiou. Tiou miou, tiou miou. Miaou, Miaou, miaou, mia.
Mia ou mia ne pas miaou. Miaou miaou pas mia. Tia miaou mes pas
moi. Toi moi est un chat. Chat un chat mes pas toi. Je suis chat mes
pas toi. Toi un pate mes pas moi. Mois un pate sent toi. Toi, toi, toi,
toi. Je suis chat me pas toi.

    Avec mes amitie pour un homme me pas Cocto.

    Waslaw Nijinsky.

TO JESUS

In this letter Nijinsky begins by saying that he is Jesus—"Je suis gèsue"—but
then becomes more interested in the similarity of the sounds *sue* and *suis*.

—J.A.

Au Gèsue

Je suis gèsue
Je suis gèsue
Je suis gesue
Je suis gesue
Je suis un sue
Je suis un sue
Je suis je suis je suis je suis
Suis je suis je suis je suis
Je suis suis je suis suis je
Je ne veux pas sent je suis
Je me suis je suis je suis

NOTES ON CONTRIBUTORS

JOAN ACOCELLA, author of *Mark Morris* (Farrar, Straus & Giroux), is the dance critic of the *Wall Street Journal*. She also writes for *The New Yorker* and *The New York Review of Books*. She is at work on a biography of Mikhail Baryshnikov. Her edition of *The Diary of Vaslav Nijinsky: Unexpurgated Edition* is forthcoming from Farrar, Straus & Giroux.

Expressing strong emotion through simple and concise language, ANNA AKHMATOVA's (1889–1966) love lyrics made her popular before the Revolution. After the Bolshevik takeover in 1917, she refused to abandon Russia, although her works were not allowed to be published for many years. In her later poems, she became the voice of the collective suffering of her people, who lived through war, revolution and the Stalinist Terror.

ESTHER ALLEN is currently translating a novel by Marie Darrieussecq tentatively titled *Gone*, which will be published by the New Press.

JAROSLAW ANDERS is deputy chief of the Polish Service of the Voice of America. Among his translations are *Barbarians in the Garden* by Zbigniew Herbert, *Rondo* by Kazimierz Brandys and *Subtenant* by Hannah Krall.

CAMILLA BAGG is the daughter of Mary Butts. She is currently editing a number of Butts's unpublished works in collaboration with Nathalie Blondel.

DJUNA BARNES (1892–1982) is best known for her novel *Nightwood* (1936), a tragic novel about the gay expatriate life in Paris during the 1920s, which was acclaimed by T. S. Eliot, Dylan Thomas and others. Barnes's many works also include *Ryder* and *The Antiphon*. She was also an accomplished journalist, artist and playwright. Djuna Barnes, "Eighteen Poems," copyright © 1998, The Authors League Fund as literary executor of the Estate of Djuna Barnes.

THOMAS BERNHARD (1931–1989) was a novelist, playwright and poet whose works include *Gargoyles, Correction, Woodcutters, The Lime Works, Wittgenstein's Nephew, The Loser* and, most recently, a collection of plays, *Histrionics*, and of stories, *The Voice Imitator*. The winner of many distinguished prizes, Bernhard, who lived in Austria, is widely considered to be one of the most important writers of his generation.

ELIZABETH BISHOP (1911–1979) is now generally regarded as one of the principal American poets of the century. In her lifetime, she won both the Pulitzer Prize and the National Book Award. Her books include *The Complete Poems 1927–1997, The Collected Prose* and *The Diary of Helena Morley*. *Edgar Allan Poe & the Jukebox: Uncollected and Unfinished Poems*, edited by Alice Quinn, will be published by Farrar, Straus & Giroux in the fall of 1999.

Born in 1907, French novelist, critic and theorist MAURICE BLANCHOT has published more than twenty-five volumes, many of which have been translated into several languages. He began his career as a journalist in the 1930s and went on to write the short, enigmatic works designated as *"Récits,"* such as *Death Sentence, When the Time Comes* and *The Last Man.* He has profoundly influenced more than two generations of French writers and thinkers. Blanchot lives near Paris.

NATHALIE BLONDEL is Mary Butts Research Fellow at Oxford Brookes University, England. She is the editor of *With and Without Buttons: The Selected Stories of Mary Butts* and the author of *Mary Butts: Scenes from the Life* (McPherson), the authorized biography. She is currently preparing an edition of Mary Butts's journals for Yale University Press.

HERMANN BROCH (1886–1951) was born in Austria but after the 1938 annexation fled to England and later to the United States. Among Broch's masterpieces are the novels *The Sleepwalkers, The Death of Virgil, The Spell* and *The Guiltless.* Few of his theoretical writings have appeared in English, with the notable exception of *Hugo Hofmannsthal and His Time: The European Imagination 1860–1920.* In 1950 he was nominated for the Nobel Prize.

One of the greatest writers of the twentieth century, novelist and playwright MIKHAIL BULGAKOV (1891–1940) is known for such novels as *The Master and Margarita* and *The White Guard* and the plays *The Days of the Turbins* and *Flight.* Born in Kiev, he moved to Moscow in 1921 and spent virtually the rest of his life there.

MARY BUTTS (1890–1937), English Modernist woman of letters, was the author of novels, poems, essays, stories, historical fiction and autobiography. "Fumerie" forms part of the ongoing project to bring her unpublished writings into print. Her short story "The Master's Last Dancing" (*The New Yorker*) and the essay "Bloomsbury" (*Modernism/Modernity*) appeared earlier this year.

TRUMAN CAPOTE (1924–1984) established himself as one of America's foremost writers with the publication of *Other Voices, Other Rooms.* Among his other works are *A Tree of Night, The Grass Harp, Breakfast at Tiffany's, A Christmas Memory* and perhaps his most famous book, *In Cold Blood.* Capote's unfinished novel, *Answered Prayers,* was published posthumously in 1987.

CONSTANTINE P. CAVAFY (1863–1933), the renowned Greek poet, was born in Constantinople, but spent most of his adult life in Alexandria, Egypt, the city that provides a background to so many of his poems. Cavafy's *Collected Poems* (Princeton) was translated by Edmund Keeley.

ANTON CHEKHOV (1860–1904) is often referred to as the father of the modern short story, and his work as a dramatist is equally important. His classic plays *The Cherry Orchard, The Seagull, Three Sisters* and *Uncle Vanya* are among the most performed in the world.

377

Born in Transylvania, E. M. CIORAN (1911–1995) was the son of a Christian ortho-dox priest. He started to publish in Romania in 1932 and lived the next two years in Germany as a sympathizer of the Nazi regime. In 1936, he moved to France, where his philosophical work earned him praise as a great stylist of the French language. Cioran's books translated into English include *Anathemas and Admirations*, *The Trouble With Being Born*, *A Short History of Decay* and *History and Utopia*, all translated by Richard Howard. He lived in Paris until the end of his life. E. M. Cioran, *Cahiers 1957–1972*, copyright © 1997 Editions Gallimard, to be published by Arcade Press.

PETER CONSTANTINE has written seven books on the languages and cultures of the Far East. His most recent book of translations, *Six Early Stories* by Thomas Mann (Sun & Moon), was awarded the 1998 PEN/Book of the Month Club Translation Prize. Some of the Chekhov stories in this issue are scheduled to appear this fall in *The Undiscovered Chekhov: 38 New Stories* (Seven Stories).

LOUIS COUPERUS (1863–1923) wrote eighteen works of long fiction, of which *The Books of Small Souls* and *Old People and the Things That Pass* are among the most well known. He was a celebrated writer during his own lifetime, both in his native country of The Netherlands and abroad.

JOHN C. DAVIS teaches translation at the British Council, Athens. Earlier this year, his translations of medieval Greek texts were read by Alan Bates at the Byzantine Festival in London, while his translation of a lament on Constantinople was set to music by John Tavener.

LYDIA DAVIS is the author of *Break It Down* and *The End of the Story*, as well as *Almost No Memory* (Farrar, Straus & Giroux). *Almost No Memory* has just appeared in paperback from Ecco Press. She has translated numerous books from French by writers including Maurice Blanchot, Michel Leiris and Pierre Jean Jouve.

VOLODYMYR DIBROVA is a Ukrainian writer and translator now teaching at Har-vard University. His book *Peltse and Pentameron* appeared in English transla-tion in 1996, published by Northwestern University Press. Himself a fiction writer and playwright, Dibrova has also translated Beckett and Ionesco into Ukrainian.

DUNCAN DOBBELMANN is a writer and translator who lives in Brooklyn. He is currently writing his dissertation on George Oppen at the Graduate Center of the City University of New York.

FYODOR DOSTOEVSKY (1821–1881) is one of the most influential novelists of the last century, the first to explore the psychology of character as a principle of com-position. Among his major works are *Poor Folk*, *Notes from the House of the Dead*, *Crime and Punishment*, *The Idiot*, *The Possessed* and *The Brothers Karamazov*.

MICHAEL EMMERICH graduated from Princeton University in June. He has studied in Japan at the Kyoto Center for Japanese Studies, and will return to Japan in April to pursue a graduate degree. This is his first publication.

KYRIL FITZLYON translated Constantine Baustovski's autobiography, *The Restless Years*, from Russian and *The Memoirs of Princess Dashkov* from French as well as works by Leo Tolstoy and Anton Chekhov. He writes for *The New York Times Book Review*, *The L.A. Times Book Review* and the *Times Literary Supplement*. He lives in London.

JEFF FORT is a graduate student in comparative literature at the University of California at Berkeley. He is completing a dissertation on Kafka, Blanchot and Beckett.

SARAH FUNKE is currently cataloguing the Nabokov family collection of his works for Glenn Horowitz Bookseller, New York.

SUSAN GILLESPIE has published translations of work by, among others, Theodor Adorno and industrialist Robert Bosch. She is director of the Institute of International Liberal Education at Bard College.

ZINAIDA GIPPIUS (1869–1945) is the foremost Russian female Symbolist writer. After the Bolshevik Revolution, she left Russia for Paris, where she lived and wrote until her death. Among her works available in English are *Between Paris and St. Petersburg: Selected Diaries* and *Selected Works of Zinaida Gippius*, both edited and translated by Temira Pachmuss (University of Illinois Press).

ANNETA GREENLEE teaches Russian language and literature at City University of New York and New York University. Zinaida Gippius is the subject of her doctoral dissertation.

PHILLIP HERRING is professor emeritus of English at the University of Wisconsin-Madison and lives in Austin, Texas, where he works at the Harry Ransom Humanities Research Center. He is the author of *Djuna: The Life and Works of Djuna Barnes* (Viking Penguin).

GITTA HONEGGER is chair of the Department of Drama at the Catholic University of America, and is the American representative of the Thomas Bernhard International Foundation. She is completing a book on Bernhard, *Whereof One Cannot Speak . . . The Making of an Austrian*, to be published by Yale University Press.

RICHARD HOWARD is a poet and translator. He teaches in the Writing Division of the School of the Arts, Columbia University.

EUGÈNE IONESCO's (1909–1994) many remarkable works include *Rhinoceros, The Bald Soprano, Jack or the Submission, The Chairs, Antidotes*, as well as other plays, memoirs, children's books, and even a satirical biography of Victor Hugo. In his later years, he tried his hand at the plastic arts.

YASUNARI KAWABATA (1899–1972) was born in Osaka, Japan. The author of dozens of novels, including *Snow Country, The Sound of the Mountain, Beauty and Sadness, The Lake* and *The Master of Go*, and of hundreds of short stories, he was the first Japanese author to receive the Nobel Prize in literature. He died near his home in Kamakura, four years after he accepted the prize.

MICHEL LEIRIS (1901–1990), early French Surrealist, poet, novelist, ethnographer, art critic and memoirist, was the author of many works including the four-volume "autobiographical essay" *Rules of the Game, Manhood* and the massive chronicle *L'Afrique Fantôme*. He lived for most of his life in Paris.

NORMAN MANEA is writer in residence and Francis Flournoy Professor in European Studies and Cultures at Bard College. Author of *The Black Envelope*, among other works, his next book, *Variations on a Self-Portrait*, will be published by Farrar, Straus & Giroux.

SUSAN MATTHIAS, a translator of modern Greek literature, has had works published in the *Harvard Review* and the *Journal of Modern Greek Studies*. She is studying for her Ph.D. in comparative literature at New York University.

BRADFORD MORROW is the editor of *Conjunctions* and author of four novels, *Come Sunday*, *Trinity Fields*, *Giovanni's Gift* (all published by Penguin) and *The Almanac Branch* (W. W. Norton), which was a finalist for the PEN/Faulkner Award. In May 1998, he received an Academy Award in Literature from the American Academy of Arts and Letters. He teaches at Bard College.

ROBERT MUSIL (1880–1942) was the author of two novels, *Young Törless* and the epic *The Man without Qualities*, a number of short stories and miscellaneous pieces, two plays, *The Visionaries* and *Vinzenz*, and a considerable number of important essays on European culture. Born in Austria-Hungary, he lived in Berlin and Vienna, then fled to Switzerland, where he died.

VLADIMIR NABOKOV (1899–1977) was born in St. Petersburg and educated in French and Russian literature at Trinity College, Cambridge. Nearly two decades in Berlin and Paris yielded a substantial body of Russian work. His work gained international recognition with *Lolita* in 1955 and he wrote the masterpieces *Pale Fire* in 1962 and *Ada* in 1969, as well as dozens of other remarkable works.

VASLAV NIJINSKY (1889–1950) came to national fame as a principal dancer in Serge Diaghilev's Ballets Russes. After a falling out between the two men—who had lived openly as lovers for some time—Nijinsky struggled to build a career on his own. From 1912 to 1913 Nijinsky produced three ballets—*The Afternoon of a Faun*, *Jeux* and *The Rite of Spring* (to Stravinsky's score). In December 1917, Nijinsky, the most famous male dancer in the Western world, moved into a Swiss villa with his wife and three-year-old daughter and began to go insane.

BURTON PIKE is professor of comparative literature and German at the Graduate School of the City University of New York. His most recent work was as co-translator, with Sophie Wilkins, of Musil's *The Man without Qualities* (Knopf). He also co-translated, with David S. Luft, a collection of Musil's essays, *Precision and Soul* (University of Chicago), and edited the volume *Robert Musil: Selected Writings* (Continuum).

The Milanese poet ANTONIA POZZI (1912–1938) died by her own hand. She left behind several hundred poems, none of which was published during her lifetime.

MINNA PROCTOR is a fiction writer and translator. Her translations of Federigo Tozzi won the 1997 PEN Renato Poggioli Award for a translation in progress. Her translation of a collection of Tozzi's stories will be published by New Directions.

MARCEL PROUST (1871–1922) was the author of *Les plaisirs and les jours*; an unfinished novel, *Jean Santeuil*, first published in 1954; translator of John Ruskin's *The Bible of Amiens* and *Sesame and Lilies*; and, most famously, author of the masterpiece *À la recherche du temps perdu*.

ALICE QUINN is the poetry editor of *The New Yorker* as well as an editor in the fiction department.

ROBERTA REEDER is the author of *Anna Akhmatova: Poet and Prophet,* published by St. Martin's Press in 1994. She is also editor of *The Complete Poems of Anna Akhmatova,* published by Zephyr Press, which is now available in a new enlarged edition published in 1997.

GEORGE SEFERIS (1900–1971) is best known for his poetry, but he also was an influential critic of modern Greek literature. His *Complete Poems of George Seferis* (Anvil) was translated by Edmund Keeley and Philip Sherrard. Seferis won the Novel Prize for Literature in 1963.

Born in Argentina, OSIAS STUTMAN has lived in New York since 1972 and is a scientist by trade (professor of immunology at Cornell and the Sloan Kettering Institute). His Spanish translation of the poetry of Djuna Barnes will be published in Barcelona by early 1999.

The work of Tuscan novelist, poet, historian and essayist FEDERIGO TOZZI (1883–1920) has been sparsely translated. The short stories included in this issue of *Conjunctions* were originally published posthumously in Italy in various collections. His novel *Eyes Shut,* translated by Kenneth Cox, was published in 1990 by Carcanet.

PAUL VAN OSTAIJEN (1896–1928) published three collections of poetry during his short lifetime: *Music-Hall, The Signal* and *Occupied City.* Two additional volumes of poetry were published posthumously, as were collections of his many prose "grotesques" and critical essays.

LAWRENCE VENUTI's latest books are *The Scandals of Translation: Towards an Ethics of Difference* (Routledge) and his translation of *Finite Intuition: Selected Poetry and Prose of Milo De Angelis* (Sun & Moon).

Back issues of
CONJUNCTIONS

"A must read"—*The Village Voice*

A limited number of back issues are available to those who would like to discover for themselves the range of innovative writing published in CONJUNCTIONS over the course of more than fifteen years.

CONJUNCTIONS:1. *James Laughlin Festschrift.* Paul Bowles, Gary Snyder, John Hawkes, Robert Creeley, Thom Gunn, Denise Levertov, Tennessee Williams, James Purdy, William Everson, Jerome Rothenberg, George Oppen, Joel Oppenheimer, Eva Hesse, Michael McClure, Octavio Paz, Hayden Carruth, over 50 others. Kenneth Rexroth interview. 304 pages.

CONJUNCTIONS:2. Nathaniel Tarn, William H. Gass, Mei-mei Berssenbrugge, Walter Abish, Gustaf Sobin, Edward Dorn, Kay Boyle, Kenneth Irby, Thomas Meyer, Gilbert Sorrentino, Carl Rakosi, and others. H.D.'s letters to Sylvia Dobson. Czeslaw Milosz interview. 232 pages.

CONJUNCTIONS:3. Guy Davenport, Michael Palmer, Don Van Vliet, Michel Deguy, Toby Olson, René Char, Coleman Dowell, Cid Corman, Ann Lauterbach, Robert Fitzgerald, Jackson Mac Low, Cecile Abish, Anne Waldman, and others. James Purdy interview. 232 pages.*

CONJUNCTIONS:4. Luis Buñuel, Aimé Césaire, Armand Schwerner, Rae Armantrout, Harold Schimmel, Gerrit Lansing, Jonathan Williams, Ron Silliman, Theodore Enslin, and others. Excerpts from Kenneth Rexroth's unpublished autobiography. Robert Duncan and William H. Gass interviews. 232 pages.

CONJUNCTIONS:5. Coleman Dowell, Nathaniel Mackey, Kenneth Gangemi, Paul Bowles, Hayden Carruth, John Taggart, Guy Mendes, John Ashbery, Francesco Clemente, and others. Lorine Niedecker's letters to Cid Corman. Barry Hannah and Basil Bunting interviews. 248 pages.

CONJUNCTIONS:6. Joseph McElroy, Ron Loewinsohn, Susan Howe, William Wegman, Barbara Tedlock, Edmond Jabès, Jerome Rothenberg, Keith Waldrop, James Clifford, Janet Rodney, and others. The *Symposium of the Whole* papers. Irving Layton interview. 320 pages.*

CONJUNCTIONS:7. John Hawkes, Mary Caponegro, Leslie Scalapino, Marjorie Welish, Gerrit Lansing, Douglas Messerli, Gilbert Sorrentino, and others. *Writers Interview Writers:* Robert Duncan/Michael McClure, Jonathan Williams/Ronald Johnson, Edmund White/Edouard Roditi. 284 pages.*

CONJUNCTIONS:8. Robert Duncan, Coleman Dowell, Barbara Einzig, R.B. Kitaj, Paul Metcalf, Barbara Guest, Robert Kelly, Claude Royet-Journoud, Guy Davenport, Karin Lessing, Hilda Morley, and others. *Basil Bunting Tribute,* guest-edited by Jonathan Williams, nearly 50 contributors. 272 pages.*

CONJUNCTIONS:9. William S. Burroughs, Dennis Silk, Michel Deguy, Peter Cole, Paul West, Laura Moriarty, Michael Palmer, Hayden Carruth, Mei-mei Berssenbrugge, Thomas Meyer, Aaron Shurin, Barbara Tedlock, and others. Edmond Jabés interview. 296 pages.

CONJUNCTIONS:10. *Fifth Anniversary Issue.* Walter Abish, Bruce Duffy, Keith Waldrop, Harry Mathews, Kenward Elmslie, Beverley Dahlen, Jan Groover, Ronald Johnson, David Rattray, Leslie Scalapino, George Oppen, Elizabeth Murray, and others. Joseph McElroy interview. 320 pages.*

CONJUNCTIONS:11. Lydia Davis, John Taggart, Marjorie Welish, Dennis Silk, Susan Howe, Robert Creeley, Charles Stein, Charles Bernstein, Kenneth Irby, Nathaniel Tarn, Robert Kelly, Ann Lauterbach, Joel Shapiro, Richard Tuttle, and others. Carl Rakosi interview. 296 pages.

CONJUNCTIONS:12. David Foster Wallace, Robert Coover, Georges Perec, Norma Cole, Laura Moriarty, Joseph McElroy, Yannick Murphy, Diane Williams, Harry Mathews, Trevor Winkfield, Ron Silliman, Armand Schwerner, and others. John Hawkes and Paul West interviews. 320 pages.

CONJUNCTIONS:13. Maxine Hong Kingston, Ben Okri, Jim Crace, William S. Burroughs, Guy Davenport, Barbara Tedlock, Rachel Blau DuPlessis, Walter Abish, Jackson Mac Low, Lydia Davis, Fielding Dawson, Toby Olson, Eric Fischl, and others. Robert Kelly interview. 288 pages.*

CONJUNCTIONS:14. *The New Gothic,* guest-edited by Patrick McGrath. Kathy Acker, John Edgar Wideman, Jamaica Kincaid, Peter Straub, Clegg & Guttmann, Robert Coover, Lynne Tillman, Bradford Morrow, William T. Vollmann, Gary Indiana, Mary Caponegro, Brice Marden, and others. Salman Rushdie interview. 296 pages.*

CONJUNCTIONS:15. *The Poetry Issue.* 33 poets, including Susan Howe, John Ashbery, Rachel Blau DuPlessis, Barbara Einzig, Norma Cole, John Ash, Ronald Johnson, Forrest Gander, Michael Palmer, Diane Ward, and others. Fiction by John Barth, Jay Cantor, Diane Williams, and others. Michael Ondaatje interview. 424 pages.

CONJUNCTIONS:16. *The Music Issue.* Nathaniel Mackey, Leon Botstein, Albert Goldman, Paul West, Amiri Baraka, Quincy Troupe, Lukas Foss, Walter Mosley, David Shields, Seth Morgan, Gerald Early, Clark Coolidge, Hilton Als, and others. John Abercrombie and David Starobin interview. 360 pages.

CONJUNCTIONS:25. *The New American Theater,* guest-edited by John Guare. Tony Kushner, Suzan-Lori Parks, Jon Robin Baitz, Han Ong, Mac Wellman, Paula Vogel, Eric Overmyer, Wendy Wasserstein, Christopher Durang, Donald Margulies, Ellen McLaughlin, Nicky Silver, Jonathan Marc Sherman, Joyce Carol Oates, Arthur Kopit, Doug Wright, Robert O'Hara, Erik Ehn, John Guare, Harry Kondoleon, and others. 360 pages.

CONJUNCTIONS:26. *Sticks and Stones.* Angela Carter, Ann Lauterbach, Rikki Ducornet, Paul Auster, Arthur Sze, David Mamet, Robert Coover, Rick Moody, Gary Lutz, Lois-Ann Yamanaka, Terese Svoboda, Brian Evenson, Dawn Raffel, David Ohle, Liz Tucillo, Martine Bellen, Robert Kelly, Michael Palmer, and others. 360 pages.

CONJUNCTIONS:27. *The Archipelago,* co-edited by Bradford Morrow and Robert Antoni. Gabriel García Márquez, Derek Walcott, Cristina García, Wilson Harris, Olive Senior, Senel Paz, Kamau Brathwaite, Julia Alvarez, Manno Charlemagne, Rosario Ferré, Severo Sarduy, Edwidge Danticat, Madison Smartt Bell, Fred D'Aguiar, Glenville Lovell, Mayra Montero, Lorna Goodison, Bob Shacochis, and others. 360 pages.

CONJUNCTIONS:28. *Secular Psalms,* with a special Music Theater portfolio guest-edited by Thalia Field. Maureen Howard, Julio Cortázar, Joanna Scott, David Foster Wallace, Stephen Dixon, Susan Gevirtz, Gilbert Sorrentino, Anselm Hollo, Can Xue, Harry Partch, Robert Ashley, Meredith Monk, John Moran, Alice Farley, Ann T. Greene, Ruth E. Margraff, Jeffrey Eugenides, Jackson Mac Low, and others. 380 pages.

CONJUNCTIONS:29. *Tributes,* co-edited by Martine Bellen, Lee Smith, and Bradford Morrow. Ntozake Shange, John Sayles, Nathaniel Mackey, Joanna Scott, Rick Moody, Dale Peck, Carole Maso, Peter Straub, Robert Creeley, Paul West, Quincy Troupe, Ana Castillo, Amiri Baraka, Eli Gottlieb, Joyce Carol Oates, Sven Birkerts, Siri Hustvedt, Lydia Davis, and others. 416 pages.

CONJUNCTIONS:30. *Paper Airplane,* edited by Bradford Morrow. Franz Kafka, Günter Grass, Jorie Graham, Susan Howe, Dale Peck, Susan Sontag, John Ashbery, Anne Carson, Alexander Theroux, Rosmarie Waldrop, William T. Vollmann, Robert Coover, Joanna Scott, Joyce Carol Oates, John Barth, William H. Gass, Shelley Jackson, Fred D'Aguiar, and others. 400 pages.

Send your order to:
CONJUNCTIONS, Bard College, Annandale-on-Hudson, NY 12504.
Issues 1–15 are $15.00 each, plus $3.00 shipping.
Issues 16–29 are $12.00 each, plus $3.00 shipping.

Issues with asterisks are available in very limited quantities.
Please inquire.

Mary Butts

Published in 1998

Mary Butts: Scenes from the Life

A Biography by NATHALIE BLONDEL

$35.00 cloth   600p.   Notes, index, bibliographies, 45 photos.

Published in 1998

Ashe of Rings, and Other Writings

by MARY BUTTS

Includes *Imaginary Letters, A Warning to Hikers, Traps for Unbelievers, &c.*
Preface by Nathalie Blondel $24.00 cloth   384p.

Also by Mary Butts

The Taverner Novels

Armed with Madness, Death of Felicity Taverner
Preface by Paul West   Afterword by Barbara O'Brien Wagstaff
$25 cloth, $15 paper   374p.

The Classical Novels

The Macedonian, Scenes from the Life of Cleopatra, plus three stories
Preface by Thomas McEvilley $24 cloth, $14 paper   385p.

From Altar to Chimney-piece: Selected Stories

Preface by John Ashbery $22 cloth, $12 paper   295p.

A Sacred Quest

THE LIFE AND WRITINGS OF MARY BUTTS

Essays by Robin Blaser, Gerrit Lansing, Barbara O'Brien Wagstaff; contemporary assessments by Glenway Wescott, Hugh Ross Williamson, Louis Adeane; tributes by Bryher, David Hope, Robert Duncan; bibliographies by Christopher Wagstaff and Kenneth Irby; memoirs by Hugh Ross Williamson, Camilla Bagg; interviews with Virgil Thomson, Quentin Bell, &c. by Robert H. Byington; 45-page sampler of Butts's writings.

Edited by Christopher Wagstaff $25 cloth   297p.   Eleven photos and drawings.

McPherson & Company, Publishers

Post Office Box 1126   Kingston, New York 12402

1-800-613-8219   www.mcphersonco.com   bmcpher@ulster.net

Mail Orders: add $4 shipping, NY sales tax if applicable.

NOON

EDITED BY DIANE WILLIAMS

NEW

PLEASE SEND FICTION

1369 MADISON AVENUE   SUITE 298   NEW YORK   NEW YORK   10128

THE VOICE IMITATOR

104 STORIES

BY THOMAS BERNHARD

"*The Voice Imitator* works as a mini-anthology of Bernhard's obsessions with political corruption, madness, murder, and the inability of language to capture, or relieve, the absurdity of life. Part diatribe, part black comedy and part philosophical investigation, the book strikes all the major themes in Bernhard's novels and plays. . . . A highly artistic undertaking."
—Peter Filkins, *New York Times Book Review*

Paper $10.00 Available at bookstores.

THE UNIVERSITY OF

CHICAGO PRESS

Visit www.press.uchicago.edu to read an excerpt from The Voice Imitator.

EIGHTEEN SUICIDES

SIX PAINFUL DEATHS

TWENTY-SIX MURDERS

{ *one love affair* }

THIRTEEN INSTANCES OF LUNACY

TWENTY SURPRISES

FOUR DISAPPEARANCES

TWO INSTANCES OF LIBEL

THREE CHARACTER ATTACKS

FIVE EARLY DEATHS

ONE MEMORY LAPSE

FOUR COVER-UPS

posmanbooks

Jürgen Habermas   Stanley Cavell   Julia Kristeva
Kaja Silverman   Pierre Klossowski   Edmund Husserl
Wislawa Szymborska   Jacques Lacan   Henri Bergson
David Lewis   Emmanuel Levinas   Jacques Derrida
Thomas Bernhard   Adam Zagajewski   Thierry De Duve
Manuel De Landa   Michel Tournier   Thomas Elsaesser
Wilfred Sellars   Giorgio Agamben   Denise Duhamel
Wesely Salmon   Slavoj Zizek   Paul Celan   Thom Gunn
Ismail Kadare   Rosalind Krauss   Francine Prose
Mark Cox Orhan Pamuk Donna Haraway Baron Wormser
Louise Glück   Jean-Francois Lyotard   Denis Johnson
Emmanuel Eze Russell Edson Marie Howe Avital Ronell
Olive Moore Saul Kripke Jean LaPlanche Alice Munro
Charles Wright Lydia Davis Hélène Cixous Paul Virilio

The best of scholarly and university presses

Just off the northeast corner of
Washington Square Park
One University Place, NYC 10003
Phone: 212.533.2665 Fax: 212.533.2681

web: www.posmanbooks.com / E-mail: posmanbook@aol.com

Sun & Moon Press presents...

The Winner of the 1997 National Poetry Series

TALES OF MURASAKI
and Other Poems

Martine Bellen

Selected by Rosmarie Waldrop

Order from
  Sun & Moon Press
  6026 Wilshire Boulevard
  Los Angeles, CA 90036
  323 857 1115

Please visit our website
  www.sunmoon.com

ISBN: 1-55713-378-6
$10.95